Charlotte Nash is the internationally published author of seven contemporary novels, most recently *Saving You* and *On A Starlit Ocean*. She has degrees in engineering and medicine and a PhD in creative writing, which used the neuroscience of reading to understand how cleverly-crafted technical fiction appeals to our narrative brains. As a firm believer in unlikely pairings, she is an engineer by day and writes smart, unusual love stories by night. She has taught writing through The University of Queensland, QUT, Queensland Writers Centre and the University of Technology Sydney.

Twenty-Six
Letters

Twenty-Six
Letters

Charlotte
Nash

ALLEN&UNWIN
SYDNEY · MELBOURNE · AUCKLAND · LONDON

First published in 2022

 **Queensland** Government   This project is supported by the Queensland Government through Arts Queensland.

Allen & Unwin
83 Alexander Street
Crows Nest NSW 2065
Australia
Phone: (61 2) 8425 0100
Email: info@allenandunwin.com
Web: www.allenandunwin.com

 A catalogue record for this book is available from the National Library of Australia

ISBN 978 1 76106 652 8

Set in 11.9/17.7 pt Sabon LT Pro by Bookhouse, Sydney
Printed in Australia by McPherson's Printing Group

10 9 8 7 6 5 4 3 2 1

For all the great love stories
...especially the ones we cannot tell

Chapter 1

On the last Friday of April, Wilhelmina Mann really meant to be on time. But the Gold Coast autumn mornings were still balmy, so it was easy to leave her warm bed and make her way down to the beach for the sunrise. She was only going for a quick look because she wanted to make sure today started in the best way. A reset after last Friday.

The wet sand crunched under her toes, and she spun one foot around to dig a great circle. It would wash away in an hour as the tide turned, and by then Wil would be deep in bathroom renovations. Pity. The sun was rippling up gloriously from the glassy sea, turning the scattered clouds pink and orange, and glinting golden off the high-rise glass behind the beach. A morning of ordinary wonders. Far too nice to be at work.

But she wasn't staying—she had promised herself she was going straight back to shower, dress and be at the site on time at six. Five to six, even!

She snatched up a sandy sea pen with a pleasing shape, washed her feet in the water, and turned to follow her tracks back up to the carpark. Her footsteps had made a path right through the centre of her sand circle, suggesting the trunk of a tree. Wil tipped her head, then dipped the sea pen to the sand, and swept the trunk line down to touch her circle. There. She liked the way an uneven lump of sand had made a shadow like a tiny boulder on the edge of that line. She used her toe to push up another lump, then another, forming rocks around the beginnings of tree roots.

She came back to herself a few minutes later. The sea pen and her toes were sandy, her hair escaping its band. She had made the inscribed tree into a lush canopy across the top of the sand circle, and the spreading roots into a mass across the bottom. Perfectly balanced. She smiled, satisfied, just as she registered something amiss. The sun was higher now, the mellow glow of dawn burned away into a less friendly light. Wait, that wasn't right.

She squinted to read the clock on the surf club, but it was too far away. Tipped her wrist, but she'd lost her latest watch two weeks ago, into a grout bucket. Her pockets were empty. Where was her phone?

She sprinted back to the car and, still gasping, found her phone on the passenger seat. The screen was a mess of missed calls and texts from Tony, Col and her father. The last text read *WHERE ARE YOU*. The time was already 6.32.

Wil's stomach caved. *Oh, murder!*

She threw the ignition and spun out of the carpark, nearly colliding with a passing hatchback. Her brakes squealed, her

2

knuckles tight as she yelled, 'Sorry!' over the blast of horn. On the drive home, she caught every red light.

The house was ominously silent as her rusty Corolla finally screeched into the drive. Three trucks with Cameron Butler Construction stickers had been parked there when she'd left. The two her father and Tony drove were gone, leaving the one with the tile order in the tray, which she was meant to have delivered to the job more than half an hour ago.

Barefoot, she stumbled through the side gate and winced over the sharp stones to the granny flat under the house. The room looked far less cheery than it had at 5 am. Her patchwork bedspread hung on a rumpled angle and one side of the bed was a mess of sketchbooks and pencils, because she'd fallen asleep drawing last night. A pile of dirty clothes was growing in one corner, encroaching on two stacked baskets of clean unfolded laundry. Some of the dirty pile were Rob's, from the last time he'd stayed over. Wil wrinkled her nose at them and rummaged in a basket for blue work pants and a shirt. She found some, horribly crushed. She threw them on anyway.

In the mirror she resembled a crazed eggshell. 'Could be worse,' she muttered. 'Could be worse, could be worse . . .'

Then she heard an engine growling in the driveway, before heavy boots stomped down the stone path. Okay, this was worse. Wil didn't even have time for an 'uh-oh' before the door flung open and her father appeared, sweating in his work shorts and drill shirt, his tool belt around his hips. He was wiry rather than solid, his skin flushed from the neck to jaw. Wil stood several inches over him, but she felt none of that advantage now.

'I've had tilers,' he drawled, his eyes burning, 'sitting on their arses for the last forty minutes, smoking while I pay them for nothing.'

'I'm sorry—'

He held up a hand. 'Last week you missed two pick-ups, and you backed the ute into a pole. I need reliable help, not extra costs. That's what you promised when you moved back in. You're thirty-one tomorrow, for god's sake, not sixteen.'

Wil swallowed, her voice catching. 'I'm really sorry. Complete idiot. It won't happen again.'

He sighed and walked out. She knew what he was thinking: *You say that every time.*

The day did not improve. Arriving at the job site, she saw her brother Tony up a ladder, fixing a beam in the garage. His thick neck turned in her direction and he shook his head, probably at her clothes. As if he was forty and not twenty-four. Wil clenched her teeth; it was galling to be judged by the little brother you used to rescue out of tree branches. But she kept her mouth shut. Her father was now bearing down on her truck. She practised new apologies in her head, but he didn't even look at her. He just hauled up a tile box and stomped up the stairs into the house.

Wil scrambled out and grabbed the next box. Inside, she spotted Colin rocking out to his earbuds as he plastered sheetrock near the kitchen. The air was thick with sawdust and paint fumes.

'Where'd you get to?' he asked, pulling out an earbud.

'Less talk, more work,' her father shouted. He set his box down by the stairs, his face redder than ever. He finally looked at Wil. 'Bring the rest here, then go help the tilers with the cutting.'

But as he straightened to stalk off, his hand clutched at his hip. 'Oof,' he said. He sucked a long breath.

'Your back again?' Wil set her box down and moved to look.

He shifted away from her. 'It's nothing. Go get those boxes.'

Wil glanced at Colin, but he'd turned back to work, earphones in.

When Wil returned with the next box, her father was still standing by the stairs, working a fist into his back. A little knot formed in Wil's chest. The box after that, she saw him try to climb the stairs before stepping back down again.

'You need to go see someone,' she said. 'The physio?'

He waved her away grumpily, so she went upstairs to mark and cut for the now busy tilers and ignore her worry. But half an hour later, when she came down for a fresh box, she could see him lying flat on the floor, in the space beyond the kitchen.

He was still there when everyone went on break. The knot in Wil's chest was now tight and painful. She wiped her hands on her pants and steeled herself.

'Is it worse than last time?' she said, edging closer.

'Those tiles are all done, I hope.'

'Nearly. Is it worse?'

'No,' he said, pushing up on his arm. But his face paled and he fell back, teeth clenched. 'All right. Maybe it's the same.'

Getting him up and into the truck was ten times harder than humping boxes of tiles. They rode to the physiotherapist in tense silence, his fuming anger like the heat of a campfire. If Wil asked how his back was, he stonily told her to keep driving.

'I'll wait with you,' she said in reception.

'I don't need babysitting,' he hissed. 'I need you to go back to work, and do the job you said you were going to do. It's not slack-off day.'

Wil tried not to feel wounded. 'Then I'll pick you up later.'

'If you had just come to work when you'd promised, this would never have happened.' He folded his arms. 'I'll get one of the boys to pick me up.'

After Wil retreated to the car, she sat in the driver's seat, the knot in her chest now replaced with a dull, heavy ache. She thumbed through the contacts in her phone, looking for someone to call. She stopped at her sister Kate's number, feeling the ache harden and a new, desperate knot loop around her heart. Because she knew her father's frustration with her wasn't about today, or even this week. It was what she'd done six months ago to Kate, and the years and years of disappointments before that. Because of the too many times when she'd promised to do better.

Quickly, she sent Kate a text: *Dad hurt his back again.* She couldn't send anything else.

When she pulled back into the job site, Colin had saved her a sausage roll, but Wil couldn't finish it. The knot was taking up all the space in her body. She went back to work, shifting tiles and unpacking boxes, and taking out rubbish.

Rob started texting at three. *Willy, babe! We going out tonight or what?*

She screwed up her nose at the name *Willy*. Rob had picked that up from Tony.

Can't, she wrote back, *working early tomorrow.*

Work is for losers. It's your birthday tomorrow. Be a great time. Promise. Come on!

She didn't reply.

When she eventually arrived home, aching and covered in sweat and tile dust, the first thing she saw were Rob's clothes in the dirty laundry pile. She scooped them up, smelling a faint trace of his cologne, and shoved them into the washing machine. The TV was on upstairs, and she could hear her brothers' voices. She wanted to see how her dad was, but she couldn't face him just now. Instead, she stared at the text Kate had sent back: *Okay, I'll talk to Tony.*

Tony.

She probably deserved that.

She opened the drawer beside the bed and took out an old polaroid, browned at the edges and faded. It showed a woman wearing big dark glasses and a broad smile, standing with two little girls, their arms around each other's shoulders. One was dark-haired, the other fair. In the background was a prime mover. This was her and Kate, years before Kate had left home, before there'd been this knot in Wil's chest. Wil gently touched Kate's face, then the face of the woman. Their mother, Ann. She couldn't describe what she felt when she looked at her mother, but it was old and buried, nothing like the fresh pain over Kate.

She flipped the photo over. There were no notes about where it had been taken, or when, but there was a little pen drawing in the corner, a sketch of a mother mouse holding the hands of two smaller mice. It was lovely, full of warmth, but that feeling was almost all she had of her mother.

Almost.

Wil reached further back in the drawer and pulled out the envelope. In the centre it said *Mina* in blue letters, and in the top corner *1994* was written in pencil. The glue on the closing flap had aged into a useless brown stripe, and the thin paper inside was sepia down its edges. She knew every word by heart.

Dearest Mina,

I'm so very sorry to be writing this letter at all. This was not the plan I had for my life, to leave you so soon. But then life seems to get in the way of our plans, and everything we want. I wanted you most of all. You are my sun and moon, my earth and stars. I will always love you so very much, and I will miss you every day until we see each other again. Be brave, my darling girl, hold on to yourself. The sadness will fade and good things come again.

All my love,
Mummy

Underneath was an exquisite pencil drawing of a little house in a wood, with a night sky filled with stars and a crescent moon. Light came from the windows of the house, and a thin stream of smoke from the chimney. Wil didn't need anyone to tell her it was the same hand that had drawn the picture on the back of the polaroid. She hugged the page gently to her chest, as if trying to feel the mother that had made the pen strokes.

Sometimes, she almost could. The love and beauty of the words and picture would create a soft warmth in her core, like the powdery ash of last night's fire. Other times, the letter seemed to have come from a time that had hardly been real, and so long ago that no one needed to talk about it.

Maybe she could draw some mice like these ones and send them to Kate. Except she'd draw two adult mice for Kate and Neil, and one small mouse for their daughter, Ashleigh. Only, Wil knew it wouldn't be enough. Kate would probably see it as juvenile. Too little, too late.

Wil put the photo away, cleaned up her sketchbooks, tugged the bedsheets into place, and checked on the clothes still bashing about in the washing machine. But the knot in her chest was tighter than ever, and she couldn't stand the idea of being alone with it all night.

She picked up her phone.

What time are you going? she sent to Rob.

Pick you up at 7, he messaged back.

⌒

'Did something happen?' Rob said when she slid inside his Commodore.

'I don't want to talk about it,' Wil said, sounding huffy. 'Can we just go?'

Rob thumbed the wheel. 'You were like this last week, too.'

'Like what?'

'You used to be funny. Now it's like you don't want to be here.' He shrugged. 'Should I be worried?'

She looked at his sun-bleached hair that was still damp, and smelled the board wax and body-spray on his skin, just a little overdone. He stirred nothing in her, but she knew him. She gave him a smile she didn't feel. 'I'm here now. Let's go, okay?'

The Broadbeach surf club was crowded and noisy, the atmosphere weekend happy. Rob shouted something about ordering from the bar and was quickly swallowed by the crowd. Wil spotted Rob's friends at a ring of tables, all guys like Rob and their blonde surfer girlfriends. Wil had worked with one of them a few years ago when she'd briefly had a job as a beauty therapist, but they'd never quite clicked. Still, she felt a relief when she saw them.

They briefly called hello when she slid into a vacant chair, then leaned back into their conversation over the din of the live band. Wil listened to them talk about this morning's break, and about someone's dog at the vet. She'd spent many nights like this, within conversations about nothing in particular, all underneath a heavy bassline. It was better than being home alone, but she couldn't quite lose herself the way she once had. She picked a beer coaster into pieces and didn't say much.

After an hour, when Rob put a new bourbon and coke in front of her, he slid a hand around her leg and said, 'What's wrong?'

'Nothing.' She tried to brighten, but she couldn't quite summon that, either, and she thought she saw him mouth 'Bullshit' under his breath. Wil checked her phone for the tenth time.

She saw a text from Kate. *Are you ok?* it said. Wil felt a tiny gut punch with her surprise, and took a long minute before she texted back, *Fine and dandy.*

But she wasn't. Her head was heavy with exhaustion and she wanted to go home. Rob was loudly arguing with a guy called Max about a surfer she didn't know, and the others were discussing heading to someone's place to smoke pot. She couldn't get involved in that. She'd go to the bathroom and then make an exit.

When she came out again, she ran slap into Colin.

'What are you doing here?' she blurted, then frowned. 'Is Dad okay?'

'He's watching Liverpool on the couch. I figured you were here and came to see if you needed rescuing from Awful Rob.'

'He's not that awful,' she said, with an inexplicable drive to defend him.

'We've got that Mason job starting early tomorrow,' Colin said. 'You should go home. Make your birthday this year a really good one.'

Wil sighed. 'Did Dad send you?'

'That hurts, Wil.' Colin took a breath and looked down at the floor. 'Don't bite my head off, but something's been up between you and Dad since that Sydney trip you didn't come on. I still can't believe you ditched Kate for Rob.'

What had been a knot in Wil's chest became a dumper wave holding her to the seafloor. In her mind was a flash of the old polaroid, with Kate's white-blonde hair and her mother's dark glasses. Then another image: her stepmother Carol waving as Kate left in the taxi for the airport. Colin was still talking, but Wil hadn't registered a word.

He cleared his throat. 'I said, do you want a lift?'

'It's fine,' she mumbled, desperately trying not to cry in front of him. She'd rather fork out for an Uber. 'I'll say bye to Rob and head. I'll see you at work in the morning.'

Wil picked her way back to the tables but Rob had disappeared. She stopped, disoriented, narrowly missing a collision with a man crabbing four drinks in his fingers. She was sure it had been these tables. Had Rob left already? It wouldn't be the first time.

A heavy hand tapped her on the shoulder, and she turned to find a black-clad security man. 'Come with me, outside,' he said, thrusting a meaty thumb towards the door.

'Oh, why?'

'Nothing personal, love, just when one person in the group's out, you're all out.'

Confused, Wil stumbled down the stairs and outside, where she finally spotted Rob, having a shouting match with another security man. Rob was obviously drunk, pointing his finger towards the man's chest, just shy of actually touching him. The security man looked painfully sober, his jaw working like he was chewing gum, and ready to deck Rob.

Rob's friends were hanging back, their girlfriends even further away, scuffing their shoes and looking at the ground. Wil turned to ask the security dude what had happened, but he'd crossed his arms and was giving off a you're-dead-to-me vibe. When she spun back, two police officers had stepped in front of Rob. Wil's heart clenched.

Police.

What happened next seemed to go down very fast. Rob did *something*, she didn't know what, but suddenly one of the cops had twisted him against the wall and had his arm in a good hold, and then Rob was screaming bloody murder about them breaking his arm.

Wil ran over, trying to tell the cop what Rob was saying. At least, she was pretty sure that's what she did. But the cop ignored her. It was like a dream, where she could yell and no one could hear. All she could take in was the policeman's muscled arms, and the pain in Rob's voice. The next thing, she'd laid her hand on the cop's shoulder.

She only meant to get his attention.

She realised her mistake an instant after she'd made it. The cop's partner was onto her so fast, she had barely drawn breath before she was the one cuffed and shoved in the back of the patrol car.

She was so surprised, it took her five long minutes to realise what had happened, by which time the car was driving back to the station. She'd been arrested for assaulting a police officer.

Arrested.

For assaulting a police officer.

And that was how the story really began.

Chapter 2

The police seemed very calm about the whole thing, which only intensified Wil's mortification as she sobered up and waited for the fallout.

It wasn't her first arrest. She'd made that dubious milestone at sixteen, after she and a new friend called Kelley had lifted a few headbands from a dollar shop. It wasn't really something she'd wanted to do, but Kelley had said it was no big deal and dared her. For a brief moment, the thrill of walking out with that headband in her pocket had made Wil feel completely alive. Vibrant, powerful even. Feelings that vanished the moment the cop had stopped them down the street.

The police station smelled just the same now as it had back then, an unpleasant blend of body odour and cheap coffee. The smell of shame.

She called Colin but reached his voicemail. He was probably diligently asleep already. After that failed call, all her personal things were zipped in a plastic bag and she had to wait in a bland cell. She tucked her knees up and hugged them, examining how the day had cascaded to this point. One moment of slipped attention at the beach, and lateness had turned to an injury, and to harsh words, and then to accepting Rob's invitation. And now, here she was. She could see how it all threaded together, just never in advance.

She had no idea what had happened to Rob.

It was two in the morning when she heard footsteps and male voices in the hall, and the door was unlocked. Her heart shrivelled when she saw her father outside. His face was tight, and far more grey than when he'd hurt his back earlier.

'You're being released without charge, Miss Mann,' the policeman said. 'You can come and collect your personal items.'

Wil couldn't speak on the way back to the truck, her shame a noose about her throat. Her father winced as he climbed into his seat. She tried to shut her door very softly.

'You know,' he said, his hands resting on the wheel. 'There must be a word for mugs like me who keep offering chances.'

'I'm sorry,' she croaked. 'I didn't mean—'

'Doesn't seem to matter what you say,' he went on. 'You just manage to fall into trouble. I expected it when you were sixteen but you're thirty-one now, and you've got nothing to show for the years between. Do you know what I had to do to convince those coppers not to charge you? They know the people you hang out with—one of Rob's pals is being looked at for a run of break and enters. They wanted to make an example of you. You're not a teenager making mistakes now; you're an adult who should've known better. It costs me to use my credit up like that. And I almost think it would have been better for you if I hadn't.'

Wil sat rigid, barely breathing at the horror of people thinking of her as an actual criminal. She wanted to argue she didn't even know Rob's mates, but no words would come out.

'Look at Kate,' her father said now, 'she's only two years older than you, but she's worked hard at a profession. She's supervising other nurses, she's respected. And she's married with a family. She can be proud of the life she's living. She knows how to work hard, like I do. That's what you have to do if you want to get anywhere. Not bumming around and hoping your dad will be there to fill the gaps in for you. I should have stopped that years ago. Maybe if I had, I wouldn't be getting hauled out of bed now because my tiler is in the lock-up.'

Tiler. Wil pulled her knees up again. Not *daughter.*

They drove back to the house in dreadful silence. Wil was too stunned to cry, or to have another solid thought. Her father's disappointment had sucked her feelings away, and the trip seemed to never end. When he finally pulled into the drive, he paused before getting out.

'This is the last time I'm ever going to say it. Get your act together, Wil. Quit flaking around and start working at something. I'm not putting up a room or giving you work without that. One more incident like this morning, and you're out. Out of the house, out of me bailing you out. Out of everything.'

∼

She was ten minutes early the next day. The Mason job was in a swanky house on a ridge, high over the Pacific Ocean. The view through the big windows was endless blue sky, with a golden rind of beach. A salty breeze caressed gauzy curtains as the swell lazily rumbled. Tony and Colin stopped to gawp.

Wil hunched in her hoodie and dragged her tool belt past them. She was ragged with no sleep and a hangover, and the emptiness of the night before. The air seemed to have turned chilly overnight.

She worked to warm up. For the first hour, her jobs were in the upstairs bathroom, helping the plumber because, ironically, his apprentice was late. The fact gave her no solace, especially as Rob hadn't messaged her back. The only reason she knew he was alive was because he'd tweeted about the cost of bail. Anonymous people on the internet knew as much as she did.

She was just unpacking a horrendously modern and questionably phallic tap fixture when her father appeared. He was still moving stiffly due to his back, and trailing a young woman in overalls.

'Found her, Pete. You should give better directions next time,' he said. Wil avoided his eye and focused on the tap fixture.

'Sorry, sorry, Uncle Pete!' said the woman, throwing down a tool bag. 'I ended up down that one-way estate street. I'll catch up real fast. Oh, another girl. Hi, I'm Shonna.' She marched over and offered Wil her hand.

It took Wil a beat to respond and awkwardly shift the tap. It might be ugly, but it cost an obscene amount. It wasn't worth her life to drop it. 'Wil,' she said, quickly shaking.

'Really great to meet you,' Shonna said, and Wil felt a kernel of warmth despite all the trouble she was in. She was about to start chatting when her father leaned in.

'I'll let you and Pete get on,' he said to Shonna, then added pointedly, 'Colin's waiting for you in the kitchen, Willy.'

Shonna turned on a big smile. 'No rest for us! I better hustle to make up time.'

'Move it, Willy!' yelled her father from the hall.

Wil did. Twenty minutes later, when she was unpacking a cabinet box and their father was nowhere in sight, Colin dropped his voice so she could just hear him over the radio. 'What the hell happened last night? You told me you were going home and five minutes later you're being arrested!'

'It wasn't my fault!' she hissed back. Then, as he gave her sceptical eyebrows, 'Okay, fine, it was. I didn't know you weren't allowed to touch cops! But they were hurting Rob—'

'Something I have no trouble believing.'

'And I was just trying to tell them to . . . I dunno.' She was exhausted just thinking about it. She slid the box onto the counter and rubbed her temples. 'I just wish Dad didn't know.'

Colin sighed. 'I had to tell him, Wil. He's done work for half the cops at the station. I reckoned he was a better bet to get you out than me. And he was going to find out anyway.'

In a small voice, Wil found herself saying, 'But now Kate's going to know.'

Colin took a breath to reply, but their father appeared by the stairs, running a tape measure along the floor, one hand braced on his lower back. They both went back to unpacking to the sound of the radio ad break, until he moved away again.

'He shouldn't be here,' Wil whispered. 'He should be resting.'

'You try keeping him away.' Colin lightly punched her arm, and whispered, 'Happy birthday anyway.'

'Thanks,' she said, but her birthday seemed so trivial and undeserved today.

They worked to the tunes of the local FM station for the next hour, hanging the final cabinets and preparing to start on splashbacks. As she was knocking down the last cabinet box for recycling, Wil's phone rang.

Expecting Rob, her spirits sank when she saw a private number on the screen. She cancelled the call, but two minutes later they called again.

'Hello?' she said, pinning two collapsed boxes under her arm and heading for the skip.

'Wilhelmina Mann?' The voice was male and sounded older. Polished, too, in a way that made her pause.

'Yes, this is Wil.'

'This is Bruce Turner from Turner, Little and Cody. We've met briefly a few times. Do you have a minute?'

Wil's heart started pounding. Bruce Turner was her father's lawyer. She'd occasionally seen him at job sites, and her father would mention him whenever they were negotiating contracts. This could only be about last night. She dropped the boxes near the skip. 'Ah, I suppose. What's this about?'

'Well, your father called me about what happened last night, and I'm wondering if you could come in and meet me later today.'

Her thoughts were spinning now. Were the police going to charge her after all? Did her father want her to sign something? She took a step, tripped on the boxes and barely caught herself.

'We've got a job on today,' she rushed out, trying to pick the boxes up with her phone squashed to her ear. 'I'm pretty busy.'

'I understand. And it's not urgent, but we found some correspondence in our filing that belongs to you. From your mother's estate. I would like to meet you personally about it.'

Wil slowly straightened, boxes forgotten. 'I'm sorry, what did you say?'

An hour later, Wil was sitting in Bruce Turner's office, which had deep leather seats, arctic air-conditioning and a giant oil painting of the Gold Coast shore on the wall. She sat forward on the chair, conscious of her grout and tile-dust covered clothes.

Bruce Turner was a commanding figure, with shoulders like a support beam, but elegantly dressed in a blue suit, his tie flecked with small pink fleurs-de-lis. Wil knew her father liked him for his lack of nonsense, which was almost laughable, seeing as her being here seemed to be exactly that.

'Sorry to take you away from work, even if it is a Saturday,' he said, smiling over half-rims. 'Your father must want you back pretty quickly.'

'He said he'd make an exception for you,' Wil said.

Bruce chuckled. 'I'll take that as a compliment. Now, you must be wondering what this is all about.'

He slid a thick yellow envelope across the desk. 'When your father called early this morning, my paralegal thought to cross-reference your file in our archive. Which is why we found these letters.'

Wil looked down at the envelope, then back to Bruce's face, searching for meaning in his pause. When he'd said 'correspondence', she'd imagined a stack of old bank statements. 'Letters?'

'Letters your mother wrote, for you,' he said.

'For me?'

Bruce pushed the packet towards her. 'Before we took over the old firm here, they'd had a fire in the building. There was a lot of smoke and water damage, and then the files were held by the insurance company for a couple of years. Even after we got the files back, it took years to reorganise and catalogue them. We only discovered these ones today.'

Gingerly, Wil pulled the packet off the desk, feeling the weight of it. It crackled under her fingers. One end was open, and she tipped it to peer inside. All she could see was a clear plastic cover holding yellowed envelopes, but an old smell of woodsmoke and damp paper curled in the air. The contents were a mystery, the same way her mother was. Wil felt a qualm looking at nothing more than a stack of old paper. A nothing that somehow meant so much.

'Okay,' she said slowly. 'But I got a letter already. When I was five.'

'I understand, but there were more. They were part of her will. One letter each year until you turned eighteen.'

'Okay,' she said again. But she didn't feel okay. She felt as though Bruce had opened a door in the sky, and there was another world behind it.

On the way back to work, Wil stopped at a bakery and ordered six sausage rolls while the envelope of letters sat on the passenger seat. She was still trying to process what Bruce had said.

Letters. One a year until she was eighteen.

Even when she'd thought the correspondence might be bank statements, the idea of seeing her mother's name on something so ordinary had seemed capable of making her real. But real in a way that was safe, a way to look in the mirror at a reflection of her mother.

But now, letters. More letters.

They weren't a reflection. They were looking into the sun.

She pulled back up to the Mason house and cracked the window to let out the smell of pastry, but she couldn't make herself climb out. She scanned the windows of the house, searching for her father watching her, then glanced at the packet.

It was easy to slide the clear plastic wallet onto the seat, Bruce Turner's card slotted in a window on the front. She turned the pile over and stared at the envelope on the top.

It was the same type of envelope as the other letter she had. Nothing fancy, just a once-white rectangle. Surrounded with a night sky of age spots, the blue cursive script read, simply, *Mina*.

Wil's heart flinched, as though she'd touched a live wire.

Haltingly, she opened the plastic zip and pulled out the envelopes. They were bound together with a thick rubber band. Each one had the same name written on the front, and a little date in faded pencil in the top right. The first one was 1995. The next, 1996. She'd never realised the 1994 on the letter in her drawer had meant something. She flicked through, finding one envelope for each year, right up to 2007, the year she'd turned eighteen. Thirteen letters. Missing for over thirteen years. Her eyes welled.

Her mother had touched these. She hugged the pile into herself.

Somewhere in the house, a tile saw started up, which sounded like the feeling in her chest. A horrible, jagged thing that kept burning her throat and throwing tears into her eyes. She had grabbed the steering wheel, squeezing to stop from screaming, when a face appeared in the passenger window.

'Hi, there!'

Wil jumped. It was Shonna, the plumber's apprentice. She knocked on the glass. 'You okay in there? Need a hand carrying anything?'

Wil snatched up the bakery bag and pushed her door open, flustered. She turned away from the car a moment, trying to gather herself.

'Got sausage rolls,' she said, holding the bag up to cover any signs of crying. 'Got to help everyone get their cholesterol!'

'Great. But not for me, I don't eat meat.'

Shonna couldn't have known how much this was a lifeline. Wil held it and pulled herself back. 'Oh, I didn't think. And I could have bought cake, too. I guess I could go back, or maybe Colin would. Dad will want me to get back to work.'

She wondered if Shonna could tell she was rambling.

'Hey, no worries,' Shonna said. 'Pete's sending me to the hardware so I'll pick up a couple of spinach and feta triangles on the way back. Don't sweat it.' She gave Wil a big grin. 'So how about a drink later? Colin said it was your birthday, so totally my shout. I just moved to the coast and I don't really know anyone. I need pointing in the right direction of fun things to do. Figured us girls should stick together.'

'I, ah, can't tonight,' Wil said, folding in on herself as her father came out the door. 'Another time.'

'Oh right, you have plans already,' Shonna said, smacking herself lightly on the forehead. 'My bad, should have thought. Happy birthday, though.' She waved and jogged off to Pete's truck.

'What did Bruce want?' her dad said, glancing at the retreating Shonna.

'Nothing important,' Wil said quickly. 'I thought I should get back to work now.'

Cameron considered her a moment, then grunted. 'He'll probably send a good bill. Okay, let's get on.' Then, after a pause, 'Happy birthday.'

But her birthday was the furthest thing from Wil's mind. All she could think about was the envelopes with her name on them, what was in them, and when this horrible overwhelming feeling would go away.

Chapter 3

The letters stayed in the car and Wil tried to go back to work. Only, she'd be halfway through mixing a bucket of mortar, or breaking down an empty box, and suddenly that drawing of the night sky she knew so well from the letter in her drawer would be before her eyes again, with its restful scene, and those words of love, and she'd find herself losing time like she had at the beach yesterday.

With effort, she would pull herself back to task. But then sudden anger would come, itching in her hands, and she'd be slamming paint tins and swearing under her breath.

'What's up with you?' Tony demanded at one point.

'Nothing,' Wil said, deliberately putting the next tin down softly. But she muttered about him under her breath, grievances she normally let go. Like how her father often talked up Tony's work achievements around her, as if it would motivate Wil to hear how her younger brother had succeeded where she had failed. Or how she'd caught Tony laughing about her with his mates, once, when she'd been working in her father's office and kept sending the wrong invoices. She remembered the awful jealousy she'd felt growing up, over Tony and Colin's special place in her father and Carol's marriage. Only, back then, she'd always had Kate to lean on.

The thought of Kate made it worse, the knot around her heart tighter than ever.

Wil was wrung out by home time. She changed into soft trackpants and her oldest, most comforting T-shirt, but she couldn't settle. She paced her room, picking up laundry. Opened and closed the old bar fridge twice, even though it was empty. She took up a sketchbook and pencil, usually a sure way to lose herself for at least an hour, but she couldn't start anything.

Finally, she dug in her drawer and pulled out the 1994 letter, and laid it on the bed. Then she extracted the new packet from her bag, and gingerly tipped out the thirteen others. She lined them up. The first letter looked so slender next to the rest, and she had the feeling of looking up a steep dune, with her feet sinking into soft sand before a hard climb. Slowly, she reached for the one marked 1995 and slid out the pages.

Dear Mina,

Happy 6th birthday, my darling girl. The last year must have held many new things for you. I think starting school must be the biggest one. I remember when you started playgroup, and then kindy, you always went along bravely, even though you didn't know what you'd find there. And in part, I'm writing this letter because of school. I wish I could have seen you in your uniform, and picked you up at the end of the day, and put all your drawings on the fridge. I always loved the stories you told me about the pictures you made.

But I know playgroup and kindy weren't as easy for you as they were for Kate, and you might find that school is the same.

Some people find school isn't easy. That's what it was like for me. My school was a bit different to yours, though. I came from a small village in England, which is on the other side of the world. The village is called South Bandinby, which is just near a bigger city called Lincoln. Kate might help you look it up in the atlas.

It has just one road that goes in a circle, with most of the houses on the outside. But all around that are green fields, full of crops and sheep, as far as you can see.

In winter, when I was growing up, it often snowed and the fields were all white. Sometimes the steep hill up to the main road was so deep with snow that no one could drive it! That must seem very strange to you, living in Australia.

Our schoolhouse was just one room, a small building among the houses. School was never something I really enjoyed. I found it hard to pay attention, and our teacher was very strict. It was even worse in winter, where we had just this tiny stove in the corner that didn't make us warm. I used to pretend I was a little mouse who had a nest in the wall, all lined with soft wool and snug and warm. But even in summer, I was always looking out the windows, or not hearing what the teacher said, and in trouble. My parents were workers in the village and, in those days, the teachers often thought that workers, and their children, weren't good for anything.

That will probably seem strange and unfair to you, but our village was like that. There was a lord, who was like the boss, and who owned all the land. Then came the farmers, who planted the crops and kept the sheep. And then the workers, who did all the hard work for the farmers. That was really very important, but many people thought worker children like me weren't very clever.

Sometimes you meet people like that, who will think you can't do things. And that can make you feel like you can't. But sometimes it's just that they aren't the best people to teach you.

That's why I met your teacher, Miss Morton, to see if she would be a good teacher for you. I liked her straightaway. She seemed to understand me, and I thought she would be good for you, and make your school experience so much better than mine.

I also hope that you make friends at school, but don't worry if you don't. It took me a very long time to make friends, and before that I just had my brothers. There were five of them, all older than me, and we weren't close. It's lovely that you and Kate always look after each other. And I hope you will always have that. But I think we also need those friends who aren't our family, because they can show us different things. You will meet someone like that, I'm sure, but I can't say when.

For now, I am going to leave this letter. There will be another. Be brave, my darling girl.

Love,
Mummy

Underneath, her mother had drawn a little mouse wearing glasses and a pair of overalls, and sitting on a toadstool. The mouse had a giant pencil in one hand, an open book in his lap, and was grinning. In the background, a roaring fire lit a cosy room of cushions and an oversized plate holding a wedge of cheese.

Wil put the letter down, her mind swimming. What was all this about a Miss Morton being her teacher? Wil's first-grade teacher had been a white-haired woman who'd often sent Wil to sit on the time-out mat. Had that been Miss Morton? Wil couldn't remember, but she didn't think so.

She reached for the next letter, marked 1996.

Dear Mina,

Happy 7th birthday, darling girl. Christmas and Easter have come and gone again (I hope lots of chocolate?), and I so wish I could have been there to see you opening presents and hunting for eggs in the garden. You won't remember, I'm sure, but we first hunted for Easter eggs when you were two and Kate was four. It was at the beach in Perth, early in the morning before the sand got hot. We all sat in the shade and ate chocolate. How different that was to Easter when I was growing up!

When I was young, we went to church at Easter. My mother, father and brothers and I would all walk up the lane to the church, which was made of grey stone, and sat on a little hill beside the village houses.

A lady everyone called Granny Maxwell would play the organ, and we would sing hymns. The whole village would be there, from Lord Elston and his two boys up the front to all of us worker families at the back.

For me, the service just seemed to go on and on and on, a bit like school. I would imagine all kinds of fun places and games to pass the time. Outside the windows was a huge tree by a wall, so I'd imagine climbing it and looking down into a fairy kingdom just outside the village. A hidden fairy kingdom that only I could see. Or I'd imagine climbing right over the wall and into the manor house (that was the big house where Lord Elston lived) and visiting a friendly dragon who lived in the cellar.

Of course, I was never allowed to actually do those things. Growing up in that tiny village was very hard because I didn't really fit in. The other kids at school didn't want to play my games, and my older brothers were always off doing things on the farm, things that I wasn't allowed to do.

We lived in a small cottage with no TV, and I had no real idea about life outside the village. My brothers would sneakily listen to the radio sometimes, and once I was listening too, from the top of the stairs, and I heard a Beatles song called 'Twist and Shout'. Ask Kate to find it for you? She has all my tapes.

Something about that song was really exciting to me. It seemed to come from a faraway place, a long way from where I was. I think that was when I first started to really think about leaving the village and what would come after school.

I'm writing this because I think you might be like me, and find it hard to fit in. Maybe other people don't want to play your games, too. That might not be true. But if it is, I want you to know that you are just the way you're meant to be.

The world is a big place with many different types of people,
and you will fit in with some of them just fine.
  Be brave, my darling.

Love,
  Mummy

This time, the sketch on the letter was of a pretty stone church, set among leaning headstones. The church sat on a rise, with a square belltower at one end and a long nave with arched windows. A tree with spreading boughs framed the building, reaching across a heavy stone wall that bounded the right side of the picture. Little sprites and fairies were drawn among the branches and along the wall.

Wil read the letter again. It wasn't the music that seemed to come from a different universe, it was these words. Easter egg hunts on a Perth beach? Kate having all her mother's tapes? Wil didn't know they'd ever been to Perth, that there had ever been tapes. But most of all, it was all that stuff about not fitting in, and not being able to pay attention. That was exactly what Wil had been like. And yet, no one had ever said anything like this to her before.

With a shaking hand, she flipped to the next letter, marked 1997.

Dear Mina,

  Happy 8th birthday, my darling girl. I thought in this letter
I would tell you a little more about my village, and about my
first best friend, because we met when we were eight.

Her name was Susie, and Granny Maxwell was her grandmother. She'd lived in Lincoln city before the village, which is only a short drive now but when I was growing up it seemed a long way away, like the fairy kingdom. She had found school difficult, too, and she liked to go adventuring.

So it wasn't long before we were going everywhere together. Sometimes, we'd walk up the hill and cross the big road to an old airfield, where we'd play fighter pilots in the abandoned building there. Sometimes, we'd go down the path (called the 'bridleway') towards North Bandinby (which was the next village north of South Bandinby—creative names!) and play fairy kingdoms in the lumpy field.

But most often, we went to the wood.

The wood is different to the bush in Australia. It sits in the middle of the fields, and doesn't look big from the outside. But inside, it can be dark, with the trees growing close together. Susie and I loved searching for fairy circles, which are rings of mushrooms, or wild blackberries, or sitting on logs making up stories about elves and witches.

We had to be careful of nettles, which are stinging plants, and we hid if any of the boys or the village men turned up to hunt, but that just made it more exciting. We could spend hours in there, and then be in trouble for disappearing. On summer school holidays, when my parents were busy with the farm harvest, we'd often only come out of the wood when the sun was going down. The sky would be all orange, and the fields and rooftops rimmed in golden sunlight. It felt like a magical time.

I was so sad when Susie moved away again. All the good things in the day disappeared with her. None of the jobs in the house or garden could hold my attention. I was more annoyed than ever that my brothers were going off to jobs outside the village, or visiting friends far away. It's hard to watch your older siblings do things first, and you might find that with Kate, too. Your turn comes though, even when it seems it might not.

I wrote to Susie for a long time, and I did eventually see her again. I will tell you more about that another time.

For now, though, I wonder how things are for you? Do you have a good friend, or have you lost one? Is Kate doing things you want to do and can't? Are you still living in the house with the blue door? Do you have a special place for adventures?

I wish I could hear all these things from you, that I could still comfort you when something makes you sad, and celebrate the fun things. You can tell me these things, if you want, and I promise to hear them, wherever I am now.

With all my love,
Mum

Underneath, her mother had sketched two little girls, holding hands beneath dark overhanging trees. They were laughing together, a fairy ring of mushrooms circling their feet.

Wil remembered the one close friend she'd had in primary school. She'd thought they'd be friends forever, until that girl had discovered the cool kids, who were listening to Hanson and the Backstreet Boys and the Spice Girls on their portable CD players, and sneakily playing with their Tamagotchi pets in class. Wil hadn't known how to be cool, and with three children then in the Butler house, and sketchy economic times for her father's business, there were no CDs or electronic toys. Wil had found herself excluded. But even before that, she and her friend hadn't had adventures together. She'd never had a friend who matched her mother's description of Susie.

Being frustrated over Kate doing things first, however—that, she knew all too well. The knot tightened around her heart, again, and she needed relief from it.

Wil dropped the letter, turned on her bedside lamp and thumbed through her phone. For the second time in as many days, she paused at Kate's number before quickly moving to Rob. She tried him and got voicemail. Again. He didn't respond to a text.

Dusk was settling into dark now. Her fingers hovered over the bright screen. She tapped on the blank search bar and typed *South Bandinby*.

Maps quickly brought up a view of a tiny loop of road, branching west off a north–south arterial with a B number. Turning on the satellite picture, she could make out the shape of the church to the north of the loop, and a cluster of other buildings. To the south was a dark rectangle, which could be the wood. It was so strange to think this was where her mother had grown up; stranger still to have known nothing about it until today.

A knock came on the door.

'Dinner call,' said Colin, poking his head into the room. 'I'm about to order the pizza. You want the usual?'

'Not hungry,' Wil said.

'But it's your birthday dinner! You can't just sit down here reading. What is that anyway?'

'Nothing important.' She casually pulled a sketchbook on top of the envelopes.

'Come on, come up,' he said.

Wil shook her head, but Colin hovered. 'How'd you like that Shonna girl? She's Pete's niece. Seemed nice.'

'Yeah, she seemed nice.' She wanted him to go, so naturally he didn't.

'I thought you two might get along.' He stepped inside the door and leaned on the wall, clearly bent on convincing her to do the birthday dinner.

Wil dropped her phone. 'Did we ever live in a house with a blue door?' she asked.

Colin's eyebrows popped. 'Where did that come from?'

'It would have been ages ago, when Kate and I were little. I don't remember a lot from back then.'

'No blue doors that I remember,' he said, tapping his chin. 'But I'm the wrong one to ask. I'm eight years younger than you, remember.'

'Oh, I remember that.'

He grinned. 'Why don't you ask Kate?'

'Yeah, maybe.'

Colin took a breath to say something, then let it go. 'You really not hungry?'

'Nah,' Wil said. 'And forget I said anything, okay?'

'Okay.' He pushed himself off the wall, but he looked back at her before he disappeared.

Wil waited until she heard him go back up the stairs before she took out the next letter, marked 1998, and ran her finger over the writing on the cover. A crack had opened in the abstract idea she had of her mother. And through that crack, Wil could glimpse not only the person her father would never talk about, but the kind of mother Ann Mann might have been. It was so much more solid than the scarce memory Wil had of her.

In the back of her mind there was caution: if her father would never talk about her mother, if she had been like Wil as a child, would that mean she was disappointing as an adult?

But that worry seemed far removed from the reading so far, and she wasn't going to let it stop her from reading more.

⌒

Dear Mina,

Happy 9th birthday, darling girl.

Now that you're a little older, I thought I should tell you about your name. You probably know Kate was named after her grandmother, Katherine. So where did Wilhelmina come from?

I must confess, I never liked my own name: Ann Mann. How plain is that? My first name and last name are nearly the same! Ann was so common, too. I knew three other Anns in school, and another two women in the village. I have a whole family tree of Anns—grandmothers and aunts. I'm not even Anne with an 'e', which is a joke from a wonderful book you might want to read: Anne of Green Gables. *I didn't read it until I was much older than you, but Anne in the story was often in strife like I was, and I always liked how, despite her difficult start to life, she found a wonderful place in the end. She always wanted a different name, too!*

I was in London when I first read about Queen Wilhelmina. She was famous in the Second World War, but it was the name that stayed with me. Later, in New York, I came across another Wilhelmina, a model called Wilhelmina Cooper.

For a long time after that, I carried the name around in my mind. It seemed to have such promise in it. Then, the moment I saw you, I knew that it was yours.

I don't know if you'll thank me for it. It's hard to stand out sometimes. But I had a sense you would stand out anyway. And you could make your own history.

Perhaps that won't make a lot of sense, so I'll try to explain. History often matters a lot, both with names and with what we think we're allowed to do. In my village, Lord Elston's family had history like that. They had been lords in the village for hundreds of years! And while there were a lot of Anns in the village (and Elizabeths and Emmas too), in Lord Elston's family, the men were all called John, Henry or Thomas.

And all those Johns, Henries and Thomases owned all the land—that was their history. I've mentioned that before, I think, but it's probably a little strange to think of one person owning everything across two entire towns, and everyone else having to ask that person if they are allowed to live there. But that was how South Bandinby worked, and probably still does.

You remember when I told you about looking out of the church window at the wall under the big tree? On the other side of that wall was the manor house, where the Elstons lived. It was a stone building, far bigger than any of the village houses, with gardens all around and huge trees between it and the road.

I was fascinated with the manor house growing up. We didn't often see Lord Elston, or his wife, or his two boys (Thomas and John), so I always wanted to know what they were doing in their big house. I was sure it must be so exciting.

I didn't understand why we weren't just allowed to go in there. We all lived in the same village, and I went to many of the other houses. But somehow we weren't supposed to be friends with the Elstons. And the only reason, really, was because no one ever had been before. Which I've always thought was a silly reason for anything.

I'm saying this because you might notice that people often do things just because it's what people have always done. I was expected to stay near the village, and do what my mother had done, as her mother had, and hers. Just as Lord Elston was supposed to keep living in his house and running his land, and his sons were meant to do that too.

But those things weren't rules. And if I'd followed them, I'd never have had the life I had, and I never would have read the name Wilhelmina, and I would never have had you.

So if you ever find someone expecting you to do something, or be something, just because that's what they expect, maybe you can remember that it's not a rule, and there might be a better way for you.

As always, I love you, my darling girl. Be brave. I miss you.

Love,

   Mum

At the bottom of the last page, Ann had drawn the manor house, with a long line of dry-stone wall in the foreground. The wall was capped with its own tiled roof, making it look like a battlement. The house itself was elegant, with large windows and a sloping roof, a building made for snowy winters.

But even that distant, old-world manor house made more sense than the way her mother saw her in these letters.

Wil pushed herself up and paced around the room. Don't worry about not fitting in? Be brave? Find friends and don't do what people expect?

All that people expected of Wil was for her to make mistakes. And her name having promise? Please. Ann had been right about one thing: her name had made Wil stand out. It had followed her through school offices and detention rooms. It was the name that came home on lacklustre report cards and was written on a lengthy school file. She'd felt relief in finally settling on Wil, which cut away every unneeded syllable.

This was all garbage. Long-ago letters from someone who didn't know her at all.

So why did it make her so angry?

Wil stopped pacing, her fists balled into her legs, realising that tears were running rivers down her face. She swiped at them with her sleeve. The letters were still stacked on the bed. God, this was ridiculous. She didn't need this.

In two quick steps, she yanked the bedside drawer open and shunted the lot of them inside, among the stacks of old loyalty cards and broken headphones, spare shoelaces and USB sticks. She banged the drawer closed, and then sat on the table, as if the drawer might open again on its own.

When her blurry eyes cleared, she spotted a white rectangle that had fallen to the floor: Bruce's card. He'd said to call if she wanted.

Oh, she was going to, all right.

Chapter 4

The long wait through the next work day did nothing to help Wil's mood. By the time the appointment rolled around on Monday afternoon, she was feeling so punchy she backed her Corolla into a pole in the Turner, Little & Cody carpark, and couldn't sit still in their white-tiled reception. The girl behind the desk watched her with wary eyes. Wil desperately wanted a drink to loosen the fist in her stomach. She kept forgetting what she had planned to say.

By the time Bruce called her in, she was ready to burst.

'I don't understand,' she started. 'Those letters were written for my birthdays. Each year. From when I was five. But the fire you mentioned didn't happen until 2003. I looked it up. So why didn't I get them before that?'

She clamped her teeth to stop the wobble in her voice.

Bruce nodded. 'This is awkward and potentially upsetting,' he said, pulling out a slim file. 'I didn't know all the details when we spoke the other day. You are correct, those letters

41

were intended for you while you were growing up. It was part of your mother's wishes . . . only it was felt at the time that giving you the letters may not have been in your best interests.'

'What does that mean?'

Bruce shifted in his chair. 'Your father had some professional advice that said it might be damaging for you to receive letters each year. It was felt they might not allow you to move on. So he stepped in to have them held until you were eighteen. And before that time, well, the fire happened.'

Wil blinked, aware she wasn't absorbing something he was saying. 'But I got the first one. Why would they give me one, and not the others?'

Bruce spread his hands. 'There was probably no reason to hold the first one. Especially with your mother having died right before your birthday. It must have been some time afterwards that your father sought advice about the other letters.'

'I'm sorry, what?'

'I said, it must have been some time—'

'No, go back. She died right before my birthday?'

Bruce paused. 'Yes, the day before. I'm sorry, I thought that was something you knew.'

'No,' Wil whispered. It was clear now how little she knew. Or rather, how much had been kept from her. Her hands trembled, her throat beating with her own pulse. She couldn't begin to form a thought, much less a sentence.

Bruce Turner pushed a box of tissues across the table. 'This is clearly distressing,' he said. 'It's a lot to take in, during what is already a stressful few days. I feel for you.'

Wil didn't know why, but his kindness and his calmness were working against her now. Her body was so tense, all she wanted to do was smash the crystal decanter sitting on his side-board to get some relief.

After another pause, Bruce said, 'I assume, then, that you've read them?'

'Some,' Wil whispered, but she felt far away, caught in imagining her mother writing the letters, and then them being locked in a filing cabinet during all these years. 'But my father, he had them . . . put away?'

Bruce nodded, slowly and uncomfortably.

'What else? What else don't I know?'

He pushed the slim file across the desk. 'You can see for yourself. There's a copy of your mother's will in here, but it's fairly straightforward. Apart from your letters, there were some other letters and a few items of jewellery and some music and personal effects left to your sister, Kate. Nothing else, I'm sorry.'

'Wait, Kate had letters? *Letters*. Like, more than one?'

Bruce nodded.

'And were those held back from her?'

Bruce shifted in his seat again. 'I don't see any indication they were.'

Wil laughed bitterly. Kate had never mentioned letters. Ever. 'Right. So this is "nothing else". Any other fun discoveries in the files?'

She pressed a hand to her burning cheek, hearing her own hysteria. She was embarrassed but too upset to stop. 'I mean, is it not enough that she's the favourite anyway? The one with everything together? No, she has to have had all the things she was meant to have, too.'

'I can understand how that must seem terribly unfair,' Bruce said.

Wil suddenly slumped, as if all the things she'd learned in the last few days had become an unliftable load. Slowly, she slid the folder from his desk and hugged it to her chest.

'I just don't understand how this happened,' she whispered. 'How can my luck be this bad?'

Bruce sighed. 'I know this must be dragging up a lot of old emotions. And without speaking out of turn, I know this has been a difficult time between you and your father. It would be a shame if this added to the trouble.'

'But he never says anything about her,' Wil blurted. 'Did he hate her? Does he hate me? Is that why he never talks about her at all? Why he did this?'

Bruce shook his head, and for a long minute, he seemed to grasp for words. 'Look, I didn't know your mother at all. Your father and I didn't meet until many years after she was gone. And he's never talked about her. Except once, briefly, at a Christmas party.'

Wil froze, hanging on every word.

'He'd had one too many at the time, and I was there as a friend, not as his lawyer, which is the only reason I'm mentioning it,' Bruce said. 'He talked about their life, that they'd worked together, but that it had all been ruined somehow. Which is a lot of people's stories. I do think he loved her, Wil. Perhaps more than he can say. But, regardless of what they thought of each other, it's not a reflection on you. Those letters are a gift to you. Delivered late, but still. It's up to you what to do with that gift.'

When Bruce pushed the door open, he told her to take care and call again if she wanted to. But all Wil could feel was that she'd come in search of answers, trying to make sense of her confusion over the letters, thinking this was only about her mother, and some other imagined life that could have been. But none of that had been resolved. Instead, it was far worse. Secrets had been kept from her. Not only involving her father, but Kate, too.

⌒

Dear Mina,

Happy 10th birthday, darling girl. What a proud day, to write your age with two digits! I remember the first time I could do that, and it seemed as though bigger things were so much closer.

I think every year is a celebration. I wanted to be like Granny Maxwell, with wild white hair and a cane. I wanted to tell people I was eighty-three, or ninety-three! Having only made it to thirty, I'm rather disappointed.

I hope I'm not upsetting you to say that. I wanted these letters to be something happy, a little piece of me I can leave with you. By the time you're reading this letter, several years will have passed since I did, and I hope that the grief is easing into time. It does get easier.

I thought I'd tell you a funny story in this letter, about something that happened when I was ten. It's also something that happened at the manor house, and I've been thinking a lot about the manor since I finished the last letter. This story is about the first time I saw inside it.

Once a year, the Elstons held a party for the church committee, and Lady Elston herself hosted it in the manor house garden. To me, Lady Elston seemed very posh—she wore beautiful clothes and huge pearls, and her hair was glossy and neat. Never with sticks or leaves in it, like mine! She and Lord Elston often travelled away, to London or even France, so when she was in the village it was like the queen was in town.

When I was ten, I was invited to the garden party. How on earth did that happen? Well, it was because I'd been given the job of turning the sheet music for Granny Maxwell when she played the organ. I had absolutely no talent for music, but I could turn a page when Granny Maxwell nodded, and my mother was so fed up with me disappearing from the house that she was happy for Granny Maxwell to take some charge of me. Maybe my mother thought all those hours of practising in the church, and by the piano in Granny Maxwell's cottage, would do me good. I'm sorry to report that it just gave me more time to think about the fairy kingdom. Granny Maxwell would stomp her cane on the ground when I was distracted and missed the page turn, which was often.

But, as poor a page turner as I was, I was invited to the party. It was the first time I'd walked through the manor gates. The garden was magical, with little ponds and flowerbeds under spreading trees, and archways leading off into deeper green wonderlands behind the wall. But that was nothing on the house itself, all grand with its bright red door.

I just couldn't help myself. All the adults were busy talking, so it wasn't hard to slip around the corner to the back of the house. That was where the kitchen door faced another little cottage (I learned later that was for the gamekeeper) with hedges in front. A perfect hiding spot.

From the hedges, it was easy to just walk through the kitchen door and into the house.

I don't know exactly what I was expecting. Big paintings on the walls maybe? Stacks of gold on a desk in the library? A curving staircase that Lady Elston would descend in a ballgown? An actual dragon in the cellar?

Well, I was a bit disappointed to find none of those things. But it was definitely fancier than any of the village houses. The kitchen was huge, with these heavy wood cabinets with wood so polished that it shimmered. There was a separate dining room, which was amazing to me because we only had a fold-out table in the kitchen in our house. The curtains and carpets were thick like new.

I only meant to take a quick look. But, as I've said before, I often couldn't stop myself, and before I knew what I was doing I'd climbed all the way up the stairs. I knew I'd gone too far when I came to a room with pale blue walls and a single neatly made bed with a plush quilt. It was a child's room; a whole room just for them! There was a row of toy trucks neatly lined up under the window, through which I could hear the party outside. It was then I realised how much trouble I would be in to be caught there.

I crept back down the stairs—and let me tell you, every one of them creaked so loudly! Then I had to hide by the stairs when the cook came back to the kitchen, and I only just made it outside again without anyone seeing me, and just in time for the photo.

Now, I'm not telling you this because I think what I did was smart or good. It's just that sometimes adults forget that they ever did silly things when they were growing up, and I try not to. Maybe because I did so many silly things, and because I want you to trust that I understand when you make mistakes. That you can tell me if you broke that window and blamed it on the dog. Or took something you shouldn't have. I know I can't answer you, but you can tell me all the same. I like to think that when someone loves you as much as I love you, they never really leave you.

Until next year. Be brave, darling girl.

Love,

   Mum

There wasn't a drawing this time. Instead, inside the letter was a photo. Or, rather, a photocopy of a photo. The reproduction was grainy, but the picture was clear enough: a group of people in blocky coats and stewardess hats, sideburns and shirtdresses—as if fashion was lagging a decade behind in South Bandinby—all posing in front of an ornate door crowned with a sunburst, and flanked on both sides with square-paned windows. Both floors of windows were just visible in the blockwork of the building. The door's surface was deep grey in the photocopy, but Wil could imagine it as a scarlet shade of red.

It only took Wil a second to spot the girl wearing a guilty expression at the far right of the photo. She stared at that face for a long time, shocked at how much the expression looked like her own school photographs. Her mother's features, however, looked more like Kate's, with the thick fringe and heart-shaped chin. More delicate, like Kate.

It was hard to imagine that face making mistakes. Wil couldn't help thinking of the shoplifting she'd done at sixteen. Would her mother really have understood that?

Would it have happened if she'd read this letter when she was meant to?

She checked her watch: nearly eight-thirty. She could hear the TV on upstairs, with a warble of commentary over the constant roar of a stadium soccer crowd. Wil had calmed down since leaving Bruce's office, but the sense of betrayal hadn't gone. She vacillated between her phone and going upstairs. Finally, she bit her lip and called Kate.

'Can't talk long,' Kate said, dispensing with hello. 'Dead tired. Just got off a double shift and Ash isn't sleeping well. What's up?'

Wil's heart was thudding so hard she thought Kate must be able to hear it. There was a difficult pause. When they'd been teenagers Kate would have been onto Wil in a second with these signals that something was up. But not anymore.

'Is this about your run-in with the cops? I imagine Dad is livid.'

Wil paused. So, Kate knew. 'Did he tell you?'

'Tony did. I thought you said you were done with those friends? Colin says they're a pack of losers. Sounds like Dad's ready to kick you out.'

'They're only part-time friends,' Wil said, but she didn't want to talk about that.

'Uh-huh. How's Dad's back? Is he taking it easy?'

'He's watching the soccer,' Wil said, glancing at the letters, knowing she was dancing around her purpose. 'And he's back at work.'

'Of course he is. Oh, happy birthday for Saturday,' Kate said. 'Meant to text you, sorry. Did your present arrive?'

'What present?'

'Oh. I ordered it online. Pretend I didn't say anything.' Kate yawned. 'I'll go in a sec. I need to nap.'

'Did you ever get a letter from Mum?' Wil blurted.

There was a long pause. Wil tried to fill it. 'I mean, after she, you know . . .'

'Died?' Kate finally said, an edge in her voice. 'Why are you asking?'

'Did you?'

Another pause. 'Yes.'

Silence hung between them. Wil looked up at the ceiling, every word feeling like pulling her own molars. 'Why didn't you say anything? I let you read my letter when we were kids.'

'I'd rather not talk about it,' Kate said. 'It was a long time ago now, Wil.'

'What about other letters? You got more, didn't you? Were they on your birthdays?'

Kate gave a flustered sigh. 'Look, there was one when I graduated from uni, okay? And one when Neil and I got married, and another when I had Ashleigh.'

'What?'

'But you wouldn't know anything about that, seeing as you didn't come to the christening.'

That edge in Kate's voice was honed now. A week ago, Wil would have been wounded by the reminder about the christening. That was what her father couldn't forgive her for. But her pain now was so much bigger, full of the reminders of Kate's milestones that she never felt she'd reach, and the letters she hadn't known about. The hurt of loss and betrayal ate the space between them.

'Sorry,' Kate said, huffing a breath. 'I don't mean to bring it up again. I mean, I was hurt at the time, but you do you. I'm fine with it.'

Wil didn't believe this, but it eased the knot anyway. Then abruptly, Kate caught up. 'Why did you ask about birthdays?'

'I got letters, too. This week,' Wil rushed out. 'From a lawyer. But I was supposed to get them years ago. For birthdays.'

'From her?'

'Yeah.'

'Wait, how many letters are we talking about?'

Wil took a breath, suddenly unwilling to meet Kate's lack of disclosure with information of her own. 'A few.'

'And what's in them?'

Wil floundered. 'It's nothing important, I guess. Just stories from her village, of growing up there. Do you have her tapes?'

'Her what?'

'Music tapes.'

'Oh. Somewhere, I think.'

'God, why didn't you tell me?' Wil said, as the hurt slammed back with double force. She bit back tears and took a shaky breath. She felt even worse when Kate didn't reply, because she could feel her sister mustering her firm, reasonable adult voice. That voice only made Wil feel more insane.

'Look, Wil,' Kate said, calmly and a little too slowly. 'I'm sorry if you're hurt. But you know Mum wasn't the most stable character. You won't remember all the moving around, but I do. It's awful that we lost her, but she's been gone for more than twenty years, and we were lucky to have Carol. Maybe you need to take a few deep breaths.'

Wil clamped her teeth as Carol's name gave her another flash of anger. 'I guess.' The words were tight, as pleasant as chewing glass.

'Okay,' Kate said, as if that ended things. 'So, you still seeing that guy? Rob?'

But Wil had hardened to the conversation. 'I'll let you get to bed.'

After she hung up, Wil sat fingering the letter marked 2000, listening to the game upstairs. She felt charged, like she wanted to pick a fight.

Wil crept up the stairs in her sock feet and peered into the living room, checking if Tony was watching the game, too. But no, her father was there by himself, spread out flat along the three-seater, halfway down a Carlton Draught, and scrolling on his phone. The soccer was clearly over and now, on screen, a rugby scrum was packing in.

'Dad?'

'Mmm?' His eyes remained on the phone screen.

Wil edged around and sat on the chaise. Her bravado had left her somewhere on the way upstairs and she was casting around for how to open.

After a few seconds, her father grabbed the remote and pressed mute. 'What are you after?'

'Nothing, really. I mean, not nothing. It's just about seeing Bruce Turner.'

Instantly, her father's eyes flicked up from his screen. 'You said that was just a conversation. And I don't need to hear any advice he gave you. Bruce is a good bloke, so you can keep it between you. I did call them this morning about contracts and he didn't mention anything, so it's done. Leave it there.'

She bit her lip. 'It's about the letters.'

Her dad reached for the remote and shut the television off, his face difficult to read. With effort, he pushed himself up to a sitting position. Wil watched the way his actions were overly deliberate. She wasn't sure if he was half-drunk or just in pain.

'Which letters?' he said, but Wil could tell he knew what she meant.

'The birthday letters. From Mum. Bruce gave them to me.'

Her father went still, staring at his beer, as if he was about to ream an underdelivering contractor. His voice came out tense. 'They told me they were lost. In that fire.'

Wil, who'd been ready to accuse him of having withheld the letters, paused. He sounded angry, but not at her.

'Have you read them?' he asked suddenly.

'Some.'

'They make sense?'

'They're just stories about her growing up,' she said, carefully, 'in South Bandinby.'

The mood shifted from tense to frosty. Her father winced as he rolled and stood up. '*That* place.'

'You know it?'

He reached for his beer and drank it down to the bottom, a little foam splashing on his shirt as he finished. He wiped it with the back of his hand. 'The only time I set foot in that place was when that Susie girl died back in eighty-six. Liverpool won the Premier League that year. That's how I remember.'

Wil thought of the little pencil sketch of the two girls in the forest and felt a dreadful sadness. 'Susie? She died?'

'Aneurysm.'

Wil put a hand over her mouth. But she'd never seen her father talk like this—about things that were long past and just a degree away from her mother. She wanted him to keep talking.

'You knew her?'

He shook his head.

'What about the Elstons, the ones who lived in the manor house?' Wil tried to slow down, but she couldn't help rushing.

His body stiffened again and his accent thickened. 'Toffee-nosed buggers. They're nothing but trouble, those lordy types who think they're better than everyone else and don't do no work. Too up themselves for folks like us.'

'Did you ever—'

She broke off as her father stalked away. He chinked the beer bottle down on the kitchen bench and leaned over his hands on the counter. Finally, he looked up.

'This is old stuff, Wil,' he said. 'Old stuff. How does any of it help with what we talked about? With getting your life together and working on something that matters? I made myself clear. Nothing changes that.'

Wil had a new, curious experience in that moment. She could feel a barrier between them that was far older than the trouble she had fallen into since she was sixteen; a barrier as high as the manor house wall itself. It ran all the way back to the day her mother had died. And now, abruptly, she was back in that day.

She hadn't thought about it in years, and had never had concrete memories of it, just bright blurs of a room and people. But now she had a blinding certainty of wanting to stay with her mother, wanting it with all her soul, and that her father had taken her away. She had a flash of running. She certainly wanted to run from this feeling, of the pressure in her chest, of wanting to cry until she burst.

Then she was back in the now, and he was staring at her, waiting for a reply.

'You were clear,' she said, her voice tiny.

'And what was I clear about?'

'To apply myself. Get my life together, or I'm out.'

He moved back to the couch, slowly picked up the remote and flicked on the rugby again. 'New job starts tomorrow. Every chance to make it a good one.'

Chapter 5

Back in her room, Wil paced, trying to feel the same desperation she'd had on Saturday to make good on her promise to do better. Her father might be right—what good had the letters brought when it came to making better choices?

And that weird memory just now? Maybe she was just inventing things. Inventing the feeling of him keeping her away from her mother, because that's what he'd done with the letters. God, she felt like a mental case, even more than normal.

She sat on the bed and gripped the edge of the mattress, taking the breaths that Kate had suggested. She had to calm down. She was on her last chance here.

She didn't realise that she'd moved her hand to touch the letters until she was already opening one. She paused, but she felt much calmer. Bruce had said they were a gift. And they were just stories, weren't they? What harm could a story do?

Dear Mina,

Happy 11th birthday, my darling girl. I hope that you've had cake and good fun, perhaps a party or a special dinner to celebrate?

I thought I would tell you a story about a different part of the village, and about a very special friend of mine.

If you look up South Bandinby in an atlas, you might see a blue line running through the village. In Australia, it would be a creek and it would have a name. In the village, we just called it 'the beck', which is an old Viking word for stream. There were lots of Vikings in that part of England once upon a time. If you enjoy history, you might want to learn more about that.

Anyway, the beck began somewhere underground on the manor, and flowed out under the manor wall into the village, then all the way down to the fens, which just means a kind of swampy area. The wood had lost its magic for me after Susie moved out of the village and, by the time I was the age you are now, all my older brothers had left home, working in factories or on other farms. So I was often alone, and, just as often, I would go to the beck.

It had a narrow path by the side, and from there you could just see the church belltower through the trees. There were little duck families on the water. In summer, the bees would be droning in the grass, and in winter the water would break through the snow. I would still make up stories in my head, but fairies and dragons were starting to be less interesting. I wanted something new, and I wanted a friend to share it with.

Being lonely is the hardest thing to feel. It's so much more than being sad. You can feel lonely even when you're not alone, even with people who love you. Especially if you have

*something you can't tell them or that they won't understand.
It was often like that for me in the village, but the beck made
me feel better at those times.*

Wil took a breath, and looked away, realising loneliness was
what she so often felt. With Rob and his friends, with her father
and brothers, and in so many other places, including at school
when she was growing up. Kate had been the person who'd
made that feeling go away back then. Now, Kate had her own
life and Wil went to the beach, or drew in her books, or both
at the same time. Loneliness was the feeling she had every time
she looked in her contacts list and had no one to call.

And then, I found Bridget.
*When I was eleven, I finished at the village school, and
started at a comprehensive in Welton, another town nearby.
It was exciting, that first year, going outside the village every
day. The school was built on an old bomber command station
from the Second World War, so it seemed very grown up
to be there, especially if we walked through the shops and
pubs in town (one pub was supposed to be haunted). The old
air-raid shelters were still there for exploring, too (through
a fence—I was still having trouble controlling myself).
And Susie was in school there, so it felt almost like old
times again.*

*I also didn't do awfully in everything for once. I never
seemed to get maths to stick in my head, but I borrowed
books from the library and read them on the bus ride to and
from the village, and so my English marks improved. And I
did quite well in sewing, which was one part of what they*

called 'domestic science' (the other half, cooking, is quite another story!).

The best thing of all, though, was that Welton was where the children of the Royal Air Force men went, because there was an air base (called Scampton) not far away. Bridget's father was an officer there, and one day she caught me and Susie stepping through the fence towards the old air-raid shelters. She was the one who suggested she bring her radio and we play cards there, and we became immediate friends.

Bridget seemed so different to me at first. She had been all around the world with her family, because her father would be posted to a new job every year or two. She'd seen places I had never even dreamed about. I knew vaguely from eavesdropping on my brothers that I liked popular music, like the Rolling Stones, Elvis and the Beatles (that might sound terribly uncool to you now?). But I'd never imagined going to a concert, or what it would be like to actually cross the ocean and see a city like New York. I couldn't imagine how big the world really was.

Susie and I could listen to Bridget's stories for hours, about living in America and Manila, and India. And the funny thing was, she seemed to enjoy us just as much, maybe because we knew all the secret places to go in town. I don't think I was lonely a day that year.

I started to worry as the next summer rolled around, though, because I knew that Bridget wouldn't be at our school forever—her father would be posted somewhere else and she would move away. We prepared ourselves for that, promising to write, and I knew Susie and I would still have each other.

*We were excited for Bridget, but still worried. Which is
like growing up—excitement and sometimes worry, at the
same time.*

*I have such a clear memory of this with you. When you
were nearly four, you told me you didn't want to grow up.
When I asked you why, you said because it was scary. You
looked so anxious, in a way Kate had never been at the
same age. I think you were maybe watching Kate starting
school and it seemed so overwhelming to you. I gave you
a big hug and told you that we all feel scared of things
sometimes and that I would always be here for you.*

*That's part of why I'm writing these letters, because I
promised you that. And now you're nearly at high school.
I know growing up can feel a bit fast sometimes. I hope you
and Kate can help each other, and that you have friends at
school. And if not, because that happens sometimes, then
don't give up. It will get better. I promise.*

Be brave, my darling girl,

Love,

   Mum

Wil closed her eyes at the end of the letter. If her mother
could see that almost five-year-old Wil wasn't ready to grow
up, maybe she had been hopeless from the beginning. She still
didn't do well with grown-up things, like being on time and
collecting the right orders. Maybe she couldn't blame her father
for the things he said, given she was yet to reach the 'it will
get better' part. Maybe it was time to get her life together like
he wanted.

She pushed the drawer closed on the next thick envelope and set two alarms.

⁓

Wil arrived at the job site five minutes before seven the next morning, and found herself unexpectedly alone in the driveway. The owners had just bought this split-level house in a growing hinterland estate, where gum trees had been allowed to stay on the oversized blocks. The couple wanted to do some renovations before they moved in. The house looked like a typical suburban lowset with a tile roof. But the block dropped away towards a creek bed behind the property, so the front door opened into the upper level, and the lower was tucked underneath. The couple had hired Wil's father to gut and rebuild the kitchen, and update the tiles and fixtures in the bathrooms. As Wil retrieved the keys from the power box, she could hear currawongs calling in the green belt off the back deck. They sounded as hopeful as she felt. It was a new day.

Her phone bleeped with a text from her father: *Out of bed yet?*

I'm here already, she sent back. *Have keys.*

After a pause, he sent back: *Taking a minute for pills to kick in and swinging past Mason job to check in. Col picking up cabinet order, be there in 40 to start kitchen demo. Take a look around.*

Wil tucked the phone in her cargo pants pocket and stepped through the door, feeling twitchy. She couldn't sit around for a half-hour on the clock. That was exactly what her father had been mad about the other day when she'd failed to bring the tile order.

She could start the demo at least. She went back to the truck and pulled out a prying bar, sledgehammer and drop sheets, turned off the power and water, then stepped through the empty echoing spaces to the kitchen. The house looked nearly new, it was just lacking appliances. The colour scheme in the kitchen was awful—standard, off-the-plans awful, with cheap manufactured counters—but there wasn't anything wrong with it.

But if Wil had a dollar for every perfectly functional kitchen that she'd helped make into rubble, she could have retired by now. Most people didn't bother to save anything, because that just added to labour costs. Rough was cheap. So she laid the sheets over the polished wood floors, and picked the island bench to start with.

She put a loud music beat into her earbuds and got to work.

It took only five minutes to pop the first row of cabinets from the wall, rough stack them on the drop sheet, and chip the nasty white square backsplash tiles off underneath. The sink came out with a great wallop from the sledgie, and the window trim with the prying bar, so she could chip off more tiles. She was busy giving the counter on the island bench some encouraging taps with the sledgehammer when, abruptly, her earbuds were yanked out and she came face to face with her father, his face volcanic with fury.

'What the hell are you doing?' he asked. At least, that's what he would have said in the PG-rated movie of what happened.

'Getting started,' Wil said, panting. 'Kitchen demo.'

But something about his face made her stomach roll.

'I *said* "look around",' he roared. 'Not come in here and screw this job up before we've even started!'

'I know how to do this.'

'Oh yes,' he said, pacing around, examining the mess and throwing his hands up. 'You're doing an excellent job. In the wrong bloody room!'

Wil's stomach heaved. 'What?'

'It's the *downstairs* kitchen. In the granny flat. *That's* the one we're knocking down. The one with the dated décor, not the one that was just renovated last year!'

'Oh god,' she whispered, looking over the damage. The cabinets could maybe be put back up again, neglecting the cracked panels, but those tiles couldn't be saved. The sink was busted, and the countertop on the island was cracked. That would mean replacing all the counters. She saw dollar signs and hours of labour, bundled into the growing ball of her father's rage. All her blood fell towards the earth.

'I'll fix it,' she said, desperately. 'I'll redo it all myself.'

'Yes, you bloody will,' he said. 'Out of your own pocket. And you'll explain to the owners how this happened.'

'Give me their number,' she said, taking two steps back from the tight circle her father was pacing. 'Dad, I'm really—'

'You're always sorry and I'm always soft. Jesus, after the other night!'

Wil felt tears creeping up on her again. 'I just wanted to help, like you said,' she whispered. 'I'll fix it.'

'I'm giving you til Monday.'

She'd never seen his anger so hot, and yet so dangerously contained. The words seemed to squeeze out of him under great throttled pressure. It was more frightening than him unleashing. Her phone pinged as he texted her the client's number.

'Do it now,' he said tightly.

But as she turned away, he said, 'One other thing.' His voice was cold and tempered now. 'I said until Monday. That's four days to fix this. That's also four days to get out of the house.'

⌒

The client was spectacularly mad. The only thing that made it bearable was that her father's ultimatum was worse. By the time Wil had worked out what she could salvage from the demo, her meagre savings account would be utterly consumed. And that left finding somewhere to live a bleak and hopeless prospect.

Crickets sang loudly and joyfully, oblivious to her troubles, as she trudged home that night. She thought about Rob and his friends. She didn't want to crash on any of their couches. Most of them were already freeloading off someone else. As for Rob, he was living in his van most of the time and didn't like sharing his space.

Her stomach coiled when she saw the stack of moving boxes and a roll of tape that had been left on her bed. She'd half been hoping it was a joke, or that he'd calm down and reconsider. But he'd taken time out of work to do this, and that meant he was serious.

'Knock, knock?'

Wil looked up and took a moment to recognise Shonna, now in jeans instead of overalls, and carrying shopping bags. She raised a six-pack of cider. 'I heard you were in trouble. I've come to offer solace.'

'Who told you?'

'Colin. I think he used the term "demo-gate". Can I come in?'

Shonna eased inside and closed the door, settling herself on the bed. She put the bags on the floor with an easy familiarity.

'I figured it might be the night for that drink. These are even cold. Want one?'

Shonna reminded Wil of Kate—at least, a long-ago Kate who knew when Wil needed someone to stick around. So she took the offered cider bottle, twisted the cap off and sank down into the bed. 'Thanks. You haven't got a room for rent in those bags, do you?'

'I see the moving boxes,' Shonna said. 'So Colin wasn't joking about your old man kicking you out.'

'One too many screw-ups,' Wil said, already a quarter down the bottle, and finding Shonna one of those rare people who was easy to talk to. 'My tiling skills and ability to collect lunches aren't quite enough to make up for wrecking kitchens.'

Shonna laughed and nodded. 'There, you see? Making jokes. You must be on your way to healing.'

Wil snorted, and took another long drink of the cider. It was starting to put that nice fireside glow inside her, however temporary the feeling was. 'Can't see much healing in this one.'

'His reaction does seem a bit extreme. I mean, you're fixing it, right?'

'I see that Colin didn't tell you I was arrested.'

Shonna's eyes popped. 'For the kitchen?'

Wil chuckled, really feeling the cider. 'Nope. Last Friday. Second time, actually. I'm not exactly the child my dad boasts about at barbecues.' She peered at the cider label. 'Wow, that's strong. You aren't having one?'

Shonna had pulled another bottle from her shopping. 'Lemonade for me. Boring, I know. So what happened the first time? That must be a story.'

Wil pushed herself up on the bed, tongue loosening further. 'Shoplifting. My friend Kelley dared me and I did it, then we got busted for it.'

Shonna chuckled. 'When was this?'

'When I was sixteen, right after Kate left.'

'Kate?'

'My sister,' Wil said quickly. 'She went to live in Sydney.'

'Are you still friends with Kelley?'

Wil snorted. 'I don't think we were ever friends. Kind of a sign, really, when someone's urging you to break the law, don't you think?'

'Fair point. Dirty move.' Shonna took a swig from the lemonade bottle.

'Oh, I have a dirtier one,' Wil said. 'Not long after that, I went out with this guy who was on at me the whole time to sleep with him. When I finally did at a party, five minutes later he said, "Thanks, you're all right, but I'm really into Carla."'

'Omagod!' Shonna put her hand over her mouth. 'Dirty bastard! That wasn't your first time, was it?'

Wil swallowed. 'I think it's best we don't talk about it.'

'Bastard,' Shonna said firmly. 'What was his name? So that I can ask the universe to pox him.'

'Scotty Dunn,' Wil said, remembering all too vividly. His name still tasted like ash. She sank the cider and took up another.

'Dirty Scotty Dunn,' Shonna said with slow distaste. 'That's a serious run of bad luck, though, especially right after your sister moved away.'

'Don't think it has much to do with luck,' Wil muttered. She thought desperately of a way to stop talking about herself. 'Did you, ah, say you're new on the coast?'

'Yeah, just moved down last month.' Shonna paused. 'I had to move out of my parents' house, and my uncle was going to take me on as an apprentice anyway, so ... here I am. Hey, where's that?'

'What?' Wil twisted around to see what Shonna was pointing at and felt her stomach drop. It was the photo of the manor house in South Bandinby, with the church group posed in front, the one with the guilty-looking Ann.

'Oh, it's a village in England,' Wil said, wishing she'd put the photo away. Shonna had already scooted across the bed and picked it up.

'Cool old house. Family photo?'

'Not exactly. But that's my mother, there.' Wil slow blinked. She hadn't meant to say anything about it. She pulled her knees up.

'Look at these mad hairstyles and clothes. How vintage!' Shonna said, studying the photo intently. Then she seemed to become aware of Wil's discomfort. 'Sorry, didn't mean to pry. I just love old photos. You look a lot like her.'

'I do?'

'Sure.' Shonna glanced back at the photo, and laughed again. 'And who's the little guy sneaking in at the window there?'

'What little guy?'

'Here,' Shonna said, pointing to the upstairs window at the edge of the shot. 'It's pretty grainy, but there's a boy looking down at the group. See?'

Wil peered. Now Shonna had pointed it out, she could see there definitely was a boy in the window. 'I didn't even notice that.'

'Whose house is it?'

'It's the manor house,' Wil answered.

'What does that mean?'

'It was in Mum's village. The house of the local lord, you know, who owned the land. Lord Elston. That's him, there, I think, in the front.'

'Oh, wow, like *Downton Abbey*.'

'Sort of, I guess. But not that big. The village is pretty tiny.'

She'd looked it up on Wikipedia and driven round it using Google maps more than once. The images of rolling green fields, the church and the single street had made her mother's description into a three-dimensional image, but it still hadn't seemed like a real place.

'Maybe he's a ghost,' Shonna said, excitedly, 'the ghost of the manor house!'

'Ha,' Wil said.

Shonna took one look at Wil and all the excitement dimmed. She replaced the photo on the table. 'So . . . she's not around, your mum? I sort of caught the vibe from Colin that his mum and yours are different. He said Cameron had two divorces behind him.'

Wil, intending to just take a sip, found herself polishing off the cider bottle again. A warm haze followed, where she felt like a ghost herself, her body floating.

'She died,' she said.

'Oh,' Shonna said slowly. 'I'm sorry. And now I know why you just gave me that look with the whole ghost thing. Way insensitive.'

'It was a long time ago,' Wil said, imitating Kate. She set the second empty bottle down on the nightstand.

'Can I ask what happened?'

'Cancer,' Wil said. 'When I was five. Actually, she died the day before my birthday, apparently.'

Shonna's mouth dropped open in horror. 'Oh my god, that's *awful*.'

'Yeah. Another thing I just found out.' Wil heard herself slur. 'I mean, I've never known much about her. Kate told me a long time ago that Mum and Dad split before I was born, and she said they were . . . unstable, which is why we're Manns like her, and Tony and Col are Butlers. But no details. Dad never says anything about her, so I just imagined they hadn't gotten along, and all that was before I was around anyway. But you think I'd remember she died the day before my birthday, right?'

Shonna frowned, considering. 'I don't know. I don't really have any memories around that age,' she said, then paused. 'Is Kate older than you?'

'Two years.'

'So two younger brothers and an older sister,' Shonna said.

'Half-brothers. Dad married Carol when I was little. She's their mum. But she divorced Dad about six years ago and moved to Sydney for her job, like Kate. Kate's got a baby and a mortgage now, and Carol just down the road.'

Even Wil could hear the pain in her voice. She remembered what it had been like to go to Kate's wedding and not feel part of her life anymore. Even worse when Kate had taken Neil's name. Wil hadn't realised until then how much having that tiny link to Kate and their mother had meant.

'Are you guys close?'

Wil sucked a breath. Shonna wasn't really like the younger Kate that Wil remembered. She had the same openness and warmth, but she had a fearless energy for exploring, as if she wasn't afraid of leading Wil into difficult places. 'When we were younger. But she left home as soon as she could to go do nursing. Carol's idea, cause she's a nurse too.'

'Sounds like you had a tough time after she left.'

Wil shrugged.

'And your dad doesn't talk about your mum?'

Wil shook her head, feeling as though the tide of the big emotions around her father and Kate and everything were lapping at her chin. She bit her lip and glanced over to the bedside table. 'You know where that photo came from? Mum wrote me letters. I had one from when I was little, but there were more I was supposed to get. Fourteen altogether. I only just got them, because Dad had decided I shouldn't have them earlier.'

She briefly described her visits to Bruce Turner's office. Shonna seemed momentarily lost for words. 'I'm not even sure I want to read the rest of them,' Wil finished. 'Maybe Dad was right. It won't help me.'

Shonna cleared her throat. 'How could that be true about letters from your mum? You obviously love her, even if you can't remember her.'

Wil had to clench her teeth against a desperate choking sadness. That memory that had surfaced with her father yesterday was lurking again. She turned away so Shonna wouldn't see her tears and extracted the polaroid from the drawer and dropped it on the bedspread. She sniffed. 'That's her, there. And us.'

Shonna took the photo carefully, and without looking at Wil said, 'This is really heavy stuff. Not to be all woo-woo, but it's fine if you don't want to go there. Or go there, whatever you want. No judgement. Pete's a bit new-age,' she added.

'He says stuff like that and it helps. You wouldn't think that about a plumber, would you?'

Wil laughed with her. 'No, I totally wouldn't.' In the relief of the laughter, she shook her head. 'Sometimes I wish I could—' She broke off before she could say, *remember her voice*, and bawl her eyes out. 'How about let's not go there?'

'Fine. You know, that's a Mack truck,' Shonna said, pointing to the big tyre in the background of the photo. 'You can see the bulldog on the hood, right there. Unusual setting for a photo.'

Wil shrugged. 'Yeah, I know.'

'Oh no, I went back there, didn't I?' Shonna stood up. 'You want me to go, don't you? People tell me I'm too forward, and I don't mean to be.'

'No, wait,' Wil said, hearing her mother's words about loneliness in her head. She wasn't ready to be by herself, and she sensed Shonna wasn't either. 'Make you a deal—let's have another drink, and we won't talk about her, or about getting kicked out of the house, or arrested, or anything like that.'

Shonna brightened. 'Great! What shall we move on to instead?'

'Your family?'

'Hmm,' she said. 'My alcoholic mother, or my absent, truck-driving father? I have the full bingo card.'

'Oh,' Wil said slowly, catching the obvious pain in Shonna's not-quite-smile. 'How about we don't talk and watch something instead?'

'Perfect, can't go wrong with that.' Shonna laughed and pulled herself up. She took a pillow, then glanced at Wil. 'You know . . .'

'What?'

'I swear this is the last thing I'll say about it, but if you don't read them, won't you wonder?'

'Sometimes it's better to wonder,' Wil said, and took a drag on a fresh cider.

'You think?'

'Sure. Better than finding out and being disappointed.' And though it must be the cider talking, absently Wil thought that really was the anthem of the last fifteen years of her life. Being tipsy, the sting of that realisation barely registered. She was beginning to understand why people developed a drinking habit. It was lovely to be able to say things that normally hurt so much and barely flinch.

'You must have been so special to her,' Shonna said, with a wistful tone, looking over at the photos on the side table. 'God, sorry, I'll be quiet now.'

'It's okay,' Wil said. But as Shonna browsed Netflix, Wil was eyeing the letters, just visible in the open drawer. The next one was a lot thicker than the ones she'd already read. If she didn't read it, she might wonder, but she was suddenly more afraid of what the reading might actually do to her. Things hadn't been going well before. And now, she had all the old problems, plus a new sea of uncharted emotions to navigate. She knew from experience that things could always get worse.

'*Black Mirror* or *Outlander*?' Shonna asked. 'It's either mildly depressing social reflection or gruff men with nice Scots accents in kilts.'

'You choose,' Wil said, pushing the drawer firmly shut.

Chapter 6

Wil kept the drawer shut the next morning, and tried not to think about the letters as she set about correcting her demolition mistake.

The tension with her father didn't help. He stalked around the job site in grim, silent disapproval, which just made Wil cold and jumpy. By the time everyone was clocking off for the day, she was worn out.

Back home, shivering, she stuck her mother's letters in a backpack and took a rusty pushbike down to Broadbeach, and sat on the edge of the sun-warmed boardwalk. She didn't intend to read the letters, she just didn't like the idea of going anywhere without them.

After ten minutes of listening to the waves, she was calmer, but no closer to working out her next move. Her failings sat heavy on her heart, and the conversation with Shonna kept intruding into her thoughts, along with the image of her and Kate in front of the Mack truck. None of that helped with finding somewhere to live and a new job, which only made both more daunting and hopeless. The only thing that she had to soothe her were her mother's words.

Which is why she opened the letter marked 2001.

Dear Mina,

Happy 12th birthday, my darling girl. I miss you. Have I said that enough?

I know I don't have the first idea what these years have been like for you, and you'll now be such a long way from the little girl I knew. But I know you're a strong and capable person. I'm sure of that because I knew you better than anyone else. I don't know why I felt so compelled to write that just now ... maybe because, from time to time, we all doubt ourselves, and I want you to always know that I never doubted you.

I want to tell you another story about the village, in part because it's about stories, which I always loved, and in part because it was so surprising and pulls together many of the things I've said about the village in the previous letters.

In the letter for your eighth birthday, I mentioned a lumpy field where Susie and I would sometimes go to play. In England, a lumpy field often means buried history, because buildings were abandoned there long ago and eventually covered over. That's exactly what our lumpy field was.

I also mentioned that there was another village called North Bandinby, which is of course to the north of South Bandinby. North and South—makes sense, doesn't it? The walk between the two villages was straight up the bridleway path between the fields, which began beside the churchyard.

It takes about twenty minutes. The lumpy field was about halfway, off to the side of the path.

From a young age, I understood that the lumpy field was once another village called Middle Bandinby, which had been abandoned in the Middle Ages during the plague (which must have been so awful). Eventually, the buildings fell down and the ground built up over them, but the story of the village kept being told. Farmers didn't plough the lumpy field. I was never sure if that was because there were stones underneath from the old houses, or if no one wanted to disturb the ground. But either way, this neglect made it a natural place for me to go. A little secret space in the fields, with a stand of trees you could climb inside. And sometimes, you could find treasures in the dirt.

One long afternoon, just as school had broken up for that year, I went to the lumpy field. It was harvest season, so my parents were working all day long. I was supposed to be studying, but instead I was in the weeping branches of the trees, watching the blue sky through the branches and listening to the planes from Scampton airfield overhead.

You will understand my surprise, then, when I heard rustling and someone else burst into the tree stand. In the panic of the moment, I thought I was in trouble, but it was actually just a boy, not much older than me.

I say 'just a boy', but in South Bandinby, John Elston was hardly 'just' anything. He was Lord Elston's second son, so he may as well have been from another planet. He and his brother went to fancy schools in London. They had holidays in France and to their other estate in Jamaica. The closest I had ever been to him was watching the back of his head in the front pews of the church at Easter.

So I was shocked when he stood there, in smart-looking trousers, and said in his posh accent, 'Why, Ann Mann!'

I didn't know how he knew my name, because I'd never really given him two thoughts in my life. And he looked so odd, out in the fields in his smart trousers. Which is probably why I said, 'Why, John Elston. What on earth are you doing here?'

To which he said, 'This is my land!' And before I could say anything back, he added, 'But then, you're used to trespassing, aren't you?'

'I've been coming here for years,' I said, painfully aware of how common my accent was next to his. 'What's it to you?'

He grinned, and said, 'I wasn't talking about here.'

You remember the story I told you about the garden party at the manor, and how I thought no one saw me sneak into the house? Well, turns out John had seen me, and because of that, he had taken it upon himself to find out who I was. At the time, I was terrified to learn this, wondering what kind of punishment I might be in for. I'd never been in trouble with Lord Elston before, who may as well have been God. But John said that he'd keep my secret if I gave him another in exchange.

This was more imagination than I'd expected from the lord's son. It felt more like the games that Bridget and Susie and I played, and I was getting out of trouble, too.

But the only 'secret' thing I could think of was the story about Middle Bandinby and the plague. And I completely forgot he was a son in the unbroken line of Elstons who'd probably been lords when Middle Bandinby had still actually existed. I thought I had blown it when he told me drily that he knew the story already. But then, to my surprise, he climbed up the tree and pointed out a particular lump that he said was the remains of the church, and another spot where he'd found part of a pot. He seemed more interested in discussing the story than in our deal. For over an hour, we talked about what it might have been like to live in Middle Bandinby, and where everything would be best placed. There was no make-believe of fairy kingdoms. John was very practical, but I knew how a farmhouse ran, so we brought different parts to the conversation. At the end of it, I felt bad for having snuck into his house, because he didn't seem like the lord's son anymore. He seemed so much like me.

I've never been able to find any records of Middle Bandinby, though I have looked in newspapers and library files. The story survived because all the people in the village told it to each other. It was the first story John and I told each other. And now, I've passed the story to you. If you ever travel to England, you might like to find the lumpy field and imagine it like I did. And tell that story to someone else, if you don't find it silly. I like the idea that a tiny village in the middle of England, which hasn't existed in hundreds of years, still lives on in our memories.

Until next year. Be brave, my darling girl.

Much love,
Mum

Wil hardly noticed the joggers or the drifting spray from the nearby beach showers. She was deep in a lost village. She scrambled to open the next letter.

Dear Mina,

Happy 13th birthday, my darling girl. You cannot imagine how I am bursting with pride even writing this, imagining you as a teenager now!

I so wanted to still be with you. I would give anything to have seen moody moods, to have you roll your eyes at me, to have you ... oh, I don't know, try to get a piercing or a tattoo, or sneak out to a party. Did I make you smile? Or am I just so uncool? Honestly, I was looking forward to it. Mostly because I remember how confusing being a teenager was, how the aloneness was worse, especially from my parents and brothers. I wanted to be there for you, even if you didn't want me there. Even if we fought. Even if you hated me. Because nothing would have stopped me loving you.

Even under the late afternoon sun, Wil felt a tearing sadness, and had to read on through blurred eyes.

Granny Maxwell was the only one I remember being kind to me when I was thirteen and fourteen. Some days were like a storm inside my head, and my parents had so much work they couldn't spend any time with me (something I didn't realise until later).

Thank goodness I had Susie and Bridget, and sometimes John. But they lived in other places. One thing I never had was a sister, so I really hope that you and Kate can depend on each other. Because friends are wonderful, but a sister you get for life. That bond, I hope, can outlast anything, even the things that sometimes friendships can't. Whether it's moving away or hurting each other.

I know you and Kate are different people. She was the one who lined up all her books on the shelf by name, and you pulled them down and carpeted the floor with each one opened to your favourite picture. She waited patiently until biscuits were cooked and cool; you ate the dough and burned your tongue. But you'll always have blood between you, like you'll always have it with me.

Until next year. Be brave, my darling girl.

Love,

Mum

The lifeguards were packing up their flags now. Wil watched them, turning the letter in her fingers. She and Kate had done a nipper season when they were kids with another club not far from here. Kate had taken it very seriously, paying rapt attention to the instructors, even if she was reluctant to go into the bigger waves. Wil remembered taking off into the surf on her own.

She could remember the delight of the foamy waves on her skin, and the rough hand that had hauled her out and told her not to run off. Back then, she couldn't explain why she'd just jumped in, much less remember why now.

But it had been Kate who'd comforted her. Kate who'd said she didn't want to continue the next season, despite their father wanting them to. They had had that bond, once. But what did that matter now, when they barely got along?

Wil opened the next letter, marked 2003.

Dear Mina,

Happy 14th birthday, my darling girl. I spent a long time thinking today about what you might be like at fourteen. Whether you're tall like I thought you would be, and whether your feet stopped growing at an easy-to-buy size. (I made some interventions with a minor goddess on that one, but if it didn't work, I'm sorry, the gods are fickle. And maybe by now shoes come in any size?)

Shoes are on my mind because I had exactly two pairs when I was fourteen and I decided to run away from home. By then, John and I had been meeting at Middle Bandinby, or sometimes by the wood, for nearly a year, whenever he was home on term breaks or odd weekends. We were good friends, both of us lonely for company and hungry for bigger horizons, but in very different ways.

It had started with me telling him the stories Bridget had told us about living in foreign places, and he would tell me all about his boarding school in London, or the sports his older brother Thomas was playing. Our what-would-it-be-like games turned to cafes in Paris, or hunting weekends in a German castle. I often forgot that John had actually been on holidays to the south of France and the Caribbean, and that some distant relatives of his probably had been lording over a German castle in the not-too-distant past. So one chilly autumn day in the wood, when the blackberries were gone, I said, 'Let's do it! Let's just go up to the road and take a bus. We'll go away and never come back.'

He didn't miss a beat. 'I know which train to catch to London,' he said. 'And I have some money.'

We kept going, filling in the plan with more and more detail. We'd be across the Channel eating croissants by tomorrow evening. Then we agreed to meet at the road the next morning, in time to take the bus into town. I barely slept that night. I kept thinking of my spare shoes and a change of clothes in my bag, and wondering if that would be enough. And if my parents would miss me. But I was too excited to think very much about that. The next morning, I told my mother I was going to help Granny Maxwell practise, and I was up at the road with fifteen minutes to spare.

John never came, of course. I waited and waited, until I could see the bus coming, always thinking he would run up the road just in time. Then, I had to decide whether to just get on myself. But that hadn't been the plan, and courage failed me in that moment.

I can still remember how my chest burned hot, like coals at the very centre of a fire, as I went back down the road. I was mortified to have been abandoned, and the pain felt like it would never go away. I didn't see John for nearly a fortnight after that, when we ran into each other by chance, by the wooded bank of the beck, and it was too late for me to avoid him.

'You never came,' I said. I almost didn't want to speak to him, I was so hurt.

He looked confused, then he laughed. 'You didn't think we were really going to run away?'

At first, I was ashamed. I was always the one who got carried away and, once again, it seemed that I had misunderstood. That I hadn't realised he thought it was just a game. But later I thought more about it. I knew him. I was sure he'd been serious, because he had. Much later, I understood that John felt a very strong bond to his family, so he could never have left his life behind just like that. I didn't feel that way about my family, which made me more than a little jealous of him.

He did say he was sorry. But at that age, all my feelings—the shame, the betrayal, the jealousy, the disappointments—they all seemed so intense. Maybe because it was the first time I'd really felt them, maybe because they were part of figuring out who I was. I think that's the main job of being a teenager. You're between how you were as a child and how you will be as an adult, and trying to work out how to make the transition. Achieving that seems to be how we know ourselves.

I wanted to be there for you during your defining moments, regardless of whether you would have shared them with me or not. I loved that you and Kate and I had created such a close family, so different to the one I'd grown up in. I was always very proud of that—the three of us, together. And wherever I am now, I still love you just the same.

Until next year. Be brave, my darling girl.

Love,

   Mum

               ⌒

Dear Mina,

Happy 15th birthday, my darling girl. I can hardly believe that, when you read this, you'll be ten years older than when I had to leave you. You won't be a girl anymore—you'll nearly be heading into the world as a woman. Maybe you feel ready for that, and impatient. Or maybe you won't. When I was your age, it was a little of both. I needn't bore you with more details of how much I wanted to be out of the village, that much I'm sure I've made clear. What did come as a surprise, though, were any thoughts of wanting to stay. And my fifteenth year was the year that happened.

John and I had long recovered our friendship after the running-away disappointment, and we had been skirting around plans for the life that waited for us after school was over. He was serious and practical, and some of that had rubbed off on me. I was a little less impulsive than I had once been, and I had seen the benefit of planning. From this I discovered that looking forward to something could sometimes be as much fun as the thing itself. I think, too, that I'd rubbed off on him, because his future plans became a lot more daring and adventurous than they once had been.

John talked about joining the army, or the navy, and seeing the world that way. I was wildly jealous of this idea. I knew by now that a different set of rules often applied to men—it was the seventies, and they seemed allowed to travel and do exciting jobs, while women stayed home. At least, all the ones I knew did.

That inequality grated at me, and the more John talked about his plans and his freedom, the more I resented him. I would start arguments with him over nothing, which would often end with him exclaiming, 'You, Mann, are impossible!' and storming off. And I would swear at him and promise myself we would never be friends again.

I think someone must have heard one of these exchanges. Or simply that, in a small village, people eventually were going to notice us heading towards the same places, or away from them. Because not terribly long after that, my mother sat me down for a talk.

Now, I should explain at this point that I had never looked at John romantically. I'd catch him sometimes smiling at me and I'd think he was plotting something provocative to say, especially because he'd often give me that smile when he thought I wasn't looking or when we'd had a fight. I never thought he wanted anything else. I think perhaps the idea that Lord Elston's son would be interested in me was just too impossible to even consider.

So, when my mother sternly (though awkwardly) cautioned me for my behaviour, and all the trouble I might get into with John Elston, I realised that she thought John was something else entirely to me. I guess the idea we might have been friends was too impossible an idea for her; she found it far more likely the lord's son was taking advantage.

That conversation had a strange effect on me. Every time I saw John from then on, I had trouble seeing him as just my friend. I noticed how he looked at me, as though I was the only person in the world. It was as if my mother, in trying to warn me off, had actually put the idea of love in my head.

That was the beginning of our romance, and of our plans to be together (planning on his side, mostly suppressed excitement on mine). Our relationship seemed possible because John's older brother, Thomas, would eventually inherit the estate, and John would have to find his own path somewhere else. What better thing was there for him to do than join the army and serve his country, and for us to share these grand adventures together?

My resentment towards him dissolved as we made these plans. As if in sharing our dreams, we stopped being competitors and started being a team. That's what trust is, really. It's sharing the things that are closest and dearest to us.

I thought about this many times when I was deciding whether or not to write you these letters. I don't know for sure that it's a good thing—will you want to hear from me every year like this? Or is it a sad reminder, when I should let you move on?

But in the end, I also have to trust that you know how to best look after yourself. I thought you always had a good sense of that. Perhaps this letter is sitting unopened somewhere, because you chose not to read it. And if that is what happens, so be it.

But if you are reading this, then I would say that love can be confusing. It can make you crazy. But in that confusion, ask yourself if this is someone you want to share things with, and who will share them in turn with you. Without reservation. I think those people are the ones that will mean something to you for all of your life, even if your time together doesn't last.

And last of all, remember that a mother's love is different to romantic love—it's endless and always here for you, even when I can't be. We shared everything together, you and Kate and I, from the very start. Nothing can ever undo that.

Until next year. Be brave, my darling girl.

Love,

Mum

Wil blew out a great shuddery breath as she finished the last lines. Daylight was fading fast on the beach, streaks of apricot backlighting the indigo horizon. Behind her, evening joggers and dog walkers crunched past, and early drinkers chatted happily in the beachside bars, oblivious to the turmoil in Wil's thoughts. There were only three letters left—two thick ones, and one very thin. She didn't want to read them right now. The mention of disappointments in the letters had really driven a nail into her despair, and other lines had stirred up emotions over all the misadventures of her youth.

What would it have been like if Ann had still been alive when Wil had been a confused and unruly teenager? Or if she'd had these letters? How would her mother have handled the shoplifting incident? Or the dumping from Scotty Dunn?

. . . would she even have been with Scotty Dunn?

Wil barely remembered anything about her mother, and yet the voice she heard reading these words was softly familiar, an echo from some unremembered time, and with a wisdom Wil knew she still lacked. And this voice of her mother seemed . . . real. *She* seemed real, and right, in a way no one else did. Carol, her father's second wife, had been what everyone called a 'good person'. She'd taken all the children to church on Sundays, cooked meals every night and never shouted, even when Wil didn't meet her expectations to do homework or keep rooms clean. Still, Wil had gone to Kate for comfort. Kate had felt right; Carol never had.

And then Carol had encouraged Kate to go to Sydney, and Kate had gone, like it was nothing at all.

Wil sat staring at the beach, fists rigid in the sand at the thought. The anger crashed through her like a wave, ebbing to sadness. For the first time though, she didn't feel defeated. Yes, she was sore all over from work, with broken nails and broken relationships. No, she didn't have answers for her pressing problems. She didn't really believe what her mother had said about being strong and capable, at least not in the way Kate was. But maybe she was capable of something, beyond fixing mistakes.

She stood and brushed the sand off her jeans. The question was, what?

Chapter 7

On the ride home in the clanking Corolla, while she was contemplating what she could do, the radio station struck up a Cold 30 countdown dedicated to 1994. Wil snorted. What were the chances they'd pick the year her mother had died? She was about to switch the station when they started playing Denis Leary's 'Asshole'. Her hand stalled, and a minute later she was singing along—with gusto in the chorus—and thinking about Rob. A rollercoaster week had gone by since the Friday night of the arrest, right through the letters and demo-gate. All while he'd not answered any of her calls or texts, but still managed to find time to insta-post the wave break each morning, with hashtags like #beachlife #epicvibes and #livingthedream.

Living the dream. Seriously.

While ghosting her.

Wil belted out the last chorus loud enough to attract stares from the next car at the lights. She barely cared. At least the curdled feeling in her stomach over Rob had lifted. Next came Salt-N-Pepa's 'Whatta Man', and she sang to that one too, only less enthusiastically, because it just reminded her of what Rob definitely wasn't.

That realisation was still fresh as she arrived home. In her soon to be ex-room, she flicked the radio on and dug around for the old box under her bed. She didn't have many mementos from her school years—mediocre report cards and school diaries full of blank pages hadn't been things to treasure. But she had kept her sketchbooks, full of little hand-drawn comics and interesting doodles. She was surprised looking at them now how immature they were—full of uneven, hesitant lines and awkward shading.

When she held a pencil now, she felt much more certain about what she was doing. But it was really the only skill that she had improved on since school. Wil had never shopped for bedsheets, or a rug, or come close to any of the grown-up things Kate did. Her life seemed to have stopped somewhere, locked away from the bigger world adults inhabited. Maybe like her mother had felt in the village.

Cut 'N' Move began singing 'Give It Up'. Wil threw a pillow at the radio, which jumped but kept playing. Maybe it was a sign.

As the song wound to an end, her phone rang. Rob's face was finally on the caller screen. She'd been waiting a week for this call, but now she didn't want it. A rare clarity formed before she answered.

'Why haven't you called me back?' she said, turning down the radio.

'Whoa, Willy, babe! Easy there,' Rob said, full of Friday night energy.

'Easy? So it's okay for you to go surfing and post pics, but not call me back? I got arrested sticking up for you!' Another thought occurred to her. 'You just left me there! Would've been much better if you'd bailed me out and not my father!'

'Hey, chill out. I had to split. You know I have priors— couldn't hang around with the cops. Then there was this whole work situation.'

Wil let him go on about an overinflated drama at 'work', knowing it was all bollocks. He'd been smoking and surfing all week. She could hear it in his voice. Bryan Adams was now crooning 'Please Forgive Me' on the radio, but Wil was unmoved. Screw that.

'Save your wankery for someone else,' she said, cutting him off. 'You're lying.'

'What's wrong with you?'

Her mother's words about sharing were suddenly bright in her mind. 'Oh, let's see. How about we circle back to you being a complete dick who gets kicked out of a pub and then bailed up by the police? Then not caring enough about your girlfriend to check in for a week? You missed my birthday. I can't believe I was worried about you.'

Rob laughed, missing her tone. 'Yeah, how crazy was that night? You bundled in a patrol car. Don't worry, bad girls are hot!'

Wil wrinkled her nose. 'I'm sorry, what?'

'Heard something about you smashing up a kitchen with a sledgehammer, too. You coming out tonight?'

'No.'

90

'Come on, Willy. It's always a good time.'

Wil was suddenly amazed this had ever worked on her. 'I'm not going anywhere again with someone who can't call, who doesn't give enough of a shit to tell me what they've really been doing all week. We're so done.'

Rob gave a whistle. 'What, you on the rag or something?'

She hung up on him. And, with only a moment's hesitation, blocked his number. Then, she sat staring at the phone, horrified at all the booty calls she'd answered from him. What was wrong with her?

She fished his clothes from the clean basket and dropped them in the bin. She'd rather burn them, but some odd piece of sense told her that lighting fires was pushing her luck right now.

The soft wailing of Bon Jovi's 'Always' came on, signalling the Cold 30 was reaching its number-one end. Epic love songs weren't Wil's taste, but it turned her thoughts towards her mother and John. Clearly something had happened to them because Ann had ended up with Cameron, on the other side of the world. Somehow, her mother must have broken out of the village, but had it been with John?

Wil fingered the letters. Only three left, and the last one was very thin. Would she even find out what had happened in those pages?

⌒

Dear Mina,

Happy 16th birthday, my darling girl.

As I write these letters further into the future, I find it harder to know what to say to you, what might have meaning to the person you are now. I am taking what I know of you, which I feel in my heart, and imagining. I hope you'll forgive me if I get anything wrong.

I've thought a lot today about something I'll doubt you remember, which is you playing with one of the nurses here at the hospice. You've always been cautious about other people, which might be why you and Kate are so close—she's the person you've known the longest. But Marionette is one of those rare people that you warmed to straightaway. Maybe because she is a confident person about herself, so she can let other people be who they are, too.

Yesterday when you were here, and Marionette was showing you a book, you suddenly said, 'Girls have to kiss boys when they get bigger.'

And Marionette said, 'Who says that?'

You shrugged and said it was a girl in your kindy class, and that you thought it was a silly idea. Marionette laughed and told you that girls don't have to do anything if they don't want to, and then you had a big conversation about what you could do, which involved both surfing and riding unicorns—so very you.

You might be embarrassed by that story, but it made me think that your feelings on romance will likely have changed by now, though whether you are interested in boys or girls or whatever isn't really my business. Instead, I'm going to tell you a story of mine. It's going to start with romance (and maybe this is an 'Eww, gross, Mum', letter—sorry about that) but it's really about something else entirely.

So, John and I grew closer the year I turned sixteen, though it was difficult for us to see each other. We had no friends in common, and now we knew people were watching *us. We met up with Susie outside of the village a few times, when Susie and I were supposed to be on our way to a youth group meeting at Scampton, or a dance, or a football game. I was nervous about John meeting Susie, because I didn't know how he would behave. But Bridget's father had left the RAF and taken a diplomatic post in London, so Susie and I were both feeling the loss of her, and I wanted this new group of friends to work out.*

I needn't have worried. John was great company—a little arrogant and opinionated, but with humour that made up for it—and for a while the three of us saw each other regularly. We all listened to music and talked about movie stars, and Susie became the only person who really knew about my romance with John.

I left school at the end of that year, which probably wasn't the best decision, but I was such a poor student everyone thought I should just head out to work. That was when incredibly (to me at least), I was offered a job at the manor house.

I don't know now if it was a coincidence this happened, or if my mother had a hand in it, or if Lady Elston herself suspected something was going on. Both of them might have felt that having me nearby with plenty to do would be best. The job itself was fairly awful—I was helping in the kitchens and with cleaning around the estate, under Cook's direction. She believed in very hard work and wasn't impressed with my tendency to daydream. She yelled at me more than once for staring at the wood grain on the kitchen cupboards, because I liked the way it shimmered, and for burning food in the oven because I'd forgotten to check on it. I'm sure she asked for me to be sacked.

But sometimes I was lucky and it was William (the gamekeeper) who had the job of directing my work, and he was a gentle soul who I became friendly with. We felt more like a team, and I did a bit better with him. And Cook couldn't have her eye on me all the time. Whenever she would disappear on errands or days off, somehow John—if he was home—would find me.

I came to know the house and the estate very well that year, every hidden nook. Behind the house and the gamekeeper's lodge were several walled gardens, all with sheds, and there were new stables (and old ones with a walled rose garden in front). There was also a vast greenhouse and a pump room near the source of the beck, and a handful of small cottages for the foreman and the live-in staff. John didn't often risk us going upstairs in the house, because it was so much harder to come up with an excuse for my being there, but he did show me his room, once, the one I'd seen rudely that first time. I was really touched by that.

There was nothing sordid about our meetings. We talked, and kissed, but mostly talked—about books and music and what the world was like; what we were like. Drifting together, like the tide, all through the estate. And one afternoon, when Cook was out in Welton, John took me to the rose garden and proposed.

If you weren't expecting that, neither was I. Briefly I was happy, the pure kind of happiness that can lift you above any problem. I really believed that a life together was going to happen. John said that he wasn't interested in what his family thought, that he was free to make his own path, and that he chose me. I believed him. After all, I knew he wasn't put off by discomfort—he could have nettle welts up his arms and not complain about it. Disapproval seemed trivial, and it all seemed settled.

Of course, it wasn't. When I tell you about getting engaged at sixteen, I hope your first thought is, Was she crazy? *Probably, I was. Or just naïve. It should have been a warning sign to me when he said he wanted to keep it secret. But for the year it lasted, it was the first time in my life I remember feeling such mature excitement.*

It also changed me. The biggest thing was that I learned how to work, for I now realised that making my way outside the village would require money, and there wasn't any other way to get it except to work. The job at the manor house did not pay well, but that taught me frugality, too. If I could encourage you in one thing, it would be to learn the same things now yourself. If you haven't already, find that part-time job. Studying is important, but so is learning how to work. It will prepare you for the less glamorous parts of adulthood, and it will give you confidence.

It doesn't matter if you have no experience. If you have skills to offer, great, but my biggest tip is to tell your employer that you like to work. That often played well for me, even when it wasn't true, and I learned how to love it along the way.

Until next year. Be brave, my darling girl.

Love,

    Mum

Wil sucked a breath at the sting of the message around work, but the revelation of the engagement pushed her on. She fumbled in her haste to open the next letter, marked 2006.

Dear Mina,

Happy 17th birthday, my darling girl. If I have counted correctly, this is your senior year of high school. When you reach your graduation, I'd like to think that, somewhere, I'll be looking down on you, very, very proud.

I did actually finish high school myself, just many years after I first had the chance. Late really is better than never. But now that you are soon about to go out into the world yourself, I want to tell you how I finally left the village.

I continued to work at the manor house for a year, most of it secretly engaged to John, until the position was retrenched. By then it really was time to move on. John and I were taking more and more risks to meet. The village might have been good at keeping secrets from outsiders, but if someone found out about us, everyone would know. Luckily, my job at the manor house helped me find another in Lincoln city.

I worked in a tearoom, right on Steep Hill, which is the very heart of the town. I'm sure it won't surprise you that the hill was, in fact, very steep, climbing all the way from the river to the cathedral, which is in the area called 'Uphill' (all the names are clever, as you can see). It's a beautiful place—all old cobblestones, narrow low doors (I hit my head many times) and strange little steep staircases, like out of a fantasy story. The cathedral is right on top of Lincoln Cliff, along with the castle, and I could just imagine it in medieval times with all the Vikings about, at the same time Middle Bandinby had existed, or further back to the Romans even.

'Downhill' on the other hand was a more lower-class area, so I felt quite elevated working near the top of Steep Hill, even if I did have to climb it every day. And if you're sitting there thinking, 'How steep could it be?', go there and try it!

Finally, with that job in the teashop, my life felt as though it was beginning. I had John and a plan.

Of course, it wasn't as easy as that.

I haven't said much up until now about John's brother, Thomas, but he was quite important in all this because he was the one who was going to inherit the estate. This fact left John without title or income, and therefore free. However, Thomas wasn't turning out to be a reliable heir. He had a reputation for bad behaviour, of being 'a bit of a bounder'. That's what I overheard some older ladies in the tearoom saying one day. It was said he showed no great interest for either the estate or his family responsibilities to marry, or really for women in general. What I didn't understand until much later was that Thomas was probably gay. It was only just the eighties, and such a thing was really shameful back then. I never much understood why it was anyone's business, but I did appreciate that as the heir to a noble estate, with a long line of heirs to maintain, it wasn't what the lord would have wished for.

And that was why the weight fell on John. With his brother having little interest in the estate, he felt he might not be able to leave after all; that he was needed to help manage things and to encourage his brother to act appropriately. I didn't believe this. I thought John would leave because he could. Because he wanted to. And maybe, because of me.

We had planned to marry in 1981, as soon as I turned eighteen, knowing our parents would never approve it earlier. It was to be a very low-key ceremony in town, and we would briefly stay in Lincoln before moving on to wherever John would be based.

I had my bag packed, because I clearly hadn't learned anything the last time around. The first sign there was a problem was when John arrived at the tearoom without his bag. You know the phrase 'Fool me once, shame on you; fool me twice, shame on me'? At least he turned up this time, and didn't leave me waiting at a bus stop. He tried to explain, but I was so angry, so hurt. I'd waited and waited. I'd built dreams in my head that were all made for two. We went for a walk over the cobbles through Bailgate as he talked. We were in the shadow of the cathedral. All I could think was that we looked like we were just out shopping, but my whole world was falling apart.

John begged me to just wait, another year maybe, or until such-and-such a thing was settled with his brother and the estate. And I wanted to believe him. I didn't want to lose him—the one person who had given me the confidence to plan a life outside the village. So for two long weeks, I went back to my routine: to the bed in my parents' house, and to work in town.

But it wasn't the same. After those two weeks, I finally accepted that John would never leave the village. And that he would never marry a commoner like me. Whatever these bonds were to his family, and to their land (which my family had worked on for generations), they were stronger than the love we had for each other. That was a bitter realisation. But I also knew I couldn't stay where I was, to be constantly reminded of him. I didn't want resentment to take root in me, as it had in my parents, who seemed caged by the village.

So I wrote to Bridget in London, asking for help, a place to stay. As soon as I had my reply, I booked my train ticket. And that was how I left home: on a frosty morning, the sky pale grey like a dove's feathers. It was spring, but the sun was late in coming that year. I can remember shivering as I stood at the top of the road, waiting for the bus to the station, and looking down on the beck one last time. The wood was threadbare, and the church belltower and the manor house were visible through the skeleton trees. I wished that I'd just had one more chance to see all the new lime-green leaves bursting out, because I didn't think I would ever go back.

I did only two things before I left. The first was to go to that stand of trees in the lumpy field of Middle Bandinby and carve my name into one of the trunks. The other was to sneak into the rose garden at the manor house and take a near-blooming rose. Both little acts of defiance, but I guess also an exchange: leaving something of myself there, and taking something with me. Generations of my family had lived there. Which is your family, too. And if I couldn't have John, then I would take something of his with me. I asked Susie to tell him I'd gone. I didn't want to say goodbye.

Spring did come, of course, once I reached London. I will tell you more about London later, but the point of this story isn't about London, it's about what it took to get on the bus and the train to get there. I was so afraid, because I wasn't *supposed to go alone. And I've thought about that moment many times, knowing I'm not there with you anymore, as you get close to going out into the world yourself.*

Even being an impulsive person, I found it hard. But the idea of leaving wasn't a whim that I'd had one day. I'd been thinking about it for years, and it wouldn't leave me alone. Those are the kinds of leaps that are worth making. The ones that make you want to work hard, to struggle if you must for them.

I don't know what yours will be, I have no idea the shape of your life now, but I hope that you have them. I cannot imagine that the tenacious, intelligent, persistent girl I was forced to leave could be any other way.

Until next year. Be brave, my darling girl.

Love,
   Mum

Inside the envelope was a pressed flower in a fold of blotting paper, its petals aged to a creamy yellow.

⌒

Wil let the letter fall into her lap, tears stinging her eyelids. Tenacious? Persistent? She was none of those things. She'd never had ideas that wouldn't leave her alone, even by thirty. She'd been an ordinary, C-grade student and hadn't even graduated high school. She'd left to work for her father, doing the administration for his business, and she hadn't even been capable at that. She knew he'd had high hopes of her taking the pressure off him while her brothers were still a long way from finishing school. But she'd been no good with spreadsheets and invoices, and after two years of creating problems someone else had to fix, he'd hired an admin temp and moved her onto the tools.

When she showed some promise, he'd organised an apprenticeship with one of his carpenter mates, which she eventually ruined in the same way she managed to ruin most things. Having lost the apprenticeship, she'd waited tables and worked behind bars for a while, and picked up work with her father when he needed extra hands, as a trades assistant. She'd talked about finding another apprenticeship, but never got around to it. Instead, there'd been a patchwork of years in skate shops and bars, a flight of forgettable share houses, various unfinished TAFE courses, jobs in cleaning and beauty therapy, surfing and drawing, and whatever odd work her father had going. She'd watched that spark of enthusiasm in his eye dim more with each passing year. Somehow she'd known, when she'd ditched Ashleigh's christening, that she was on the final straw with him.

So it really wasn't surprising that it had all led here—to being a thirty-something screw-up who was about to be homeless. Reading these letters was giving her a sense of her mother, but it was also opening a gulf between what her mother had expected of her and what she really was. There was a despair in knowing she couldn't be any different.

Could she?

Maybe if she'd read these letters when she was meant to, she'd have felt less lost. Maybe then she'd have chosen differently when all her schoolmates were doing their homework, or going off to university, or on overseas gap years. Maybe she'd have had a plan, so that when Kate suddenly left it wouldn't have felt like the end of the world.

But that wasn't what had happened.

She fingered the last letter, the very thin one, meant for her eighteenth birthday. The envelope had a brown tidemark on the corner where 2007 was just visible, and the paper crackled in her fingers as she unfolded the single sheet. The very idea of it was a misery, worse because it was the last. She meant only to read the first line and put it away again if it held any more of her mother's misguided ideas about her. But the difference in tone immediately caught her.

> *Dear Mina,*
>
> *Happy 18th birthday, my darling girl.*
>
> *This letter is a little different. I have written all the others thinking of you as a girl growing up, and as a way to remain in your life, even in such a small thing as a birthday letter. I told you the stories I probably would have told you if I had lived, because I think it's important to know where you come from. But there is also something very important that I need to ask of you.*
>
> *Families can be very good at holding secrets. I think it must come from a time when everyone lived in tiny villages, like South Bandinby, and had to sit next to the same people in church and work with them in the fields, day in and day out. It must have felt safer to keep things quiet. I don't believe in that. Lives are sometimes ruined for secrets. And I have more than one.*
>
> *But that doesn't mean they are easy to hear. I wanted you to be ready, to be old enough to think about whether*

you want to know. The choice is yours. But if you are willing to go forward, to hear about what happened in London and afterwards, then there is another set of letters. As I write this, I am not sure how many there will be, but it will be as many as I need to put all of it down. I will have them put in a special place in the South Bandinby church, a spot that only John and I know about. They will be safe there. I need you to go there to find them, because a place isn't real until it's been under your feet, and it will be a measure of whether you're really ready, if you make that journey. And I need to know that you've stood in that church ground, on that earth that we both came from.

Those words, my darling girl, will explain everything, just as I would have if I had still been with you now. You may hate me for it, or love me for it, but either way you'll know everything. And then I can ask you to do one last thing for me, if you so choose.

With much love and hope,
  Mum

In the space after the sign-off was a floor plan of a church, its nave running across the page with boxy additions for what looked like an entrance porch and a side chapel. In the drawing was a dashed line, leading across the nave from the entrance and into the little side area, where a circle was drawn. Next to the circle was written, *Pull out at bottom (tips), look down.*

Wil stared at it. Of all the things this letter could contain, she hadn't expected this. There were *more* letters? More to know?

She swiped the last tears out of her eyes, thinking of her father having nothing to say about her mother. And even Kate being so reluctant to talk about her. Had Ann become some kind of notorious figure? Had she done horrible things? Was there some secret trust fund waiting in an offshore account, or a buried deed to a house in South Bandinby?

In all likelihood, her mother had simply hurt the people in her life. Kate remembered her not being stable and moving around a lot. And Wil knew all about being unreliable; that might be the only thing she shared with her mother. Maybe her mother just couldn't help herself from ruining things, like Wil couldn't seem to.

Except the person Wil heard writing these letters sounded organised and together, even if her judgement of her own daughter had been wrong. And that organised, together woman, twenty-six years ago, had written something she wanted Wil to read.

Wil grabbed her phone. She already knew that the internet was useless for her mother: there were too many Ann Manns to find any trace of one who had been gone since before social media. She'd already looked at South Bandinby's brief Wikipedia page, describing its location, the listed-building status of the church, and the Elston family mausoleum. Now, she revisited it and lingered on the pictures of the church, its worn stone grey-green against trees and fields. She followed links to several heritage registers with entries for the church. Some had internal photos, but none seemed to be of the area circled in her mother's letter. The register entries were dry, noting the building's age but also its history of poor maintenance. Another link mentioned interest from a TV series called *Saving History* that wanted to film there, and the possibility of funding a restoration. The

Elstons had apparently refused. Wil imagined her mother wryly commenting on the Elston pride.

A link to the Elstons led to another brief Wikipedia page, with a long list of Barons Elston. A few notable ones had their own pages, all from the 1700s. But most, like the current, seventeenth Baron Elston, Thomas, had no link. There was nothing about John.

None of this helped Wil when it came to actually setting foot inside the church, and the mentions of deterioration and restoration work only made her jumpy; in the jobs she'd worked with her father, they'd sometimes found things left behind in the walls. A tin of old coins, costume jewellery, old banknotes and account books. Her mother's letters had been in the church for more than twenty years. Wil couldn't risk someone else finding them, if they hadn't already. She had to work out how to get there, and soon.

Chapter 8

Despite the restless urgency she felt, Wil still had to drag herself up at five the next morning and address the ruined kitchen. She was tired and distracted, a dangerous combination when she had to prep for the cabinets and benchtop arriving this morning. Those alone had cleaned out most of her cash. But as long as both items were finished today, she could complete the tiling and clean-up by tomorrow.

So, naturally, the benchtop didn't arrive and two delivered cabinet boxes were the wrong style, so Wil spent a panicked hour and a half driving to the showrooms and haggling, extracting promises they would rectify the problem today, even though it was Saturday. It was the kind of thing she'd seen Tony and her father do many times, but she'd never felt the weight of a timetable entirely on her own. Driven on by her deadline, she finally pulled it off. Because she couldn't be late. Not if she wanted her plan to reach the church to work out.

At five-thirty, wrung out and shaky, she cornered Colin washing his truck in the driveway at home.

'How goes demo-gate?' he asked.

'Can I borrow your laptop?'

He frowned. 'No one will answer trade questions until Monday.'

'I know that. I'm doing research.'

'What kind?'

'The not-your-business kind.'

Col narrowed his eyes but handed the laptop over. Back in her room, Wil rested the laptop on the moving boxes and brought up the maps of the village again. It was nearly three hundred kilometres up-country from London. There was a train to Lincoln, but after that there was only an infrequent bus and even that didn't go straight to the village. She chewed a pencil, fighting the urge to dive off into sketching with the hope a solution would present itself without effort. But she didn't have time for that. There were no hotels in, or really anywhere near, the village, not even an Airbnb. That would leave her with a cheap hotel in Lincoln and needing a car, which all added up. Then there was getting to London, which would cost almost two grand. She scratched all the numbers down on the back of one of the cabinet receipts, and drew a line under it. She sucked on the pencil, then went back and added ten per cent. That was what her father would do. That was the number she'd need.

On Monday, Wil tried to pick a good moment to talk to her father. She felt good about her prospects: everything was perfect with the kitchen, even if it had taken until after five yesterday. She'd sent photos to the client, who was happy, and she'd apologised for the mistake more times than was probably comfortable. She'd moved her packed boxes to the garage last night, so her father would have seen she was ready to go when he came down this morning. She'd been on time to the site, and when he'd come in, he'd flicked his eyes over the re-do without complaint, which was a good sign. On the other hand, he was unstoppably busy. Just when he looked like he was free, he'd taken another call and disappeared down the stairs to where Shonna and her uncle were now working on the downstairs en suite.

Before he came back, Wil had to unpack the cabinet delivery for the downstairs kitchen—the one that she should have demolished. She then ran to the hardware for a sealant she needed to finish her work. When she came back, Tony and Colin were muttering about the new island being out of square, so she helped with the correction, and then went off to confirm other deliveries due today and tomorrow. This last thing wasn't really her job anymore, but she wanted to be as helpful as possible. Her chest was all light with hope as she touched the list in her pocket again. Her father was still on the phone.

Finally, at three in the afternoon, she found him at his makeshift office on the outdoor table, and just hanging up a call.

'I'm going on a snack run. Want anything?' she said.

'Did you get that air-con delivery confirmed?'

'I tried. I'm waiting for a call back.'

'Give them fifteen minutes,' Cameron said, jabbing out a text. 'Then call them back again. Pie and peas.'

'Okay.' She hovered, shifting from foot to foot.

'What?'

'Nothing.'

She beat a cowardly retreat to the bakery and another half an hour went by before she circled back, just as her father was sliding the pie out of its bag at the outdoor deck table.

'Delivery's confirmed now,' she said.

'You keep ogling what I'm doing out here,' he said, around a mouthful. 'So spit it out. What's the problem?'

'The upstairs kitchen is done,' she said.

'I saw.'

'The client's happy with it. So I was wondering—'

'I meant it about moving out. This doesn't change that. It's better for you.'

'Not that.' She took a breath. 'I wondered if I could get a loan. For a few thousand. I'll pay you back.'

There was a pause. 'That's normally how loans work,' he said dryly.

Wil pulled the list out of her pocket, her heart dancing, and glanced at the number again. 'Just to cover the money I spent on the kitchen. Temporarily.'

Her father stared at her. 'What for?'

'Well . . .'

'Rent? Bond? Weed? What?'

Later, she reflected it would have been much easier to lie. She could have just told him she needed bond for a new place. But she wasn't like that. 'I need to make a trip.'

A second later, he'd snatched the list out of her hands.

'Flights, trains,' he read. 'So it's a holiday you're angling for. And you want me to pay for it?' He laughed. 'You know, if you put anywhere near as much effort into your work as you did

into this list, you'd be on your way. Answer's no. Good job on
the kitchen. You can pack up for the day.'

Wil stood there, feeling a raging impulse to defy him. 'I need
to go to the village,' she said. 'It's not a holiday.'

'Pull the other one,' he said.

'I want to see the place that Mum came from. I need to see
it. I'm serious.'

'You need a serious head examination,' he said. 'What do
you think you'll find there? Bunch of stuffy old buildings and
sheep fields.'

Her voice rose. 'Maybe I wouldn't need to go if *you* hadn't
kept the letters from me!'

His jaw quilted. 'For your own benefit. As I'm sure Bruce
explained to you. A case you're only making stronger now.'

She stared him down, her face on fire, feeling as bitter as
she had at sixteen, after Kate had left and she'd had to face his
disappointment at her every mistake. A time when she could
have had these letters and her mother's words to comfort her.

'I hate you,' she whispered.

'Make sure you're gone before I get home,' he said, turning
his back and putting his phone to his ear. Then he took his pie
into the laundry and slammed the door.

An hour later, Wil was back at the house, a heavy weight in
her stomach as she moved the boxes to her car. There weren't
many. One was half-full of sketchbooks; another contained
curling paperbacks, the contents of her bedside table drawer,
and a shell collection. Another with clothes. She couldn't fit
her surfboard, so she left it to collect later. But she couldn't
imagine wanting to surf again; nothing seemed possible now
that her plan was in ruins. She slid the letters into the tattered

backpack that she kept on as she packed the car. Where was she even going to go? Her thoughts kept wandering dangerously towards Rob's number in her phone, before retreating in disgust. She'd chosen a wonderful time to develop standards. She'd just have to sleep in her car. She picked up the last box, giving the room a last rueful glance.

'Knock, knock.'

Wil looked around a box to find Shonna at the door. 'Couldn't help overhearing earlier,' she said. 'Do you need a place to stay?'

An hour later, sitting on the couch in Shonna's apartment, Wil was staring into her phone, contemplating her mistakes and regretting the hope she'd had of her father. She'd misread the moment, thinking there was something new between them. Not a good something perhaps, but different. Positive, at least. But either she'd been wrong, or it was too fragile for what she'd asked.

'I'm going to order a pizza,' Shonna said. 'What kind do you like?'

Wil didn't respond.

'Are you looking for jobs?' Shonna said, peering at Wil's phone. 'Because let me tell you, the phrase "motivated self-starter" is code for "willing to work overtime for no money". Hey, it was a joke.'

'Ha,' Wil said.

Shonna peered over her shoulder. 'Hey, that's not jobs, it's hotels. You don't have to do that! I said you could stay here as long as you wanted.'

Wil put her phone down. 'It's a hotel in England.'

Shonna's eyebrows popped. 'Oh, was *that* what you wanted the money for? To go to England. Because of your mum's letters?'

Wil knew her face gave her away.

Shonna flopped down on the couch. 'This is exciting!'

'It's not going to happen,' Wil said. 'That kitchen fix-up cleaned me out, and Dad wouldn't give me a loan. So I'm back to bar work and other stuff. Take ages to save for a ticket.'

Wil had done bar work before and knew how tight her money would be. It was one of the reasons she'd always gone back to building. And odds were, she would find some way to screw up the jobs and burn through any savings in between.

Her stomach caved at the idea of finding herself living in Rob's van in a year's time, while the rest of her mother's letters were still locked in the old church. Or worse, being found by renovators. Lost forever. She swallowed, itching with horrible restless energy.

A tap came at the door and Colin barged in, hauling a bag from the bottle shop. 'Have to hand it to you, Wil. You know how to make a departure. Dad's gone fully nuclear.'

Wil covered her face. 'How bad?'

'Non-stop football marathon on the TV, drinking scotch straight from the bottle. What did you say to him?'

'I asked for a loan,' Wil said, faint with regret. 'And then I accused him of withholding the letters from me. And told him that I hated him.'

Colin whistled. 'Jeebus, Wil.'

'She wants to go to England, Col. See the village her mum came from. Isn't that romantic?'

'I don't get it,' Colin said slowly. 'Where did this come from? Is this something to do with you asking about a house with a blue door?'

'You didn't tell him?' Shonna said.

'Tell me what?'

Wil took a breath. 'I found out that Mum wrote me all these letters that I was supposed to get when I was growing up. But Dad didn't let me have them, and I just got them the other day. From Bruce Turner after . . . you know, getting arrested. And the last letter says Mum wanted me to go to the village to find something.'

'Oooh, really? What?' Shonna said.

Wil felt as though she was on an express train, with no stations where she could get off. 'Something in the church.'

Shonna was so excited she couldn't contain herself. But Col held his hands up. 'Wait, wait, back up. Dad didn't let you have them? Why?'

'Thought they'd unhinge me. That worked out well, wouldn't you say?'

Col's frown deepened. 'But that just doesn't seem like him.'

'Did you know that Mum died the day before I turned five?' Wil asked, unable to stop herself.

'She did?'

'Yep. Bruce Turner told me. Don't you think it's weird I didn't know that?'

'I guess, yeah. You really didn't know? That's heavy.'

Wil shrugged. If she said anything, she was going to cry.

'But what does she want you to find in the church?' Shonna asked, desperate for details.

Wil produced the fourteenth letter, rather than having to explain the details. Shonna treated it like a museum piece as she pored over it like a sleuth. Finally, she shook her head. 'How amazing is this? Family connections waiting in long-lost letters! Col, why don't you lend her the money?'

'What?' Colin looked up from gently fingering the letter's edges.

'She's your sister, right? And she's got a mission to complete.'

Wil glanced at Colin, without any hope. He was careful with his money, and he didn't believe in lending to friends, let alone family. Even as her favourite brother, he knew she was a flake as much as anyone. Wil could see it written across his face.

'How much did you ask Dad for?' Colin finally said.

Wil told him.

'Man, no wonder he flipped. How were you planning to pay him back?'

Wil shrugged. 'Charm my way back into the building business, and not demo any more kitchens?'

Col snorted. 'Jeez, you're a train wreck, you know that, Wil? An occasionally entertaining train wreck. But—'

'Occasionally?' Wil said. 'Wow, must be a good week for me.'

Col laughed.

'But?' said Shonna, dragging the word out so as to not let Colin escape.

Col wrinkled his forehead and compressed his mouth. '*But.* I've never seen you want anything bad enough to ask Dad for money before. And his ultimatums never make a difference to you. Maybe you need to do this. I'll give you the money on two conditions.'

Wil slapped her hand across her mouth to keep the hope from flying right out of her. 'What?' she asked, breathless.

'First, you absolutely pay me back. I'll take it out of you in favours and T-shirts if nothing else is available.'

'And second?'

'You don't breathe a word to Dad. He finds out I lent you money, he'll disown me too. And I need his contacts. I'm not ready to couch surf.'

Shonna leapt into the air with a victory fist pump worthy of finals tennis. 'Wil, you're in business!'

Chapter 9

A week later, on a crisp morning, Wil almost missed her first glimpse of South Bandinby. Bleary from the long flight, and wrung out with negotiating her way across the behemoth of London city to the connecting train, she'd finally stepped out under the Lincoln sky at dusk last night. She'd been imagining some kind of profound experience at being so near where her mother had come from, but she'd barely had enough energy to drag her case to the Travelodge and collapse into the bland bed. But this morning, she'd woken to blue skies and soft light shining down on the cathedral on the hill, and she'd suppressed a shiver of excitement.

She was here.

She collected a tiny hire car and set off north, onto a B-road that should run straight past the village road. The land was a fairytale, all emerald fields and border hedges, fog thick in the hollows with misty wisps hanging on to hill edges. Gazing out the window, Wil found it hard to pay attention when there was so much wonder. Stands of trees stood shaggy green against the sky, and sheep huddled in fluffy packs against the dew.

Mesmerised by the scenery, she also found she couldn't tell one stretch of green hedge or stone wall from another, and that with an impatient lorry riding her tail, she missed half of the GPS instructions.

'Turn left,' said the GPS.

Wil braked, but she'd already missed it. There was nothing but a towering hedgerow alongside. She jumped when the lorry blasted its horn and she pulled left too fast and bumped along the shoulder. When the car finally stopped, she was hunched over the wheel, her heart thumping. The lorry roared away into the distance through the wipers screeching across the windscreen. She fiddled to turn them off with shaking hands; this car inexplicably had wipers in the same spot her indicator was back home, and she was jangly from nerves and cheap coffee. She blew out a breath. That was when she saw the break in the hedgerow.

There was a building down the hill through that break, its blocky tower just emerging from a pocket of mist. Wil's heart lurched as she threw her door open. She'd seen that tower before—it was the South Bandinby church. She was sure of it. As if she'd smelled the damp green scent of the fields before.

Slowly, the mist rolled back like a winter blanket, and then Wil could see the manor house, the treed line of the beck, the loop of the village road and, far to the left, the dark thumbprint of the wood. She shivered, her heart rising through her body.

Her mother's village.

Wil knew from her research that South Bandinby was different to most other villages. It had no pub, no post office, no shops, and it sat down from the road. Tight, and close. No wonder her mother had chafed to leave. Across the road, Wil could make out a simple bus stop, with a sign and bench. She stared at it, not quite able to believe it was the same place her mother had mentioned in the letters. It seemed both so unreal and yet so familiar.

And just down the hill in that church, more letters were waiting.

Wil reversed back along the shoulder to the missed turn and eased the car down the narrow road, bouncing over lumps of pavement and potholes. Grass grew tall in the ditches, giving the road a wild quality. She swung left at the fork and crept around the village loop, passing the stone cottages on the outside. To her right was a fenced green space with a stream running through it.

Oh! She paused. Not a stream. The beck.

But apart from the moving water, she didn't see much activity—a glimpse of someone up a drive taking a bin out. And another opening a window up high. But no cars or pedestrians.

A narrower road teed in to the left, down which Wil could see what must be the wood. She stayed on the loop, rolling past more cottages and then came a long building behind a leaning wooden fence. The schoolhouse! Then, the loop turned again, and she looked up the rise straight at the church.

The car's wheels crunched into the ditch by a little gabled noticeboard at the gate. Wil climbed out and peered inside at the notices of service times, and a parish council meeting roster. A page at the top declaring the church as open from 'dawn 'til dusk' was terribly faded, but the roster's dates were recent—evidence of activity. Wil glanced back at the unmoving village, wondering if anyone was watching.

The gate eased open at her touch, and the path led up the hill and through the graveyard. The headstones were worthy of a Halloween set, all leaning and barely readable. Wil hardly noticed. She was deep in the wonder of her mother having walked up this path so many times. Had it looked the same, then, with the gravestones running all the way to the massive stone wall? But of course it had, because there was the fairy tree. And there, behind that wall and more trees, was the manor house. Wil stared at the house as her heart thudded out the seconds. Was Thomas, Lord Elston, in there at this moment? Was John?

She left the path and paced towards the manor, her body pulled with an uneasy curiosity. Up close, the wall needed work. It had its own tiled roof, exactly as her mother had drawn it, but one section had fallen down. Two massive cracks ran through it in other places, as if the barrier that once set the manor apart from the villagers wasn't as well maintained as it once had been. Wil felt an urge to climb it and to run away all at once.

It was almost too quiet—she could hear the distant rush of the traffic up on the B-road and the twit of an unfamiliar bird flitting among the gravestones. As she retreated to the church door, she half-expected someone to leap out and demand to know her business.

But no one did. The temperature dropped as soon as she stepped under the vaulted roof. Goosebumps ran up her arms. She craned her neck to look at the ceiling, which was ornate with wooden arches and painted friezes. The rough-hewn beams seemed ancient, and she could see tool marks in the stones. The rendered wall on her left held several coats of arms. She didn't know any of them from a football club logo, but the sense of ancient weight was heavy. It was odd then to see the mismatched trestle tables piled with hymnbooks in the entry and a smudged visitors' register alongside a tray of homemade jam for sale. Then again, looking closer, she could see peeling plaster and water marks, and where stained glass panels had been replaced with plain. It smelled damp, too, as if the roof could use resealing. It was a shame to see the evidence of such an old building breaking down, but she took some encouragement from this that any renovations were yet to start.

Wil pulled the letter from her pocket and tried to orient herself to her mother's map. She drifted into the central aisle, loving how the stone floor was worn from centuries of human feet, and glanced left, expecting to walk through the pews, but they were blocked. Maybe that had changed.

She backed up and quickly found a way around the pews, past a stack of folding tables and into the side chapel. It was only a small space and, to her relief, a column hid her from the main nave and the door. On the wall ahead was a memorial to the airmen of the Great War, who had flown out of the local airfield. It hung on vertical wooden panels. Plastic chairs had been stacked on one side, another folded-up trestle table on the other. This was where her mother had circled.

'Pull out at bottom? Tips?' she murmured. Her eyes came back to the vertical panels. They were studded with ironwork along their edges, little knobs of metal on their dull wooden skins. They looked sturdy and definitely not movable, but she couldn't see with the table in the way. Glancing over her shoulder, Wil hefted the table to the side and squatted to look at the bases of the panels. She poked at one with her finger.

'Can I help you?'

Wil jerked and bobbed upright, cheeks blazing. A woman with white hair and pale skin was standing beside the stone column like an apparition, eyes narrowed at Wil.

'Oh!' Wil said. 'I was just . . . admiring the architecture! All very solid, er, construction in this place. Pretty old, huh? I just came to see the church today, and I just thought, well, this looks interesting.' She swallowed, knowing she sounded as guilty as her mother had looked in that old picture.

The woman's frown knotted her brows. 'You're with that man next door, I suppose?' she demanded.

'What? No, I'm not with anyone . . .' Wil grappled for words as the woman continued her scorching visual assessment. Wil suddenly noted the garden shears clamped in her pale fingers. 'I was just, ah, looking. At the church. The sign said it was open. See, I have a connection to the village. From a while ago, but still.'

She shrugged helplessly, desperate not to be thrown out.

'So you *are* with that man next door. Well, you can tell him he's not to send people to sneak around for him.' The woman punctuated the point with the shears. The movement of her cardigan shifted a crooked name tag into view, which read *Rose*. 'His Lordship's been quite clear about that.'

Wil held up her hands. 'Man next door? Do you mean in the manor house?'

'Manor house? What do you want with the manor house?' Rose said. 'I'm talking about that man in the church cottage,

Charlotte Nash

next door.' She pointed the shears off in the opposite direction. '*Mister* Hunter.'

'I swear I don't know who that is. I just assumed you meant the manor house, you know, because it's right there. Next door.' She gestured helplessly towards the wall.

Rose straightened, her face displaying a flurry of sceptical thoughts before settling into an expression of mild surprise. 'So you *don't* know David Hunter? You're a tourist, that's what you're saying?'

'David who? And not exactly. I mean, yes, I guess so?'

Wil knew she'd buckle under further questioning, so it was lucky Rose said, 'Information sheets are fifty p, and the preserves are two pounds. Supports the upkeep of the church, so we encourage all the visitors to be generous. Sign the book, too, before you go. That's a must, dear.'

Rose shuffled away, towards a table now heaped with fresh-cut flowers and empty vases. Wil blinked at it; how long had she been staring at the panels for Rose to walk in here with all that? She couldn't go investigating now. She had no choice but to walk around, pretending to admire the church as Rose made arrangements. It quickly became clear that Rose had settled in for an extended session that would outlast any reasonable time for a tourist stop. Wil pretended as long as she could, not taking in a single detail of what she saw, but eventually she had no choice but to retreat to the door, her feet dragging.

The sunlight outside felt like a defeat.

'Don't forget the register!' called Rose. 'And the preserves!'

Wil reluctantly backtracked and scratched her name into the visitor book, then, with Rose's gaze still boring into her, dug in her wallet. She only had a five-pound note, so she slid it into

122

the tray and picked up a jam jar, thinking, *I went all the way to England and all I got was this lousy jam.*

She paused again on the porch threshold in the faint hope Rose might be about to take a break, but the woman was only halfway into her second arrangement, fussing around the blooms and foliage. Darn it, she would have to come back.

She scuffed her shoes on the porch stone in frustration, then paused, looking down. A flat stone the size of a newspaper page was set into the side of the porch floor and inscribed. It read:

> *Remember, man, as you pass by*
> *As you are now so once was I*
> *As I am now so you must be*
> *Therefore prepare to follow me*

Wil paused, staring at the 'man', trying to tell if someone had scratched another 'n' at the end to make 'mann', or if it was just the way the light fell.

⌒

Wil drove around the village loop three times, then down the long fen lane past the wood and back, and still Rose's hatchback remained parked at the church gate. Wil went back up the hill to the B-road and pulled off the side again near the break in the hedgerow. She reread the letters, while every fifteen minutes trotting out to peer down at the church. Rose's car never moved. Finally, with fatigue catching her up, Wil had to go back to the Travelodge in Lincoln.

She intended to return to the village after lunch, but jet lag dragged her under until dark, leaving a long wait until the next morning. At least by the time the sun was up, she'd caught up on sleep, and the sky was dressed in brightest blue. In the sunshine, the greens were emerald and lime, teal and mint; the beck sparkled like diamonds among the trees. Wil hummed happily, confident that she knew where she was going now. But as she drove down the village road, Wil gave a cry and thumped the wheel. Now *two* cars were parked outside the church gate.

Driving any more loops would make her seem like a serious stalker, but she couldn't face leaving again without any success. So she parked, well behind the other cars, alongside a narrow path that ran north into overgrown grass below the church-yard, and up into the fields. A small sign marked it as a public bridleway. Perfect. Her mother had mentioned the bridleway. She could stall awhile heading up there.

Wil slipped around her car and began up the path. It passed a cottage to the left, a boxy Land Rover parked in its yard. To the right, she could peer up into the churchyard and see what was going on, which was nothing at the moment. When she looked ahead, she could see buildings in the far distance. Oh, right. That was North Bandinby, the next village. So this was the way to Middle Bandinby.

Wil thought of her mother, stepping up this same path to the lumpy field, playing in the trees there, and carving her name in one before leaving home. Wil inhaled deeply, as if the memory was in the air waiting to be breathed. Her footsteps ate up the ground.

After the churchyard the bridleway ran straight as a stringline through a gate and then beside a field knee-high in some crop with deep green leaves. The verges were overgrown with weeds, and bumblebees bounced drunkenly among the wayside flowers, while sheep grazed through a fence sown with tall trees. The land ached with quiet and yet buzzed with life.

The path rolled over a dip and then rose uphill again. The sheep paddock ended, and the buildings of North Bandinby drew close enough for Wil to make out their dull brown bricks. She was definitely about halfway between the villages now. She spun in a slow circle, scanning the fields. They were sown with wheat, the green grain heads knee-high and as even as a still-morning ocean.

So where was this lumpy field?

Little stands of trees sat in the distance, both east and west. Which way had her mother said it was? Had she even said? Wil had expected the place to be obvious, but it wasn't.

She chose east, heading along the boundary of the sheep field towards the B-road on the hill above. After several long minutes, she realised the illusion of distance. The field was huge, the distance to those trees closing with aching slowness.

She was halfway down the paddock fence when she saw a tractor in the distance, turning the corner and rumbling towards her. Wil glanced around. She couldn't go anywhere, unless she wanted to leap into the wheatfield or shimmy over the sheep fence. But there was something about the bearing of the tractor driver, the determined hunch of his back over the wheel, the roar of the approaching engine, that made her want to run.

As the huge wheels bore down, she flattened herself against the fence, making plenty of room for him to pass. But the driver lurched to a stop beside her, the engine rattling and roaring. His flat cap perched above fleshy ears, his raised eyebrows like a pair of hedgerows.

'Oi! Giranooing owdear?' he yelled, shaking his fist.

Wil was pinned, like a butterfly in a museum case. 'What?' she mouthed.

'Gooaroo!'

She put her hands over her ears. Either he was speaking gibberish, or all speech was being lost in the engine noise. Either way, she knew she was in trouble.

The engine abruptly clattered to a stop, and a tense silence fell.

'Well?' he barked. 'Are you deaf?'

Very bloody nearly. 'I'm sorry, I didn't hear anything you said,' she stammered.

'Public bridleway's that way,' he said, stabbing a finger behind her. 'You're trespassing.'

Wil felt her blood drain to her shoes. First assaulting police, now trespassing. She was a felon on two continents. 'I'm sorry . . . I was just, just looking for—'

'I don't care what y're looking for. There's no metal detectors allowed out here, no horse-riding, no tramping. No going after Roman coins or pot sherds or nothing. This is private land, and you can piss right off.'

Wil bristled. Maybe it was because between her father and Rose at the church, she'd had enough of people's bad opinions. Or maybe it was because it seemed unfair to be intimidated by a man who had the advantage of giant machinery. Or maybe there was something about this land, where her mother had once dared to play and cross walls, that wouldn't let her quail. 'I was just looking for a village,' she said, sounding pissed off herself.

'You'll find one if you stay on the damn bridleway. Out of my field.'

'I'm not *in* the field,' she shot back. 'I'm on this potholed pathway. And it's an old village, buried under a lumpy field. Middle Bandinby. It's supposed to be right around here.'

His brows knotted together. 'You with that man in the church cottage?'

Again with the man in the cottage! Wil threw up her hands. 'I don't know who that is! I just arrived in the country a few days ago, and somehow everyone thinks I'm with some man in a cottage!'

He was peering at her now, as though her face had the answer to a dozen questions concerning the fabric of the universe. 'Who are you?'

'Wilhelmina Mann,' she said. 'My—'

He sat back in his seat and stabbed a finger, pointing back along the sheep paddock. 'Girlie, you got two minutes to get yourself off my property, or there'll be worse things coming your way than a John Deere. Hop to it.'

And the tractor roared back to life.

Chapter 10

Wil didn't need further encouragement. She wasn't going to square off with a tractor, and memories of the lock-up back on the Gold Coast were a bit too fresh. She didn't have anyone here to bail her out. The fields looked much less beautiful as she stumbled back towards the bridleway—managing, of course, to find every rock and divot to step on. But at least by the time she burst back onto the main path, the tractor's engine was a distant if ominous grumble.

She turned back to stare at it. The farmer hadn't actually moved. He was just sitting there with the engine running. Probably on his phone, calling the village police to look out for a tall, awkward girl trespassing in the fields. Perfect.

Wil turned back down the bridleway, deflated and confused. Was it just an English village thing to be so hostile? Her mother had said it was a secretive type of place, but Wil had expected that to have changed, at least a bit. She'd seen satellite dishes on the cottage roofs; some people at least must have the internet, and be aware that the world was a more tolerant place these days. First Rose's suspicion, now this. Well, to be fair, Rose had nearly caught her. But just now she'd only been walking. How threatening could that be? When she reached the gate back down by the churchyard, she stopped to peer ahead, making sure there weren't any police cars waiting in the road.

But the gate was too tall for peering around. She stepped backwards along the boundary fence to get a better view, and neatly trod on a rock, rolled her foot and tumbled back into the weeds and flowers in the ditch. A surprised bumblebee bounced off her shoulder. Wil sat a moment in the dirt, smelling the crushed green, and laughed. *Perfect. Really, this day couldn't go any better.*

Then came the stinging, and then a roaring fire, all along her legs and across her hands. Wil scrambled up and shot away from the weeds, scraping at her skin. What the hell was happening? Had she been stung? Her body felt as though she'd fallen in a nest of bees. She danced on the spot, shaking her hands, brushing at her legs, but the fire only spread.

She fumbled with the gate catch and left the field, but the pain was so bad she could hardly bend her knees to walk. Her hands were breaking out in some kind of rash, pale lumps rising from angry red skin. She could feel the tears pouring down her face, her breath coming in bare hitches. *Murder!*

All she could think about was plunging into cool water to wash down the fire. How far was it to the beck? Maybe she could run there. But she couldn't remember if it was left or right at the bottom of the path, and anyway that path seemed to be stretching away into the distance.

Then to her right, she spotted salvation. Down a little hill was a bordered pond by a cottage. Wil stumbled towards it, sloshing in, shoes and all, before sinking down to cover her arms and legs. Her knees sank into what felt like silty mud, but she hardly cared. It was cool. She whimpered in relief, spreading the mud up over her arms and lying back in the water to catch her breath, her head on the side like it was a spa bath.

'Nice morning for a swim?'

Wil started. She cracked an eyelid to find a man staring down at her. A very attractive man with dark blond hair and an angular face. Her stomach folded in on itself and sank into the silty bottom of the pool.

'Shit,' she muttered, attempting to get out. But as soon as her arm cleared the water, the stinging itch roared to life again. Lord, what had she touched? And where was an esky of ice or a snowdrift when you needed one? 'Sorry, it's my skin, it's burning,' she said. 'I fell into the edge of the path over there and into an ant nest or something.'

'You found the nettle patch, didn't you?' he said, sounding more amused than annoyed, despite the authority of his English accent. 'Look, stop scratching at it, you'll make it worse. And come out of the pond. I've no idea what's living in there.'

With his help, Wil managed to lurch ungracefully out of the sucking silt. She stood, dripping black mud onto the emerald-green grass of the cottage yard like some kind of swamp monster.

'Well, aren't you a picture?' he said.

'I've been called worse,' Wil said, through clenched teeth. 'God, it's still burning.'

'This way.' He made off for the cottage door. 'Quick.'

Wil followed, aware as she stepped through the cottage door that she was dropping mud on beautiful slate flagstones in his hallway. She heard a shower start up to the left. Peering around a jamb, she saw him through the door of a bathroom. There were mud marks on his jeans and on the back of his nicely tailored shirt as he adjusted the taps.

He beckoned her over. Wil didn't have time to think, her mind occupied with the seven fires of hell burning across her arms and legs.

'Water's cold,' he said. 'Let it run over your skin until the stinging stops, then wash it with soap. I'll find a cloth. And a towel.'

Five seconds later, she was under the water still in her shorts and shirt, her mind clearing as the cold dampened the pain. Her clothes were a muddy ruin, the dark silt still running down the plughole. But her dignity was in worse shape.

She heard his footsteps coming back beyond the shower curtain. 'Thank you,' she called out, doubly embarrassed at his kindness. 'I made an awful mess out there. I'll clean it up, I swear.'

'Do you not know what nettles look like?' he said, from nearby. She peered around the curtain to see he was holding out a washcloth. 'Then again, with that accent, I suppose you're not acquainted with the hazards of the countryside. I'm going to guess you're from Sydney.'

Wil reached for the cloth and thanked him—trying not to stare at his face, and the athletic lines of his body, especially as he was politely turning his face to the wall. He had the kind of presence that made her want to stare. She swiped gingerly at her left leg to distract herself. The heat of the nettles was waning, replaced by the burning embarrassment of having ended up in a strange man's shower.

'Gold Coast, actually,' she said. 'And I don't remember anything at the airport about nettles.'

He chuckled, though he sounded further away, as if he'd retreated to the door. 'About knee-high,' he said. 'Fluffy top, pointed leaves, look a bit like mint but with a serious bite. Murder in the summer.'

'There should be some kind of public notice,' she complained, switching the washcloth to her other leg. 'You know, *Public bridleway, beware the nettles*. I mean, come on, all you Brits know the stuff that'll kill you in Australia: spiders, snakes, stingrays. How is it possible that people have lived for thousands of years where there's a *plant* that can disable you in a second? And growing beside a public path? Ow!'

'Easy there, take your time.' He laughed. 'Perhaps over the generations us locals have learned about long pants?'

He was teasing. She glanced around the curtain to roll her eyes at him, but got stuck on his smile when their eyes met. He had the most arresting face, made for photographs. She pulled back. 'Long pants next time, check.'

After a pause, he said, 'You know, I saw you up at the church yesterday, and going up the bridleway earlier. Not many people come through this village, much less a tall girl from Australia coming twice in two days.'

'Family connection,' she said quickly, with another peek around the curtain.

He'd sat down against the wall, as if settling in for a good story. 'Oh? Do tell?'

'It's a long story,' she said.

'I rather like those.'

Wil blushed at the way he said it. She fixed on the wall to recover and noticed that most of the tiles above the water line had been pulled down. When she peered around the curtain again, the missing tiles were evident everywhere, and the sink was missing its tap. It looked ready for renovation.

Wil glanced back at him. 'I'll just make an idiot of myself if I start telling it. Especially to a perfect stranger.'

'David Hunter,' he said. 'There, we're not strangers. At least, not perfect ones. And are you going to?'

'What?'

'Make an idiot out of yourself?'

'And add to the idiocy of being found in your duck pond? No, thank you.'

'You're funny,' he said. 'By far the best thing I've ever found in that duck pond. All right, how about your name to start?'

'Wil Mann,' she said.

'Wil? Short for?'

'Wilhelmina,' she said, scrunching her nose as she said it. 'I'd offer to shake your hand, but . . .'

'I'll not be offended. You keep on with that soap. Now, Wilhelmina Mann. What a good name for a storyteller. How about a hint on this saga?'

She sighed, but she couldn't be silent here under the water, in all her wet clothes, with him just by the door. 'Well, I came to South Bandinby because . . . my mother is from here. But so far, I've been suspected of poking around the church and been accused of trespassing in the fields, and all I have to show for it is a jar of rather dubious jam and these nettle injuries. That's the broad strokes.'

David laughed, which sounded sympathetic and comforting, as if all the ills of the world could be turned into good things. 'So you've met the locals. They're not a receiving bunch. Believe me, I know.'

Wil frowned, then abruptly yanked the curtain aside to point at him. 'Oh! *You're* the man next door!'

'I'm what?'

'Yesterday in the church, and just now in the field, I was asked if I was with "the man next door". That's you. David Hunter.'

'Ah . . . yes, my researchers didn't exactly make any friends here.'

Wil snapped the curtain closed in symbolic rebuke of the difficulties he'd caused her. 'So *you're* the reason I might have just been mowed down with a tractor?'

'Well, not the *whole* reason,' he said, sounding sheepish. 'But probably that's my bad, yes. You don't know who I am?'

Wil shut off the water, wondering what to do about her clothes. She didn't want to strip off, but at least the nettle stings had faded into tolerable itching. She hid behind the curtain. 'Nope. Who are you?'

'I have a cable show called *Saving History*, so I tend to get recognised. Terribly arrogant to say so,' he said. 'But it does happen a bit. Not that it's helped me here. Rather the reverse. There's a towel and some dry clothes on the mat for you now, and a bucket for your wet clothes.'

'Oh, I remember something about that,' she said, slowly easing her shorts over the welts. 'The Elstons weren't keen on letting a TV show in. Why's the show interested in South Bandinby anyway?'

'Tell you what, I'll give you some privacy, and then we'll wash and dry your clothes while I tell you about it.'

~

'Believe it or not, I live here,' David said, when she'd taken the sitting chair beside an enormous stone hearth. He sank into an old tan couch opposite. 'This cottage came up for sale five years ago. Saw it by chance on a real estate site and fell in love with it. It needed enormous work—all the stone repointed, rotting timbers to replace, plumbing, wiring, everything. I think it had been sitting vacant for nearly a decade. Only trouble is that my work hasn't allowed me much time to be here to do it. I'm still finishing things.'

He shrugged.

'If you've been here for five years, why's everyone asking me if I'm doing work for you now?'

'Ah.' He nodded out an arched window, through which Wil could see the church and its leaning headstones. 'You see that church out there? I couldn't believe it when I first drove in and saw it just sitting there. It has an original Anglo-Saxon era tower and south porch—you see that blockwork? There are Medieval additions, of course, and some ill-considered renovations in more modern times, but, overall, it's an incredible building. A perfect example of how Roman architecture had far less influence on English churches than is generally thought.'

Wil frowned at the building, not following. 'Really?'

'Oh yeah,' he said, his body animating. 'When most people think about glorious English churches, they think they're derived from Roman architecture. But that's only one influence. There's Byzantine and Celtic as well, and some features

135

are hotly debated. The tower, for example. That doesn't come from European influence. It could be an addition to make it a defensive position, from the Viking era. Or it could be the English answer to Byzantine domes.' He broke off, as if becoming aware she was staring at him again. 'Sorry, I'm getting technical. It's just you wouldn't think to find something like that, sitting in this little village. Such a layered story of so many different people and philosophies and art styles, all written in stonework. I'd love to have the chance to really investigate the history of that building, and preserve it. So to do that, I started the research process for the show, and, well . . . that didn't exactly go as planned.'

'Someone threaten to run you down in a tractor too?' she said, but she looked at the church with new eyes. She had no idea what Roman or Byzantine architecture even was, but she could well imagine what stories it might tell. She felt a filling pride that her mother was one of them.

David grinned. 'Not exactly. But let's just say Lord Elston hasn't yet allowed me an audience. We've tried reaching out to the Jamaican estate, too, where his younger brother John lives, but he doesn't respond either, and the cordial nods I used to get in Sunday church have been replaced with pointed suggestions to buy the jam.'

Wil felt the momentary snap of attention at hearing John's name, then she smiled, and returned her gaze to the church. 'It is pretty amazing.'

'I hope you're talking about the church, because that's not how I'd describe the jam,' he said. They shared a smile. 'I'm sorry I didn't have anything smaller. The dryer will be finished in half an hour.'

'It's fine,' Wil said, pushing up the sleeves of the T-shirt and jeans he'd lent her, which were two sizes too big. The awkwardness she felt in wearing his clothes was waning the more they talked, but thank goodness she'd left the letters in the car. They could have been a wet ruined mess too. 'So . . . what did your researchers find out? You know, before they were run out of town.'

'Not a great deal unfortunately. We have everything that's from official channels, of course—listed-building records for the church and the manor house, genealogy for the Elston family, some limited archaeological work. But oral histories from the residents . . . there, I've pretty much drawn a blank.'

'Oh?' Wil said, feeling strangely deflated. 'Really, nothing?'

'It's unusual,' David said with a sigh. 'In villages like this, there's often at least a few people who've lived here all their lives. They've never moved more than a few miles from where they were born. And the lord has oversight on who can move in, so that tends to keep things even more static. But about twenty years ago, Lord Elston relaxed the old approvals processes. Now lots of the village cottages are the country weekend houses of Londoners. The few people who have been here longer are tight-lipped. It's been difficult to trace anyone who lived here before that. We have found a few, though.'

'What did they say?' Wil said, mentally calculating. Her mother had left the village in 1980, before this great exodus.

'Surprisingly not too many stories about the church, given how much time many of them probably spent in it as children. Some had family stories about great-great-grandfathers working on the renovations. Some had a few photos of older relatives from decades ago. And of course, there's the Middle Bandinby story.'

Wil's head jerked up. 'You know about that?'

'Sure. Why?'

'It's where I was going this morning, when I was shooed off by Farmer Friendly.'

David laughed. 'You are the history fan. Wonderful story, isn't it? And tragic.'

'My—I mean, I thought that there weren't any records of it?'

'Oh, there are lots of records, all the way back to the Doomsday Book. But they're confusing because these villages went by many names. And unfortunately, there wasn't any formal archaeological work done until recently, when ploughing had already damaged a lot of the site.'

Wil frowned. 'I thought they didn't plough it?'

'You do know about this, don't you? They didn't used to. The couple of villagers we found were clear about that, too. Most of them remembered going to see the lumpy field as a childhood lark. But that's another thing that's changed in the last twenty years. More modern farming equipment, loss of superstition about contamination. Go back a generation and people still believed the plague could come out of the ground, as if it was lurking there like a curse. You'd think an abandoned medieval village would attract more academic interest, but it never did.'

Wil's heart tugged. 'So it's gone?'

'Not entirely. Look, if you're interested, I can have someone bring the records up here. You'd be welcome to take a look.'

Wil swallowed. 'Thanks. But I was looking for something more recent.'

'Oh?' he said. 'So Middle Bandinby wasn't your primary objective?'

Wil considered him a long minute, his open curious face. The last hour of the conversation had been like talking to someone she'd known for years, awkward introduction in the duck pond aside. But he was on television, she reminded herself, and almost a stranger. Her real objective was far too personal to tell.

She shrugged. 'I was hoping to get time to look around the church without the locals peering over my shoulder, I guess. My, ah, mum came from the village, and I wanted to, ah, take my time. But someone always seems to be there.'

'You bought the jam, didn't you?'

Wil laughed. 'Worse.'

'What could be worse?' He raised his eyebrows.

'I paid five pounds. I nearly died when I converted it back to dollars.'

David put a hand over his face, suppressing a laugh. 'No one escapes Rose.'

Wil smiled, but she felt a familiar impulse to just keep talking.

'I think my clothes will be dry enough now,' she said, rising out of her chair and making it to the dryer before he could make any reply. Her shorts and soft bra were still damp, but the shirt was dry enough and she needed to escape the pressure of having to tell him why she was really here. She definitely didn't want to talk about the letters. It would be safer to be back in the field with a tractor-wielding farmer.

David was waiting when she emerged from the bathroom, her clothes clinging.

'You really won't stay?' he said, seeming disappointed. 'You're welcome to dry those completely.'

'The Travelodge has a dryer,' she said, knowing it was time to go. Her shoes at the door were still sodden, so she picked them up in her hand. Hopefully she could make it back to the car without stepping on nettles. Only when she was on the garden path did she turn and look back to find him watching her from the doorway. He'd never changed his muddy jeans.

'Thank you so much. Sorry about your pond,' she said, and turned to go.

'Wait.'

She stopped.

'It's the parish council meeting in the church right now. If you give it another ten minutes, they usually retire back to someone's house for tea. Church would be all yours, then. There's almost never tourists.'

'Oh, okay,' Wil said.

'Don't worry, I won't ask you to come back in to wait. You'll be able to see better from your car, and it's probably best you not be seen coming out of this house.'

Wil smiled, relieved of her worries.

'One more thing,' he said. 'Dock leaves. Should you find yourself in the nettles again, look for dock leaves.'

He raised a hand and waved, then turned inside.

～

David was right. Eight minutes after Wil slid into her car, she spotted movement at the church door, and six people slowly spilled down the step, carrying folders and shoulder bags. Wil slumped lower when she saw Rose, who was the most loaded down, with two bags and a vase in each hand. But none of the parish counsellors looked in Wil's direction. They all turned east towards the beck side of the road. Wil watched as Rose loaded her items into her car and pulled away, waving to the others as she went.

Wil's stomach dipped as the rest slowly disappeared around the curve in the road. She scrambled out and forced herself to amble up the verge, going carefully over the stones, and even pause by the noticeboard, and at a gravestone, neither of which she read. Once inside the darkened doorway, she stopped and tested the silence. Peered past the jam table into the side chapel, and took two steps down the nave. No lurking parishioners now. She really was alone.

Her bare feet were quiet across the flagstones to the memorial, and she gritted her teeth as she pulled on the iron stud at the base of the wood board. It gave a little. She stopped to huff a breath, trying to calm down, then used her other hand to push at the top.

The board swung up with a squeak that made her jump. She glanced around guiltily, but Rose didn't erupt from behind a column, so Wil dipped her head behind the board, heart thundering. Darkness back there. She used her phone to shine a light and found a smooth stone cavity behind the board. Right at the bottom was a wood cover with a finger hole at one end.

Wil stared at the tideline of skin oils around that finger grip. This was it. The place her mother had meant her to find. Her finger fitted perfectly into the grip.

She pulled the cover away and shone the phone light down into the space. It was about the size of a small shoebox. Grey stone. And completely empty.

Chapter 11

When Wil woke the next morning, she momentarily forgot where she was. She had a familiar empty feeling that always led to wondering if there was time to get to the beach before work. Then she slowly registered the bland beige of the tight Travelodge room, and remembered. The emptiness spread into every fibre of her body, making her just as hollow as that hiding hole had been.

She had tried all the other panels behind the memorial, of course, but none of them had moved, and she'd searched all around the chapel, hoping that her mother had meant some other spot. But there was nothing else to find. The letters simply weren't there.

Perhaps they had never been. Maybe her mother had died before she'd finished writing them, or maybe, in the years since Wil was meant to get them, the spot had been found, and someone else had those letters. Just as she'd feared.

She felt stupid for having been so hopeful. The letters could be buried in a landfill, next to banana skins and meat tray wrappers. Or in the hands of a lucky finder who showed them to friends saying, 'Hey, look what I found in this old church!' If they had been finished at all.

Wil slumped back on the bed, the devastation of the missing story, the missing pieces of her mother, of hope dangled and then snatched away again, descending on her. Eventually her phone rang. Listlessly she checked the screen. Colin.

'What?' she groaned.

'I hadn't heard from you,' he said through a scratchy connection. 'I lend you the money to fly halfway around the world and suddenly you forget about your favourite brother?'

'Sorry, Col,' she said. 'It's been . . . a bit mental.'

'How goes the mission? You at the village yet?'

'Sort of,' Wil said. She couldn't bring herself to voice the failure.

'Shonna's asking about you. She wants to know if you'll still be staying when you get back.'

But Wil couldn't see past her disappointment. There didn't seem to be a tomorrow.

'Also, Rob's been calling,' Colin said.

Wil jerked to sitting. 'Why? I dumped him.'

'You did?'

'Yeah.'

Colin whooped. 'I can finally throw that party! And tell him to sod off. If I'd known this trip was going to be this good for you, I'd have funded it two months ago.'

'Very funny.'

'You don't sound that great, Willy. What's going on?'

Wil bit her lip, trying not to cry. 'It's just harder than I thought it would be,' she sniffed. 'I got chased by some grumpy old guy on a tractor, and then I ended up falling into nettles and then into a pond, where of course the owner of the cottage found me covered in mud.'

Colin laughed. 'I wouldn't expect any less. I hope the owner had a sense of humour.'

'Yeah, I suppose. You want to know what's worse? I embarrassed myself in front of some minor celebrity. The owner's a guy called David Hunter. Apparently he's on TV. He was pretty nice about the whole thing though. Let me use his dryer.'

An odd pause came before Colin said, 'Not *the* David Hunter?'

'Who's *the* David Hunter?'

'Wil, Jeebus. He's not a minor celebrity. He played for *England*. Gave old Becks a run for his money when he was on form, before he blew out his knee. Clichéd way to go, really. They used to call them "the two Davids", you know? Beckham and Hunter? Dad still thinks he was robbed.'

'I didn't know he was a footballer,' Wil said. 'He said he had a TV show. *History* something.'

'*Saving History*. Shonna has the box set at her place. Lots of David Hunter talking smartypants about old buildings and how to shore them up, and all their local history. It's, like, only second to *Grand Designs*. You've seriously never heard of it?'

'No.'

Colin grunted. 'Well, so are you going to the church today?'

Wil said that she was, and hoped she sounded sincere as she hung up. She hugged herself. She knew this escapade was already at an end, and she felt desolate, but also stupid. Her mother had been gone for twenty-six years, and the mysterious extra letters may as well have never existed. She'd dug herself into a money hole with Colin for nothing.

She hauled herself up, numb at the thought of how much worse she'd made her situation. She'd better pack up and leave before she had to pay for another night.

She'd just finished collecting her discarded clothes when a knock came. Expecting housekeeping, she opened the door and stepped back in surprise.

'What are you doing here?' she said.

David Hunter was standing on her doorstep.

$\backsim$

'Do you know how hard it is to find someone when all you have to go on is that they're staying at the Travelodge?' he said, as Wil ushered him inside, grateful he'd caught her at the end of cleaning up and not at the beginning.

'There are two Travelodges,' he went on. 'After I called all the rooms at the first one—because reception most unkindly refused to tell me anything about their guests—I decided to drive down here and knock on doors at this one instead.'

'Why would you do that?'

'Do you know, I think my face is more recognisable than I think, given that in my doorknocking I had not one, but two offers to come in for a wee drink, and one a more sordid proposal that I won't repeat in the company of a lady. But, here I am, victorious at the end of my quest.'

He grinned, and Wil smiled despite herself. 'Are you drunk?'

'Not even slightly,' he said, quite serious now. 'But I might have gotten myself a little worked up, afraid that you may have left already, and before I could deliver this.'

From his pocket he drew out a plain-looking yellow envelope, the type that official documents came in. It had been opened, but a second envelope inside was still intact.

Wil's heart tumbled as soon as she saw the blue fountain pen letters spelling *Mina* on the front. In the top left corner was *2008, 1 of 11.*

'Where did you get this?' she asked, nearly breathless. Had his researchers stumbled on the letters after all?

'Someone dropped it through my letter slot last night. Given the fact that you're the only visitor I've had who could possibly be Mina, I assumed someone wanted to get it to you. And given your reaction, I seem to have been right.'

'Oh my god,' Wil whispered, patting around for the bed so she could sit down. She was still trying to navigate from despairing depths of imagining the letters had never existed to holding one in her hand just ten minutes later. It was giving her terrible whiplash.

'I should go,' David said.

'No, no, wait.' She was so grateful to him for bringing this, right when she was about to give up, and so giddy at the thought her hopes might not be completely empty. But who on earth had sent it? And where were the others?

'You do look like the kind of happiness I'd like to bottle,' David said. 'Care to share what's so exciting?'

'I need to read this,' Wil said, easing the seal of the envelope open and pulling out the folded sheets. 'Would you wait? I'll need to ask you a few things.'

He gave her a slow smile. 'Anything for the woman I found in my duck pond.'

~

Dear Mina,

I've written these letters so that you can choose to read them year by year if you wish. If that's the case, then happy 19th birthday, my darling girl. However, I think it's equally likely that you may read them all at once, because even as a little girl, if there was something to know, you always wanted to have it all now.

That was what life was like for me that first year I was completely away from the village, through 1981. London seemed the other side of the world to me, a huge city full of so many things to do and see. Bridget and I lived in a tiny basement flat not far from King's Road. Even though it had almost no windows and a postage stamp kitchen, we could never have afforded to live there on our wages. Bridget's uncle owned it, and his generosity enabled two young ladies to see the bigger world.

And didn't I see it. Bridget worked in a boutique (called Seditionaries), and I found a job as an usher in a theatre, which was perfect. Bridget snaffled us clothes and taught me how to dress—punk, mod, you name it—and I snuck her into movies. I think I spent the better part of that year in the dark! Movies were so wonderful, and I always felt transported into other places. I remember sitting in the aisle watching The Shining, Friday the 13th, *and a whole slew of horror movies that Bridget refused, and seeing* The Empire Strikes Back *and* Raiders of the Lost Ark *fourteen times.*

I may have had a crush on Harrison Ford. I took my usher job very seriously, because it was the first work I loved. The power of having that little torch to take people to their seats after the lights went down! And to calmly ask people who'd actually bought the cheap front seats but then snuck into the middle to please move, thank you very much!

When I wasn't working, we were often going to concerts. Bridget found most bands through the musicians who passed through the boutique, and later as she took the ethos of her workplace to heart (it was quite political and emphasised staying informed) we went to the British Museum and bookshops, and we'd spend the days between work learning, reading and playing music, and then talking about all the things we'd read and listened to. We had intelligent conversations about Brave New World *and* 1984, *which at the time felt like the looming near-future. (Feels odd to say that now, more than ten years later ... if you ever read these books, see what you think.)*

It was a crazy time, happy and bittersweet. On occasional weekends, Susie and John would come down on the train, and we would all spend time together. It was generally good fun, though John and I had to pretend we hadn't broken each other's hearts. Well, I was pretending. I can't say what he felt. But there were times, where we were alone for a few minutes, that I could sense the pressure of the things he wanted to say to me.

I never let him. I couldn't look back now I was out in the world. I didn't dare, and risk that deep burning ache for him being fanned back into flame. Because at the end of those weekends, he would be gone again, and it would have left me putting that fire out over and over.

He always returned to the village. His father was not well, and Thomas was having to assume many of the lord's roles with the estate, in which John was forever helping. He talked about how that would all be done with soon, that Thomas would be ready to stand on his own, and then John was going to travel—to Australia, New Zealand even! Places that really were on the other side of the world. But he'd say these things in front of everyone else, when we were sharing a bottle of wine and talking up the futures we'd all have. Never in private. Maybe he'd learned that in public you could make assertions that didn't have to be acted on. While in private, between the two of us, declarations carried weight. That was how we'd come unstuck together: making promises we hadn't kept. But I always meant what I said, and did what I meant, and between the two of us there would never be space for mere speculation again.

Still, he continued to come down. And from time to time, I saw Thomas in London, too. The first time, I thought I was seeing things. Bridget and I were leaving a club in Chelsea one night, and I saw someone I thought was John. I almost called out to him, but another second later I realised it was Thomas, with a group of friends I didn't know. Weeks later, I mentioned having seen him to John, and John turned pale.

That's when I realised something secret hung around the Elston house. At the time, I didn't care much what it was. I saw Thomas a few more times here and there, always on a weekend when John wasn't in London. I didn't tell John about any of those other times, and not just because of his reaction *the first time. John always seemed a little disapproving towards me in those days—I think he was conservative in his heart, and seeing me dressed as a punk was rather an affront to him. I was done caring what he thought of me (or at least, pretending that I was) but I would still catch him looking at me in that old way that made my stomach flutter. I took comfort from the idea that he might be envying my freedom, but I didn't want to invite any more disapproval. So I kept Thomas sightings quiet.*

As the wedding of Lady Diana and Prince Charles approached, though, I found I had once again drifted back into John's close company, and he had drifted back to me. His family were devoted royalists, and Lord and Lady Elston, Thomas and John were all invited to the BIG DAY. That came with more trips to London for John, which I enjoyed at first, but otherwise I can't say I bought into the hype. All these people were lining the streets to watch a fairytale, while the man I loved would go to the party without me. I think that finally spoiled us. A day where supposedly the whole nation came together only emphasised how divided John and I really were.

London seemed too small for me after that. In a little over a year, the city had gone from a new universe to a place too close to the village. It seems ironic now, watching Charles and Diana's fairytale implode over the last few years, that I let their wedding get to me so much. I guess it just goes to show that what you see in public is rarely the whole story. Or even the right story. In public, Thomas was Baron Elston's heir, an eligible bachelor, and John was his equally eligible brother, two poster boys for the aristocracy. In private,

Thomas had a penchant for alternative London nightlife and John had been secretly engaged to me, the peasant-nobody daughter of a village worker.

I don't know if anyone in our lives really sees all our faces. We're all more complex than what most of our friends can even allow in us. But I was tired of that kind of double life. And I couldn't play it again with John. I knew I was in danger of being in love with him all over again, and he with me. Probably I was already too late. So I had to leave before he broke my heart a second time.

I bought my ticket across the Channel. Bridget was very disappointed to be losing me and our London life, to be upsetting the weekends with Susie and John. But I was determined. I felt it was easier to be miserable than be the kind of happy that's tainted with always waiting, either for the better days to show up, or for it to all end.

I wanted the kind of love I could believe in, that would be freely given. And that year, I hadn't found it. So I moved to Paris—the city of love. I will tell you more about that in my next letter.

Until then, be brave, my darling girl.

Love,

Mum

Chapter 12

Wil lowered the letter and found David waiting, a small smile on his lips. It was strange to be observed in this moment by someone she hardly knew, but she was so grateful to him for bringing the letters that it didn't matter.

'I'm morbidly curious. What do you need to ask?' he said.

'Well, who sent this? Was it someone in the village?'

'I have no idea. Didn't hear or see anyone. There's over a hundred people living in the village, much as it doesn't look that way. I'd put my money on a local, but I don't know who.'

She hopped up. 'But how would anyone know who I am?'

She frowned at him, wondering if he'd somehow orchestrated this. After all, he was the only person who knew her name. What if one of his researchers *had* found the letters in the church? Unless . . .

She clicked her fingers. 'Maybe it was that farmer, the one I ran across in the fields. I told him my name, too.'

'Was that before or after the nearly running you over part?'

'Before, I think,' she said. 'You don't think that's why he tried to run me over?'

David laughed. 'Those who wish you ill don't usually turn around and bring precious artefacts. Sounds as though we can rule him out.' He paused. 'Are you going to tell me what this is all about? Because, excuse me being a research nerd, but if you're asking who sent it, then either the letter isn't signed, or you know whoever signed it isn't around anymore. Judging from how old it looks, I'd guess the latter.'

Wil took a breath, afraid that if she started, the whole story would come tumbling out. Certain details of it were too personal to tell, like the secret hiding place in the church, or the details of her mother's early death. But if there really were more letters, then she wanted to find who had them. And maybe David could help, especially if he'd already spoken to everyone in the village.

She thought about Rose, and the other parish counsellors she'd watched walk up the road. Maybe one of them had seen her come out of David's house, or sitting in front of it in her car. Or anyone else in the houses and cottages around the fields could have seen her driving circuits. But how would any of them know who she was? She looked up to find David waiting, his eyebrows raised. He looked as if he was expecting an answer.

'Did you say something?' she said.

He laughed. 'Confusion. Definitely a sign of low blood sugar. I asked if you were hungry. How do you feel about pub food? Stories are better told over a meal.'

'Pub food?'

'Yes. Proper English pub, not those monstrosities you have in Australia. There's a place not too far away, very discreet. Can I buy you a drink?'

'Given I slept through breakfast and lunch, that might not be a good idea.'

'Early dinner, then.'

The pub was called The White Horse, and was set on a corner approaching the village of Nettleham, about twenty minutes from town. It had white rendered walls and dark beams, and a little brook bubbling past the back door, which was where David went in. They slid into a quiet booth in a corner, out of sight of the main bar, where a few red-faced locals were nursing pints and staring pensively at a football match.

Soon, Wil had a pint and a menu, and only then realised this might have been a mistake. Perfect conditions for oversharing.

'So,' David began, raising his glass. 'To mysterious letters and ignorance of nettles.'

Wil clinked her glass to his, but however charming he might be, she was apprehensive. She took her time choosing the pie and chips, trying to think how she could avoid laying her mother out in the open. The silence was almost painful.

'You really don't want to talk to me, do you?' David said when he returned from ordering at the bar. 'It's okay—I can spot reluctance at ten paces.'

'Sorry,' Wil said. 'I don't mean to be rude.'

'I understand. Whatever you're doing is private. If you don't want to tell me the story, I can just watch Arsenal over your shoulder.' He checked his watch with a small smile. 'I'm about due for an annual dose of regretting-the-life-that-almost-was. May as well get it over with.'

Wil thawed. Oh, why did he have to be funny?

'My brother told me you were a footballer. How long's it been since you played?' She noted the intense focus the other bar patrons had fixed on the game. Her father wore that face when he watched football. She'd never thought about the incredible pressure that must come from knowing people all round the world were watching you like that.

David took a breath as though he was about to make a joke, then said flatly, 'Nearly fifteen years. Which sounds like an age. But feels like a moment ago, too.'

'Do you miss it?'

'Here we are.' The server appeared by the table, and the question hung unanswered between them. She put down the meals, Wil's plate groaning with a pie, peas and chunky chips. David had ordered the same thing. Once the server had left, he picked up a chip and squeezed it.

'How much do you know about football, Mina? Being Australian I would bet on cricket and rugby, maybe, since you tend to wallop us at both of them, but soccer?'

'My dad's English. He stays up until stupid hours to watch matches on satellite. I know that much. But I don't go by Mina.'

'What do you go by?'

Don't say Willy. 'My brother calls me Willy. He thinks it's hilarious because there's so many boys in the house, but I hate it.'

'I can't imagine why,' David said dryly. 'Doesn't really suit you.'

Wil shrugged, building a tower out of her chips. 'My name's never really suited me. What kind of name is *Wilhelmina*? I mean, I'm tall and I wear overalls all day. Wilhelmina sounds like someone in fancy dress, or with a fascinating Insta account, or who at least has their life together.'

She hunched. She hadn't even started her pint yet, and already she was talking away like an idiot. David must think she was a lunatic. But when she glanced at him, he was just staring back at her with a slight crease between his brows. She couldn't read his expression. 'Sorry,' she said. 'I'm being boring.'

'Not at all. Names mean everything. You must have some attachment to yours if you've held on to it this long. You could have changed it.'

She sat back. Despite never liking her name, she'd never considered changing it. Then she thought of what her mother had said about her name, and the tiny thaw she'd felt towards it. 'Maybe,' she said.

'Besides, people who have their life together tend to be boring. You must have interesting stories to tell.'

Wil grunted. 'Maybe on that, too.'

He grinned. 'Tell you one thing though, Miss Wilhelmina Mann, you may be English by blood, but football didn't make it into your circulation. Otherwise, you wouldn't ask if I miss it.' He sat back, tapping his fingers on his glass. 'But since you are asking, as it turns out, I don't miss it as much as you might think. At least, not now. I miss my teammates. I miss the excitement, sometimes. But I've moved on. Mostly. Just didn't get the sort of exit I was hoping for. On the right day, that can feel like regret.'

'My brother said you hurt your knee.'

He gave her a crooked smile, and she wondered if it was a bad memory for him, or because she'd just revealed she'd talked about him with Colin for a second time. 'Let's not speak of it while boys are playing,' he said. 'Bad luck. What's your brother's name?'

'Colin,' she said. 'He's great. He's the reason I could come here at all.'

David's mouth curved, as if reflecting the affection Wil felt. 'Thank goodness for brothers.'

Before Wil could say anything more, David reached into his pocket and pulled out a folded envelope. 'Before I forget, I promised you this,' he said, unfolding several sheets. 'Records about Middle Bandinby.'

Wil leaned forward, eager to see. 'Oh, what are these?' she said, fingering printouts of several sandy-coloured, patterned objects.

'Finds from a field walk at the site. One is a broken tile. It's only a fragment, but the texture is amazing, isn't it? Like dragon scales.'

'Yeah.' Wil ran her fingers over it. 'I love it.'

'And this other one is stonework, probably from a church, a curved edge. Very elegant. Pity we don't have more photos. If I could get permission from the estate, we could do some more serious work on the area.' He moved some photos out from under the sheets. 'And here's some aerial shots, taken in the fifties.'

Wil traced the lines of boxy foundations, clearly visible in the fallow grass. 'But it doesn't look like this now?'

'Not since it's been ploughed over,' he said. 'And here's the entries from the Doomsday Book.'

'Middle Bandinby,' Wil read. 'Lord in 1086: Gilbert the Fat.' She looked up at David. 'Really?'

David laughed. 'Perfect, isn't it? Give me your number and I'll text you the photos.'

'Is Gilbert the Fat related to Lord Elston?' Wil asked, after she'd told him her number.

'Trust me, it's not something I've brought up. The Elstons can trace their lineage a long way, but not quite that far. Fortunately.'

Wil sipped her pint, turning through the other sheets, pretending to look at them while madly thinking what to say to him, especially now she felt she owed him twice over. She'd never thought so much before opening her mouth to talk. Finally when she had the words, she swallowed, feeling she was about to jump from a great height.

'You wanted to know about the letter,' she said.

'Mmm?'

'Well . . . it's from my mother. She . . . we lost her a long time ago, before I can really remember, but she came from South Bandinby. I think I said that already. So I'm here to see what I could find of her.'

David sat back with a look of genuine amazement. 'After all this time,' he murmured. 'After all this time, someone had a letter of hers? And they found out who you were and got it to you? Our scriptwriters couldn't make this up.' He leaned forward again. 'And does the letter have any clues about who might have had it? Who was it addressed to?'

Wil paused, realising he'd misunderstood her, but not sure how much to correct him. She kept to the hard facts. 'I know my mother had two schoolfriends. One of them is dead, I think, but there was another called Bridget, who went to the same school as my mum in Welton. She moved away with her family though, and I don't have a last name for her. But this letter says that my mother lived with her in London, around 1981. Mum mentions the name of a shop where Bridget worked.'

There, that was okay. It felt safer to talk about Bridget.

'Which shop?' David asked.

'Something called Seditionaries. It's probably closed now. And I don't suppose Bridget ever came back to the village.'

'There's no one who goes by Bridget now, I can tell you that much,' David said. Then he grinned suddenly. 'But that store isn't closed. It just goes by a different name. You want World's End, in King's Road.'

'How on earth could you know that?'

'My dad was into the London punk scene in the late seventies. Everyone knew that shop, it's Vivienne Westwood's store. I met her at a party, once. I think the store was called Sex when Dad first went there. He likes telling that story at family gatherings. How is it you *don't* know it?'

'Who's Vivienne Westwood?'

'I see.'

Wil threw a chip at him. 'But what's the chance of anyone there remembering a salesgirl from forty years ago?'

'You'd be surprised what people remember. It's getting them to tell you that's the problem.' He smiled, and Wil wondered suddenly if he could tell how much she'd withheld. 'Do you look like your mother?'

Wil felt a burst of unexpected grief, like a star exploding in her chest. 'Um, I'm not sure,' she mumbled, rubbing her ribs with the heel of her hand. 'I don't have many photos of her.'

'And I hit a nerve,' David said. 'Sorry. The reason I asked is that sometimes familiarity helps people remember. In a small village like South Bandinby, the locals aren't the kind of people who'll open their door to a TV crew and tell you their whole backstory. You need to spend time with them, and if you look like someone they once knew, all the better. Because you're not really a stranger at all. You're long-lost family.'

'Didn't you say you've been in the village five years?'

'Fair point,' he said, dryly. 'But I have the problem of having a public profile, and I'm asking for huge things: let us dig under your church and expose your lost village on national television. You, on the other hand, are just looking for who might have sent you a letter. They've already made the first move.'

'So what are you suggesting?'

'Church. It's Sunday tomorrow. Go and make your face known. Hopefully whoever sent the letter is there, too.'

'And what do I say to them?'

'Nothing, if you don't want to. In fact, that's probably best. If you ask them directly, they'll probably deny knowing anything about it.'

'They would?'

'Well, someone put that letter through my door instead of giving it to me in person. That suggests they wanted to be anonymous. Maybe because of how they got it, who knows? People will lie about anything if the true story doesn't work for them. It's the ultimate form of self-protection.' He smiled. 'That's why you're keeping the real story to yourself, isn't it?'

❧

Wil woke the next morning far too early for church, and instead found herself returning to the searches she'd done on David last night. The images that returned were mostly of a younger and painfully leaner version of him in his club colours, on the field. Pictures of him running, and with teammates, and taking kicks at the ball. *Boring*. Wil scrolled past those. But a number of other images were of a much more mature-looking David, taken in a field with an old church or castle or crumbling wall behind him. In these ones, he was usually wearing a long military-style coat, the collar turned up. He seemed so different to the soccer player.

Idly, Wil tapped on a video link, and the *Saving History* opening credits played. It was odd to watch him appear on screen, striding across an old stone bridge. 'Mills were an essential feature of every medieval village, owned by the lord and leased for a fee to the miller,' said on-screen David, pausing to lean on the bridge. 'The Doomsday Book records over five thousand watermills. They could be constructed in a multitude of ways, on natural watercourses, or with manmade earthworks, and were hubs of industry and the economy. Almost all of these incredible machines have disappeared. But today on *Saving History*, just a hundred yards down this stream, we're going to witness the reconstruction of a very special watermill, with an unexpected and surprising history of murder, intrigue and politics.'

The shot panned out and up, swooping around to show David gazing downstream. The full episode wasn't available, but Wil found another five videos like it. In one, David was speaking French with a stonemason. In another, he was going over plans with a reconstructive architect. He seemed incredibly smart and awfully distracting. Nothing like a footballer. She read far enough into his Wikipedia page to discover he'd retrained after his professional career ended before she noticed the time and had to scramble to her car.

As she parked in the lane opposite the church, a single bell was ringing out the service, a rather mournful note that went with the grey morning. The church itself seemed at home under the heavy sky, and the village buildings hunkered down against the threatening drizzle. Wil shivered in her too-thin jacket and tried to fathom hundreds of years of people tramping up to these doors through rain and mist, and failed. The day she'd received the first letter already seemed a lifetime ago; it was impossible to grasp such early times. She tried instead to imagine her mother trudging up this grey path as a girl, on her way to turn Granny Maxwell's pages. The idea seemed awfully bleak and limiting. No wonder she'd wanted to leave.

Wil saw only two figures ahead through the church door, but then movement caught her eye and she spotted David emerging from his cottage. He gave her a discreet wave and waited. It had been his suggestion that they not be seen together in the congregation. That would be better for Wil's odds, or as he'd put it, make her look 'good by comparison'.

Her heart started up a drumbeat as she approached the door. Her eyes grazed over the rhyme carved in the porch flagstone, and came to rest on a woman handing out hymnbooks, who was wearing a cardigan as grey as the flagstones over a mint-green dress. 'Welcome,' she said to Wil, handing over a book stuffed with papers. Wil glanced back after she'd passed. Could that be the person who'd sent the letter?

Wil inspected the scant congregation next, mulling on where to sit. Six people were scattered through the first few pews, with another six towards the back. Fortunately, none of them looked like Farmer Friendly. Wil chose an empty pew in the middle and slid into the seat. It reminded her of the church Carol had taken them all to as kids, where Wil had suffered through Sunday school. At least, the pews did. The churches themselves couldn't have been more different. She imagined the two churches having a throwdown fight, South Bandinby's stained glass and stone weight against the white plaster and neon-blue cross of Broadbeach Uniting, and had to stifle a giggle.

As someone turned to look, she quickly glanced out the nearest window and saw the huge tree by the wall. She stilled. It was the same tree her mother had imagined fairies in, the same one she had drawn. Tears pricked Wil's eyes and she looked away, blinking.

A priest in robes was busily turning the pages of a double-brick Bible on the pulpit. And there was Rose, moving down the aisle, handing out flyers from a bundle gripped under her arm.

Wil swallowed as Rose reached her.

'So, you've come back again,' Rose whispered, handing over a song sheet and a service order. She seemed more friendly when not holding pruning shears. 'How was the jam?'

'Lovely,' lied Wil, who hadn't tried it.

'You feel free to take another. Not that we'll begrudge any generous donation. But five pounds for one is rather too much.' Rose smiled. Wil tentatively smiled back, before Rose's gaze shifted and her mouth pulled tight. 'Oh, *he's* come,' she said.

Wil glanced around to see David backlit in the porch doorway. How was it possible that he could look as though he was in a photoshoot when just coming to church? It must be the hair, the way it stood up like that. Or maybe it was all those videos she'd watched of him. Rose made off in his direction.

Wil wrenched her attention back to the front so as not to appear too interested. Out of the corner of her eye, she spied David slide into a pew on the other side of the aisle.

Wil studied the backs of the heads of the people she could see. They were all grey-haired, but for one woman with two tweenage children, who were already trying to kick each other. It was a long way from the packed pews of her mother's story. She found it impossible to imagine any of them knew who she was. Wil almost missed Rose cane-walking slowly back down the aisle, and sliding into the organist's chair. Next thing, she was playing the rousing bars of the first hymn.

As the tiny congregation shook itself awake, Wil stared, a funny feeling stirring in her gut. She flipped to the service order, and searched past the church notices to where it said *Organist: Rose Maxwell.*

Maxwell!

Wil tried to guess how old Rose was, and to calculate the years since her mother had been in the village, which she kept mucking up and having to start again. But even doing it four times over, right through a dry sermon on charity, she couldn't see that Rose could be Granny Maxwell. A relative, maybe.

Her mother had been right about the eternity of time in the church; it seemed to take an age for everyone to drift away. Wil hovered, waiting until she could approach Rose, who was tidying up the prayer books in an antique bookcase.

'I see you, hanging about there,' Rose said, giving Wil a shrewd eye. 'Not a name you hear every day, Wilhelmina.'

Wil started with a surge of excitement. 'How did you know?'

She was sure Rose was about to confess to being the letter sender, but the woman jerked her chin at the table near the door. 'I always read the visitor register. Mann, though, that's a common name around here.'

'My mother used to turn the pages for Granny Maxwell playing the organ,' Wil rushed out. 'I wondered if she was your mother.'

Rose's brow furrowed, then she gave a bark of laughter. 'There's only been one Granny Maxwell in this village in my life, and that's me.'

'But, how is that possible? You can't be that old!' Wil slapped a hand over her mouth. 'I mean, that's not what I meant—'

'Ninety-six this October, I'll have you know.' Rose pulled her glasses up from their chain and peered hard at Wil. 'Well, bless me, if you aren't her daughter. Only Ann would talk like that. She always had a tongue faster than her brain could keep up with.'

'But you don't look a day over sixty.'

Rose laughed. 'Get away with you. Though I suppose I've had more luck in my years than your poor mother.'

Wil's own laugh broke off as the grief flared again. She tried to smile.

'Anyway,' Rose said, briskly skirting the awkwardness without acknowledging it. 'You've come to see where she came from, then?'

Wil nodded, still unable to speak.

'And you're sure you're not working with David Hunter?'

'No,' Wil whispered, though that felt slightly less true than last time. She cleared her throat. 'I wondered if anyone else in the village remembers my mother, or might have been friends with her. Might have any . . . stories for me.'

Rose's jaw worked as she considered.

'Anything you could remember,' Wil rushed on. 'I know she had a friend called Bridget, and she was also friends with John El—'

Rose held up a hand. 'Come take a turn with me outside,' she said quickly.

Out in the gravestones, a light drizzle was falling. The water puffed Wil's hair into a wild frizz and clung like jewels on the thick pile of Rose's cardigan, but Rose paid it no mind as she caned through the damp grass to the western edge of the yard.

She stopped at a place with a clear view of David's duck pond, and the first part of the bridleway.

Rose pointed at the path with her cane. 'I can't tell you the number of times I saw Ann come this way, head down and muttering to herself, or swinging a stick into the hedgerow. She was all grating edges as a girl. Half away with the fairies. Useless as a page turner. Not a musical note in her body.'

Wil held her breath, taking each detail as an uncertain gift.

'She always wanted to be gone away from here, anyone could see that. I suppose it's a pity she didn't have any relations who would have boarded her out, given her some diversion, some remedy for her wanderlust. But she was kind. She and my granddaughter got up to all kinds of mischief.'

'Susie?'

'Aye. God rest her. She died very much too young.' Then, after a pause, too long for it to have been more than an afterthought, 'As did Ann, I heard.'

Wil had to suck back the slug of emotion again, this time with new frustration. Her mother had been gone so many years. When was it going to stop hurting this much? Finally, she managed, 'My father said she came back for Susie's funeral. Is that right?'

'Who did she marry, then? Your father?' Rose asked, eyes sharp for gossip.

'Oh, Cameron Butler. He's a builder,' Wil said. 'On the Gold Coast. In Australia. But they—'

Rose grunted. 'Butler, eh? Where'd they meet?'

Wil foundered. 'I don't actually know,' she said. Another note in the silent opera of her mother's past. 'But he came from London. Maybe they met there.'

Rose scoffed. 'Oh, London, eh? And yes, she came back for the funeral. She wasn't here long, though. Don't know that we exchanged more than a few words then. Awful time.'

'What about John?' Wil asked. 'Mum said—'

'John Elston's been gone away from here for a good many years. And them what's over that manor wall don't come down into the village. Best to stay out of that mess. His Lordship's away most these days, too, and the oldest on his staff's only been here ten years.'

Rose glanced back to the church. Wil ploughed on, desperate for the old woman to keep talking. 'What about Bridget? Mum said she and Susie were both friends with someone called Bridget at school.'

'She said, did she? You can't have been more than a few years old when she passed. But you remember things she said?'

'Family story,' Wil said, quickly.

'Ah.' Rose turned her eyes back to the fields. 'Oh, aye. Bridget. Father in the RAF up at Scampton. They were only here a few years. But she and Susie kept in touch awhile after, as I understand it. Maybe Ann did, too. But there's no one in the village anymore who'd have known Ann. Her brothers all moved away, and they were older than her and not close. Susie's funeral was the last time she was here. Most of the young folk from that time moved away—they don't want to work on farms anymore, and the olds retire out somewhere, so they don't need to drive to Tesco. Most people here now, this is their country house, you know? Live in London all week, then merry on up on the weekends. Dreadful. No wonder no one comes to church.'

'Bridget never came back?'

'Not that I saw. I think she was at Susie's wedding, down in London. Don't know where that girl was, otherwise, then or now. It's a long time ago.'

'You don't remember her last name, do you?'

Rose scrunched up her face, thinking. She suddenly looked very tired. Wil tried not to let her emotions swing wildly from hope to defeat.

'Can't put it to my mind, and I've my garden to do after a wee rest. Go along with you, now. Think about that jam, though. I can look after myself.'

Dismissed, Wil picked her way back through the headstones, now darkly capped with rain. She glanced around once. Granny Maxwell hadn't moved. She was bent over her cane, looking down on the bridleway. Catching Wil's eye on her, she said, 'Oh, wait there.'

She moved stiffly over the grass to the church porch, taking a good while to move up the one step.

'Spencer,' she said, before she went in. 'Bridget Spencer. No relation to the earl.'

Back at her hotel, Wil paced a little, reread the letters, and googled Bridget Spencer, finding a depressing number of young women who couldn't be a schoolmate of her mother's. Besides, Bridget could well have married and changed her last name. It seemed a dubious lead, but she didn't know what else to do.

Her phone rang as she was contemplating a sandwich from a vending machine for lunch.

'I meant to call you before now,' David said. 'But a production meeting ran long.'

'How did you even get my number?'

'You gave it to me. For the Middle Bandinby photos, remember?'

Wil immediately did, and felt stupid. 'Oh, yeah.'

'I noted you talking to Rose Maxwell for a good while. Do I take it you've succeeded where I have failed?'

Wil bit her lip. 'I'm not so sure about that.'

'Any information's a lead.' He paused. 'Hey, you want to come back to the village? Talk through what you found out? Maybe I can help.'

Half an hour later, he let her into the cottage and ushered her into the room with the huge stone hearth. 'I don't know whether to be jealous that you managed to befriend Rose so quickly, or happy for your success.'

'I wouldn't call it that,' Wil said. 'She did know my name, but from the church register, and she remembered my mother, but she hadn't put us together until we were talking. And otherwise she only told me things I already knew. Unless that was because I said she couldn't be as old as she was. I just can't stop my mouth sometimes.'

David laughed. 'Whatever gets the job done.'

'She did tell me one thing: my mother's friend who worked at that London store, Bridget, her last name is Spencer. But also that Bridget's never been back to the village, so she couldn't have been the one who put the letter in your box.'

David slid a slim computer from its case. 'Keep talking. I'll check a few things. What year was your mother born?'

'Why?' asked Wil, feeling her guard rise.

'I'm assuming she and Bridget were the same age, because they were at school together. It might help me find a record.'

'Oh. She was born in 1963. But I already searched for Bridget on social media.'

David focused on the laptop. Wil picked up the glass of water he'd set before her, then put it down again. 'I suppose I could take the train back to London and ask at the shop? Or is it too much of a long shot?'

'Doesn't really matter what I think. The researchers who work on the show all have different methods. When I do it, I chase the thing that I'm drawn to. Sometimes it's the hottest lead, sometimes just the most fascinating. Sometimes I want to sit behind a computer, and sometimes I want to get on a train. But an old letter turning up mysteriously is fascinating enough for anything. Now, I can't find a birth record that matches a Bridget Spencer anywhere in the county from 1962 to 1964. But you said they moved around. It's possible she was born in another county, or overseas.'

Wow, he was sharp, and remembered everything. Wil nodded. 'Mum said her father was in the air force.'

'Ah. We could try the school in Welton, but many of the schools records in that era are in deep storage. Could take a while. If we had her birthplace, we could narrow the search enough to make sure there's no death record.'

There was a beat where Wil hung suspended, his enthusiasm enough to make up for all the doubt she felt. 'I guess the most fascinating thing for me is who sent that letter. And if they have more.'

His eyebrows flickered with interest. 'More? I still don't quite understand what the letter was. An old one of Bridget's? Something like that?'

Wil bit her lip. She'd have to tell him about the other letters if she started on this, and that felt like stripping off her own skin.

'What did I say?' he said. 'You made a face.'

'It's nothing,' she said. 'I do that.'

He sat back from the computer. 'I have a feeling what you're looking for . . . it's something much bigger than I realised. Something very important to you.'

She could only nod, embarrassed by the emotion that kept bursting up out of nowhere like a geyser. And that it showed on her face.

'Do you want me to go?' he said.

'It's your house!'

'Not saying it wouldn't be awkward.'

She laughed, the tension broken.

He gave her a look full of compassion. 'Look, I get it. History matters. These stories are all we have about how we came to be. *Of course* it matters. But that doesn't mean those stories

171

are anyone else's business. God, I can't believe I'm saying that. My producer would shoot me.'

Wil took a deep breath, smelling the resiny wood of the cottage. Maybe, once, her mother had even stood in this room. She had certainly walked down the path outside, many times, on her way to meet John, or in the hopes she was stepping towards brighter days. And she had wanted Wil to come here, to find the letters. The whole story seemed suddenly too large to hold in. Too large not to have his help.

'Okay . . . a few weeks ago, I suddenly received a stack of letters that my mum wrote for me. I was supposed to get one every year until I was eighteen, only I'm thirty-one now. The first ones were just about her growing up in this village and at school. But the last one said she needed to tell me something important and for me to do something for her. I had to come to the village to collect more letters. Only, they weren't here.'

'How were you supposed to get these other letters? From a person?'

She hesitated. 'From the church.'

His eyebrows shot skywards. 'This bloody church,' he muttered, but his eyes were dancing with excitement. 'Where? Some kind of drop point?'

Again, Wil hesitated, and this time, she shook her head. She wasn't going to tell him about the secret spot. 'It doesn't matter. They weren't there. I thought maybe they never had been, until you brought me one. Maybe whoever had that one, has the rest.'

'So, let me get this straight,' David said slowly. 'You're a decade late to collect letters that your mother promised you, and presumably entrusted to someone who knew the village.

And yet, a day or so after you've arrived, one of those letters just appears?'

'Pretty much, yes.'

David fell back into his chair, as though he'd scored a corner goal. He raised his hands. 'I've done shows with an army of professional researchers that didn't pull a story like that! What did the letter say?'

Wil shrugged, dragged along with his optimism. She was unnerved at the mention of the TV show, but she wouldn't have the letter if he hadn't tracked her down. 'It was about living in London when she first left the village. And working as an usher in a theatre. Nothing too dramatic.'

Her fingers found the letter, tucked in her jacket pocket. Slowly she drew it out. 'Would you . . . would you like to read it?'

She knew she would regret the offer later. She could feel it in the way her muscles nearly refused to move the paper towards him. But he kept his eyes on hers the whole time, as if allowing her to change her mind at any moment.

He was careful with the old paper, and read with deep concentration, that little crease pulling between his brows again. Wil had to remind herself to breathe. It would have been less embarrassing to be a potential date on *Naked Attraction*.

Finally, he sat back, letting the pages relax into their long-held folds. 'She's something, isn't she, your mother?' he said. 'She writes with such insight, like she knows herself really well.'

Wil nodded, not trusting herself to speak.

'And such a lot of sadness,' he said, his eyes falling back on the letter. 'Do you hear that, too? Or is it just me?'

'No, I hear it,' Wil said. 'Funny, that's not the thing I thought you'd notice first.'

'What, you thought I'd notice that she had had a relationship with John Elston? Quite escaped my attention, what with being deeply interested in his family's church and estate and all that, and living in his village.'

Wil snorted. 'Don't make fun.'

'I'm not. She makes good points. All that stuff about complexity, and how we all have it, but how tiresome it is to deny it. That's why I love history. It's stuffed with complexities and secrets. It's like Christmas morning all the time.'

Wil leaned forward and retrieved the letter, regret rushing through her blood. 'Please, I don't want that. This isn't a gift for everyone to see.'

She got up, needing to put space between the two of them, as if distance could erase the information she'd just given him.

'Wilhelmina.'

She dropped the letter and, in her haste to recover it, stood and cracked her head against something unforgivingly hard, like stone. Or oak. Or her own impulsiveness. She buckled, tiny firecrackers exploding in her vision.

'Ow,' she moaned.

She felt David's hand on her arm, another on her shoulder. Guiding her back to the chair. 'Sit,' he said, then he was gone. She heard rifling in the kitchen. He came back with something wrapped in a tea towel and held it against her crown.

'That mantel is solid elm. Must have hurt.'

'Not as much as my pride,' she whispered, but at least the pain had blocked out the angst. 'After this and the duck pond, you must think I'm a disaster zone.'

'Quite the contrary, I assure you,' he said.

A few seconds later, when Wil was able to open her eyes again, she found him still crouched before her, that crease between his eyebrows now a knot of concern. He held out two white tablets. 'Here. I haven't got anything stronger than ibuprofen, but you're welcome to it.'

He waited until she'd taken the offered tablets and a glass of water.

'Let me also assure you again,' he said, 'that I will keep your letters in my most secret of secret vaults.'

'I don't really know you,' she said. 'But I've watched some of your shows. They're always about secrets.'

'You've watched, huh?'

'Well, the first five minutes of them, anyway.'

He snorted softly. 'Fair enough.'

She went to get up, but his hand stopped her, briefly covering hers. 'You're not a disaster. I think it's brave, trying to understand your place in your family after so many years. And for sharing that letter with me. I'm touched. Really. It's a precious thing you have left of her.'

Wil was grasping for something to say when a loud knock came on the cottage door. She raised her eyebrows at David, who shrugged, and went down the hall to answer it. Wil could hear a man's voice, but couldn't catch what he was saying.

David finally came back, looking incredulous, as though someone had just offered to sell him a unicorn.

'Do you know who that was?' he said.

'No?' Wil peered out the window to see if she could glimpse the visitor heading up the road.

'It was the manor estate foreman. I've been summoned for a meeting with Lord Elston tomorrow morning.'

'You're kidding?'

'Gets better. And I quote, I'm "to bring Ms Wilhelmina Mann with me, if I please". How's that for Christmas morning?'

Chapter 13

The next day, the sun burned away the clouds and threw the greens and browns of the countryside into vibrant shades. Wil felt as though she were entering an oil painting as they walked up to the manor estate gates. The slate grey of the stone wall was dotted with bright lime moss, and the grandeur of the palisade gate softened under the dappled light filtering through the spreading boughs of the border trees.

She had parked outside David's cottage as the ship had truly sailed on pretending they didn't know each other. They said little as they climbed the hill. Wil could scarcely have formed a sentence with all the questions racing through her head. Like, what could have prompted Lord Elston to call this meeting? David had been trying to speak with him for months without success. Was he going to give them a dressing-down? But about what? And what would he be like, this man whose brother had once been her mother's greatest love? This man who her mother had speculated had an unconventional life in after-hours London?

He would be in his sixties now. Would it be tea and cake around the kitchen table? Or would he be sitting in his library, in a powdering gown and smoking cigars, while fifteen cats ran about the place? Either seemed likely.

'Penny for your thoughts?' David asked softly, as they approached the gate. 'I can't say I know how this is going to go.'

'I have no idea what to say,' Wil said. 'I have a dozen questions, but knowing me I'll clam up and say something stupid. You just watch.'

David chuckled under his breath, and Wil's heart lurched as a man appeared behind the gate. But it couldn't be Lord Elston; this man was much older. He wore trousers and a flat cap tucked down over a weathered face.

'Morning, Bill,' David said. 'This is Wilhelmina Mann. Bill's the foreman of the estate,' he added, glancing at her.

Bill gave Wil a shy nod under the cap and pulled the gate wide. She could see the corner of the manor house, ahead through the greenery.

'You'll find His Lordship expectin' you in the front garden, up that path thar,' he said, and tipped his cap. Wil tried not to grin. It was like a period movie. Did people even wear hats like that anymore, non-ironically?

They crunched down a narrow path, bordered with two pretty ponds full of waterlilies and rimmed with boxed hedges. Then, they emerged onto an expansive lawn, with the manor house façade dominating the northern side. Wil was struck with déjà vu. That door, those windows. It was the backdrop of the photo at the garden party. Her eyes flew to the upstairs window, where young John had looked down on that party, where her mother had nearly been caught trespassing in the house.

Well, hadn't she done a bit of trespassing herself, now?

She turned away, and her gaze fell on a man standing by yet another pond, behind an easel like an artist cliché. He was also wearing a flat cap, in a rather dull tweed, and a pale blue button-down shirt and fawn trousers. He looked a picture of aristocratic breeding, framed by the ancient wall and the towering trees of the garden behind. But as they approached, Wil stopped and took a step back, confused. *That* wasn't Lord Elston. *That* was the man who'd chased her off in his tractor.

David was the one who stepped forward, offering his hand. 'Lord Elston, David Hunter,' he said. 'Thank you for taking the time.'

Lord Elston's body hardly moved as he extended his own hand, his gaze running quickly over David and then over Wil, who tried and failed not to stare. Those eyebrows could catch a snowdrift, and it was hard not to have flashbacks of roaring engines and then sprinting over the broken ground like a lost rabbit, only to fall into a nettle patch. And then a duck pond.

'I see you've brought the rambler,' Lord Elston said, his voice carrying dry amusement. 'She can go over ground quite nicely, this one.'

'I don't follow . . .' David frowned.

'Tractor,' Wil said quickly, then dropped her voice. 'Farmer Friendly?'

'Oh,' David said, sneaking a glance at the lord to catch his reaction, but the man had turned away from the easel, the canvas completely blank, and was striding across the grass, beckoning over his shoulder. Clearly a man used to being obeyed.

David and Wil jogged to keep up, until Lord Elston pulled up by a potting shed. It was built into a wall that divided the manor grounds from the church boundary. Wil could see the aerial map of the estate in her mind, its grounds partitioned with walls like this. She'd looked at it so many times, but she'd not realised that the partitions were taller than she was.

'This estate has been in my family for generations,' Lord Elston said, one proprietary hand resting on the shed. 'Been carved up from time to time—had to meet the bloody death taxes, you know—but a very long, long unbroken line.'

'Yes,' David said, because it seemed there was nothing else to say. 'Your family has an exceptionally long-standing bond with this land, one that few others in the country could match. An important legacy.'

Lord Elston looked him up and down again, unimpressed. 'Yes,' he said slowly. 'You know, I watched you play for England, back in '03. Had quite the career ahead of you, then.'

'My knee had other ideas,' David said, a little too smoothly, too rehearsed.

'And now you're in television,' Lord Elston said, making it sound as though television were synonymous with drug dealing, or the republican movement. 'And you want to make this place into entertainment and spectacle. Dig up some titillation from the past to amuse the viewers.'

'Not at all—'

'Oh, so you're *not* in television?'

Wil's eyes widened. *Wow, Lord Elston can be bitchy.*

David smiled, clearly amused. 'Oh, I most certainly am, whatever its evils. But I'm not in the business of spectacle.

I care very deeply about each place we feature, and I've lived in this village for five years myself, as you know.'

'Oh, five years. Indeed?' Sarcasm. Even Wil could hear it.

'Granted, I spend a lot of time away.'

Wil watched this exchange in fascination. The entitled aristocrat going up against the former all-star footballer, who must be used to adoring interviewers, but was obviously too much of a gentleman and a strategist to be ruffled.

'But you'll find me patient,' David finished. 'And persistent. You think I was determined on the field? I'm just as committed to preserving that church, and all the history and legacy it represents, despite how I'm thought of personally.'

Lord Elston grunted, and turned his gaze on the church. A quick look down at the ground, a quick pop of his eyebrows. '*All* it represents, hmm?' he said, as if to himself. Then he swung round to Wil.

'And what do you do, young lady, when you're not tramping through my fields?'

Wil, who'd been distracted by a butterfly, had to ask him to repeat the question. 'Oh, I work in construction, mostly,' she said, feeling very foolish.

'Construction, eh? Carpenter?'

'Sometimes, when I need to be. But I can do plumbing and electrical stuff, too. Not that you're meant to without a licence. I mean ...' Wil huffed a breath. 'Ah, mostly, I'm a tiler. Sometimes I've done handpainted tiles, special patterns, that sort of thing. I mean, I've done it once or twice. Most of the time it's just horrible modern stuff. Glossy subways, that sort of thing.'

She broke off, squeezing her eyes shut. She just couldn't hold her tongue.

'Working for yourself? Or for Mr Hunter?'

'Working for my father, mostly, who's a builder,' she said quickly, sensing that that her status was being evaluated in addition to her association with David, 'though I've done a bit of private work, here and there. And every other job, too. Bartender, lifeguard, signwriter . . . I can mix a mean martini!'

In her head, a little red light started blinking, a warning that she was not only getting nowhere, but digging herself into a hole. *Shut it down, Wil.* She bit her lip. While David might accrue some points for being a former national sporting hero, she would earn none as the wayward, handy bartending daughter of an antipodean ex-pat. And yes, Lord Elston's stare had distinctly glazed, his eyeballs glossier than a shower tile she'd no doubt have told him all about if she'd kept talking.

'Well, let's walk through,' Lord Elston said, after the embarrassing pause.

Wil managed to keep her mouth shut through the rest of a tour of the immediate grounds. She wondered why she'd even been invited, except that it was clear Lord Elston was taking every opportunity to evaluate David. As an assumed co-conspirator, it made sense he was checking her out, too. Fortunately, David did most of the talking, what sounded like careful observations of the architecture. Wil would only have betrayed her ignorance, and she wasn't sure if that would support her denials of working for David or simply reflect badly on him. She found herself slipping behind their voices, drifting through thoughts of her mother, and the strangeness of being in the same place described in the letters. Beyond the shed was another walled garden, beyond that a long grassy field, also walled, and dominated on the western side with a large greenhouse. The wall behind the greenhouse had fallen in, and the damage was what pulled Wil back to the voices.

'Rabbits,' Lord Elston was saying. 'They tunnel underneath and bring down the lot. Over here, we turn back to the stables.'

The stables were a tile-roofed, pale rendered building, though they seemed to be for storage instead of horses. Wil was about to turn away when she spotted the overgrown rose garden. Her fingers went immediately to her pocket, where she kept the pressed flower from the letters, carefully folded in a tissue. *Be brave.*

'Lord Elston,' she said.

'Mmm?' He barely turned in his stride back towards the house.

'My mother once worked in the manor house, years ago. In the kitchens, I think. I was wondering if you . . .'

He glanced at her. 'Your mother. Worked for Cook, did she? Lots of the village girls did that.'

'Her name was Ann Mann,' Wil rushed out. 'Maybe you remember her? Your brother John knew her quite well. So I wondered if—'

He stopped suddenly, his expression severe under his bushy eyebrows. 'You wondered what?'

She stumbled on her words and careened off having to mention the letters or any of their details to him. 'If he would, he would talk . . .'

'My brother lives in Jamaica, Miss Mann, where he has such a fine life that anything beyond a two-yearly Christmas card exceeds his concern for this estate or anyone on it. Though I'm sure Mr Hunter has already made that clear, given how—' Lord Elston gave her a clearly appraising look '—*collegiate* the two of you are. Now, round this wall is the gamekeeper's cottage.'

They crunched around a gap in the wall to find a low-roofed lodge facing the back of the manor house, whose two storeys and staring windows dominated the lane. Wil nursed her desperation at his dismissal, but then Lord Elston paused.

'The house kitchens are right through that door, Miss Mann,' he said, pointing to the door at the back of the house. 'But there's nothing much to see. Been torn out for a renovation, at my mother's request. And now you'll forgive me, but I've a business call to attend to. Bill will show you out.'

Wil jumped as the elderly foreman appeared from the gamekeeper's lodge. Before she knew it, Lord Elston had crunched back across the stones and disappeared into the house. Then they were back outside the palisade gate, with Bill tipping his cap and thanking them for their time.

~

'What was all that about?' Wil asked, as they picked their way down the drive.

'Evaluation, and a bit of grandstanding,' David said, as they reached the road. 'He's used to giving the orders. But ignoring me hasn't made me go away, so I think he thought he'd see for himself if I was serious. I hope I gave the impression I was. It could be a good sign.'

'But why invite me there, too?'

'He clearly thinks we're in cahoots. And since he saw you first poking about on his land, I suspect he thinks I've brought you in as some new strategy.'

184

'Can't think that's likely now,' Wil muttered, as they both stepped to the side to let a red Royal Mail van pass. 'After spilling my unimpressive resumé all over his feet. God! I told you that's what would happen.'

'Well, on the plus side, you did an excellent job of making yourself non-threatening.'

Wil scowled at him, while David grinned.

'Seriously though, Mina, your resumé won't matter to him. He probably thinks anyone who works for a living is beneath him. He can't help it.'

Wil stopped and looked back at the manor, now just a pale suggestion of a house behind the trees. 'Tell you what makes *him* less threatening: imagining him forty years younger, and in tight jeans in a London nightclub.'

David laughed. 'Complexity, right? Maybe he has a whole box of old photos he'd never want to come out. But, either way, this is a real step forward for me. And I'm glad you got to see the manor, even if only from the outside.'

'Yeah, I noticed how he did the "Oh the kitchens are there, but you shall not see" bit. I don't know why I thought he'd let me inside,' she said, as they stopped beside her rental car.

David shrugged. 'Give it time. He might.'

Wil hesitated with her hand on the door, an idea suddenly flying into her mind. 'The foreman, Bill? I didn't even think to ask him if he knew my mother. She mentions someone called William at the house she was friendly with. Could that be him?'

'Hate to disappoint, but he's one I did manage to speak to,' David said. 'Bill's only been at the estate ten years, and couldn't offer me much, though he was perfectly willing to talk to us. Came down from another estate somewhere in the north where he worked for decades. Said he wanted the warmer weather, here. William's more common a name than Ann and Elizabeth.'

'Oh, right, I guess it is,' Wil said, disappointed. The moment seemed over; time to drive away and think about what to do next, like contacting the school about Bridget, or planning a trip down to London before her cash ran out, or doorknocking the entire village on the chance David had missed something. But she didn't climb into the car. She wanted David to say something else so that she didn't have to go.

'Do you want to come in?' David said. 'I've an idea I want to run past you.'

'I'd better get back,' she found herself saying, even though she didn't know what she was doing.

And that was that. David waved and went in the gate to his cottage. Wil slid behind the wheel and pulled down the lane towards the fens, to the road junction where she could turn around. It was quicker than going around the loop. But when she came back up the hill, feeling wretched at having to drive away, David was standing in the middle of the road.

Wil pulled up with an unnecessary squeal of brakes. He was holding aloft an envelope.

Dear Mina,

Happy 20th birthday, my darling girl. When I last left off, I was heading for Paris. As I write this now, they are preparing to open the 'Chunnel', which is twelve years too late for me to have avoided the hideous ferry crossing I had.

It was near Christmas, 1981. A grey winter, and the ocean seemed the same colour as the sky. The ferry stank of diesel and the sea rolled the whole way. I always thought I'd be of strong constitution and never get seasick, but I spent most of the journey turning my stomach inside out. Part of that certainly was the relentless rolling and pitching and that fume smell. But another part was just terror. I'd never been so far from home. I may as well have been in the ocean without a lifeline.

Paris in winter is not the magical place that everyone imagines. The fountains were boarded up, the air damp and cold. I was bold because I had to be. I needed to find work, so I walked into any shop I liked the look of and asked for a job. After being chased out (with a broom in one case!) I was finally given an outrageously underpaid position in a patisserie, washing up out the back, which required no French at all (except the curses I'd brought with me from England).

It was an attractive shop in the front, with cabinets of delicacies that I would never be able to afford. Out the back, it was a mountain of sticky pans—caramel was the absolute worst—and a floor covered with ground dough pieces and marzipan.

Somewhere in my mind, I'd thought that just leaving John and England behind would be enough for me to land on my feet. I didn't realise that being miserable in an unfamiliar place was ten times worse than being miserable at home. I did not meet any charming French men to make me forget John. Oh, there was plenty of interest, but not in a chivalrous way. I dodged the hands of the pastry chef at the beginning of every shift. And I lived in a little broom closet of a room over the shop. That Christmas was the saddest I've ever had.

But never despair, things did improve. A few months later, when the spring leaves came out and it stopped raining, I was sick of myself. I'd made my decision, so I'd just have to make the best of it.

I took my sketchbook to the museums and drew, surrounded by the great masters. I think that was what brought me back to myself. Then, by chance, in the Jardin du Luxembourg, I met an English family who needed an au pair and they agreed to try me out for a month. They entertained their ex-pat friends often, so that left me in charge of their two lovely children.

Now, I'm sure that when they hired me they hoped that I would be a more scholarly influence than I was. I'd told them that I'd worked in the theatre in London, and in a baron's household, which, while true, gave me far more credit than was my due. But I did know how to have fun, and make up games and adventures, and draw pictures, and I was so unsupervised that I don't think either of the parents knew what the children and I were doing.

Michael and Heather and I would visit museums and parks and have picnics by the Seine. It was so much more delightful than scrubbing pans. We would lurk under bridges pretending to be trolls. I would take them to school, pick them up, and fill their weekends with stories and trees to climb. It was utterly exhausting, don't get me wrong. When they were at school, I would take my sketchbook down to the river and would often wake up in a panic, not realising I'd been asleep. But they saved me from loneliness, and regret. I don't know if they would remember me now, but I remember them.

Maybe they remember me deep in their souls, in the parts of ourselves we can't declare but that are still undeniably us.

Maybe that's what I am to you now, too. Someone you don't really remember, but who is indivisibly part of you. And that's fine, really. We don't have to be conscious of everything that makes us up. Just to understand that there are parts of how we came to be that we cannot say. That the soul is deeper than what we can bring into words.

So that is how the summer passed in Paris, and much of the autumn, too. It was as the year was sliding towards winter again that the unexpected happened: I had a letter from John.

He must have prised my address from Bridget, because she was the only person who knew where I was. And the next week, he was there.

The family had had so little trouble with me they were only too happy to accommodate a day off. I met John at Gare du Nord, and despite all the talking-to I'd given myself, we still ended up just standing there and staring at each other for a ridiculous time. As if we had to wait for a montage of all our history to pass before we could speak.

But I couldn't go back down that road again and, fortunately, it didn't appear that John wanted to, either. He said that he'd wanted to see me in person, by which I understood that he wanted a friend. Someone who'd known him well, who had roots back into his childhood and could understand what he was going to say.

His father had died. He told me quite matter-of-factly, as if they'd been distant relations. But that was how John was— holding everything back, never allowing it to burst across the bank he'd built to hold it. His brother Thomas was Lord Elston now, and so amidst the upheaval of their grief had come the unexpected transfer of the estate management, and concerns about how on earth they were going to cover the death tax. He talked a long time about selling part of the estate, or even the property in Jamaica. And how useless Thomas was in making any of the decisions. I felt for John; I wanted to be able to relieve him of the burden, which I've come to know is a marker of loving someone. You want them to be happy, even if that means you aren't.

He began the day in a kind of daze. But gradually, as we walked around in the falling leaves, among the monuments, he came to life again, in the way I remembered him from our earliest friendship. It was such an exquisite day—there we were, in the city of love, as close and companionable as we had ever been. And yet, it was also an end for us. Like autumn trees shedding last year's leaves to prepare for winter, there was no going back in time. We parted with empty promises to keep in touch. Both of us knew we were not the kind of people who could write to each other. We were visceral. I could never express myself particularly well to him, and he certainly couldn't say all the things he felt. But when we were next to each other, we understood. From the moment he left, I had the feeling I wanted to leave Paris as well. I didn't want to walk past that place by the river, or that one, and think about the two of us standing there. And know that we never would again.

Not very long after this, Heather and Michael's father was offered a promotion to New York City, and they asked me to go with them. I didn't even think about it. So I crossed

*the Atlantic, my first time on a plane! And we arrived in the
Big Apple just in time for Christmas 1982. I was a long way
from home again, but this time I had Michael and Heather
to hold me together. And I spoke the language, not a small
thing. It was a year that spun me, that bent my path in a new
direction, which is the story for next time.*

Until then, be brave, my darling girl.

Love,

Mum

Chapter 14

Wil came back to herself as she finished the letter. She was curled in David's leather armchair, the one facing the stone hearth and its solid elm mantel that she'd already tested with her head. Outside, the afternoon sun made silver ripples on the pond, the insects humming in the grass. Inside, the cottage was cool and comfortable.

David padded in with a wine bottle, and raised it in question.

Wil shook her head. 'Not yet.'

'Any leads? I mean, apart from this confirming the mystery sender has more letters.'

'She talks about Lord Elston dying in 1982. But most of it is about her moving to Paris and working as an au pair for a family there, and then she moved to New York with them. Isn't that incredible?'

Wil dropped the letter in her lap. She'd wondered if it would begin getting into whatever the important thing was her mother wanted her to know, but instead it had just blown her idea of her mother wide open. Wil hadn't consciously assumed her mother's history, but a straight line from England to Sydney was more or less what she'd expected. That perhaps she would have met her father in London, and then both of them would have relocated. She'd never expected Paris and New York. Never expected the same uncertainties about money and work Wil herself understood. It was simultaneously a profound connection and a deep sadness.

'I'm thinking a mixed bag for you, given your face,' David said.

Wil immediately smiled to hide however she looked. David returned the smile as he set down two glasses of sparkling water.

'No new leads on contacts. She only mentions the children's first names.'

'Okay,' he said. 'So, go back to the start and list out your possibilities. Who's a candidate for having these letters?' he said, sliding into the armchair. 'And, more importantly, what criteria make them a candidate?'

'What criteria?'

'Where do they have to be, and when, to make it likely they have the letters?'

Wil glanced out the window, to where the church sat immobile on its hill, framed with trees that must be generations removed from the ones that had stood here when it was built. Her caution of trusting David was flaring again, but none of this information was really new. And she was desperate to find out more.

'Well . . .' she said, slowly, 'I guess I'm looking for who she was close to when she was writing the letters. Who she'd have trusted with them.'

'So, very close to the end.'

Wil swallowed. 'Yes. And that's a problem because all the ones I have so far are about her much earlier life. The only person she's mentioned at the hospice is a nurse called Marionette. Damn, I hadn't thought about her.'

The word 'hospice' had given her a jolt as it left her mouth, and with it came that old fizz of pain and memory that she'd felt arguing with her father. The indistinct shapes of people and rooms. The feeling of running, of being filled up with grief. She sucked a long shaky breath. She was glad that David wasn't looking at her this time. He'd jumped up and gone to the kitchen.

'Okay,' he said, returning with a leather-bound notebook. He opened it to a blank page. 'Let's write it out. We do this sometimes when we're researching a piece and we've hit a wall.'

'You do?' The memory was still with her, echoing like a heartbeat, but focusing on him faded it enough to concentrate.

'I should say, "the researchers do this". There's way too much background in each episode for one person. But I've watched them work.'

Wil took another breath as he began drawing. 'You're trying to find out what's in these letters,' he said, 'so that means finding who has them, correct?'

'Yes.'

He drew a circle at the top with *Ann gave Mina's letters to . . . ?* inside.

'I told you, I don't go by Mina.'

David crossed it out. 'Shall I write Willy? Wilhelmina isn't going to fit.'

'Let's move on.'

He grinned. 'Okay, so there's Marionette—how do I spell that?'

Wil told him, and he jotted it down underneath and then added a bunch of blank dot points.

'Now, who else did she definitely know at the time she was writing? What about your father?'

Wil made a face. 'He knew about the letters, but he never wanted me to have them. And I don't think they were on good terms.' She didn't know that for sure, but sure enough. It was part of the nebulous memory.

'Let's write him down anyway. Here.'

He handed across the book and pen. Wil wrote *Cameron Butler*, each letter stirring a pot of conflicting emotions, and at the next point, feeling it was ridiculous, *Kate*.

'Who's Kate?'

'That's my sister. But she's only two years older than me.'

'What if your mother left the letters to her?'

Wil looked down at the floor. In the same way she knew her father and mother had been in conflict at the end, she knew Kate couldn't be who she was looking for. Sending the letters was an act far more intimate than their relationship could allow. The thought tore at Wil, like a grater rasping down her breastbone.

But she didn't say any of that to David. 'I already asked her about the letters. Besides, she's back in Australia and doesn't know I'm here.'

David gave her a gentle smile. 'Not close?'

Wil shook her head. 'I can't think of anyone else.'

'That's a short list,' he said. 'But okay, let's make a second column for anyone who knew her well at other times. We can try to find out if they were in contact with her near the end, too.'

Wil began a new column: *Bridget*, she wrote. Then, *John*. She didn't write Susie's name, because Susie had died before her mother, but added *Rose* and *William*. She tapped the page. It didn't seem a promising list. 'I don't know if I'll find Bridget, yet. And Rose doesn't seem likely—she talked about my mother pretty easily, but said she hadn't seen her in years. But she's been here the longest. Maybe she knows something she didn't say.'

'Now you're thinking,' David said. 'She might know where William went, too, though he might have passed away.'

But Wil was still staring at the list. 'Oh! I'm an idiot.'

'Mmm? Why?'

'I forgot: Mum said that the spot in the church was something only she and John knew about. They obviously parted ways, and I don't think it could be him if he's been in Jamaica for years, but they were very close, once. Maybe he would know.'

The moment she said it, Wil regretted the disclosure about the church hiding spot, but she couldn't take it back. David had gone still, as though his thoughts required all his energy.

'Well, that could be significant,' he said eventually. 'Especially when you consider that the second letter was posted, not dropped in person.'

'Oh, I forgot that, too,' Wil said, looking around for the envelope. 'Where was it sent from?'

'Local post stamp, unfortunately,' David said, pulling the outer envelope from under the table, but he seemed unenthused as he said, 'It's not impossible it came through someone else's hands.'

'You don't think it could be Lord Elston himself?'

David made a face, as though considering an unlikely situation. 'It's just John hasn't shown any interest here in years,' David said. 'And while the family is always tight-lipped, there's wide rumours of a rift between Lord Elston and John that goes all the way back to when John left England. Some people speculate it was because John was overbearing in wanting to run the estate when it wasn't his place. He had a reasonable profile for a while, and Thomas could easily have felt threatened. It's quite interesting, but it's a whole other story. And given the animosity—you heard what Thomas said yourself—I find it hard to believe he'd help John.'

Wil made a disappointed sound in her throat. They both sat back, looking at the names. Finally, David leaned forward, broke the page out of his book, and handed it to her. 'Does this give you any clarity on what you're doing next?'

Wil wrinkled her nose. 'I suppose I should have a go at finding Marionette, but that probably means talking to my father again. And I need to charm Rose Maxwell into telling me about William. She seems to know everything else about the village.'

'May I suggest a jar of homemade preserves?' David said.

'Smartarse.' Wil threw the pen at him. He ducked, giving her a quick-flash smile that unexpectedly made her stomach disappear. She pushed away any thoughts that she found him attractive and went back to staring furiously at the list.

'I suppose,' she said after a long minute, 'anyone else in the village could have found the letters.'

'Not impossible. Less likely they'd know who you were, though.'

'Unless I look like her, which is what you asked before.'

'That I did,' he said, considering her. 'How about deploying some new technology on the problem? I could organise to rig a camera on the box, so if another one is dropped in person we can see who it is. It would be worth it, even if it took a few weeks. The show could cover the cost.'

Wil chewed her lip, his words a thump back to reality. 'You might have to send the footage to me back in Australia, though.'

'You're not leaving?'

'I'm nearly out of cash. Three more days and I'll be camping in the fields.'

David opened his mouth to respond when they both heard a *click*, *click* outside, and then a soft tapping on the cottage door.

'What new lead awaits?' David whispered, and padded down the hall.

Wil craned to see, admiring David's departing back. For a man who was fifteen years out from his professional sporting career, and nearing forty, he was fit. He had the kind of body any twenty-year-old builder would devote serious time to admiring in the mirror. Put him in a pair of King Gees and give him a nail gun, and he could fool anyone on a job site. In fact, do the King Gees and nail gun without a shirt, and he could have thousands of followers on Instagram. As he opened the door, the sun lit up his profile like a studio light. Wil had a second to feel her heart flip before she saw who was on the porch.

'Afternoon, Mr Hunter,' Granny Maxwell said, her cane leading through the door.

'Rose,' David said, not quite covering his surprise. 'To what do I owe the pleasure?'

'Taking you up on that offer to see the renovations,' she said. 'I've known everyone who's lived here in the last fifty years. Humour an old woman in a bit of nostalgia?'

Behind Rose, David caught Wil's eye and gave the hands-up gesture, but Wil already sensed the subtext: Rose was here to see what was going on. Wil swiftly tucked the letter down the side of the chair cushion, just as Rose reached the end of the hall and saw her.

'Well, now, Wilhelmina, isn't this cosy? You've met young Mr Hunter, then?' Rose twisted to give David a shrewd glance. 'Told me she didn't know you.'

Wil managed to stand up awkwardly, as though she was seventeen and her father had caught her with a boy in her room. Protests of how it looked formed on her tongue. Fortunately, Rose was too busy inspecting the cottage. 'Oh, that mantel's changed, hasn't it? Why haven't you used the original? And that stonework. That's different, too.'

'Different, yes, but I've used sixteenth-century detailing to honour the cottage's roots as a converted barn, and it's hard to be authentic without reinserting the stables. Now, you'll want to see the added bathroom?'

'Well, I hope it's more impressive than this.'

Wil hung back as David patiently escorted Rose around the renovations and she pronounced her judgements. To avoid feeling useless, Wil slipped into the kitchen and washed up the glasses. There were handpainted tiles behind the Aga, an agricultural celebration of wheatfield gold and hedgerow green, twisted in a pattern that was almost heraldic. She traced her finger over the lines, marvelling at it. Clearly custom work, and set off by the flawless craftmanship of wooden cabinets faced in recovered timber. She dried her hands and ran them over the beauty of the darkened dents and scratches, which married so beautifully to a house that had stood here for five hundred years.

'You like it?'

Wil hadn't even heard David come back from seeing Rose out. She dropped her hands. 'It looks like it was meant to be here. Who did these tiles?'

'An artist I found up-county who specialises in agricultural pieces. I wanted to connect the kitchen to the fields outside. For most of the life of this cottage, everything prepared in it would have come in from the garden, or one of those fields. From an historical standpoint, supermarkets are the aberration around here.'

'And the wood?'

'Recovered from a shed we had to demolish in the yard. But that was already recycled from something much older.'

Wil ran her hands over the surfaces, appreciating the hours of work in the cabinetry. 'Let me guess, Rose thinks it's not good enough?'

David grinned. 'I hardly care. I've been trying for months to interest anyone in what I'm doing here, and then you show up and all of a sudden people are coming to my door. I made that offer to show her around months ago. I'm starting to think you're answering every prayer I've ever made in that church.'

Wil shook her head. 'I must sound like a dirty liar, the way I protested I had no idea who you were. Which, in my defence, I didn't at the time. Now I must look like one of your associates.'

'About that,' David said, with a rare pause as if unsure how to phrase his words. 'I have spare rooms here. What would you say to shifting your research operation from the Travelodge?'

Wil blinked. 'And stay here?'

'If your presence really is rattling someone into action, what better move than to stay in the village yourself? And it means you don't have to up sticks and go home yet.'

Wil took a breath, torn. She already felt a debt to him. She didn't want that feeling to grow. 'I can't take a room for nothing.'

'Didn't say you could have it for nothing,' he said with a grin. 'You'll notice that I have a lot of work that isn't finished. Bathroom tiles. Woodwork. You help me out with your skills, you can take the room. It has its own bathroom,' he added in a rush. 'I don't spend much time here in the year, so I'd been considering letting it out, before I caught wind of village disapproval and thought I'd better not.'

'And you don't think my moving in would attract disapproval?'

'Oh, it most certainly will. But I kind of enjoy Rose Maxwell's disapproval.'

'You don't know that I'm any good at what I do,' she argued.

He smiled slowly. 'No, but I can tell from the way you were looking at my kitchen that we have similar tastes. That's good enough to start.'

Wil wavered, but she was almost out of cash and pragmatism won.

'Before I say yes, you'd better show me this work,' she said. 'I don't want to find out I'm rebuilding the whole place single-handed.'

'Could you do that, do you think?'

'I don't think I could even lift the end of one of these beams,' she said, looking up at the stout oak holding up the top floor. 'But bathrooms, those I can do.'

'Then right this way, Miss Mann. I'll show you the work, and then I'm going to go into the off-licence in Nettleham. We need a stronger drink.'

⌒

Wil woke the next morning to the sound of sparrows outside the window. She cracked an eyelid, taking in the rake of the roof beams intruding through the ceiling. She'd collected one of those with her head last night, thankfully in a different place to the mantel blow. Being tall was not an advantage in these old buildings. But the beautiful warm wood and creamy render more than made up for it. The room overlooked the fields, and the window seat was stuffed with cosy cushions.

She had a memory of laughing after knocking her head on that beam, and David's sympathy, then him telling her she had to choose between more ibuprofen and the wine because she couldn't mix the two. Lord, how much had she drunk?

They'd sat by the hearth with the bottle, him mostly telling stories about episodes of *Saving History* and the antics of shooting it, while she asked questions she now couldn't really remember. Wil sat up, testing her head. Not hungover. But odds were she'd made an idiot of herself.

She threw her legs out of the covers and listened to the silence in the house. She wanted to avoid any awkward meeting when David woke up. Would he be wearing flannel pyjamas? Or, oh god, nothing? Wil raked her fingers down her face and crept out. She hadn't thought this through.

The stairway creaked like a horror movie as she descended, but the kitchen and living room were mercifully empty. Her list from yesterday was still on the coffee table. Wil read through it again. The shortness of it bothered her, and she took up a pencil and added Susie's name, even though Susie couldn't have had the letters. Couldn't have, because she'd already been *buried*. Wil lifted her gaze to the headstones in the churchyard, their tops just visible through the window. Sadness flitted through her, as quick and surprising as a swallow darting through a barn. Her mother wasn't there with the church, with generations of her family and friends, like Susie Maxwell was. Instead, she'd died a long way from here and been cremated, her ashes scattered in the Gold Coast sea. Wil had no idea if that's what she'd wanted.

The soft grey sky was daubed with pink blobs of sunrise cloud as Wil climbed the hill to the churchyard. The grass was growing long between the outer rows, in need of a mow, but a few closer headstones showed recent tending with new flowers. Those in between had grown over with lichens, with the soft stone weathered rough. Wil stopped at the inscription in the church porch.

'Remember, man, as you pass by, as you are now, so once was I,' she murmured. There was definitely an extra 'n' scratched into the first line. 'As I am now so you must be, therefore prepare to follow me.'

Her mother must have read that many times; it was impossible to miss. Had she ever thought about it when she'd been the one preparing to follow? Wil huffed a breath against threatening tears and paced away into the rows. The first few headstones she passed showed dates in the seventeen and eighteen hundreds, at least the ones that she could read. Susie's should be much more recent. She moved along, finding some Manns, and Richardsons, Greenes and Wrights, too. But no Maxwells. No Susies at all. Or Susans. Or Suzannahs. When she reached the far corner near the wall, Wil pulled up, frowning. Her mother had come back here for Susie's funeral, so Susie must be here. She tramped back down the rows, right around the church, stopping again at each headstone. Still nothing.

Maybe she had missed something. But it wasn't a huge place. She could see from one end to the other, from the edge of the churchyard to the broken top section of the manor wall.

Wil set off through the long grass to the wall without a thought about what she was doing, except that it would be easier to see from the top of the wall. The broken section was easy to climb, like a staircase, then one big step and she was on top. The churchyard oak arched over her head, reaching its long boughs beyond the wall, as if having its roots in the churchyard wouldn't keep the tree from aspiring to own the manor as well.

Wil tipped her head back. The view from here was gorgeous wherever she looked—up into the canopy with its lush green and woodland browns, or out over the fields that rolled in postcard patchwork. Not quite like watching the sunrise over the beach, but the same sense of beautiful natural freedom. No wonder John's family had an immovable attachment to the place. What was it like to be lord over all of this? Or just be the brother of one?

Maybe that was what John hadn't been able to stand, after all. And he'd had to leave the country to make peace with it.

She reached her hands to the nearest thick bough, which was only just over waist height, still absorbed in her thoughts of jealous brothers. A breeze kissed her skin, inviting her to climb further. It wouldn't be much trouble. Lazily she glanced at the manor house, only intending to appreciate the view that way, and jumped in fright.

Lord Elston stood watching her like a grim statue on his perfect green lawn, one eyebrow cocked like a shotgun. A black dog lay obediently at his feet. There was an awful silence, in which Wil felt her blood thrumming in her throat.

'I was just telling Bill the rabbits were frightful this year,' he said. 'But then they usually go *under* the walls.'

'I'm so sorry,' Wil stammered, realising she was standing on *his* wall, about to climb into *his* tree. Well, the church's tree, but it was his church, wasn't it? *What on earth possessed me?* She was too mortified for anything but truth. 'I was looking for a headstone and I couldn't, erm, find it. I thought I might see better from up here.'

'And here I was expecting you to say you'd tripped and fell.'

Wil shrugged hopelessly. They faced each other for a few long seconds, Wil's elevated position feeling increasingly juvenile as she tried to find something fascinating to say about his boots, which were heavy and thick with shards of dewy grass.

'Whose grave were you looking for?' he asked finally.

'Susie Maxwell,' Wil said, encouraged that he wasn't shouting for Bill to release the hounds.

Lord Elston blinked.

'She was a friend of my mother's,' Wil went on. 'My mother came home for her funeral years ago, so I assumed Susie would be buried here. Only I can't seem to find her.'

Lord Elston looked down at the dog, who regarded him with panting dedication, and then back to her. His eyes were stony, but she couldn't read him. 'You've not looked hard enough,' he said. 'I trust you can find your way down again.'

He turned for the house.

'Wait!'

He paused with such a look of annoyance that Wil's heart hammered at her own gall. 'Did you know my mother?' The question was as heavy with desperation as the dew on the grass. She hated how weak it sounded, but Lord Elston gave her a considering glance.

'Ann Mann?' he said. 'My brother knew her. I only saw her when she worked here at the house. Years ago. And not since.'

Wil's heart soared and sagged at once. She tried to think of something to say, anything that might draw even a shard of memory from him. But he suddenly tipped his head, as though he'd just had a realisation.

'You're here awfully early this morning,' he said. 'Didn't hear any cars come down. But that green thing you're driving is in the road.'

The fact was undeniable. She could see the hire car easily from where she was.

'I, uh, stayed here last night,' she said, then, unable to stop herself, 'At the cottage. David's cottage. He offered to let me stay if I'd do some work for him. Renovation work, that is. Nothing strange, or weird! Um . . . see, I was running out of money and . . .' *Oh dear god.* She bit her lip.

'Renovation work,' he said. 'Because you're in construction, not in television, you said. Father's a builder.'

'Yes, that's right. I can do just about anything, which I think I said before.' Her face glowed hot with mortification.

'Family knows you're here, then?'

'What? Oh . . . sort of.'

'Sort of?'

'I didn't really tell them, no. Just my brother Colin. He lent me the money. It was just that I needed to find out some things about my mother. And it was kind of private, so I didn't want to . . .'

She trailed off, only because she had to breathe, but it was enough to stop. She was aware there was nothing salvageable about this conversation. She was standing on a wall, rambling, for goodness sake. And he was like a bloodhound, catching any little thing she said and somehow prompting her to spill all kinds of random thoughts. She must look like a complete fool. But Lord Elston lifted his chin, as though he grudgingly approved of her secrecy. Well, he would, wouldn't he? Being the lord of the most unforthcoming village in history. Secrecy might be the only virtue he knew.

'Mother meant a lot to you, I suppose,' he said, though grudgingly. The dog looked between him and Wil, and gave a soft whine. Wil imagined it was waiting for instructions, perhaps to be allowed to sic her, but all she could do was nod.

'I'll, uh, be going then,' she croaked, crouching awkwardly. The drop into the churchyard looked a bit far from this angle, and she couldn't judge the ground through the long grass.

Behind her, he chuckled. 'You know, I think I do recall seeing your mother come to the house over this exact wall, once. Probably late. That was when one of the tree branches used to dip low enough for a handhold. Same branch came down in a storm a few years back and knocked that part of the wall out. Maybe there's something in apples not falling far from the tree.'

With that, he called the dog. Wil stared after his departing back, until the flat cap and grassy boots disappeared around the side of the house.

She blew out her breath and edged back to the broken part of the wall. After stumbling down, she spent another twenty fruitless minutes searching the churchyard while trying to calm herself, until she saw Rose Maxwell coming along the village road, bucket in hand. Wil quickly slipped back to the cottage. The sun was so much higher now—any awkwardness with David was far preferable to asking Rose about her own granddaughter's grave.

Wil found David in the kitchen, pouring black brew into a mug and dressed in a polo shirt and jeans. The room smelled of coffee beans and a hint of warm caramel. 'There you are,' he said. 'Figured you'd gone tramping again. Any luck?'

Wil shook her head, grateful there was no strange vibe after last night. 'Unless you count nearly being done for trespassing. *Again.*'

'Not in the same place?'

Wil slid into a bar stool at the kitchen island. 'Much worse.'

'What could be worse?' he said, pushing a mug towards her. 'Because the last one got us into the manor grounds. This could be good.'

She shook her head. 'Not with the years it must have taken off my life.'

He laughed, but then, abruptly, he stopped and held up a finger. 'Did you hear something?'

'What?'

'I thought I heard . . .' He put his mug down and bolted for the front door, faster than Wil imagined he'd moved on the ball during his career. She saw him skid on the flagstones in the entry and disappear behind the wall. When she heard him open the door, she finally realised what he meant and bolted after him.

He was halfway down the path by that point, shading his eyes against the sun as he spun around. 'Do you see anyone?'

Wil could only see a few figures moving deep down the village road, too far away, and Rose already at the church door. And besides, she couldn't pay attention to anything other than the envelope in his hand.

'They must have really scarpered,' David said, coming back to the door and handing it over. 'This should take your mind off the trespassing.'

⌒

Dear Mina,

Happy 21st birthday, my darling girl. When I was growing up, twenty-one was the age everyone considered you an adult, a strange symbol really, because we'd been doing adult things for years already. Working, marrying, paying taxes. This letter is a bit about all of those things.

So in 1983 I landed in New York, still as a live-in nanny. New York was vastly different to London or Paris, and I think that affected my employers too. Their apartment was in the Upper East Side, which was very clean and insulated from everywhere else, and I wasn't permitted to take the children beyond certain streets. For a while, when I took Michael and Heather to Central Park, the edges felt like a fence I was always looking over and wondering what was out there.

What was downtown Manhattan like? Or across the Hudson,
in Brooklyn?

My fence didn't last long. By the time the summer rolled
around, the two children had been enrolled in boarding
school and shipped back to England, and I was out of a job.

That was probably the most lost I'd been since leaving
home. I'd been alone and in a tight spot in Paris, too, but
Paris had a European gentility. It hadn't towered over me
like New York did. Paris might have had catacombs, but only
in New York did I feel it was possible to disappear under a
sea of concrete. I was lucky that I met an artist who was
at the Parsons School of Design. She let me sleep in her
shared room for a week, and introduced me to a crowd of
photographers, filmmakers and musicians, all bright up-and-
coming types, who were connected through friends and clubs
all through Manhattan. For six months I subsisted in that
scene, doing all kinds of jobs—graveyard shifts at all-night
coffee places, stretching canvases, cleaning at a Kung Fu
movie theatre, running errands. I ended up in some places
that now I can hardly believe—dancing with gay men in
nightclubs, watching people trade cocaine in bathrooms, and
once collecting glasses at an uptown party with Richard Gere
and Diana Ross.

It was often exciting, full of new ideas from the most
interesting people I've ever met. But I was also a long way
from 'me'. Everything always felt as though a storm was
coming, and I hated that edginess. I didn't like staying up all
night and not knowing who might be in the apartment with
me or where my next paycheque was coming from. It was

the first time I thought about the wide open fields of South Bandinby, the wholesome country houses, the clean work and the ducks on the water in the beck, and wanted it more than a gritty, uncertain life in the city.

And yet I stayed, waiting for . . . something, something. Then in November, news arrived with a letter from Bridget. My correspondence had been lax with the round-the-clock schedule I'd had as an au pair, and she had my address only because I'd suddenly—in a fit of nostalgia—sent her a letter myself. She wrote back, saying she was glad I'd written because she needed to tell me something, and would I call her?

I ended using a callbox in Union Square, feeding it coins at a ridiculous rate. And that was how I found out that Susie had married John.

'What?' David said.

Wil held up a hand, backtracking several paragraphs to read it over again.

'You just gasped and said, "Oh my god,"' he said.

'Wait, shhh!' Wil's heart was pounding.

I can't remember much else of what happened that week. I don't even remember how the conversation ended. Quite possibly, I left the phone receiver dangling by the cord with Bridget still on the other end, like a scene in the movies.

The news was a deep heart punch, and I walked around feeling as though I couldn't catch my breath for days. It wasn't just that Susie, my best friend for so many years, had married the man I once thought I would love forever. It was that all his scruples, apparently centred on the disapproval of his family choosing someone 'beneath him', had disappeared so abruptly.

I realised then that when his father died, so had the source of most disapproval. I kept replaying in my mind, over and over, that day in Paris when John had come to see me, when he had been still fresh in his grief. Had I missed something, then? In his reserve, had he actually been investigating the possibility of us being together again? If I had kept in touch with him as we'd promised, could this have been different?

I was in such a muddle, even though it had been me who'd wanted to leave. Because I thought I was done with him. And yet, the irony was that my heart broke most completely when he chose my friend over me. I thought I'd protected myself by holding back from him, by telling myself I hadn't wanted him, and it was the biggest lie I'd ever told. The truth was I did love him, and I would forever. I didn't want the heartbreak again, but the love I had no choice in. I don't know what to tell you about that. Sometimes we're just crazy, in love most especially. The emotion is so strong you think you must do something to relieve it. Even something stupid.

When I started to be aware of my surroundings again, winter had fallen on New York, and there were Christmas lights in the windows. It was cold and bleak, worse than any snow-in I could remember in the village. I couldn't get warm, probably because I wasn't eating. Food just didn't seem to have taste. Other things turned bleak, too. I was aware by the new year of 1984 that the oblivion of the drug and party scene was seeming attractive to me, where it never had before. This was even with the black cloud of fear that descended when men started to die of AIDS. I had seen people I knew become lost in that scene. And I sensed that if I stayed I would lose myself too.

I never wanted to leave a place more in my life, but I didn't know where to go. Certainly not home now—it was too close to John. Then, on a Sunday in January, I was walking past a shop window with a television and on came this ad, with Paul Hogan. I didn't know who he was then. All I saw was this blond man on a clean beach with white sand and turquoise water. Then a yacht on a harbour, and this man was saying I'd have the time of my life in Australia, that every day was a good day there. With the dirty snow on my shoes, I took him at his word and decided that I was going to Australia.

It was the perfect idea. Clean, sunny and literally on the other side of the world to John and Susie. I slept on a friend's floor for two months, pooling every cent I had for the fare. One of the advantages of not embracing the drug scene was I had some cash to start with. I rode a bus from New York to LA, which gave me entirely too much time to think about my mistakes, and boarded the plane from there.

The moment I stepped out into the Sydney autumn heat something inside me began to heal. For the first time since I'd left home, I felt I'd arrived where I was supposed to be. It made me think of the poem in The Lord of the Rings, *the only book I could think of with enough pages to have occupied me on the journey. It's not my favourite novel, Mina, but sometimes it's good when you're going on a journey of uncertain outcome to read about people doing the same thing. I felt less alone, I suppose.*

In any case, in that poem, there's a line that goes, 'Not all those who wander are lost'. Sydney was the first time I thought that maybe I was a wanderer, not just someone who had lost their reasons to stay at home. And that is where I will take up next time.

Until then, be brave, my darling girl.

Love,

Mum

Chapter 15

'I can't believe it,' Wil said. 'How could he do that?'

'So, you didn't know Rose Maxwell's granddaughter was Suzannah Elston?' David asked, reading over the paragraph.

'No,' Wil said, dropping her elbows onto the kitchen's island bench. She was so overcome, she didn't even think much of him reading the letter. 'What do you know about her? I mean, how could John have married Mum's best friend? And Rose didn't mention anything about it. And . . . I just—how could that even happen?'

David poured her a cup of black tea and pushed it across the bench. 'That's a lot of questions. I'm still getting over that she was your mother's other schoolfriend.'

'It's a lot of everything!'

Wil reached for the pages and slid them back together, tucking them under her hands. She pulled out the list with Susie's added name and shook her head. A thought flashed into her mind of Kate, encouraging her to start working with their father, right before announcing she was moving to Sydney. The betrayal had felt just like this grubby feeling she had now. 'It just sounded like they were such good friends. Now I don't know what to think of Susie.'

'People are always more complex than you think,' David said carefully, echoing the earlier letter, then paused. 'But as for Susie, we didn't find very much. Our research was focused on the direct line of the Elston ancestry, not the last fifty years, and not brothers and branches. We did know John Elston's wife was Suzannah Maxwell, of course, but we hadn't dug into her childhood history. They married in the early eighties and she died very young—brain aneurysm, I think—only a few years later, around eighty-six. It's a sore point for the family, for a few reasons, not least the press.'

'That tracks with my mother being back here for the funeral. Rose did confirm that. You know, it was strange my father even mentioned it. He *never* talks about her.' Wil swallowed before emotion about *that* could spill into this already turbulent moment. 'But why didn't I see Susie's grave in the churchyard? Shouldn't it be there?'

David tapped a spoon against his chin. 'I think I can explain that. Want me to show you?'

Wil sat up straight. 'What's that noise?'

She could hear a kind of rumble, like a kettle coming to the boil. But it was far off, out on the road. She slipped off the stool and crossed the living room to the window that looked out on Fen Lane. The rumble amplified and a second later a blue tractor emerged from the trees, bouncing on its fat wheels down the lane. Wil froze. It was the same tractor from the fields. Behind the wheel, unmistakably, was Lord Elston, his face intent, as though he were lining up a rabbit that had dared wander across his path, perhaps guilty of undermining one of his walls. Wil's heart made a dive for her shoes.

'God, he's coming to kill me,' she whispered.

David peered over her shoulder. 'Man looks like he's on a mission. That trespassing you mentioned earlier . . . wouldn't have been on his property, would it?'

'No,' Wil said. 'Because I absolutely did not climb up the broken wall between the church and the manor. And I absolutely was not caught red-handed about to climb into the tree by Lord Elston himself.'

David whistled. 'Don't worry, what's the worst he can do?'

'I dunno. Demand I come outside, and then run me over?'

At this, the tractor lurched to a stop in the lane outside the cottage, blocking both Wil's escape to her car, and any other vehicle that might want to use the road. If you were lord of the village, Wil imagined nobody told you where to park.

A figure climbed down from behind the cab, like a Victorian footman, and tottered up the path. Wil recognised Bill, the estate foreman, complete with flat cap. A second later, the doorbell rang.

'I'll go,' David offered, gallantly. 'Maybe he's come to offer us access to the church.'

'Yes, I'm sure my wall-scaling changed his mind on that. I'd better go. But if I'm not back in ten minutes, call triple zero.'

'It's triple nine here.'

'That's why you stay behind,' she called out, her feet dragging to the foyer. She tried to relax her face before opening the door. 'Good morning,' she said, trying for bright but sounding suspicious.

The foreman removed his cap. 'Miss Mann. His Lordship requests your company for a short excursion.'

Wil peered past Bill, as if she hadn't already seen the rumbling tractor from the window. 'On his chariot,' she said, then dropped her voice. 'Do I have to?'

Bill smiled, more conspiratorially than Wil would have expected. 'I know it isn't perhaps . . . usual, but the tractor is the best for this excursion. There's a wee bit of boggy ground up thar in the fields. I think you'd be interested, Miss, and it would mean a great deal to His Lordship if you'd accompany him.'

Wil doubted the last sentiment, but she took one look back, where David was waiting in the hall with raised eyebrows, and then bravely stepped outside. She'd have to face the consequences. She'd already been arrested this year, and destroyed an expensive kitchen, and survived both. This might just be her run of three. Bill at least seemed a calming personality. Surely Lord Elston couldn't murder her with him around.

Which was why Wil was alarmed when Bill cheerily waved and headed slowly back up the lane towards the manor house. Lord Elston jerked his thumb at a padded bench fitted up behind the main seat, bolted on like a retrofit. Yes, Wil thought as she climbed up, because tractors didn't come factory-fitted for footmen.

At least Lord Elston waited until she was seated. 'Hold on,' he barked over the engine, and they were off.

Wil gripped the canopy strut for dear life as they bounced down the lane, her nose full of diesel fumes and dust. Then they hooked a turn up a grassy drive, swaying over the bumps until they rattled up to a gate. Lord Elston himself climbed down to open it, leaving Wil feeling unexpectedly useless.

They took off again, up the hill, past the shimmering fields of green wheat. Wil looked across and back, and saw the church tower thrust up on the rise. They were running parallel to the public bridleway she'd taken towards North Bandinby, and when the tractor reached the crest of the hill, Lord Elston swung east, heading back towards the B-road up on the ridge.

Wait. Was he . . . ?

'Where are we going?' she shouted.

In answer, he pointed vaguely out into the fields beneath the ridge of the B-road. They passed over the junction in the bridleway and ran alongside the sheep paddock, where woolly faces turned towards them. This was as far as Wil had reached the other day, and all the information in her head was now crashing together into thought soup. She'd just read about John marrying Susie, and now she had to claw her way back to what she'd been thinking when she walked up here that day, so much deeper in her mother's childhood and the deeper history of the villages.

A stand of trees ahead grew and grew, until the tractor jerked to a halt, and the engine clattered into silence. A breeze shook the shaggy branches, lifting the hairs on the back of Wil's neck.

Suddenly, she knew—they'd reached Middle Bandinby.

Wil wasn't clear on whether Lord Elston was respecting the dead, or just revelling in his dominion over the long-abandoned village, but he sat unmoving for a good long while. Finally, Wil cleared her throat.

'Why did you bring me here?'

'You wanted to come to Middle Bandinby, didn't you? So go on, look.'

His voice was tight. Ah, so this was one of those *keep your enemies closer* situations. She'd trespassed on his land twice, and he was convinced she was working for David, so he'd decided it was easier to supervise her. She climbed down, feeling self-conscious and ripe for making some inevitable mistake, not unlike she had at work with her father watching her a bit too closely.

She tried to orient herself to the trees and the field around it, thick with wheat. If she squinted hard, she could imagine a small rise in the stalks out there, but otherwise . . . nothing.

'This isn't how she described it,' she heard herself say, unable to hide her disappointment. 'I can't imagine a village being here at all.'

The tractor creaked as Lord Elston climbed down. 'How *who* described it?'

'My mother,' Wil said. 'She said this was a lumpy field, and that she would come here to play in those trees among the hills. With other kids from the village.'

No need to mention any romantic rendezvous with Lord Elston's brother.

Lord Elston grunted. 'It looks different now. It's all been ploughed in.'

His candour surprised her. Wil felt a deep pang. 'But why? All that history—'

'Has been in the ground for hundreds of years, with no one much caring about it. My brother might have left it fallow, but I'm in the one in the chair.'

He stalked past her towards the trees. 'If you go in the back, there,' he said, pointing, 'there's a way inside, through the nettles.'

Wil looked down at her cut-off jean shorts. Obviously, she was still a long way from thinking things through. Warily, she picked her way around the trees, whose branches dipped right to the ground, until her back was to the B-road on the ridge. And there, indeed, was a bare earth path under a higher branch. All she had to do was stoop and edge underneath.

She emerged into a surprisingly vaulted space within the trees. Someone had obviously sheared off any branch that impeded movement in the leafy cave, and the higher branches closed in the roof. The ground was packed down solid. In fact, the trees seemed too young to have stood here very long. Then Wil noted the stumps of older, removed trees, now purposed into sitting places. On the top of one was a small pile of treasures: shards of what looked like crockery, and little round wafers of dark metal with split edges like the dry rim of rolled dough. Wil picked one up, and brushed her thumb across a curve of stamped letters. *A coin*. Even she knew it was superbly old, like something from a textbook, with a grey patina across its worn face. And not just one, a whole pile of them.

There were names carved in the living trunk above, scratchy children's capitals: *Boris*, said one. *Hamilton 2012*, another. And there, on a stump cut higher than the others, was *Ann*. The letters had blurred with time, and ran sloping to the right, but she could make out clearly enough: *Ann Mann left this place 1980*.

Wil reached a trembling hand to the letters, tracing each mark with her finger. Tears sprang into her eyes as she imagined her mother sitting here, forty years ago, and carving those words with a broken heart. Wil blinked and, for just a moment, she was back in the hospice again, her chest full to burst, an intake of air she'd taken to cry that couldn't be released. She blew out a long breath, pushing that feeling away, away, away. But it held for long seconds, only ebbing with an aching slowness.

She looked back at the words in the tree, feeling the layers and layers of story underneath them that she may never know. Wil felt both an endless grief over not having had enough time with her mother, and a great fear that she would never have a life her mother would have been proud of.

Then again, her mother kept saying, *Be brave*, like a woman who knew what that meant. Like it might be the answer to everything.

⌒

She emerged from the trees to find Lord Elston sitting in the tractor seat and smoking a pipe, puffs of grey smoke disappearing over the wheat.

'You find the treasure, then?' he asked.

She nodded, though he couldn't know that it was the carving and not the tiny hoard that she'd valued. 'Those coins look really old,' she said, still trying to sniff away the tears.

'Roman. They come up out of the fields in the ploughing,' he said. 'Stopped collecting them years ago. They're a children's plaything now.'

Even Wil, who had barely paid attention in school, knew about the Roman Empire. It was one of Colin's favourite subjects, and he'd made her watch *Gladiator* more times than she could count.

'I didn't realise the Romans came here,' she said, even though her mother had mentioned it in a letter.

'Course they did. Best agricultural land in the country? Saxons, Normans, Romans, Vikings—they were all here. Fighting over my land.'

Wil looked at him, presiding over this statement from his steel draught horse. She could almost see all those generations of land-hungry tribes running through his veins. He could just as easily have been astride a flesh-and-blood horse in any decade in the last two thousand years.

But then, as she looked away across the fields, she thought, *And through my veins.* Her mother had said their family never moved far from the villages they were born in, so that meant Wil was as rooted in the country as Lord Elston was. It was only convention that held him above her, just like the convention that led men to believe she wouldn't know the business end of a hammer. *Be brave.*

'Lord Elston,' she said. 'Your brother John knew my mother. Would he talk to me?'

Lord Elston tapped the pipe out. 'My brother John is a recluse living in what's left of the estate in Jamaica.'

'I heard that, but just a phone call—'

'You're an artisan, aren't you, Miss Mann?'

'I'm sorry, what?'

'You. Are an artisan.'

Wil stared back at him. 'Well, no.'

'You told me yourself you have done tiling work, with bespoke designs. And that Mr Hunter has employed you for his own property.'

'Yes . . . but . . .'

'And you also mentioned that you knew your mother once worked in the house kitchen.'

'Yes?' *Where on earth is this going?*

'Then I have a potential commission for you, for the kitchens, something appropriate to this place, its history and station. We've had three submissions to date and none of them show an understanding of the area.'

'Why me? I don't even live here.'

Lord Elston laughed and leaned down, his grey eyes shrewd. 'Because I see that look in your eye, Miss Mann, when I say, "This is my land". I might have the title, but you don't really believe in that kind of ownership. You know that your family was here just as long as mine. And in your heart, you'd like to say so.'

Wil opened her mouth in surprise, then shut it again. 'I wasn't thinking that at all,' she lied.

'Oh, of course not. Such things wouldn't be in your mind while scaling a wall. You have bigger fish to fry. Though what they are, I do not know.'

'I'm not up to anything, I swear. I just came to the village because of my mother.'

He stared at her. Wil held his gaze, caught in a game of eye-lock chicken. She had no idea what he thought she was doing to advance David's agenda, but it must be fairly dire.

As if he could hear her thoughts, he said, 'Well, maybe I'd like to keep a closer eye on what Mr Hunter's associate is doing. See if her work is up to scratch.'

'Sorry,' she said, bristling at being railroaded. 'But I've already committed to work at the church cottage. I can find my own way back there.'

She turned down the track along the sheep field, wanting to get away now. He was spoiling this moment with her mother's memory, using it as a way to control her.

'I'd wager Mr Hunter wouldn't object if it meant some cooperation for his project.'

Wil stopped and spun back, amazed. *Bribery!* Suddenly, she thought about her mother, her dreams crushed not once but several times, and all because the son of a Lord Elston had placed his priorities higher than hers. Because of which side of the wall they'd been born on. And now here was the current Lord Elston, using the same logic.

'Sorry,' she said. 'I keep my promises.'

Well, she didn't really, but maybe she would bloody well start!

'And if I could contact my errant brother,' he said. 'What if that was on the table?'

Wil wavered. Damn him. 'Is it?'

'Don't walk back. The path's bogged after the rain.'

Wil nearly did anyway, but she was wearing sneakers and shorts. Some of the potholes looked as if they could swallow her to the waist. She hugged herself as she stalked back to the tractor, and climbed up.

Lord Elston settled into the driver's seat, and sat with his hand on the key, as though he was thinking hard. Or contemplating murder; it was hard to tell.

'He'd want to know, precisely, what it was about,' Lord Elston said. 'He tired of the press after Susie's death, the bastards. We agree on that point. He wouldn't want anything to do with a television show.'

Wil made silent faces. Then she realised Lord Elston could see her in his side mirror. *Great.* She closed her eyes and sighed.

'I only want to know about my mother. She wanted me to do something for her, but I'm over a decade late in finding out. I'm looking for who was in contact with her in 1994. Or her close friends, like Bridget Spencer. I know that John knew them both at one time. That's all. Nothing about Susie. Nothing about the show.'

Lord Elston grunted, and the tractor roared to life.

Chapter 16

'So let me get this straight,' David said. 'After being caught trespassing, twice, Lord Elston took you personally to the Middle Bandinby site, and then he offered you work inside his house. Does that make any sense to you?'

There was an edgy, almost exasperated tone in his voice. They were walking up the church path an hour later, after Wil had come back to the cottage and spent twenty minutes in the shower thinking furiously about the decision she'd just made. Even now, as they reached the door, she still didn't really know what logic had compelled her to accept.

'I bet he thinks he's getting in the way of your plans,' she said, dropping her voice in the quiet of the church's stone-shrouded space. 'By taking my time away from you and all the secret squirrel stuff I must be doing for you. And it's not exactly inside his house. He just wants a design. He barely let me in the door when he showed me the kitchen. Something about "not letting expectations disrupt my process". I think he was mocking me. When he showed me out, I asked Bill what was going on, and he told me they don't sport shoot on the estate anymore. I had no idea what that meant, but Bill laughed and I think he was saying Lord Elston is bored and has moved on to messing with people instead. Though then all I could imagine is Lord Elston with a hunting dog and a rifle.'

David grunted and moved off down the church aisle, not acknowledging the joke. He'd been like this since she got back, the usual parry of their conversation dimmed.

'Anyway, the kitchen's massive and nearly completely gutted. I haven't any idea where to start. He's given me two days to do some sketches, and I'm to "present them the morning after that". Sketches! When I haven't any dimensions, just a glimpse of the room. Does he think I have a fancy photographic memory? Maybe he'll just say it's all bad and the deal will be off. I don't get anywhere, and he wastes my time and gets to laugh. Where are we going?'

David was walking a little too far ahead to seem interested in what she was saying, but he pointed to the end of the nave, beyond the carved wooden screens and to the left of the altar, where a black iron palisade fence barred a small chapel. As she drew up to the fence, Wil could see carved marble inside.

'What is this?' she asked, wrapping her hands around the chapel bars.

'Elston family mausoleum. I think the reason you couldn't find Susie out in the churchyard was because she's buried here.' But he seemed moody, and distracted, his hands clenching on the bars as he stared into the chapel.

'Why's it fenced off?'

David snorted. 'Out of bounds to the hoi polloi, why else?'

Okay, he was definitely in a mood. She'd never heard him be bitchy about Lord Elston before, despite all the frustrations. He always seemed so collected and professional.

'What's wrong?' she asked, tentative, because she was so used to it being her fault when people were annoyed.

He gave her a furtive sidelong glance, then looked away. 'Nothing.'

Great, I'm definitely in the shit. She sighed and turned back to the iron gate.

'Pity we can't get in,' she said, touching the sturdy padlock.

'If you'd lived here as long as I have, you'd have learned a few things,' David said, and tugged down sharply on the lock. It clicked open, and a second later he had it neatly removed and the gate swung open. 'I also might have oiled the hinges. It's important to maintain old things, and squeaking does rather prevent being covert.'

Wil imagined Lord Elston, in his walking boots and flat cap, catching them poking about his private family burial ground, and the potential pyrotechnics that might ensue, especially with David in his touchy mood. She followed reluctantly.

The chapel was spartan compared to the rest of the church, with plain rendered walls hung with only the Elston family crest: a blue river running through a shield. But it hardly needed anything else next to the creamy marble, which was shot through with pink and grey veins and carved into columns and Romanesque friezes. The air was cold and a touch musty, as if packed with the spirits of departed generations, all of them too taken with the exquisite marble tomb to pass over. Wil was certain that, if she'd asked, David could tell her who had carved it, when, and its place in a grand architectural taxonomy of crypts. But she sensed it was better not to ask right now.

It took only seconds to find the freshest carving on the marble, to *Suzannah Elston, 1963–1986, loving wife and mother.*

Wil stepped back, all thoughts of architecture gone.

'Mother,' she whispered. She hadn't realised that John and Susie had had children in their brief marriage. More children who had lost their mother before they could even remember them. She felt sick in her heart. Then she thought of Lord Elston telling her she wasn't looking hard enough for Susie's resting place. What a peculiar way of talking about your sister-in-law. Had he disapproved of Susie, in the same way Wil's mother assumed the family would disapprove of her?

'I called my researcher to check the details,' David said, his voice low and sad, and momentarily without its edge. 'There was a lot of press interest in Susie and John when they married. The Elstons were devoted royalists so some of the Royal Family attended. They were an attractive couple, too, took a good photo. When she died, it was a tragedy, which attracted all the Fleet Street parasites. No wonder they're touchy about publicity.'

His tone made gooseflesh stand on Wil's arms. There were suddenly too many awful things to be remembered here. 'Can we go, please?'

With the mausoleum once again locked, Wil expected to be on their way out, but David sank into the front pew and tipped his head back to stare at the vaulted ceiling, as though asking for deliverance from his sour mood.

She flopped down beside him. 'I really am sorry,' she said after a minute, trying to guess at what she'd done wrong.

'I know I'm a disaster who just blunders into these things, and I didn't mean to make it hard for you to—'

'It's not that.'

'Oh. Okay.'

She followed his gaze up to where the handpainted blue on the wooden rafters was fading to grey. It took David a while to speak.

'I just don't like him playing games with you. You have a lot at stake here, hopes of finding answers. I don't like him . . . I don't know, messing with that.'

'Oh.' Wil blinked in surprise. She hadn't expected him to resent Lord Elston's interest because he cared about what it was doing to *her*.

'In any case, that's not the point. Did you want to see Susie's tombstone for a reason? Check she's really dead?'

'Ha.'

'You have to admire how I'm not asking to know where this secret letter-drop place is.'

She laughed. He was clearly trying to joke and move the conversation on, despite it falling flat because of the tension. So Wil tried to do the same.

'I just needed to make what Mum said about Susie real, somehow. Maybe even to wonder what it would have been like if she was buried here, too. When I was at Middle Bandinby . . .' She tried to find the words to describe the flashes of long ago memory she had sometimes, and how they reached into both love and fear together, and failed. 'Or I'm procrastinating. I'm really good at that. I still have to approach Rose. And Dad, about Marionette. Oh, and I've got two days before I'm supposed to turn up at the manor house with sketches and convince Lord Elston to contact his brother, which could be the best lead of all. And also somehow a conversation I don't want to have.'

David leaned back. 'Then you'd better come back down to the cottage. You need to get to work.'

⌒

Wil spent the rest of the day cross-legged in her room's window seat, alternating between staring out over the fields and sketching in her book. And then tearing the sketches out and madly starting again.

She had no idea what she was doing. Not only in satisfying what Lord Elston had asked for, which must be something like David had done in his kitchen—a design that honoured the estate and its long history—but in just basic things, like understanding English design conventions. For instance, David had a washing machine in his kitchen, which was ridiculous. And she couldn't ask him about it, because he'd gone down to London for a meeting with the production team and wouldn't be back until tomorrow.

She was also avoiding calling her father. She glanced at her phone, but instead she turned to a new page, abandoning the last kitchen concept in favour of sketching the fields, and then the grove at Middle Bandinby. An hour later, with her lap covered in pencil shavings, she was sketching Middle Bandinby itself— at least, how she imagined it could have looked, with the ridge towering up beside it like a battlement and a stony church like the one next door. Except this church had a roof with dragon scale edges, inspired by the tile piece David had shown her. She pencilled in the distant cluster of North Bandinby buildings, then idly sketched a faint loop around it, like a crop circle. That looked interesting. She added another around Middle Bandinby, and the edge of another in the foreground, as if the observer were striding through the manor grounds and nearing the edge of their own village. She traced a line between the first two circles, then another to join the last. Rough path shading came next, and making the lines into borders between fields. In the distance, she smudged in a suggestion of a horse and plough. Nearer, the huge wheels of a tractor, though she didn't quite like where she'd placed it. She pencilled in a dust cloud to balance it, her pencil flying.

Around 2 pm, she finally steeled herself to pick up the phone, then realised it was nearly midnight in Australia. Deflated, she went back to sketching, the hours falling away as the sun made its long arc across the sky. When it was still light at 9 pm, despite her body aching from hunching over the drawings, she felt curiously settled. *Be brave.* The working day had started in Australia. She dialled.

'Cameron Butler,' he answered, the line sounding hollow on his car's Bluetooth connection.

'Dad,' Wil said. 'So, how have—'

'Willy. I expected to hear from you sooner.' He sounded almost conciliatory. Either someone had just paid a large outstanding invoice or Manchester United had triumphed in a game overnight.

'Oh, you were?' she said.

'How are you getting on? Shonna said you were staying with her.'

'Uh, yeah.' She was afraid to tell him where she was, and awful for withholding it. 'I've been meaning to call. I had something I wanted to—'

'We're having a barbecue Sunday, at twelve for lunch. Kate's coming up from Sydney with the family. I assume she told you. You'll be here?'

Wil closed her eyes. 'Um, about that. I need to ask you something.'

'Shoot.'

'You won't get mad?' She hated how young she sounded.

'What'd you break this time?' he said, but his voice was still wry and light, as if he didn't care that she broke things, as long as they weren't *his* things.

'Nothing!' Wil tried to laugh, but her heart was thumping, afraid for how he was about to react. She heard the sound of his truck indicator ticking. 'But it's about . . . those letters.'

There was a long pause, and Wil heard the truck's brakes squeak. He'd pulled over.

'You got work at the moment, Wil?'

'Actually, I have two jobs. Some bathroom tiling and a kitchen design.'

He grunted, as if surprised. 'What's the question?'

'Well.' She took a breath. 'In the letters, Mum mentions a nurse she knew at the hospice called Marionette. I wondered if you remembered her.'

'No.'

Too fast.

'Are you sure?'

'Your mother and I weren't on good terms, then. I didn't hang around the place.'

Wil felt an unexpected wrench in her gut, as if that old grief had ripped open again. It swallowed her next words.

'Is that all?' he said finally.

'No,' she croaked. 'The hospice. What was it called?'

'They knocked it down years ago. Is that all?'

'I guess so,' she whispered.

'Then we'll see you Sunday. Bring a salad.'

'Sure.'

But he didn't hang up. Instead, she heard a few breaths, and a creaking that could have been his hands working the leather on his steering wheel. When he spoke, his voice was tired, but gentler.

'Look, Wil, I know this seems important to you. But the past is the past, all right? I'm glad to hear you're keeping busy, getting stuck into work. See you Sunday.'

The line clicked softly.

Wil cradled the phone. Outside the window, the late twilight was spreading across the sky, drawing the cottage into a world of darkening fields. In the muted greens and greys, the boundary between times past and present seemed so thin, as if she could fade into time itself, walk up the path and find Middle Bandinby actually there, or meet her own mother on the bridleway. She jumped when her phone rang again. Colin's face was on the screen.

'Wil,' he said, his voiced hushed. 'Was that you Dad was talking to?'

'Yeah. Where are you?' Her mind was still emerging from the dreamy twilight.

'Hiding in the toilet block at the beach. He's letting us take a day off. We finished up at the Masons' yesterday, and there's a sweet swell this morning. He drove us down here himself.'

'So that was why he was in such a good mood.'

'What are you going to do about Sunday?' Colin hissed. 'You obviously didn't tell him about being on the other side of the world. No chance you'll be home by then?'

'No.'

'Crud,' Colin said. 'I figured you'd be out of money by now. I thought you were going to ask for more.'

'I'm making progress. And I got some work, which helps with the money. Also I saved a bit because I'm kinda living in David Hunter's house.'

There was a bang down the line and some swearing. 'I'm sorry, what?'

'You heard me.'

Colin started laughing, then abruptly cut off and quietened himself. 'Are you serious? If I didn't have to get out of here soon, I'd be asking for dirty details.'

'Hey, the details are all clean!'

'Sure. Look, Wil, I'd better—'

'Col . . . you don't know what hospice my mum was in, do you?'

'I don't.' He paused. 'Is that what you were asking Dad? When he said they knocked it down?'

'Yeah.' Wil tried not to fall back into despair. She glanced back outside, but the dreamy quality was gone. She didn't want Colin to go and leave her alone in the David-less house.

'Why did you want to find the hospice?'

'A nurse Mum mentioned in the letters called Marionette.'

'Marionette? That's not a common name. Like Wilhelmina. Your mum must have loved her.'

Wil laughed despite herself. 'Yeah, I guess.'

'You know, you should ask my mum. She's pretty good with details.'

Wil wrinkled her nose. 'I don't want to talk to Carol. And she wasn't there anyway.'

Col sighed. 'You want me to do some digging? If they knocked the place down, someone in the demo crews probably knows about it. I can ask.'

'If you want to. Just . . . be careful of Dad, Col. I don't want him mad at you, too.'

'He's gonna be thermonuclear when you come down with explosive gastro this Sunday.'

'Gross, Col!'

'Hey, you want a gastro story bad enough to avoid a family barbecue, right? Don't undersell it.'

~

The next morning, Wil abandoned her sketching and left the church cottage with a basket covered in a checked cloth. She had to huddle against the drizzle in a raincoat she'd found hanging in David's mud room.

The wood loomed in the distance as she dodged around puddles on Fen Lane. Given she was visiting a grandmother, the whole thing would have been very Red Riding Hood, if the raincoat hadn't been daffodil yellow. Rose Maxwell would see her coming a mile off.

Rose's house was on the corner with the loop of the village road, the same house that Wil assumed her mother had visited to endure page-turning purgatory. As she knocked on the door, Wil couldn't help noticing the house provided the ideal position to observe any comings and goings in the village street. The upstairs back windows would have a view towards the church, the manor and the beck, while the front overlooked the school.

'Miss Mann,' Rose said, opening the door. 'I'm afraid you've caught me at rather a—my, what's that I smell?'

'Fresh scones,' Wil said, offering up the basket, which did waft with a suitably enticing smell of baking and butter. 'I thought that they'd make a good pairing with your jam.'

Rose stared at her a long moment, and Wil could only imagine what reassessments were going on in her head. 'You cook, then? Your mother couldn't cook a boiled egg.'

'Not really,' Wil said, encouraged at the voluntary mention of her mother. 'It's the one thing I learned to bake at school. It's Lady Flo's recipe.'

'Lady Flo?'

'She was the wife of Sir Joh. He was a politician in Australia. Quite notorious really—' Wil was about to ramble on when she remembered that Sir Joh had been as bent as a mis-hit nail and rather keen on demolishing heritage buildings. He probably wouldn't meet with Rose's approval. Instead, she pulled back the tea towel to display the shiny golden scone tops. No need to mention it was the second batch, the first lying blackened in David's bin because she'd been carried away sketching and forgotten to check on them. 'I brought clotted cream, too.'

'Well, don't stand out there in the rain,' Rose said, stepping back. 'Leave your shoes there, and hang the coat.'

As she did, Wil had a chance to see into a cramped lounge room, which was dominated by a dark wood piano with a leaning stool. A motorised armchair sat to the side, draped in a crocheted throw the colour of the summer sky. Beyond she could see a small kitchen, with enough room for a round gate-leg table. The walls were crammed with photo frames, unfamiliar faces smiling out. Rose was putting out plates on the kitchen table and brewing tea. Wil slid into a seat and tried to imagine her mother standing next to that piano, turning pages.

'Yes, that's where she used to stand, when we practised here instead of walking to the church,' Rose said, using her cane to lower herself into the opposite chair. 'I suppose you've come to ask me more about Bridget. Find her, did you?'

'Actually, no. I wanted to ask you about some other things. I didn't realise that Susie married John Elston.'

Rose paused, her bone-handled knife poised to skewer her scone. 'You know that, do you?'

'I . . . do,' Wil said, weakly. It wasn't the question she'd meant to ask. But then she'd seen all the photographs, and it had just tumbled out. Even so, probably better not to admit to Nancy Drew-ing in the Elston mausoleum, or reveal the letters that the information had come from.

'I suppose that David Hunter pulled up the old newspaper entries,' Rose said, saving Wil. Rose plunged in her knife and sawed the scone, scattering fine crumbs. 'There wouldn't be anyone here who'd remember it now. It wasn't a secret, but it was a bad business. I don't like to think about it.'

'But you said the last time you saw my mother was when she came for the funeral?'

Rose nodded, carefully spooning jam onto her scone with a slightly shaking hand. 'I was surprised to see her, actually. I knew they must have fallen out because Ann never came to

Susie's wedding. I think she might have been living in New Zealand, then. I suppose that would have been a long way to come back, but the way they used to be, I couldn't have imagined her not coming if they'd still been friendly.'

Wil forgot her scone. 'New Zealand?'

'Yes, I'd forgotten she said that until just now. She was just married herself then, Ann was. Or maybe I have my years mixed up. But I was surprised to hear it. She was such a flyaway, I never imagined she'd walk down the aisle with anyone.'

'Sounds like you talked a bit while she was here.'

Rose made a so-so hand gesture as she chewed. 'In passing. It was a dreadful time. John had a heavy load of responsibilities, and their poor little boy had to be cared for. The Dowager Lady Elston took over much of his raising, while they were still here.'

'So you didn't see him yourself?' Wil asked, a lump lodged in her chest.

For just a moment, Rose's eyes flickered. 'Oh, aye, he was my great-grandson and I helped where I could. But John never really recovered. He took that diplomatic post in Jamaica only a year later, took wee Henry with him, and he's hardly been back since. Probably for the best, after the friction with his brother. Then the staff all changed over at the big house and it felt as though nothing was ever the same again. Oh, that scone is quite lovely. Don't leave them all for me, now. Eat something yourself.'

Wil picked up her knife. For someone who didn't want to think about it, Rose certainly seemed to have warmed to her subject. Wil's head was spinning with the details. Her mother had been in New York when she heard of John and Susie's wedding, and said she was heading to Australia, so where did New Zealand come in?

'Of course it was the press that made it worse. Rumours about Thomas Elston, then a tragic death—'

'What rumours?'

Rose waved a hand. 'Not being a suitable lord, not like his father. Conflict with his brother, who they painted as though he'd have done a better job. Tabloid rubbish. But the photographers were always trying to catch a shot of Susie, and then they hung around after she passed away. The papers made it out like the family had a curse. Dreadful people.'

'I'm so sorry,' Wil said, slicing a sliver of clotted cream. She spread it across her scone but had no appetite at all. 'I . . .' She tried to say how she felt for little Henry, but the feeling couldn't fit into words.

'Still, the whole business had one upside. It was a wake-up call for Thomas. He pulled himself together, stepped up into his place as Baron Elston. He had to, for John's sake. Or maybe to prove he could manage without him. And at least little Henry was too young to remember. He's a barrister down in London now and quite well adjusted. But I've always made sure to tell him about his mother, rare times he's up here.' Rose paused, at the end of her scone, as if the idea had just made a connection. 'That's why you're really here, I imagine? You want to hear more about Ann?'

'Yes,' Wil said, stumbling around to her original purpose. 'I do. Did she ever contact you at all, in the nineties, when she was sick?'

Rose, who seemed about to launch into a well-told village story, paused. 'No, I never heard from her again after—oh wait, tell a lie. She did send me a card with a photo of her baby. Katherine, wasn't it? That must have been the year after Susie's funeral. That will be your sister, I imagine. It's over on the far wall there, in that small blue frame.'

Wil rose and went to the frame, jammed among others. In it was a faded photograph of a sleeping baby with a squashed face under a crocheted cap. She could just see the resemblance to the girl in her polaroid.

'Kate,' Wil said, quickly, stopping herself from touching the glass. She straightened. 'Was there any other time? She never mentioned anything about something she wanted after she died? Or anything about letters?'

Oh, she'd said too much. She came back to the table, her fists bunched against her legs.

'What sort of letters?' Rose said, eyes lit with interest.

Wil wondered in that moment if Rose could be the one sending the letters after all, and this apparent ignorance just an act. Certainly, if there was a reason to mete the letters out one by one, she wouldn't want Wil to know it was her. But if she really knew nothing then Wil would have to expose the whole story yet again, and this time it would probably end up going around the parish council and probably everyone else.

With great trouble, she kept her mouth shut. 'What about William at the manor?' she asked. 'My mother knew him when she worked at the big house. He was the caretaker, I think?'

'Oh, aye, old William. Gamekeeper,' Rose corrected. 'He's one that left when John Elston did. Quiet man. Never saw him much. He knew his job too well and was always out tramping the land and going about his work.'

'Any idea where he went?'

'Somewhere up north, I heard from Cook. John Elston gave him a fair reference, I know that much. Never quite understood why he didn't go with John to Jamaica. But I suppose the land's different there. Maybe nothing for him to do.'

Wil slumped. Another road leading back to John. 'I just know that there was something she wanted me to do for her. I thought if she had contacted you when she was sick, you might know. Or maybe she was in contact with someone like William, who she knew once.'

Rose heaved a sigh. 'Sorry, duckie. I'd like to tell you she did, but we hadn't been in touch in years. And I don't know how she'd have been that close to William, either. I never saw her again after '86, and that card with the photo of your sister was the last I heard from her. Kept expecting to get another once I eventually heard you'd been born, but she never did send one. But I suppose that would be asking a bit much. Life's so much busier with two.'

Chapter 17

Wil trudged back to the church cottage through all the puddles and took her sodden shoes off at the door. Under the rainy skies, and without David, the living room atmosphere was as heavy as a 6B pencil. All her drawings were scattered at the dining table, the kitchen in disarray after the baking. The air smelled faintly of burnt sugar.

Wil slid the list out from under the sketches and put a line through *Rose Maxwell*. Old arguments with Kate kept coming to mind. She sat staring at Kate's number in her phone, pushed the dial button twice and hung up both times. What would she say, anyway?

She put the Beach Boys into her earphones and set about cleaning up. By the time she'd emptied three sinks, the music had her imagining the grit between her toes was sand and that her shirt was really damp from seawater.

Only the ducks washing themselves in the pond outside spoiled the daydream, but at least she felt better. She gathered up the dirty tea towels and padded across the slate towards the front door, before remembering that the washer–dryer was back in the kitchen and not in the much more sensible mud room. Crazy English kitchens.

She stopped. There, on the floor under the mail slot, were two envelopes, brown at their edges, their surfaces spotted with raindrops. She dropped to her knees and peered through the mail slot before pulling the door open. No one was in view.

Wil weighed the letters in her hands, one thinner than the other, and closed the door again.

Dear Mina,

Happy 22nd birthday, my darling girl. I have a feeling that by the time you're reading this you'll still be living in Australia. But then, I might be biased. From the moment I lived here, with the open spaces and the sunshine and the beaches, I considered it a madness to go back to England. You always enjoyed the water so much, I can't imagine you in coats for months on end. But that's me, and you're only drawn from some parts of my madness!

Wil glanced up at the dreary English day outside and ghosted a smile. She supposed her mother had a point. Anyone who did the dishes while fantasising to Beach Boys songs couldn't claim love for the English climate.

I felt all those things about Australia even though my first job here was in a bank. Me! In a bank! I was never a star employee, but I managed not to be fired and to find a place I loved living in. It was a friendly share house not far from

Bondi, with five rooms. It saw a steady stream of overseas visitors and students, and occasionally someone on the couch as well. There was always a fresh face to talk to, or eat with. My weeks swung into a golden rhythm of heading into town to my job, followed by warm evenings around the dining table and warmer weekends on the sand. Most of the time we'd each cook something and share it. I was never much of a cook, I'm afraid, but I learned a few things from those dinners. Anytime something tasted amazing, I made the cook teach me how to do it. It's where I learned Spaggy Meatballs, which was always your favourite—

Wil gasped as a memory came back like a flashcard: sitting at a table and eating spaghetti, and squeezing a meatball in her fist until it broke. She heard a woman laughing as she picked up every little broken piece to put in her mouth. The clock ticked around as she held on to that sound. Her mother's laugh.

—and a properly good Sangria. (I've written both recipes at the end.) On my lunchbreaks, I'd breeze through the Pitt Street Mall, or walk by the harbour. I never stopped being enraptured by the way the sun could turn the water to shimmering jewels (except when I was horribly sunburned— always wear sunscreen!). And on the weekends, I lived at the beach.

There isn't much more to tell about this year of my life, because it was so happy. Isn't that funny? When things are going well, there's no story. But throw in a little heartbreak, a bit of loss, suddenly all must be explained and told. Happiness is much more ethereal than sadness. Difficult to give a form with words, difficult to hold on to, sometimes. But that year, it held for me. The Sydney 'winter' was laughable. I went about in my shirtsleeves and swam every day. Happiness is better than fat at keeping you warm.

I met many people that year. In the house. At work. At the beach. I couldn't even remember most of their names, now. But there was one that stuck. I met him on the beach in December 1984. He was from England, too—I guess the accent was a homing beacon to hear in the crowd of locals— and he was on his way to Cairns to work on boats as a dive instructor.

Within a few days, he'd offered to find me work on the boats, too, and to go to Cairns with him. His name was Cameron Butler, and it was the first time in my life I'd run towards something and not away.

Until next year. Be brave—

Wil fumbled with the second, thicker letter, tearing a wet spot on the envelope.

Dear Mina,

Happy 23rd birthday, my darling girl. I was nearly twenty-two when I stepped onto my first boat in the Cairns marina. Memories of the ferry across the English Channel had me worried, but I never felt a moment's seasickness here. It didn't matter if it was a yacht, or a cat, or a tiny tinnie, it was as though I'd been a sailor all my life.

Cameron kept his word. He sold my charms as a hostess on charter yachts where he was the divemaster. These were big, expensive boats. I nearly fell over the first time I saw one. *The manor house in South Bandinby had nothing on the polished wood, the gleaming metalwork, the boiled and starched white of every staff member on board. And I had absolutely no idea what I was doing.*

Luckily for me, the first time I was taken on, I worked under an amazing head steward called Rodney, who was not only kind but knew his job like he knew how to breathe. Maybe that's why he was so kind—he was so competent he had enough room for my hopelessness. He was cut from the cloth of an old-school butler (I could imagine him gliding around Elston Manor, except that it would have been far too small for him).

I couldn't believe how much there was to do on the yacht and that Rodney made sure it all happened—there was provisioning the galley, and maintaining furnishings and linens and crockery, supervising the staff, organising everything neatly into storage, keeping track of all the usages, coordinating with the chefs and having encyclopaedic knowledge of wines, cigars, teas and coffees. And that was before we even had any guests. With those came individual care of each person and their luggage, assisting with undocking, anticipating everyone's needs around the clock, and still managing to be charming and courteous and utterly professional at all times. In a white uniform.

I was sure it would be a disaster. 'Charming', 'organised' and 'professional' were not adjectives I'd ever used to describe myself, and nor would anyone else I'm sure. But Rodney had utter faith in me. If he was faking it, he was very good. He started me off gently, in things that didn't involve much talking to the guests. I was a real scullery maid, and all my time in that patisserie in Paris helped me cope with the work.

I loved being on the boat, though, always on the water with these fabulously interesting people coming and going, both crew and guests. I was never lonely: Cameron and I were with each other whenever we were off duty, and if I had time alone, I took my sketchbook to a secluded part of the deck and drew endless pictures. And when I was on duty, Rodney pushed me along, imparting some little bit of wisdom, like conversation pointers or ways to defuse a drunk and angry guest, and then swooping back an hour later to see how much I'd remembered. It wasn't as hard as I thought. Within a few months, I was greeting incoming guests, being subtly attentive, asking questions about their preferences and making careful notes I could follow up on later. Rodney looked smug, as if he knew I could do this all along.

I don't think I could have done his job. I didn't much care for wines (though I did develop a snooty tea palate, especially for Earl Grey, which has spoiled teabags for me to this day) and his seemed a profession for a confirmed single person. Travelling with a boat all year, with such dedication to the job, could hardly make a happy home. But I did well enough with what was mine.

And I was happy with Cameron. He was a real Londoner, and could be loud and abrasive, but he had energy and drive. He was saving money to start a business, and I admired him for that. He tried to teach me to dive, but I developed a horrible claustrophobia being so far below the surface. It was perhaps the first disappointment he had in me—that I preferred a snorkel and a pair of flippers to a scuba tank.

It didn't seem a big thing at the time. When December rolled around again that year, we were moored off one of the Whitsunday Islands. He got permission from the captain to take a tender over to the beach for lunch, so we could celebrate a year since we'd met on the beach at Bondi. It was glorious—white sand, water as clear as snow melt and just enough clouds to keep the heat out of the sun. That was when he asked me to marry him.

We were both rostered off on Boxing Day, so we were married in the chapel at Hamilton Island. And that was that. It was a defining moment, perhaps an attempt for both of us to seal that happy time with vows. I think at least that's what I was doing. But it also marked a time after which everything changed.

We both left the ship. Cameron because he would be paid more in a new position, and me because Cameron was moving and I was ready to take a step up. So in late January, we walked onto a new superyacht, bound across the Coral Sea. Cameron had a new energy about him—it was to be the last job he'd take before starting up his building business back on shore. I think it was from that moment that I started to sense a clock ticking and that our dreamlike existence on the boats was about to evaporate.

I tried to talk to Cameron about my worries, but for him working on the yachts had not been an unexpected dream, it had been a means to an end. His dream was to use his carpentry trade and to work for himself. The fact he was also a handsome qualified dive instructor with a cute British accent had given him a passport to earn money without any living expenses. But he'd had enough of that, so he wanted to leave. As his wife, I had to follow him. I had to leave friends like Rodney, who I never saw again. I tried not to feel as though a cage were hovering over me, waiting to drop. And for a while, I did manage not to feel it.

By mid-February, we had sailed into New Zealand waters in what would be our last year afloat. I will save that for the next instalment.

Until then, be brave, my darling girl.

Love,

    Mum

'Something good?'

Wil dragged her eyes up to see David, bag still in his hand, his coat's shoulders dark with rain.

She blinked, still deep in yachts, white uniforms and questions. Her parents had been married at Hamilton Island? Why had no one ever mentioned that? Or that they spent years living on boats? Her father had mentioned diving a couple of times, but she'd known nothing of this whole other life before he'd been a builder.

It took several minutes of her staring out the window at the ducks to truly come back to the present. By then, David had taken his bag and jacket upstairs, and padded back down in his socks, jeans and a worn grey T-shirt. 'Something certainly smells good,' he said. 'Did you cook?'

'I made scones to tempt Rose Maxwell,' Wil said, still distracted.

David's eyes lit. 'Any left?'

Wil didn't know if it was that unassuming grey T-shirt, or the effect of spending two letters immersed in sun and sea, but she was suddenly happy. Almost giddy, which was the most ridiculous word she could ever apply to herself. 'You're out of luck,' she said. 'Rose needed a lot of encouragement.'

'Oh.' He affected a sad face. 'I hope you got something for it. Baked goods are currency in this house.'

'Nothing really useful, except she told me that William left the estate when John went to Jamaica. Not quite what I hoped for, but then these came.'

She held up the envelopes.

He grinned at her. 'And?'

'Oh no, you have to wait, and direct me to the best supermarket. I need to pick up a few things.'

David gave her hopeful eyebrows. 'I sense more cooking.'

'I'm making Spaggy Meatballs for dinner.'

⌒

'If there's meatballs in heaven, these are them,' David said. 'I thought you said you couldn't cook.'

They were sitting at the island bench in the kitchen, stools pulled in at a corner, with two declining glasses of red framing their plates. Wil grinned and stabbed another forkful. 'It's Mum's recipe. She couldn't cook either, but she learned it from a chef school student who came through her share house in Sydney. There's a note on the recipe that says not to skip anything. In capitals. And underlined. I paid attention.'

'With a list of ingredients that long, it's probably a fair note. I've never seen fennel seeds, Dijon mustard and parmesan go into mince.'

'You clearly haven't lived,' Wil said grandly, aglow in success and red wine. 'Two culinary wins in one day . . . something must be seriously wrong with me.'

He laughed. 'I missed you in London.'

'You did?' She nearly choked on her wine, blushing furiously. 'That sounds unlikely.'

'As enticing as back-to-back production meetings sound, I just kept thinking about you. Wondering how you were doing on your hunt. Whether you were staying out of the duck pond.'

She laughed, trying to make sense of him. He was obviously joking, but it felt like flirting, him holding her eye longer than she would have expected. 'I'm doing . . . not too terribly,' she said.

'I would think so, with your luck.'

'That,' she said, pointing her fork at him, 'is not something I'm used to.'

He pretended to crack his knuckles. 'This sounds like interesting-story time.'

'Is it interesting if you demolish the wrong kitchen on the first day of a job?' she asked, then paused. 'Which, on reflection, is not a thing to tell the person who just hired you.'

David looked bemused. 'I won't tell Lord Elston if you don't. Is there more to it?'

'Innocent mistake, really,' she said. 'Well, sort of. But it's hardly new. Did I tell you about my infamous shoplifting with Kelley?' And when he shook his head, Wil told him. And despite feeling the same old mortification, something about it was different when she was telling it to him. David winced and laughed in a way that made it *almost* feel like a teenage misadventure and not an indelible mark on her character. 'In conclusion, shit not together, remember?'

'She obviously had issues,' David said. 'Anyone can have a bad friend. I myself can boast a whole suite of them.'

'But I didn't tell you about Scotty Dunn.'

David cocked an eyebrow. And so Wil told him about sleeping with Scotty at the party and him dumping her on the spot for Carla. The whole time, she was dying of embarrassment, but she couldn't stop herself. She wanted to pour all this out of herself in front of him. David made a face at the end. 'Early romances,' he said, philosophically. 'None of us get it right. It's practically standard to have a bad first time.'

'Then I present the case of Rob, my most recent romance, the man I dated for a year and who led to me being arrested, before ghosting me for a whole week.' As Wil grandly described her dumping Rob to the playlist from 1994, David was choking on his red, laughing. And Wil glowed with relief that Rob too felt like something that had happened a good while ago.

'Now I'm not saying Rob was bad luck,' she went on. 'My mother dying the day before my birthday, though, that one I think I can have.'

Suddenly, Wil found her verbal handbrake. A silence fell over the table. 'Oh, god,' she mumbled. 'I just can't help myself sometimes.'

'Oh,' David said softly. 'I'll give you that one. That is terrible luck.'

'Don't forget Scotty Dunn,' she said, trying desperately to find humour again. 'Wham-bam-thank-you-ma'am man. Boy, that's hard to say.'

'You mean idiot of the century?' David said, refilling their glasses. 'Let's try to make it harder to say.'

Wil started to laugh just as her phone rang. She turned it over to see Kate on the screen, probably after the missed calls she'd made earlier. But she couldn't face Kate now, tipsy and in the middle of a good moment. She turned the phone back on its face.

'I know my not being together isn't really luck,' she said meditatively. 'I just don't seem to be able to do any better. Messing up orders at work, knocking down the wrong kitchen. Like I can't grow up, or something.'

'But if it even feels like bad luck you need to break the run,' David said. 'Look, I played professional football for eight years, and the whole team was full of superstitions. We had weird rituals we'd do before matches. I didn't believe in any of that growing up, but it rubbed off on me when I was playing. The stakes were so high all the time. When there was a run of signs, like lost matches and bustups, you had to do something to break it.'

Wil turned her glass in her fingers. 'Like what?'

David shrugged. 'Dunno. Take a new birthday?'

He threw out the suggestion as if it was a lobbed ball, then slid off his stool to take the plates to the sink. Wil put her glass down and followed.

'Take a new birthday?'

'Why not? People change their names all the time. Why not your birthday?'

'You mean, aside from needing it for things like passports and the tax office?'

David gave her a lopsided smile. 'Details!'

'Are you drunk?'

He twisted back to inspect their glasses, still sitting on the island bench. 'Not even a little. Look, my glass is still full.'

Wil laughed at the madness of it. They were both definitely sloshed. 'Maybe I should change my name,' she said.

'If you wanted to. But I rather like your name.'

He reached a hand out to brush her hair back from her face, his fingers tracing across her cheek. Wil felt the breath catch in her chest.

'Mina, Mina, Mina,' he said. 'You know what I think of? Mina Harker, from *Dracula*.'

Wil burst out laughing. 'From *Dracula*? Oh, that's wonderful, David. I remind you of Dracula.'

She pulled back from him, disappointed. She was definitely wrong about the flirting.

'God, no,' he said, catching her hand. 'No, no. Mina collects all the letters, journals and newspaper articles, makes copies of them for the other characters. She's the one who makes it possible for Dracula to be found. She's clever and brave, just like you.'

'Oh, really. Clever and brave.'

'And also probably unimpressed at being compared to other people. You'll get it together, you know. We all do eventually.'

His palm cupped her face, and then he kissed her, his mouth a warm invitation against hers. Wil forgot thought as she kissed him back, running her hands over his shoulders and across the muscles of his back. In response, he dropped his hands down and pulled her into him. Being in his arms was like a perfect summer day on the beach. Only better, because she hadn't expected this. Hadn't expected how he could make her feel.

He pulled back to look into her eyes, and it was then she felt the doubts. Why the hell would he be interested in her?

'Uh-oh,' David said, his hands still warm on her back. 'Are you going to tell me you're with someone else?'

She shook her head and kissed him again. Oh, he felt so good, this all felt good. She was more happy now than she'd been in years. But it was also unexpected, and the doubts wouldn't leave her alone.

The next time they broke apart, she glanced at the stack of drawings, still on the edge of the table. She was supposed to show up at the manor house in the morning, hoping those drawings would grant her a ticket to John Elston. She could barely think straight about that now. The way she felt with David's arms around her, and him kissing her, threatened to make anything else a second thought.

He followed her gaze, and his arms slackened. 'Shit, sorry. I'm being too forward, aren't I?'

'I . . . um, was thinking about the morning,' she managed, feeling like an idiot traitor to the rest of her brain, which was telling her to *shut the hell up and enjoy.*

David's hand left her back. 'I was going to say I should be able to spare you by then, but I'm getting the impression you don't feel the same.'

'It's not that,' she said quickly, feeling the stab of his disappointment. 'But I, god, I didn't know you felt like this and you've seen my incompetence in conversation when I *haven't* been up all night.'

He dropped his forehead to hers and made a mock groan, but she noticed how he kept his body away from her now. 'You make a horribly fair point. Fine. Raincheck for seduction with cooking again another night, then?'

Wil tried to laugh, but she was swimming in the muddy turmoil of so many emotions. How she felt about him. What he really thought of her. How the hell she was going to stay under the same roof with him now.

'I guess that's a silver lining,' she said, biting her lip.

'It's lead lining at best, believe me.'

He was the one who walked out.

Chapter 18

The next morning, Wil's head spun as she approached the manor house gates. Two-thirds of the feeling was pure nerves. The other third was punishment for drinking red wine. She clutched the sketches, unsure whether anything that she'd drawn would work. Bill met her at the gate, doffing his cap and pointing her towards the back of the house, saying that His Lordship would meet her in the kitchen.

This did nothing to settle her nerves.

As she stepped through the kitchen door, she had a brief moment to absorb the space for the second time and was encouraged that her memory had not warped the details. The exposed beams in the high ceiling were beautiful, and a bank of three tall windows let light play across the room and into the space of a great hearth. Wil could walk inside that arch without bumping her head. But there was nothing on the aged cream-coloured walls—no cabinets or benches, except for the bare frame of one under the window. The floorboards were scuffed with use though, in a pattern that suggested where a sink and stove must once have been. If there had ever been tiles, they were gone. A hallway led to other parts of the house, including, she assumed, the ornate front door that faced the garden and had featured in the party photo. But it was the narrow stairway leading up that caught her attention. Those must be the stairs her mother had climbed.

'There you are,' Lord Elston said. He was seated at a round table to her right and surrounded with stacks of papers, his hair flattened over his ears as if he'd just taken off his cap. The table looked as though it had been recovered from a skip, a paperback propping up one leg. He beckoned her to sit. 'What do you have for me?'

Wil slid into a seat opposite and fanned out what she considered her three best ideas. 'I have some concepts here, different arrangements that feature a large sink beneath the windows, and a choice of a range on the far wall, or within the old hearth space.'

She rambled on, pointing out the obvious features of the sketches, trying to mimic the pep of designers she'd seen at her dad's worksites, while Lord Elston's eyebrows descended south. Finally, he sat back.

'Any designer monkey could have given me these. What happened to taking from the history of this land? What else do you have there?'

And before she could stop him, he'd pulled the whole sheaf of sketches across to himself and gone tearing through, meaty hands scattering pages. Wil watched in horror, as though he were rifling her underwear drawer. Finally, he paused at one page. 'What's this?'

'It's a . . . tiling pattern, based on the Roman coin lettering and the curve of the hearth arch. I hadn't finished it.'

He grunted, and slid the page to start a pile of its own. 'And this?'

'A tessellating pattern. I based it on a piece of the Middle Bandinby church.'

'David Hunter show you that?'

She nodded, and he added the drawing to the new pile. He flicked past a few more and then stopped at the one she'd thought of as a 'time lapse', building on her drawing of the three Bandinby villages, but with technology advancing: horses and scythes in the background, tractors in the foreground. He stared at it a long time.

'Did you do this?' he demanded.

'No, I left my sketchpad by the window and a fleet of flying designer monkeys did it,' she snapped. 'I mean . . . yes. Sorry.'

She covered her face in embarrassment. When she finally cracked an eye, he was still looking the drawing over. 'I like these three,' he said finally. 'I don't want to see things that are in every kitchen showroom.'

'I just thought if we knew what the overall layout was, the style of the cabinets and counters, we could work back—'

'No. We start with the details. Get those right, the rest follows.'

'Okay,' she said. He was clearly a man used to working the way he wanted to, and to hell with anyone else's process. 'Well, that drawing was just me sketching. I don't know what to do with it. It's too detailed to work on tiles.'

'So don't put it on tiles. Anything else?'

Wil twisted around, searching the kitchen for inspiration, but her mind was as blank as the walls. This wasn't going well at all.

'Do you want to reuse that frame under the window?' she said, in desperation. 'Would be a shame to lose it.'

'Hmm, yes,' he said. 'It is oak. All the designers wanted to get rid of it. So it stays. Good. Let's meet again in two days and see what you have then.'

'Wait a minute—I really need to measure. And do you have anything else that was removed from the original kitchen? I need to see that, too.'

'I doubt very much it was the original kitchen,' he said, dryly. 'As the house was built sometime around 1700. No doubt someone's modernised since then.'

She ignored his snark. 'But was anything else kept from the demo—cupboards, doors, tiles, anything at all?'

'I can have Bill turn it up, for when you next come back.'

'I can wait now,' she said, surprising herself. 'I wouldn't want to come back in another two days and see something that changes all these ideas. And I need to measure.'

He fixed her with a hard look, as if waiting for her to back down. She held his eye, not knowing where this steel in her had come from. Finally, Lord Elston twisted towards the door.

'Bill!' he bellowed. 'Where are those doors and such that came out of the kitchen here?'

Bill shuffled into the doorway. 'In by the east stables, Sir.'

'Show her, will you?'

Wil made a move towards the door.

'A moment,' Lord Elston said, standing and digging around in his coat pocket. He pulled out a worn wallet and extracted a stack of notes.

'What's this for?' she asked in confusion, as he held out the folded money.

'For your work. This must be ten hours of drawing here, something like that?'

'I guess.'

'Good. Bill will take you to the materials and provide a tape measure.'

Bill led her around the corner of the gamekeeper's cottage and towards the old stable buildings, the ones with the overgrown rose garden. 'Must be going well, Miss?' he asked as they approached.

'I can't tell. I suppose it's good Lord Elston doesn't like meetings to drag on.'

'Oh, aye,' Bill said with a chuckle. 'He's straight to the point. But he must have liked what you showed him.'

'Why do you say that?'

'If he didn't, he wouldn't be inviting you back, nor allowing you to see these. All the others asked the same questions and didn't get nowhere.'

Surprised, Wil watched Bill unlatch the little wooden slat gate into the rose garden and followed him towards a courtyard within the stables. On either side, an east and west wing was walled in red brick, with stalls visible through the arches on the ground floor and an airy loft above. Bill led east, into a cobwebby cave, and pulled a string for a single light bulb overhead.

'There you go, Miss.'

In the first stall, a stack of recovered wood leaned against the wall. Wil stepped across the packed dirt floor and touched a heavy beam, pleasingly marked with old nail holes and dents. It would clean up magnificently.

'There's cabinet doors at the far end, I think you'll find,' Bill called.

Wil moved down the pile, picking at the layers of paint on some pieces. It was a time capsule of cream, white and pale green layers, sandwiching a shade of shocking orange that must have been done in the sixties. A thick layer of white had concealed it, as if someone had come to their senses.

Wil pulled back several cabinet doors leaning together. They were all in good condition, despite the dust. Solid wood. They could be stripped, or distressed. The grain showed beautifully on their unpainted backs. She was about to move on when a patch of scratches on the inside of a door caught her eye. She pulled the panel out to see better and gasped in surprise.

They weren't scratches. They were pencil marks—shaping a fairy sitting on a toadstool, her wings a little ragged, her dress torn. The fairy's face held a cheeky grin, as if she'd torn her dress and wings in some unregrettable adventure. Wil pressed her hand over her mouth. *My mother touched this.* Wil had looked at the drawings in the letters so many times, she knew it was the same hand—less skilled, like her own work from high school, but unmistakable. She tried to imagine her mother sneakily completing the drawing in little pieces over her time in the kitchen. Or had she been left alone long enough to do it all at once? Wil glanced across to where Bill stood watching from the doorway.

'Do you mind if I take a photo of these,' she asked. 'It would help with the design.'

'Can't see why not,' Bill said.

Wil took out her phone and photographed the picture, then took a few others of the stack. She slotted the panel away, carefully between two others. It was hard to walk away from it.

Half an hour later, after she had made the necessary measurements, she and Bill crunched down the stony driveway.

'Bill,' she asked, as they approached the gate. 'How long has the kitchen been demolished like that?'

'Oh, well now,' he said, removing his cap to scratch at his head. 'Must be going on twenty-five years, maybe more.'

Wil stopped. Right around the time her mother had died. She wondered if David had the dates all wrong, had Bill all wrong. Her hopes surged. 'Twenty-five *years*?'

'Oh, aye. I wasn't here when it were torn out, mind. That's my predecessor, mentioning that it were being demolished when the IRA declared their ceasefire. That's why I know the year. Was a talking point, you can imagine, not having a kitchen.'

'Oh. And where were you before?' Wil asked, slumping again.

'Up country, near York. Bigger estate, but not so traditional as this. His Lordship is much closer to the old ways than things were up there. I like it. I'm not one for much modernising.'

'And your predecessor was a William too?' she asked, hanging on to a hope of connection. 'Rose mentioned him.'

For a moment, Bill frowned, then his brows relaxed again. 'Oh, you mean old William? No, Miss, he was gone away around the time Master John left, well before that. The estate was without a gamekeeper for a while, then, and that's why they stopped the sport shooting. That's when the position became a foremanship. My predecessor was from the dowager's staff and came up from London, until he retired about a ten-year ago.'

'So you don't know where old William is, then?'

Bill raised his cap and scratched at his head again. 'Master John would know, I imagine.'

He replaced his cap and opened the gate for her. Then he paused. 'It's good you're here, Miss Wilhelmina, if you don't mind my saying. Not right for the big house not to have a kitchen. His Lordship hasn't seen to do anything about it, what with the Dowager Lady Elston always in London nowadays, and there's facilities enough in the cottages for a single man.' He gave a shy smile, as if he might have said too much.

Wil glanced back at the huge house, considering Lord Elston. Born into a job he might not have wanted, left alone on his estate after a falling-out with his widowed brother, who left the country. Maybe he was lonely, and bossing her around was just a sport for him. But seeing that drawing of her mother's just now, and remembering her laughter yesterday, made it worth putting up with Lord Elston.

'Does there have to be a woman here to cook in a big kitchen?' she said, finally, fondly teasing because she liked Bill.

'Oh, I know it's an antique view now, but there was life in the house when we had Cook in the kitchen, and seeing to the house was always the lady's department in my day. Maybe that's why His Lordship hasn't seen to it. I wouldn't dare cross the dowager.'

When Wil returned to the church cottage, there were no letters waiting on the mat, just David on his computer at the kitchen table. She stopped to stare at him sitting there, absorbed in his screen, the intensity of their kiss last night flying through her head. All thoughts of her designs dissipated like smoke.

'How did it go?' he asked, not looking around.

'Fine. Sort of.' She couldn't find anything to say to him, especially when he seemed so calm. As though he'd forgotten.

'You want some coffee?'

'I'm good.' She was jittery enough. 'I don't suppose there's been any mail?'

'None.'

Resigned, Wil took a seat as far from him as she could without being rude and opened her sketchbook. Extracting a chewed pencil from the spiral binding, she hovered over a fresh page, her inspiration a blank, and feeling awful. Had David just moved on from everything that had happened last night?

. . . was he glad he'd had the sense to pull away from someone like her?

She put her pencil to the paper, making jagged lines, then broke the point. She couldn't remember where her sharpener was. *What a mess.* She couldn't draw like this.

'I figured I'd let you have the house to yourself this morning, before the big meeting,' he said, giving her a sidelong glance. 'But do you want to talk about last night?'

She caught his eye, buoyed with relief, and the electric attraction was back in the air between them.

'Shit,' he said, softly, his eyes not leaving hers. 'I'm in such trouble with you. What did Lord Elston have to say?'

'I have more work to do,' Wil said, quite breathless looking at him. 'He didn't like any of the concepts, only a few of the small things I was mucking around with.'

'What sort of things?' he asked, abandoning his computer and coming over. Wil's nerves spiked pleasantly.

'Well, these ones,' she said, pushing forward the three sketches and trying to avoid looking right at him, though she could feel his presence like a warming fire. 'One's based on a Roman coin from Middle Bandinby. It's curved, so I thought that could work around the hearth arch. And this one's from that church stonework you had—it's just a geometric, so it could go into a splashback or as a feature behind the range maybe.'

'And this?' he said, his fingers moving the time-lapse sketch to the side.

'Oh, that was just me playing around. It's too detailed for tiles. And I made a mess of the tractor.'

She glanced at him then, and found the way he was looking at her drawing even more unnerving.

'I want to show you something. Upstairs,' he said.

Wil followed him up the stairs, and then down the hall. He pushed open a door into what was clearly his bedroom. Her heart hammered, though his invitation hadn't sounded like a proposition. Still she snuck a look at the bed with its thick square corner posts, the stack of books on the side table, the rolling view down to the fenland. An intimate view of him. She tried to read the spines of the books.

'Wil?'

'Mmm?'

'In here.'

Caught staring, she hastily moved, stepping through the door into a grand en suite bathroom. 'Wow,' she said, shocked to a standstill. 'What is that?'

Most of the bathroom was tiled from floor to ceiling in dark greys with a rustic red fleck. Dramatic, but plain. But the wall facing the window was elaborately patterned in small tiles that resembled stained glass from a church. The design was a woman's figure, wearing robes and a crown, a sword in her right hand and what looked like a tower in her left. She was bordered with architectural Corinthian columns and patterned coloured panels. Each tile had been handpainted, like a panel of leadlight, and set with black grout.

'Saint Barbara,' David said. 'Patron saint of sudden violent death, and thus of underground miners and tunnelling engineers, that sort of thing.'

'She's lovely,' Wil said. 'But what is she doing here?'

'She's also the patron saint of architects. I figured she was good to have around.'

'Odd combination, sudden death and architects,' Wil said, fingering the tile's paintwork.

'Oh, I don't know, architects have been under threat of sudden violent death in most jobs I've worked on.'

Wil grinned, thinking of Lord Elston and her father. David had a point.

'Seriously, though, my father was a miner. When I was maybe eight, there was a cave-in at the mine where he worked. Four men he knew died. That's when I first learned about Saint Barbara. It was a hard life my dad led. When I got my first professional contract, he gave me a medallion of Saint Barbara. I think he was hoping she'd protect me enough to keep me out of the mines. Instead, I blew out my knee and she made me an architect.'

He pushed off the doorjamb and came towards her. 'I thought it might give you some ideas for the manor kitchen. Something bold can really work when you've got all that solid wood to hold it up.'

His fingers twined into hers, and Wil stepped into his embrace. 'Tell me you don't feel this?' he asked.

Then they were kissing again, oblivious to Saint Barbara, oblivious to everything except the feeling of fingers on skin.

⌒

Two hours later, Wil lay beside him, his arm around her, his fingers lazily stroking her arm while she looked out on the fens.

'I wonder if my mother ever looked at this view,' she said. 'Their farmhouse was on the fen side.'

'Maybe. Though I doubt she spent much time lying about in the early afternoon.' He checked his watch. 'I was supposed to be on a Zoom meeting half an hour ago. I bet—yes, my phone has completely blown up.'

He tossed the handset back on the side table.

'Aren't you going to call them back?'

'No,' he said, turning towards her. 'You may be dreadful for productivity, but I'm having too much of a good time.'

She grinned, deliriously happy, all doubts muted. 'I found something today,' she said, and told him about her mother's drawing on the old kitchen materials. 'After I see Lord Elston again, I'm thinking I'll go down to London and find World's End. See if there's any leads to Bridget.'

'You could call them. Less time on trains.'

Wil shook her head. 'I want to stand there and look at it, too. This village wasn't real until I came here and saw it like my mum did. Plus, I'm learning that people are much less likely to say no if you're standing in front of them.'

David ran his hand down her back. 'You're sexy when you talk like this. Want me to come with you?'

Wil felt the smile spread slowly across her face. She felt so happy in this moment. She touched the stubble on his jaw, looking into those deep blue eyes. 'Why?'

'Chance for a jaunt with a gorgeous girl in London? Yes, please. Are you going to show me that picture from the old manor kitchen?'

'I thought I'd tell you about something else first.'

'What's that?'

'You wanted to know where in the church I was supposed to get the letters.'

She felt him tense. His lips pressed to her hair. 'You sure about this?'

'There's a hidden tilting panel, behind the memorial in the side chapel. About the size of a shoebox inside. It was empty, though.'

'Huh,' he said. 'I mean, priest holes are found all over in places that were friendly to Catholics, but this estate was always loyal to the crown. And that sounds way too small for a person. I wonder what it's doing there.'

Wil took a breath. 'My mother said only she and John knew about it. Maybe he made it, or something.'

'I guess it's possible, but if it's in the stonework, it must have been there a very long time. But one thing about that does make sense.'

'What?'

'If anyone would know about a secret spot in their ancestral church, it would be one of the family, don't you think?

You can show me later. Now, where is this picture from the manor kitchen?'

'I'd have to go downstairs,' she said. 'Left my phone on the table.'

'Off you go then. I'll just watch.' He stretched back, clearly enjoying himself.

Wil stuck her tongue out at him as she pulled on her shirt and underpants, both embarrassed and enjoying being the object of his affection. She blew him a kiss as she padded out of the room and down the hall. She'd just recovered her phone when she heard the metallic *snap* of the letter slot in the front door.

Wil froze. Precious seconds passed before she thought to run for the door, to see who had delivered the envelopes that had landed on the mat. She remembered she was only in her underpants as she hauled the door open. Peering out, she couldn't see anything, except perhaps the barest hint of a leg disappearing behind the hedgerow. It took another run of seconds to sprint back upstairs to the spare room window that faced the lane. By that time, she could see nothing except the canopy of the trees.

She thumped the glass. 'Dammit.'

'Everything all right?' David called.

She trudged back to his bedroom, holding the letters aloft. 'Just delivered,' she said.

He sat up. 'Did you see who?'

'Do you think I'd be teasing you by withholding the information if I did?'

He gave her a sly smile. 'Maybe. I don't mind a little teasing. Come back to bed. If you're going to be reading, I'd rather it was next to me.'

Chapter 19

Dear Mina,

Happy 24th birthday, my darling girl. I'm going to keep counting up the years, even if you read this at eighteen. I like the idea that you might come back to it again, maybe when twenty-four does roll around. Either way, so many years will have passed between now and when you are reading this. I hope you have found things that delight you, and frustrate you ... maybe they are even the same things.

Drawing was like that for me—it was something I had to do, and yet I was often dissatisfied with what I made. Maybe that was why I kept drawing the next thing, trying always to be better. That works when you can be the one to make the change happen. Other times, it's life that makes you change.

The year in New Zealand was like that. Change was in the water we swam in, in every meal on the ship. In every look Cameron gave me.

At first, I couldn't work out what was going on.
Everything seemed the same to me. But looking back later,
I could see the long shadow John cast across our relationship.
Cameron picked up on it long before I realised.

I never made a secret of my past with John. I didn't
believe in keeping that from my husband. But maybe I said
his name in a way that Cameron didn't like. Or maybe it
was just because of who John was—Cameron is one of those
people who is suspicious of the aristocracy just because of
who they are. Or aren't—which is honest working people.
I don't know if Cameron is still like that, but that's how he
was then, and that alone might have been enough for John to
be a sore point. Or maybe it was simply that I kept in touch
with Bridget, that I wrote her long letters. And she would
write back, care of the home port when I could collect them,
sending what news she had, which often included John.

Maybe Cameron read those letters, and took issue with
the snippets of gossip about South Bandinby, about Thomas
being rumoured to have been arrested, or John and Susie's
baby. I made no attempt to keep any of that from him, but
it was also true that John still affected me. Reading about
the arrival of John and Susie's son made my stomach drop.
I tried very much to be happy for them both—they had been
my very closest friends—but that didn't stop it hurting.
I can't imagine I was good at hiding that from Cameron. So
whenever I mentioned John, or that time in my life before
Australia, Cameron would distance himself from me. And I
understand in a way ... who wants their wife to be hung up
on their ex? But it's also what put the first wedge between us.

I was devastated when I heard Susie had died. It was the first time in my life that anyone I cared about had gone from the earth, and taken with them the chance for me to say things I had never said; to mend the bridge between us that had fractured when she married John.

It was so sudden. Many things about that year have faded, but I can remember the gulls crying when the captain brought me the telegram. We were moored in Auckland at the time, stripping down the ship before the next charter. It was the start of July, a slow time for work, and Auckland was like I remembered England in the winter—a lazy sun that rose late and set early, and a knife-edge cold. All I could think about was John and little Henry, just a baby, now left without Susie forever. The bleak grief of that was colder than anything else.

I felt a desperate need to go back to the village, maybe the only time I did in my life, and the captain was happy to allow me a fortnight to go to the funeral. Cameron wasn't so happy about it. He didn't want to spend any hard-saved money on the airfare, nor did he want me going alone. In the end, I had to tell him that he wouldn't stop me going to my friend's funeral no matter what he said. I think he was shocked. I was discovering that Cameron had much more traditional views than I did on what a wife was.

But he relented, and we went, all the way from Auckland to Lincolnshire, and then to the village that Cameron had heard so much about but never seen. He had a Londoner's sense of jostle and pace, and didn't understand anything about village life. He felt utterly out of place in the fields and hedgerows. Of course he didn't say that, but I knew it from the way he held himself, the way he kept looking around as though he had lost his bearings.

The funeral was awful and upsetting. The whole village turned out to the church service, with the Elston family and Cook and William and all the manor staff in black. There was a formal service, then the family disappeared into the mausoleum for the burial. It wrenched my heart out to see the pain in John's face. Oh, he was very stoic, of course, but I can't imagine how much iron it took to put on that performance. He was never as hard-hearted as he liked to appear.

Thomas, now Lord Elston, was very much in the background, as was his habit, barely appearing at all before he vanished, leaving the Dowager Lady Elston and John to front all the mourners. Bridget was my touchstone that day. When Cameron was distracted and hanging on the edges, she sat by me, the two of us gripping each other's fingers as we cried through the hymns. All the stuffy formal funeral business couldn't capture how the three of us had once been together. Only I remembered how much Susie had meant to me when we'd played in the wood as little girls. She had given me a friendship that had carried me my whole life. And I would never be able to tell her that. It would remain secret between the world and me, like my relationship with John had been.

It surprised me when John singled me out in the congregation and invited Cameron and me back to the manor for the tea. Maybe it was because I was married now, so it was safe for him to be seen speaking to me. Maybe it was because he felt, as I did, the need to hold on to Susie by remembering we'd all been friends. Or maybe it was because he'd noticed Cameron sizing him up and wanted to show his largesse. I like to think it wasn't that.

We spent an hour in the manor garden, with the invited few, mostly relations, making hushed small talk under the spreading tree boughs. Despite the occasion, it was the most beautiful summer's afternoon. It was almost as if Susie had intervened in the weather, to make sure everyone would remember her with the sunshine. I think I must have said as much to John. It was then he told me about his plan to move to Jamaica, to take Henry to where the sun always shone, to try to find what happiness could be found after all of this. So I ended up telling him about my time on the yachts and the beauty of Australia. And I thought I saw, just for a second, that flare of regret in his eyes, as if he was wondering what kind of life we might have had together. If we had made different choices.

We parted on good terms, though it was as bittersweet as it had been in Paris. He had a hard journey ahead of him, long and lonely, looking out for the son he hadn't expected to raise alone. And I was going back to New Zealand, for our last six months of sailing life, and from there to something new again.

Cameron was only too pleased to leave the funeral behind. He stopped short of being outright rude about my having spent a long time talking to John, but I knew he held it against me. I caught myself being careful to speak to William as long as I had to John, and I don't think I ever forgave Cameron for feeling I had to do that. I often wonder if he'd been a more understanding man, less threatened by everyone and everything, if the years after might have gone differently.

In any case, lest I leave you with an entirely unfavourable view of him, I think he was very aware that he could be resentful, and he did try to make up for it. One of those times was on the few days' stopover we had in London.

We were staying with Bridget before we flew home. By this time, Bridget was studying at university, but she'd kept her contacts with fashion and record stores. That was how we ended up with tickets to the Queen concert at Wembley Stadium. It was Cameron who insisted we go, that we needed to lift our mood after all the bleakness. And for those amazing hours at Wembley, in the front third of the crowd, my grief almost did evaporate. I could imagine me and Bridget and Susie together again, singing along to the music, dancing like lunatics, happy to be in each other's company.

Cameron was transformed by it too—he went on endlessly about how much of a genius Freddie Mercury was, despite the hours we sat on the bus trying to get out of the place. I couldn't verbalise all the things I felt. But I bought a Walkman at Heathrow, and I played Queen songs all the way back to New Zealand. Now, whenever I hear 'Under Pressure', it reminds me of those last days in England, how sometimes joy and haunting sorrow can be parts in the same melody.

By Christmas that year, Cameron and I had fulfilled our contracts on the yacht, and he was fixed on a move to the Gold Coast. We would begin 1987 in a real house with a blue door, which is where the next letter takes up.

Until then, be brave, my darling girl.

Love,

Mum

⌒

Dear Mina,

Happy 25th birthday, my darling girl. If you're keeping track of the years in my story, you'll realise that we've reached the year that your sister, Kate, was born in December. Anyone will tell you that a baby brings immense change into a household, but so much change happened even before that.

I suffered dreadful dry-land sickness after leaving the yacht. Some of it was because I had just walked away from a job I'd loved, that I felt I'd mastered (to the degree I mastered anything), and was now stepping into a house and life that belonged more to my husband than to me. What was I to do with myself? At the time, the prevailing attitude was to get on and have babies, but I didn't have a great deal of control over that.

So I did the one thing that I could do no matter where I was—I drew pictures. At first, I kept drawing the things around me, or little character sketches like mice, fairies and possums, which I'd been doing for a long while. But then, when I discovered I was pregnant, I found myself going to the children's book section of the library and poring over what was there. One day I came across what I thought was a particularly poor story and had a conceited thought that I could do better! So I set about drawing a children's story. Then two. Then ten.

I didn't know what to do with them, of course. And I may not have done anything, except that a children's author came to the library one day and I worked up the courage to ask her

advice on what to do with my work. She must have thought
I was half-mad, but she politely asked me to send her what I
had. I was hugely surprised that her agent in Sydney then
called me. They weren't interested in the story I'd written,
but they liked my drawings, and not too long afterwards I had
a contract to draw the pictures for another author's book.

Cameron had always put up with my drawing. He saw it
as an expendable hobby, something I did in my spare time
and could easily put aside once I became a proper married
woman with a family. So he wasn't too happy to learn that
I now had a contract to fulfil and a baby due all in the
same month.

I did understand his point of view. He was under pressure
himself—he'd just begun the building business and was being
mucked around by subcontractors. He was worried about
money. I tried to teach myself accounting so I could help with
the books, but I wasn't much good at it—not like the other
tradies' wives he knew. After a few bungled invoices he took
the work elsewhere.

Life wasn't much fun at that time. Now that we weren't on
the yachts, Cameron and I had lost our connection, and it felt
like we had separate lives. The house he'd bought was a bit
too ambitious for what he was making, which was another
pressure. I think the money I earned drawing was the only
reason he didn't tell me to pack it in. But he resented me for
it—he thought it was his job to provide.

By the time Kate was born, I'd submitted all my drawings,
and I had a contract for another book. Kate wasn't much of a
sleeper, and I went through months in a haze, from drawing
to feeding and back again. But the part of me that had

wanted a life beyond the village was at least happy. I loved Kate, loved her deeply, and I loved drawing. It felt like I had unexpectedly found something that I could do. Something that other people wanted me to do. Eventually, I even published a few books of my own.

If you find these books now, you might have a laugh. Or perhaps a groan. Will you be embarrassed that your mother wrote such things as Misty Mouse Goes To Sea? And The Naughty Fairy of the Dark Wood?

The books are, of course, really all about the same thing— stepping away from where you came from and finding your place in the world. Taking part of your past with you, but not letting it hold you back from something new. So, basically my life, except with furry fantasy creatures. I read somewhere recently that every writer just writes the same story over and over, and so that must be mine. It seems fairly true!

I'm going to wrap up this letter here, because I have to think about the next one, which is tricky to write. If you are reading these all at once, as I think you will be, then know I thought an awful lot about what to say and, in the end, I said what I thought you needed.

Until then, be brave, my darling girl.

Love,
   Mum

⌒

'Why does she do this?' Wil complained, dropping the letter into her lap. 'Why tease with "there's something important in the next one"?'

'Well,' David said, his arm still around her, 'she thought you'd have them all to read at once, rather than having to wait on a mysterious sender.'

Wil let her head fall on his shoulder. She wanted to get up, but it was too nice here with him.

'Speaking of which,' David said. 'Does anything particular happen before one of them is sent?'

'You mean, do I go up to the churchyard and spin around three times, and then the postman magically brings one?'

'You know what I mean.'

She shrugged. 'I did wonder about that too, but I haven't noticed a pattern. But listen to this, my mother was a children's book illustrator.'

She showed the paragraph to David.

'Well, look at that. You could contact the publishers, see if they have any information for you.'

'From twenty-five years ago?'

'Sure. Where are you going?' he complained, as Wil threw back the covers.

'I can't stay in bed all day with you.'

'You can, too,' he said, tugging at her shirt.

'Sorry, internet awaits. I have to look at book websites.'

David released the shirt. 'I have a better idea. Get dressed. We're going out.'

Half an hour later, Wil was stooped over a book bin in the Lincoln Library, flipping through the stack of hardcover children's books. The room had a quiet, restful signature, the high ceilings decorated with wood panelling in the same shade as the shelves. In the children's corner, the surfaces were covered in crayon and pencil artworks by a dozen different hands. The artwork Wil was looking for was far more familiar.

'It's not here,' she said. 'That's the end of the Es.'

'Catalogue said it was in,' David said.

Wil moved on to the next bin, and there, two books in, she paused at a cover, showing a mouse in a skirt with a suitcase tucked under her arm, determinedly stomping up a gangplank onto a boat. Above the mouse, the title—*Misty Mouse Goes to Sea*—was written in rope letters. Underneath, in smaller black letters, it said *Written and illustrated by Anne Elston*.

Wil ran her fingers over those letters. So, her mother had added an 'e' to her name. But what did it say that after so many years, and so many disappointments, she'd chosen to use John's name?

'You read,' David said. 'I'm just going to have a word with the person at the counter. See if they have any others.'

Wil glanced up as he left, noting the way several people at the computers turned to stare at him. She hadn't realised how much he was recognised. Was it weird for him? On the short walk through the Lincoln streets to the library, people had turned their heads like that, too, and one man had asked for his autograph. David had taken it with a quiet grace he seemed to have been born with. No wonder he'd walked into a job in television. Wil couldn't imagine anything worse than everyone knowing who she was and the things she'd done. Only his hand around hers had stopped her from ducking away from the autograph hunter.

She turned back to her mother's book, leafing through the wide pages, the story echoing much of what her mother's letters had told her about life working on a luxury yacht. Poor Misty, the wide-eyed country mouse, did everything wrong at first, the other cabin crew animals were mean, and she nearly left for home. But then Captain Rat gave her another chance, and, in the end, her country baking impressed the crew. Wil didn't care so much about the story, but she turned back through the pages, poring over the drawings, searching for a memory of this book. Had her mother ever read it to her? If not, then why not? Maybe she'd just been too young to remember.

In a fit of wanting, she texted Kate: *Did you know Mum wrote picture books?*

Kate responded only half a minute later: *She did?*

Wil texted back: *Misty Mouse Goes to Sea? The Fairy of the Dark Wood?*

She changed screens, looking for the other titles to send, but Kate's reply beat her. *Oh, those.*

Wil felt a tug of annoyance. Kate knew. *Did she read them to us?*

This time, Kate didn't reply. After three minutes, Wil gave a frustrated sigh. She wouldn't find out if something had just come up, or if Kate was ignoring the question. Her sister had a habit of dropping conversations and never returning to them.

'That's a serious face.'

Wil looked up to find David standing over her. 'Just waiting for my sister to reply. I don't think she's going to.'

'Is this where I share my experiences of sibling friction?' he said. 'Because I have three of them.'

Wil stifled her laugh. 'Me too. An older sister and two younger half-brothers.'

'Well, aren't we a matched set,' he whispered. 'The librarian said they don't have any others in the catalogue, and she was surprised to learn Anne Elston was a local author. I guess there's not much of a lead there.'

Wil flicked to the title page and took a photo of the publisher information. 'Couldn't hurt to email them, I guess.'

'You want me to ask the research team to follow that up?' David offered. 'Then we can spend all day tomorrow in the cottage.'

'That sounds like a misuse of your budget,' she said, knowing she didn't want anyone else making those calls. 'And I do need to spend some time preparing for my next meeting with Lord Particular.'

Chapter 20

A s Wil approached the manor gates, she reflected on how much could happen in forty-eight hours. Since that first kiss with David, her life seemed transformed. She'd never felt so settled. They'd spent most of the previous day in his bedroom, content to be together. When they hadn't been in bed, she'd worked on her concepts from the window seat overlooking the fens, and he'd taken calls sitting against the headboard. Far from being distracting, his voice in the background had been soothing as she worked. When he'd hung up calls, he'd come to kiss her and tell her he liked seeing her in his shirt. By the third time, it was a joke. She'd worn it all day anyway. In the early evening they'd meandered all down the line of the beck, from the manor wall through the village, and then to the road until they'd stood before the wood. There, under a rock, Wil had left a little copy she'd done of her mother's drawing of the two girls in the wood. A belated memorial to both Susie and her mother. And David had silently held her hand all the way back.

In a bubble of his affection, she'd never felt less worried about potential mistakes. She wasn't even nervous today. Maybe Lord Elston would like what she had done, maybe he wouldn't. But she liked it, and that seemed to mean something.

She found him in the same place, at that beaten kitchen table, this time with an ancient accounting calculator and a pencil stuck over his ear, as though he might be doing his taxes.

'Miss Rambler,' he said. 'What do you have for me today?'

'I thought a lot about what you said,' Wil began. 'And I think to truly make the kitchen a reflection of the estate, of the land and the history, we need to bring the outside in. So . . .'

She slid out the large drawing, which resembled more a fantasy scape than a kitchen. 'I want to reuse that cabinet as the frame for a central island, and build the top from the recovered timbers of the old kitchen. Strip back all the layers of paint to the wood underneath. With all that natural timber as a base, we take wall tile colours from the wood's forest tones. In the room corners, we create custom tiles to build the look of trunks and roots. The high north wall will create a frame for a painted mural based on the three village drawings. And to echo that, behind the range, which we'll place inside the hearth, we'll have painted tiles that look like stained glass, representing the wood, the beck and the church. I want to mute the tones though, so that it doesn't look overdone against the mural. I've included the Roman coin motif around the arch of the hearth, but that could come out if it's overdone. I've put other touches into the carved ends of the cabinet frames, like the church tower shape, here, and the shape of the village road from the air, here. Those would need custom carving, which would be expensive, but I like the idea that there would be details you wouldn't notice at first.'

Wil took a breath and looked at his face. 'Or, if that's all massively overdone, we could pare it back.'

She stopped talking, not knowing how to read his expression. He reached for a set of bifocals, which he perched on his nose. Finally, he dropped the sheet.

'Yes, good.'

'I'm sorry?'

'Good. You're familiar with the word?'

'So, you like this?'

'That's generally what "good" means. Do you not like it?'

'I like it very much. I just wasn't expecting you to.'

Lord Elston's considerable eyebrows rose. 'But you brought it anyway. Gutsy.'

'Or stupid. I'm told they're closely related.'

Lord Elston laughed, which sounded somewhere between a bark and a bray. 'Someone once told me that most bravery was just stupidity that turned out well.'

Wil snorted. 'Sounds like something my mother would say.'

'That right?'

Before she could say anything else, Lord Elston was up and gathering the sketches. 'I'll make copies. Then we can move on to plans and finding the contractors. I have a good man who's done work here before—I'll set up a meeting.'

'Lord Elston?'

'Mmm?' He paused, one hand on the banister of the stairs.

'If you're happy with this, what about contacting John? To see if he would talk to me?'

'Yes, of course,' he said, but then disappeared, leaving Wil with the distinct impression he had no intention at all of reaching out to his brother. When he finally came creaking back down the stairs, she was compelled to try again.

'I'm sorry to keep asking,' she said. 'But I need to talk to anyone who might have had contact with my mother in the last months of her life. It's really important.'

'My brother is a complicated man, Miss Rambler,' he said. 'But come back for the next meeting, and I will see if I can get you what you need.'

With that, Wil had to be content.

⌒

'I just have this feeling he doesn't want to talk to his brother at all,' she said to David later.

'There must be a reason John's hiding out in Jamaica,' David said. 'We never did manage to make any contact ourselves, but we didn't press the point because we're interested in the church more than the family situation. I don't go chasing people still living. The show really isn't a melodrama.' He sighed. 'So, what's the next move—London?'

Wil put a circle around *Bridget* on the research plan, and crossed her fingers under the table. 'Yes. London it is.'

⌒

They caught the train down the next morning, rolling into King's Cross in the early afternoon and out into the throngs of the station. After the quiet slowness of South Bandinby, Wil felt under assault just from the sheer number of people. Only David, holding her hand the whole time, pulled her through.

'Last chance for a Harry Potter photo,' he said, as they made it outside the terminal. 'Isn't that what tourists do here?'

'Normal tourists,' Wil said. 'Not ones on weird missions to discover long-lost letters while in the company of attractive ex-footballers.'

He grinned at her, which was all the sunshine she needed. Otherwise, the weather was in a mood again, the sky concrete grey and threatening to wring rain down at any moment. The pavement was crawling with people hauling luggage into black cabs, but David strode off down the row towards a dark unmarked sedan.

'Afternoon, Mr Hunter,' said the driver as they slid into the back. He had an accent that could have been carbon-copied from Wil's father. 'To Alma Street, then?'

'Yes, thanks, Graham.'

'Any trouble with the autograph hunters at the station?'

David shook his head. 'I think it was too busy for anyone to notice. Had more in Lincoln.'

'*Graham?*' Wil mouthed, feeling weirdly out of depth. She'd imagined taking a cab.

'Graham's our studio driver in London,' David said. 'We'll drop the bags at the house, then he can take you on to World's End. Sorry I can't come with you, I'm being dragged into a production meeting.'

'Don't sound like you don't enjoy it, because I know you do,' Wil said. 'I'm still getting over the fact that you have a house in London.'

David shrugged. 'Back when I was playing it was near enough to the stadium. I liked it. Never thought about selling it.'

Half an hour later, as they walked through the bright yellow door of a neat brick terrace house, Wil thought that 'I liked it' didn't quite capture the essence of David's London house. The lower level was open plan all the way to large windows at the back, the dark green-grey walls setting off an eclectic mix of modern and antique furniture: a patchwork sofa, a sixties easy chair in lime-green, a heavy wooden coffee table with the top a single section of trunk with the bark still on. The glass was triple-glazed, the living room built-ins stuffed with books, and the kitchen was all sleek stainless steel beneath framed baking product ads from the fifties. In the dining room, a huge photo of David playing for England dominated the wall, catching him from a dashing angle as he drove forward with the ball. The whole thing was classy and unique without being overdone; exactly the kind of taste that she'd seen in wealthy people's houses back home. She was used to working in such places, not staying in them.

'I have that there to please my dad,' David said, nodding at the photo. 'I really don't like to eat looking at my glory days when I was young and attractive, if that's what you're thinking.'

Wil studied the picture. 'Actually, I was thinking you look better now.' When he didn't say anything, she glanced around and caught such a look of devotion in his eyes that she was sure she'd imagined it.

'Bedroom's upstairs,' he said. 'I'll take your bag.'

The bedroom had the same grey-green wall behind the bed, a shaggy white rug over the slate-grey stained floor and an enormous four-poster. Oh, and a private terrace overlooking the first-floor garden and the streets of Kentish Town.

David looked at none of it. He slid his arm around her, brushing her hair aside to kiss her neck. 'I changed my mind about that meeting,' he said. 'I can be late.'

'And what will Graham think?' Wil said, pulling away. Something about this house was making her feel uncomfortable.

'Who cares?' David mumbled into her neck.

'I can't ride all the way across London with him if he's thinking about whether I was just in bed with you.'

David let her go with a considering frown, then pulled her hand. Wil didn't have enough time to react before she stumbled and, with a shriek of surprise, fell into the pillowy soft mattress with him.

'There,' he said, pushing himself up on his arm. 'You were in bed with me. Now go get your things before I try to convince you to stay here.'

'Smartarse.' Wil socked him with a throw pillow embroidered with a surrealist double-decker bus and got up. She trotted downstairs and collected her backpack and took another gawp at the house. It felt surreal, too, like that out-of-focus bus on the pillow. Graham was still waiting outside, leaning against the sedan like a secret service agent.

She went back up the stairs to say goodbye. 'David? What did Graham mean by trouble with autograph hunters?'

He looked up from where he was sprawled like a starfish on the bed. Someone could photograph him just like that and use it to sell whatever product they tacked on the bottom.

'The studio doesn't like me walking around on my own in London,' he said.

'Why?'

'Some fans are a bit ... intense. More so in London. It's not a problem.'

'Oh. Okay,' she said, though she didn't really understand what he meant. Maybe he missed a critical kick sometime in his soccer career and some people still held a grudge about it. Or maybe he had a few rabid fans who hadn't accepted his career had ended. She knew soccer fans could be demented like that.

'Thought you didn't want Graham thinking we were shagging like rabbits,' he said a moment later, when she still hadn't gone.

'Going,' she said, heading for the stairs.

'Enjoy the brutalist architecture!' he called after her.

'Whatever that means,' she shouted back, and she could still hear him laughing as she reached the front door.

⌒

Despite its significance, World's End was a surprisingly tiny shop. David had told her how it had been a centre for punk fashion, back in the day, and launched the career of Vivienne Westwood. And yet, it was nestled next to an Oxfam store on an unassuming street, its front dominated by an oversized clock with the hands running in reverse at a rather frenetic pace.

'Weirdly appropriate,' Wil muttered, as she thanked Graham and stepped out of the car. Of course her journey in peeling back the years through her mother's letters would lead to a store emblematic of turning back time.

She swallowed as she noticed at least two touristy groups taking photos of the shopfront. The poor staff of the famous store were probably overwhelmed with annoyances every day and would think she was a time-waster if she just got straight to her point. So, with trembling butterflies, Wil pushed open the front door. She sensed eyes turn in her direction, but she was quickly distracted by the items on display.

She saw tartans, stripes and T-shirts. Dresses and boots and amazing combinations of prints and shapes. She was gently examining the drape of a deep green tartan shirt when someone said, 'Great choice. You shopping for yourself?'

Wil looked around to find a smiling girl in smoky eye make-up with a fifties blunt fringe. 'Sort of,' she said. 'I just liked the look of this.'

'Mmm-hmm,' the girl agreed. 'It would be perfect with those jeans you have on. Like to try it?'

'Ah . . . sure.' *Now would be the time to ask.* But Wil didn't. Instead, she went to the dressing-room, feeling even more committed to having to make a purchase. She nearly died when she saw the price tag. It was gorgeous but it would be the last of Colin's money. She hated herself for then admiring it in the mirror, as if she really was considering buying it.

'It's really lovely,' she said, biting her lip when she emerged from changing and deciding she really must be brave. 'I'm just . . . I really came in because I'm trying to find out about someone who worked here.'

'Oh?' said the girl. She didn't seem annoyed. 'Who is it? I've been here awhile.'

'Not recently. Around 1980, actually. Bridget Spencer? She was a friend of my mother's and I'm trying to find her.'

The girl's eyes widened, all white inside her smoky lids. 'Wow, that's an age ago. I wouldn't know anything about it. Bridget, you said?'

'Yes. Bridget Spencer. I know I'm probably hoping for a bit much.'

The girl shrugged. 'Look, I'll be honest, lots of people come in who remember the store from back then. But maybe that's a good thing. Actually . . .' She screwed up her face for a second, thinking. 'There's something about that name, though. Hey, Ronny?'

Another woman came in from the back of the store, rocking a mohawk of grey miniature buns.

'Does the name Bridget Spencer mean anything to you? She worked here in the eighties.'

'When it was still called Seditionaries,' Wil added. 'I'm trying to find where she might be now.'

'Bridget Spencer? Bridget, Bridget . . .' Ronny said, clucking her tongue. 'Why does that sound familiar? . . . Wait, you couldn't mean Bridget McClaren?'

The other girl snapped her fingers. 'That's who I was thinking of!'

'Who's that?' Wil asked.

'She works at the V&A as a fashion curator,' said Ronny. 'She came in a month or two ago, looking for ideas for a new exhibition. I wasn't here but there was an article about her a few days later. Jen brought it in and pinned it up, and I think the piece said she used to work here, way back in the early days. I think she left a card. Somewhere.' She disappeared into the back of the store.

Wil could hardly believe it. 'But she's Bridget McClaren?'

'Maybe she changed her name,' said the girl.

'Here we are,' said Ronny. 'I can't find the card, but here's the article.'

She handed over a printout from a magazine site, showing a woman with long flowing hair standing beside a mannequin wearing a leather jacket. The piece was a profile of Victoria and Albert Museum curator Bridget McClaren, titled 'From Punk to Retrospectives'. Wil took a photo of it, gushing thanks.

'Our pleasure,' said the girl. 'Now, what are you thinking about that shirt?'

~

'That looks like success,' Graham said kindly when Wil piled back into the car with a shopping bag twenty minutes later.

'That depends,' she said. 'If you didn't intend to buy anything, is it really a success?'

He chuckled. 'Mr Hunter sent his apologies that the meetings are probably going to run long, but that I can take you wherever you want to go.'

'How far's the Victoria and Albert Museum?'

'About ten minutes north.'

Wil brightened. 'Okay. Let me just step out a minute. I need to make a call.'

Later, she wasn't sure why she really needed to get out of the car to make the call. Probably because she didn't want Graham overhearing. If she did happen to get through to Bridget, and it *was* Bridget Spencer, she didn't want to be having conversations that could touch on the intimate details of her mother's life with someone listening in.

The call took a while. She waited on hold with the V&A, before being transferred to the Clothworker's Centre, where she had to explain a second time that, no, she didn't want to apply to view a collection, she wanted to contact Bridget McClaren.

As she waited, Wil noticed a man leaning against the wall a little down the street. She turned away from him, and when she looked back he had disappeared. The next thing she knew, a woman had come up beside her and said, 'Here, can you just hold this for a sec?'

Wil was completely bamboozled to be handed a lit cigarette.

'I'm on the phone,' she said, but she'd already taken the fag to stop it falling on the ground. The woman dug around in her bag, as if she'd lost her keys. Wil only had a second to think how bizarre this was before she realised someone was pointing a camera at her. *Snap, snap.* She heard the shutter churning through exposures. *What the . . . ?*

Then as if fag lady had found whatever was in her bag, she reached for the cigarette and with a big fake smile said, 'Thanks,' and took off. Time came to a stop, as if the clock above World's End had finally wound back to zero.

Wil could hear someone from the V&A, far away, saying, 'Hello? Hello?' but the man with the camera was still silently taking shots. Why was he doing that? All Wil could think was that someone had made a massive mistake.

Next thing, Graham appeared around the car. 'Go'orn, push off,' he said, standing between the photographer and Wil. 'That's enough. Get in the car, Miss.'

He wasn't messing around. Wil had heard that voice in the movies, used by secret service suits who were in the line of fire. She managed to fumble her way back into the car, cringing as the photographer dived back in to shoot through the glass.

Graham piled in and the car lurched away from the kerb like they had just pulled a bank robbery.

'What was that all about?' Wil said, trying to pull her seatbelt into place. Some kind of alarm was going off because it wasn't done up. But she was yanking on it so hard the spool lock kept snapping on. She forced herself to breathe. And pull it down, slowly. *Click.* Shock finally caught up to her then, and her hands started shaking.

'Photographers,' Graham said. 'Take anything they think they can sell.'

'But why did that woman give me that cigarette?' Wil pressed a hand to her head. She was *not* the fainting type. She could handle a nail gun, for god's sake.

'I'll take you back to the house, Miss,' Graham said. 'And I'll let Mr Hunter know.'

Chapter 21

When he finally got away from his meetings, David came running in the front door. Actually *running*. As if the building were on fire.

By then, Wil had had long enough to process—and a good enough drink from his well-stocked cabinet—to pretend she was largely over it. The whole incident had been so strange it was like a bad dream, which was now fading.

'What happened?' he asked, nearly skidding to a halt.

Wil looked up at him, a little bleary. Maybe she'd had one vodka too many. 'I found Bridget McClaren,' she said. 'I mean, she might not be Bridget Spencer, but it seems too much of a coincidence. Only by the time we got back here and I'd had a few of these cocktails, the V&A was closed and so I have to wait until morning to call them again.'

He raked a hand through his hair, looking wretched. 'I mean, what happened with the photographer?'

'I don't want to go over it all again, okay?'

'Did they ask you anything?'

'No,' she said, then brightened. 'Maybe they thought I was some model. I did just buy a two hundred pound shirt, mostly against my will.'

David sat on the couch, his gaze floating up to the ceiling, as if sorting ten different thoughts into their proper order. 'Okay. We're going back north tomorrow morning. Don't ever talk to those people, Mina. I'm sorry that happened. I didn't think you'd have a problem with them.'

'Someone's going to explain who they are, right? The way Graham and you are going on, I'm guessing the Illuminati?'

A little smile ghosted the edge of his lips, but vodka glow and defensive humour aside, it didn't really feel funny. From the moment she'd set foot in this beautiful house, it seemed she'd blundered into a world she knew nothing about, where she didn't belong. It was a far worse version of the doubt she'd felt back when David had first kissed her. And now there were photographers, and some backstory involving David that she sensed she didn't want to know about.

'Close,' he said. 'Paparazzi.'

'The people who take photos of celebrity cellulite on the beach and topless royals? Why would they want a photo of me?'

'I don't know.'

She waited, expecting him to make some guess, to fill her in. But he got up and made a drink for himself. She could feel him shut down on her, the same way her mother had described her father doing over John.

'We weren't going back north until tomorrow night,' she said finally.

'Production wants to re-shoot some overlay for the first episode of the next season tomorrow,' he said, standing at the window with his drink, 'so I'd have to go anyway. The location is up near York. I don't want to leave you here on your own. I'd be happier if we went back to the village for now.'

Wil didn't like the feeling of him telling her where she should go, especially because she wouldn't be able to follow through with Bridget. But she also wasn't keen to go out in the streets again.

Still, the next day, returning down the looping village lane felt like a defeat, especially after one of the studio's security men had ridden in the train with them. She'd called the V&A again to be told that Bridget was away on holiday, which annoyed her further. She could only leave a message and wait. Always waiting. The mood between her and David was arctic.

As they walked up the cottage path, Wil could hear the pressure to talk about what was going on wedged into every step.

So when David opened the cottage door, and there was an envelope resting on the mat, Wil could only stare at it, feeling flat and uncertain. She was as unprepared for more big news as she could imagine.

David was staring at it, too. His arm came briefly around her shoulders. Too briefly. 'I'll make tea,' he said.

⌒

Dear Mina,

Happy 26th birthday, my darling girl. Last I left off we had finally settled on the Gold Coast, and Kate was a baby. I was still drawing, chafing under the restrictions of motherhood and wifedom. Among all that, two important things happened in 1988. One was that Cameron and I separated for the first time. The other was that Thomas, Lord Elston, died.

'Wait, what?'

Wil sat bolt upright in the chair by the hearth, glancing at David, who raised a questioning hand from the kitchen. Wil held up a finger, diving back into the letter.

As I said before, I've debated a long time whether to tell you this part of the story, because it isn't really my secret to tell. Beyond John himself, I had no real intimacy with the Elston family and I never sought it. I didn't want the approval of people who would never have approved of me. But if I don't tell you this part, then what comes later will not make any sense.

Not that it made immediate sense to me at the time. It was John himself who sent the telegram. I've received two telegrams in my life, and both of them were about funerals. I'm not sure that makes up for not receiving one from the Queen. John's telegram didn't actually tell me what had happened, he just asked me to call him immediately and sent the number.

Of course I called him. I hadn't had any contact with him since the wake for Susie nearly two years before and I knew something awful must have happened. Maybe with little Henry. But it was that phone call that really put the nails in between me and Cameron.

Things had been rocky between us for weeks, his temper short. Not that he expressed it. He tended to stew, keeping all that frustration boiling away inside him. Every contractor who messed up a job, every client late to pay, every stray drawing of mine in the house that got in his way, or pencil shavings under his feet—all that added to the fire. Sometimes he would come home, eat a silent cold dinner and go straight back out again. I never knew where he went—probably driving down to sit by the beach with a six-pack—coming back near midnight smelling of beer and resignation. In laying out some of Cameron's faults, I don't mean to imply I had none. I absolutely did. I often made his life more difficult and was probably as unbending as he was. And I often didn't think about what I was doing or saying before it was done or said. That was just how it was then.

So when I told Cameron that I had to go back to the UK for a funeral again, all of that boiled over, and he told me not to bother coming back.

Of course, some of that reaction came from the way I handled it. I wouldn't tell him whose funeral it was or where I was going. John had explicitly asked me to come but that, if I did, I was to tell no one. Now, such prohibitions against telling aren't ironclad in a marriage. Many a secret has been shared with a husband or wife, even if it is meant not to be spoken. If the men had been in opposite places, I would have told John everything. But that in itself was the problem—my relationship with John was far older than my relationship with Cameron. It had deep roots in my childhood, in the pivotal experiences that had made me who I was. In many ways, I felt a loyalty to him far beyond the one I had for my husband, especially at a time when I thought my husband was behaving like a jerk.

And so, I kept John's secret. I left Australia with Kate, and made my way to Lincoln without telling a soul where I was going. William picked me up at the station and took me back to the manor house, where I stayed for the only time in my life. The funeral was closed, held in the old stable chapel on the grounds and not in the church.

Until I actually reached the village, I hadn't understood why it was being done this way. I even wondered if it was some elaborate ruse to escape the death taxes that John's father had been preoccupied with.

The truth was sadder and stranger—an intersection of pride and ridiculous ideas. I've told you before that Thomas was long rumoured to have an 'alternative lifestyle', a polite way of saying he was gay. The last time I'd seen him at Susie's funeral, when he'd barely made an appearance, I'd had a passing thought of how ill he looked. But I'd seen so little of him, I'd thought no more about it. Now I learned he had been sick for a long time, that he'd had AIDS, a fact that the Dowager Lady Elston had refused to acknowledge.

John told me that the two of them trading places began as a mistake, when someone else thought he was Thomas, and John hadn't corrected them. Thomas was a recluse so no one even in the village had seen him much in years. They only remembered how he'd looked as a teenager in church, and then mostly from behind. The two of them really did look awfully alike—especially when they were younger—which was how I'd confused them in London that time. So John had already taken on Thomas's role in the past couple of years as the steward of the estate, even before Susie passed, and they'd fabricated a rumour of a conflict between the pair of them to explain the family keeping a low profile.

Susie's death provided a cover to make the swap complete. Everyone knew John had gone to Jamaica, so he simply 'remained there' while 'Thomas' finally grew up and took on his responsibilities, though in a quiet way. In reality, John became Thomas, Lord Elston, and began brushing his hair like Thomas and wearing his clothes. The family were so burned over the press interest in John after Susie's death, I suppose it made a perverse kind of sense. The dowager would not leave the way open for the tabloids to write stories about her gay son who had died of the dreaded gay disease. The family would rather commit a fraud than admit that sort of truth.

These are the kinds of secrets, the kinds of awful taboos, that trap people. John never wanted to be Baron Elston, and now he was not only stuck with the job, but under someone else's name. In some ways I think he started being more visible, hoping that someone would notice and call attention to the lie, but, to this day, no one has.

I was horribly sad for him, even in the turmoil of my own marriage imploding. The only thing that pleased me was seeing the small ways that he had begun to push back against the establishment that was caging him. Like having me, a friend, stay in the manor house. No one could stop him despite the fact that everyone there—especially the dowager—thought I ranked on par with the lint in the bottom of their pockets.

I strangely didn't care. I'd gone to support John, and I knew that I was perhaps now the only friend he had in the *world, or at least the only one who had seen the long arc of his life. I was there for him, and no one else.*

I stayed for as short a time as I was able. The longer I remained, the more likely I'd be seen and questions raised about why I was there. Kate wasn't much of a crier, but it was difficult to keep only to the house while we were there.

I came back to Australia on a chilly winter night, after being gone barely a week, and to my intense surprise found Cameron waiting at the airport. At the time, my first thought was that he'd saved us from begging a bed from a friend for the night. That thought was perhaps telling . . . I was more relieved for Kate's comfort than for the hope it might signal for our marriage. But I was still glad to hear his apologies. Glad to hear he wanted to set things right between us. Everything in South Bandinby seemed more remote from me than ever. John had been my last true link to the place. And now he'd taken a path I didn't entirely understand. And so, I put him behind me.

Maybe by the time you read this, someone will have come to their senses and the whole lie will have been cleared up. John will be Baron Elston in his own right . . . but somehow I suspect not. The Elstons dig in. They commit to their purpose. How else do you have an unbroken line of them all the way back to the Middle Ages? If John is still alive, I bet he is still walking around in Thomas's name.

One of the reasons I left it very late in these letters to write down this secret is that I do not know what you will do with it. Perhaps nothing—after all, who is John Elston to you? But maybe you will feel something strong, that he is wrong somehow.

All I can say is that, as I come to the end of my life, I find myself forgiving John for being the man he is, and the man he was.

The village shaped both of us, but in very different ways. And we shaped each other—for the better, I think. I never went back to England after that, and I never saw John again. And that's a sadness that I carry with me. But I had been carrying him with me for so long it was almost—although not quite—the same as having him with me.

When I begin the next letter, though, I want to leave these sad things of mine behind and talk about you and Kate and me, and the precious years we spent together, which were the greatest joy of my life.

Until then, be brave, my darling girl.

Love,

    Mum

                                                                         ~

Wil sat staring at the pages until she became aware of David sitting across from her, waiting.

'Something happened,' he said, quite needlessly. Wil was sure that she must look the most surprised she had in her entire life, even more than when she'd been arrested. Of all the things her mother might have revealed, she hadn't been expecting that Lord Elston was John, the very man that she had been wanting to contact the entire time she'd been in the village.

She wanted to blurt this out, to ask David whether he'd known. Because surely, with a team of researchers, they must have unearthed *something*—a death certificate, a rumour . . .

but a rare qualm stopped her. This wasn't just about her mother anymore. If it was true, then the lie was being played on a grand scale. Not the kind of thing you reveal lightly to a man who works in television, even if you thought you might be falling— Wil cut that idea right off. What mattered was that her own mother had been unsure about revealing it in a private letter. So Wil couldn't just say it to anyone.

Her phone buzzed with a message. She ignored it.

'I didn't realise my parents split up when my sister was a baby,' she said, trying it as an explanation.

The look on David's face made it clear he was expecting something else, but he didn't make an issue of it. Wil returned to her churning thoughts. Did Rose Maxwell know? She didn't seem to. But then, she'd been tight-lipped on other things, and she was related to John by marriage. Could Bill know, maybe through rumours passed from his predecessors? He'd worked at the house for a decade.

Wil flipped back through the pages, mulling.

The real point was that one person certainly knew: Lord Elston himself.

All his caginess about contacting John made sense now. How long would he have gone on exploiting that, while deliberately holding back?

A fire caught under Wil's heart, fuelled with the deception. And burning in it too was that old memory of grief and running that she couldn't name. The same one that had come up when she was fighting with her father, and then again at Middle Bandinby. She clenched her fists through a wave of muddy grief and terrible anger. When her phone buzzed again, she flipped it over with too much force.

'Mina,' David said. 'What's going on?'

'I . . .' She stood, her gaze darting out the windows, across the duck pond and up over the church to the manor house. She had to leave, or she would tell him. And she had to see Lord Elston. She grabbed up all the letters as she went for the door.

'I have to go,' she called. 'I have to . . .'

She never finished the sentence. She barely stopped to force her feet into her beaten trainers, oblivious to David calling out to her to wait. Then she was running up the lane, under the boughs of the estate trees, and to the closed iron gate.

⌒

'He's not here, Miss Wilhelmina. He don't see people outside of appointments.'

Bill's eyes were wide with alarm. He stood back from the gate two whole metres, as if she were some kind of rabid animal. Wil had her hands wrapped around the iron bars, hoarse after calling 'Hello!' into the manor grounds for a solid minute. David could probably hear her all the way down at the church cottage. She forced herself to lower her voice, to be calmer than she felt.

'But I really need to talk to him,' Wil said. 'About . . . the kitchen. Yes, the design. I've run into a . . . serious problem.'

Well, that was convincing. She didn't at all sound like an out-of-breath crazy person, trying to gain admission into a noble estate house without an invitation.

But Bill's shoulders dropped a fraction. 'There now, Miss. That'll not be a worry. Plenty of time for the kitchen. You know it's been in that state for years. His Lordship isn't in a rush, he told me that himself.'

I'll bet he isn't. Wil stepped back, feeling helpless, hopeless. What could she possibly say to sway this sweet old man?

'Bill,' she said, then took a deep breath, desperate to keep a rein on what she would say. This was risky. 'Would it surprise you if I told you that John Elston isn't living in Jamaica?'

Bill's face remained impassive. A little too impassive for someone who didn't know anything. 'Oh?' he said.

'And that he never did live in Jamaica. And that over thirty years ago, there was a secret funeral here that explains why.'

Bill glanced away, over the manicured ponds to the side of the manor drive, to the thick-trunked oaks and sycamores that guarded the grounds from the ridge road. Then he stepped forward and pulled the gate open. 'I hope you know what you're doing, Miss,' he said. 'You'll find His Lordship by the beck. Follow the wall, that way.'

Wil thanked him, but there was fear in the old man's eyes. She glanced back once and found him watching her, as though imploring her not to do anything stupid. Trouble was, stupid was what she specialised in. She couldn't stop herself. She strode on down the boundary wall, towards the corner of the estate where the beck cut through the grounds and then under the wall before flowing on to the village.

She had never been to this part of the stream. When she and David had walked the length of it, they'd started below, where the wall was too high to see over. Now, through the trees planted along the banks, she spotted Lord Elston. He was in waders among the reeds crowding the water's edge, a bucket by his foot and fishing pole in hand. Over the noise of the flowing water he didn't hear her approach.

When she froze, he looked around suddenly, surprise in his expression changing to recognition.

'I certainly hope you didn't scale the wall,' he said.

'Are you John?'

Oh lord, she'd just blurted it out.

'I beg your pardon?' He seemed genuinely confused, and cupped a hand around his ear.

'Are you John?'

She said it louder, too loud, her impatience packed between the words.

He certainly heard this time. The question seemed to unbalance him, his foot sliding into a stumble as he turned in the water. She thought he would fall, but he righted himself, then made a show of hauling his feet onto the bank.

'Now I can hear better,' he said, seeming recovered and coming closer. 'Now what's this about my brother John?'

'You,' she said, out of breath with dread. 'You *are* your brother John. Thomas, Lord Elston, died in 1988.'

He laughed. 'David Hunter has been spinning stories.'

Wil pulled the stack of letters from her pocket. She'd crumpled them in her haste. 'Do you know what these are? My mother wrote me letters before she died. About her life. About her relationship with John Elston, and how he broke her heart more than once. And how in 1988, she came back to this village for a secret funeral for his brother, who he then pretended to be. Which is you. John Elston.'

They stared each other down. Wil felt as though seasons passed through that moment, with the leaves drifting between them paling like snowflakes, the tension strong enough to pull the truth right out of the long-buried past. She knew she was right.

'You knew my mother,' she said, when he didn't respond. 'So, you must have sent me these letters. She said she left them in a place only you and she knew about.'

Wil held out the letters as evidence, daring him to deny his identity before her mother's words on the paper.

Presently, he did take them. He unfolded the topmost sheets on the bundle, the last letter she had read. She saw the curving script of her mother's letters in the dappled sunlight, saw his eyes drop to move over those words.

'I can't believe it,' Wil blurted, over the rushing hum of the beck. 'All the time! Why didn't you . . . I don't know! Pretend to call from Jamaica, or something?'

He said nothing. He just stood, rigid as iron, moving through the pages. One, then another. And another. The light shifted over her mother's words as he did.

'I mean, I would never tell anyone, but after you promised to get in touch with your brother for the kitchen, you wouldn't have had to—'

'Your mother was a fantasist.'

His words cut her cold. 'What?'

The pages were moving fast through his hands now, a flip book desperate to reach its end. 'These are the ravings of an ill person, a storyteller. Nothing more.'

'You don't mean that,' Wil said, but a split had formed in her conviction.

'Where did you get these?' he asked. 'Where?'

The last word was a roar that said *danger*. Wil knew then that he hadn't sent them. 'I . . .'

'Is this why I found you snooping around in my fields?' He squared towards her in his waders, holding the letters up like incriminating evidence. 'And climbing over my walls?'

Wil had the thought then to take the letters back, and that it had been stupid to give them to him. She thought it a moment before his hands shifted, and he ripped the pages in two.

The tearing sound cut across the water, setting a pair of ducks into noisy flight. Wil had only time to feel a primal horror, as if he had reached into her chest and torn out her heart, and then he flung the pages out into the beck. For an awful second, the paper fluttered down through the light, and then bobbed on the surface like a battle-scarred armada, before the current grabbed them and the pages all tipped over the weir beneath the estate wall.

'What did you do!' Wil screamed, leaping out into the water. But she was too late. They were gone, on their way down the beck to the fens. The current was swift out in the middle, and she fell to her waist, then had to slog back to the stony edge to avoid being knocked over. By that time, all she could see was the ramrod line of Lord Elston's departing back, already halfway across the meadow. She flopped down into the water, howling fat tears that made the light into a blinding haze.

The letters were gone.

The only real, tangible link she had to her mother was gone.

Chapter 22

Bill was the one who found her, still in the water and soaked to her armpits, shaking with cold and incoherent with grief. She had no idea how long she'd sat there.

'Here now, Miss,' he said, wading over the pebbles in sensible wellington boots. Wil could only sniffle and flail. In the process of stumbling up, she knocked Bill's flat cap into the water, and it soon disappeared under the wall as well.

'I'm so sorry,' she cried, feeling despicably awful. He seemed so much older and vulnerable with his wispy hair exposed. 'Your hat!'

'It's no mind, Miss,' he said. 'I've another.'

Once she made it up onto the bank, Bill guided her back across the meadow. She expected to be turned out at the gate. However kind Bill might be, she knew she wouldn't get away with pissing off the lord of the manor.

But to her surprise, Bill guided her up the drive and towards the house.

'*No way*,' she said, pulling back. 'Just let me out the gate.'

She was not going to face off with Lord Elston again after what he'd just done. She wanted to march straight back to the church cottage and throw the precious kitchen designs into the beck, too.

'His Lordship's gone off in the Land Rover,' Bill said, still gently pressuring her elbow. 'You're soaked through. Come and dry yourself, and have a cup of tea.'

So Wil went, as much because she didn't want to explain herself to David. Bill took her to the gamekeeper's cottage behind the big house. Its northern stones were blotched with lichens, and inside, the neat room smelled of leather and oil. Bill pulled a rough wooden chair out from a desk and handed her a towel that smelled of horses. He set a kettle on the range.

'I suppose I ought to have warned you,' Bill said, as the kettle began to growl. 'But it didn't seem my place. I didn't think he'd upset you so.'

Wil sniffed, and pulled the towel tighter around her shoulders. The shivering had stopped, but the ice in her chest was frozen in. She put her head in her hands. 'This is all my fault.'

'Come now, Miss, you only brought an unpleasant truth that's none of your doing.'

'No, I mean, I shouldn't have given him the letters. Then he couldn't have ripped them up and thrown them in the river. They were the only thing I had left of my mother.' Her voice broke. 'I only just got them, and now they're gone!'

Bill's cup was trembling a little in its saucer. He set it down. 'What, all of them?'

Wil mistook his question at first, and began explaining about the letters she'd received from her mother, when abruptly she caught up. 'It was you.'

The kettle whistled, and Bill moved it off the range, pouring the water into a chipped teapot. 'Aye,' he said softly. 'It were me what sent them.'

Wil sat up, wet clothes forgotten. 'How . . . I mean, why would—? I don't understand.'

Bill smiled gently. 'You are so much like her, you know that, Miss? She'd get all tangled up with her words just like that, and couldn't get anything out if she were overexcited or afraid, or whatever it was.'

'But how is it possible you knew her? You've only been here ten years.'

Bill poured the tea out into mugs. 'Aye, Miss. That's what everyone thinks. Truth is, I came to this house when I started working, before His Lordship was even born. I learned my trade here, and I would have worked here all my life if it wasn't for the troubles back in '86. After Suzannah, God rest her, I took a long spell up north. Lord Thomas didn't want a gamekeeper, and there was naught to do in Jamaica. But then came '88. John wanted me back for the funeral, so he could trust who was here. After that though, I went back north again, until a ten-year back, when I looked different enough to return quietly, like. Now, I don't like being untruthful about having been here before, but I've been with His Lordship since he were a little'un, and I'd do anything he asked. He'd had enough trouble.'

'But . . . William was old even back then!' Wil said. 'Rose called you "old William".'

'Aye, she means "old" compared to me, Bill, the *new* William,' he said, with a chuckle. 'So as people know which one's meant.'

'Oh.'

'I remember Miss Ann so well. She wasn't someone you missed noticing. She had a real spark about her, and His Lordship was dotty about her from when they were children.' He heaved a sigh. 'And didn't that all turn out terribly, for both of them, really. Well, how could it turn out elseways?'

He set the mugs on the desk for both of them, then raised his hands up to heaven.

'So it *is* true then?' Wil asked.

'What is?'

'That Lord Elston is John, not Thomas. He said my mother was a fantasist.'

He hesitated. 'Yes, Miss. I didn't know Ann had told you as much in those letters, but she knew. One of the few who did.'

'You didn't read the letters?'

He looked horrified. 'They weren't mine to read. I held those in trust, and I was fair confused what to do with them, 'specially as Ann's instructions were so specific.'

'What did she say?'

'Well, to place them in that spot in the church. But you were supposed to come to the village years ago for them. Ann thought so, anyways. She seemed so certain you would. But you didn't, and I thought maybe you'd decided you didn't want whatever was in them, or something had happened to you. Then Mr Hunter arrived and started talking about restorations and filming and investigating, and all I could think was that

Ann wouldn't have wanted those letters found and shown, like he does in his other programs. I fair didn't know what to do. Eventually I thought it best to take them back here, out of the church, for safekeeping. But then you did come, and you were talking to Mr Hunter. And I fair didn't know what to do again.'

'Is that why you didn't send them all at once?'

'Aye. I thought it was safest, being as I didn't know what she'd said, and how you'd take whatever it was. His Lordship's secrets aren't mine to tell, Miss Wilhelmina, and I didn't know you or what might be done with Mr Hunter around. I thought it best to be cautious. He might have been the one to bring you in.'

'So why did you start sending more than one?'

Confusion wrinkled his forehead. 'Oh, they were grouped that way, when they arrived. I figured that was what Ann intended. And for my part, you seemed to be making friends with His Lordship, so I didn't see reason to split them up, like.'

He blew on his tea. Wil could smell the earthy tannins in the brew. She spun her cup. 'So you were in touch with her when she was sick?'

Bill shook his head. 'Not really, Miss. She was the kind of person who I could not see for a ten-year and then take up a conversation like it were yesterday. The last two times she came to the village, both funerals—God rest them—we talked like she were me own daughter. She was a natural mother, Ann was. Anybody could see how much she loved her little girl Katherine, who came with her that last time. Darling child, never gave any fuss.

'But I knew Ann when she were younger, and I could tell she was unhappy in herself. Things at home, I gathered, and worry about what His Lordship was going through. I was almost expecting she might end up staying, what with how close the pair of them used to be. But she didn't. And I didn't hear from her again until years later, when she called out of the blue to tell me she had a dreadful cancer and needed me to do something for her.'

'Did she say anything about what she wanted me to do for her?'

Bill shook his head. 'Nothing like that. Only what she wanted with those letters.' He took another draught of his tea, then rose and pulled a key ring from his pocket. Picking around the loop, he selected a skeleton key and slid it into a locked box that sat on a narrow bookshelf by the front door. He lifted the lid and drew out three envelopes.

'These are the last of them,' he said, then gave a sigh. 'And now my duty to Ann is done.'

Wil took the three envelopes, the moment less triumphant than it should have been. This was what she'd been trying to find all this time, and yet they came only after the loss of the rest. Why on earth hadn't she made copies? It just proved how hopeless she was.

'Thank you,' she said, sounding hollow. She rose and folded the damp towel, knowing it was time to go.

'I know this is all hard for you,' he said, before she could open the door. 'It's the hardest thing to lose a mother. I understood that when my own passed on, and I had her most of my adult life. Can't imagine what it's like when you're just a little'un.'

'I don't really remember her,' Wil said.

He shook his head. 'Maybe not that you can bring to mind. But she weren't the kind of woman to forget. You remember her, in ways you can't name. She's in your soul; she has to be. His Lordship were devastated by her passing. That was when he started ploughing all the old fields, and letting the estate fall out of repair. Everyone's been grieving her, all these years. Him most especially.'

Wil clenched her hand on the doorframe. 'How is that possible, when she said that the Elstons would never have approved of her?'

Bill rolled his eyes. 'Love don't pay no mind to approval, Miss Wilhelmina. If it did, it wouldn't cause such strife.'

Chapter 23

Wil tore back into the cottage and up the stairs to her room, barely noticing David still sitting in the lounge. He tapped on her door just as she'd slipped open the first envelope.

'Your phone's been ringing,' he said, handing it to her.

Wil glanced at the screen, at the missed calls from Col and Shonna, and chucked it on the bedside table. David retreated without a word.

Dear Mina,

Happy 27th birthday, my darling girl. Twenty-seven years ago, you were a soft bundle of love in my arms, a source of unqualified joy in what was a very tense time. Kate adored you, too. She was utterly fascinated with how tiny you were and spent hours of the day practising kisses on your forehead. It was the most gorgeous thing to see. Cameron loved you, too.

Whether he loved me again, I was less sure about. We never managed to quite repair things after the break, and I own my fault in that. When he'd told me not to come back, I'd made a shift in my head to stand on my own, and I couldn't undo it no matter how much it aggravated him. Added to that was the household chaos of toys and nappies soaking in buckets, and of being woken up all night and him going to work at six anyway. It would have been hard on anyone. But I wanted my work and my life, so I drew rather than cleaning up, and, as my worst fault in Cameron's eyes, I insisted on giving you my surname in defiance of feeling like I belonged to a man again. So Cameron was miserable, spending more and more time out of the house, and yet I couldn't give way. You were only months old when I decided we had to part. The pressure to run away had built to an unbearable level. That was when I changed Kate's name, too. We were three together, and I was never coming back.

So I took you both, my two girls, you nearly one and Kate nearly three, and we went across the country. If I thought it had been hard to pick up and leave when I was younger, it was ten times worse with two little children. I couldn't afford babysitters to look after you while I worked, and money was running out. Then, through a bit of luck and some friends of friends, I started driving big trucks, which meant I could take you both with me.

Yes, you read that right. I'm sure you don't remember, but it's true that for months starting in 1990, you and Kate travelled with me in the cab of a big rig, hauling up and down the coast of Western Australia. We washed our clothes in roadside stops, and you girls played in the cab bunk, listening to the radio crackle. When you were tired, you slept, and when I pulled into the sidings on long runs, I crawled in with you.

We met some amazing people in that time—rough people who you might be frightened of, if you just took them at their looks. Long hair and tattoos, and a fondness for swearing. But people like that heated food for us, changed tyres, gave us toys and books. I was so often sad and frightened and lonely ... and guilty too, because what sort of life was it for you both? But many times, kindness from people I didn't know gave me enough courage to press on. After a few months, we learned how to make it work, and I made a kind of peace with it. I even met another mother who was doing the same thing.

But it wasn't sustainable. As Kate approached four, it was clear that she wasn't built for that life. She hated the travelling. She wanted to be settled somewhere. You, Mina, were happy just to be wherever the three of us were. You carried Kate's Miss Bear for her or would go off to explore wherever it was we stopped that day. Kate would often refuse to come out of the truck bunk, probably because it was the only constant place in her life. She was missing out on other things, too—both of you were—the chance to play with other children, to not have a parent who spent so much of the day driving.

So, when Kate was old enough to go to kindergarten, I swallowed my pride and went back to the Gold Coast, back to the house with the blue door and back to Cameron.

At least, that's what I imagined I was doing. I had kept in touch with him in the time we'd been gone, letting him know how the two of you were and sending photos. I kept myself out of those letters and phone calls, usually made from some dusty phone box on the highway. It felt to me that you and Kate were the only binding that held me and Cameron together. And I could go back to him for the two of you.

Until next time, be brave, my darling girl.

Love,

Mum

∾

Dear Mina,

Happy 28th birthday, my darling girl. I know I've said it before, but I'll keep writing that part, no matter how old you are now.

We're approaching the end of the story now, and I wonder if you are angry at me for writing these letters. Maybe they're comforting for you. Or maybe they bring emotions that you didn't anticipate. The way life can sometimes surprise you and tilt the world on its axis.

Coming back to the Gold Coast was like that. I expected to find everything just as it had been when we left. That might have been the tunnel vision of having two small children, or knowing how determined Cameron had been to make his business work. But it wasn't like that.

Cameron had moved on. I could tell as soon as I walked in that blue door, just by the way the kitchen had been rearranged, by the vase of flowers on the dining room table. Cameron had never bought flowers in his life, even for me. I nearly walked straight back out again, but for two things.

The first was you girls—you'd been on a long journey, and I'd promised that we were going to stay with Daddy.

The second was I was simply exhausted. The kind of bone-aching tired that could not be bargained with, even to save my pride. The reason for that exhaustion, of course, turned out to be more than just the long months of single parenting, driving trucks and then travelling back across the country. It was the first flag the cancer flew, or at least the first one I was prepared to see. After all, I'd had every reason to be tired when I'd been driving. Every reason to have little niggles of pain in my legs and back.

So I moved into the downstairs flat, thinking that I just needed time to get myself on my feet, and then I would move us out again. I wouldn't stay in the house when Cameron was now seeing Carol.

But it didn't work out that way, because soon I had my diagnosis.

I actually have to thank Carol for that, because she was the one who encouraged me to see a doctor. I can't imagine what that time was like for her, poor woman. I mean, here she was, dating an up-and-coming builder whose crazy separated wife suddenly turns up back in his house with their kids in tow. I give her credit for how she handled it— she never returned any of the animosity I felt for her. She actually stopped coming to the house and told Cameron she would give him the space to resolve his relationship with me. I can't imagine how hard that was for her.

I asked her once, only recently, how she was able to do that. And she said that it wasn't for her to stand between a man and his family, and that you girls deserved that. We've got on much better in the past year—maybe it's because she can have certainty about Cameron now ... but I think it's really because I can finally acknowledge that she is actually a wonderful person who did the most honourable thing she could do in difficult circumstances.

In any case, Carol, as you know, was a nurse. We didn't talk at all when I first came back, and we didn't meet each other properly for a long while. But she came to the house one morning very apologetically, because Cameron had sent her for a forgotten chequebook. She found me up in the kitchen, trying for the third time to draw a scene for a book I had due. Nothing was working for me that day—I was so tired I could hardly hold my pencil.

I must have looked dreadful, because she asked me if I was really all right. I ended up telling her I was having trouble sleeping because it was so hot at night in the basement room. And she paused as if she'd seen something awful and asked if I was waking up in a sweat? I shrugged, because I had been waking up in a sweat for many nights. She gently told me that it wasn't that hot right now, and then less gently that I needed to see a doctor.

So, that was how I found out about my stage three ovarian cancer, because the woman my husband was dating cared enough about me not to just be smugly happy that I looked so ill. How's that for irony? Cameron hadn't said a thing.

Of course, the news knocked me over. No one expects to have cancer in their twenties, to be told they're going to die sometime in the very near future, least of all me. I'd come from farming peasants who barely talked about their ailments, if they admitted to having them at all. I'd had a few male relatives who'd dropped suddenly of a heart attack, and another couple who'd fallen to accidents. Death had always seemed to me to be a thing that fell on you like a cartoon anvil, without warning. I mean, look at Susie, there one day and gone the next. No time to think over the life she'd led, to regret and to wonder what to do with the unknown time remaining.

Because that's what I did. In between the surgery, the chemotherapy and the radiation, I thought endlessly about the things I'd done and not done. And mostly, I thought about you and Kate, and the utter unfairness of what was about to happen to you both.

Kate pretended to be stoic. But I know she was afraid. She was old enough to realise something was wrong, but not to really understand. Every day brought some new scary thing for her. You were still young enough to accept things without worrying so much.

I lived in the basement room for nearly eighteen months, going to and from appointments. Kate started school, you went to kindy, then pre-school. I hated the time apart from the both of you. When time is running out, you become greedy for every moment. But you and Kate also needed things in place that would carry on after me, and so every day I let you go just a little more, and every day I was both overjoyed and torn apart to see you again.

The decision to move to the hospice was the hardest one. And it wasn't the best option. It was just the less-bad option. Carol actually helped a lot with that. She was quite against it, especially in the beginning, because it meant more time away from you and Kate. But even she had to admit that my care had gone beyond what could be done at home and that Kate especially was afraid of the things going on.

I want you to know that I didn't want to leave without you. I had spent my life running away from places, or running towards them, and my home was always where the three of us were. But your home was that house, and it was Kate's. And I couldn't stay. I knew that I was holding myself together when you and Kate were around, making sure I was happy for you, and never showing you how much my body hurt, or how nauseated I was. I think you accepted how I was. You would crawl up next to me and just put your arms across me. Those moments broke my heart. How could I leave you?

But at the hospice, I don't have to be strong all the time. The nurses here have seen people at their absolute worst. I don't have to pretend for them. And there's a great freedom in that. I can tell them I'm scared about what will happen to you, and they won't shush me, or tell me not to talk like that, or that everything will be fine, which is Cameron's approach. I don't blame him. He's scared, too, but doesn't have the ability to express it. The nurses ask me what I am worried about for the two of you, but then what I am doing about it.

That's how these letters came to be—from a conversation with a caring woman, who I never would have met if I hadn't come here.

I have written to Kate, too, but not so long a tale as this one. When I look at her I feel that she has a clear sense about herself, that she is going to meet the world with that sense still intact. But I see myself in you, Mina. So I think you will find it hard to settle and to find how you belong. Maybe I am *wrong about that. But if not, the only thing I could think to do was to set this story down for you. Of where I came from and where you came from.*

Why? Because we are really just the story we tell ourselves. And I wanted you to know that a life that begins small, or that has many wrong turns, can still hold the most wonderful things.

And that is where I end this second-to-last letter. The next will be the last, darling Mina, and the hardest to write. I always tell you to be brave but, for this one, I might need that advice for myself.

Love,

    Mum

Wil looked up at the light fading across the fields and felt tears spill hot down her cheeks. She was curled on the bed, crammed against the headboard, the door closed. David hadn't intruded. The house was as quiet as the fields.

Or maybe that was just the grief, which had turned Wil inside out. It was bad enough to read about a past she couldn't remember—had she really lived in a long-haul truck for months as a very young child?—but to read all those things her mother had said about the cancer, and why she'd moved to the hospice, was far worse.

For the first time, Wil tried to bring up the scattered memory from the day her mother had died. But nothing would come to her except that feeling of running, that aching loss. Not only the loss of her mother dying, but the not being there. That feeling of being pulled, like in the current of the beck, sweeping her away like the stream had taken the letters.

Bloody John Elston.

Wil sniffed and hauled herself up to the window. The man who owned all the land out there had a part in all of this. He was the reason her mother had been unhappy. The reason her parents had split up, and that her mother had gone away and missed the signs that she was getting sick. This *land* had been the reason, because it all came back to that. Ruling these fields had meant more to him than love.

Wil felt then what her mother must have felt—the leaving desire, like a rope hooked into her breastbone. She dragged her case out of the cupboard and onto the bed, next to the last letter, resting unopened on the covers. She hesitated, then reached for it. She would read it. And then, she would pack and go.

She slid her finger under the back closure and pulled out the pages.

Dear Mina,

Happy 29th birthday, my darling girl. Here we are, at the last instalment. The one I must write. One of the two reasons I started to begin with. And there's no easy way to say this, so I must just write it.

John Elston is your father.

Wil clapped a hand over her mouth. What? *What?* She read the line again, and again.

I feel ridiculous writing it like that, as if it's some line from Star Wars. *And awful that this is where and how you*

*find out. If I had been able to stay with you, then I would
have found a way to tell you much sooner.*

*But I can't stay with you. The laws of nature are not going
to allow it, and I never had John's input on this. When I came
back from that last trip to the village, I had Kate to think of,
so I never told John that I was pregnant. You can judge me
for that, but I had hopes that my marriage was salvageable,
at least for Kate. When it wasn't, and the three of us left, it
didn't seem right to add another hurt into the already hurtful
split. The fact would not have been obvious to anyone else.
Then when I swallowed my pride to come back the last time,
Cameron had already moved on from me. And then I was
sick, and I was selfish enough for your sake to never bring
this secret up.*

*Cameron loved you, and it was his house you were going
to grow up in. I didn't want to risk putting that knowledge
between you and Cameron or between you and Kate.*

*I have no idea what consequences my choice has brought
you, and no idea how you feel about knowing. Maybe the
world you knew has simply ended. I'm sorry for that—
so very sorry. It can't be easy to one day think you're the
daughter of a London-born builder and the next discover
you're actually the daughter of a baron, a member of the
unbroken line of Elstons stretching back centuries over land
in an obscure village in England.*

*I don't know what you will do with this knowing. Maybe
you'll choose to tell everyone. Or no one. That I leave with
you, because only you know the shape of your life, who
knows what it will change.*

And here, I come to what I ask of you. There is, of course, my wish that you will live your life fully. That doesn't mean a life without regret, or without sadness, or without mistakes, because I don't think anyone can do that. But live it moving towards something you love. Don't run away from difficult things. Find a way to circle back to meet them.

That was what I was hoping for with John. We were always bound together, he and I. I always loved him and I still do. When I had you, you were a child of that love. And so I hoped that somehow we would find a way to circle back together, so we could make our peace before I went.

But that hasn't happened.

I regret that I won't be there for you as you grow up. That's the biggest one, the one that's between the two of us. But I also regret that I'll leave this earth without being able to say what I wished I had to John.

So if you can find it in your heart to grant me that closure, there is one more letter. You will find it under the flagstone at the porch of the South Bandinby church. At least, I assume it is there. I sent it to Bridget to place for me, and I am sure that she will have. That one is for John. You don't have to see him to deliver it if you don't want to. But if you think about all this long tale, and you want a way to meet with him, even if it's not to reveal any of the secrets I've just told you, then the letter will be perhaps the way to do that. I can't tell you what will happen if you do, but that's your choice, not mine. He is your father, and I didn't feel I had the right to pass away holding that secret with me.

And if you decide not to do it, then I will be content to know that the letter will stay with the bones of the church, until they tear it down or it falls down, whichever comes first. By the time that happens, I imagine it won't matter who reads it. But someone will. Someone will know that once, this woman called Ann Mann loved John, Baron Elston, and their only daughter, Wilhelmina. I will have a witness to the truth of that.

There is nothing left to write, my darling girl. Be brave. I loved you from before the first day I saw you, and will forever, past the last.

Your loving mother, Ann Mann

Underneath, she had written the date: 23 April 1994. Three days before she'd died.

Chapter 24

Wil couldn't move for ten long minutes. She was in a twilight daze, where thoughts half-formed and then collapsed again. Slowly, themes emerged. How could the man who'd threatened her with his tractor and cajoled her into working for him, and who'd thrown her letters into the beck—how could *that man* be her father?

And what about Cameron? How could the man who'd taught her to surf, who'd been hard and critical but had been there every day she could remember growing up, *not* be her father? Oh god . . .

Wil felt as though the structure at the centre of her very self was collapsing.

But then, wait . . . John had said her mother was a fantasist. Was that all this was? A story from a woman who wasn't well? Who'd found a way to imagine a closure with the man who'd broken her heart?

'Mina?' David called, with a soft knock on her door. 'Can I come in?'

When she didn't answer, he cracked the door. His eyes ran over her and dropped to the papers in her lap.

'You got more?' he asked. 'Where did they come from?'

Wil stared out the window. She had no idea how to answer him. If she even wanted to answer him. He took a step inside, clearly sensing the tension between them this morning had jacked up a few notches.

'You're upset,' he said. Then hesitantly, 'Did I do something?'

Wil shook her head. She felt the gulf between the person she'd been this morning, when she didn't know the secrets of Elston Manor, and now. Between when she'd been sure of her mother and when doubt had come in. And though she'd been mad at him, it wasn't David's fault. She had to say something to him.

'He threw them in the river,' she said finally.

David blinked. 'Who threw what, and in what river?'

'Lord Elston,' she said, feeling anger even as she said his name. 'Threw my letters into the beck.'

David sat on the edge of the bed. 'You might need to catch me up on what happened after you left this morning.'

'Well,' Wil said, huffing a breath. 'One of the letters led me to believe he had been lying the whole time about . . . something, so I confronted him about it, and then he threw the letters in the river.'

David pressed a hand to his face. 'You *confronted* him?'

'What can I say? I don't have five years to sit around and hope,' she said, feeling bitchy and betrayed.

'What exactly did you confront him about?'

'Well,' Wil said again, knowing she was about to step off the smaller of two big cliffs. 'Over the fact that Thomas Elston died over thirty years ago and that John Elston isn't in Jamaica at all. He's living in his brother's identity as the current Lord Elston.'

David stared at her for several long seconds. 'And what did he say?'

'He threw the letters in the river, David.'

'But how could that possibly be true—'

'Maybe it isn't,' she said in a small voice, really hoping that all of this was some giant joke. 'Maybe my mother was sick and she didn't know what she was writing. Or she was angry with John about everything and this was a way to punish him.'

'That's a hell of a departure of character, don't you think?' David said. 'What exactly did she say? How did she know?'

'She came back here for Thomas's secret funeral,' Wil said. *And shacked up with her former fiancé to conceive me.* 'She said the brothers looked alike. And that John had been standing in for Thomas for years, anyway.'

David's eyebrows rose, then he tilted his head, as if he'd just noticed the world was a few degrees off level. 'I either need to completely reassess this project,' he said slowly, 'or I need to fire some researchers.'

It was at the mention of researchers that Wil finally felt the full blow of the letters being lost. 'Oh, god, they're all gone. Why didn't I copy them?' The image of her mother's pen strokes swam before her eyes. She'd never read those words again.

Through her tears, she was aware of David standing, his hands on his hips, considering. Then he walked out of the room. She heard him go down the stairs, and the sound of a stool move in the kitchen. Then she heard him coming back.

He appeared, his face set, and handed her a wad of crisp white paper. 'Here,' he said.

For a moment, Wil didn't realise what she was looking at. Then she saw the same words she'd just been seeing in her mind, only produced in full-colour copy. Page after page. All her mother's letters.

He'd copied them.

She didn't have time to feel the relief before the anger fell. 'You copied them,' she whispered. 'Without asking me.'

'Yes,' he said, his voice tight. 'I didn't read them.'

She scanned his face, which was more grey than an overcast morning, and didn't believe him. He'd wanted them for the show. All she could think was how much of an idiot she was for having told him anything.

'Get out,' she said.

～

Wil didn't sleep much that night. David apologised for what he'd done and how it looked, but his words didn't touch her. She stayed only because she had nowhere else to go, and in the guest bed with the door firmly shut. When she came down the next morning, hoping to find the kitchen empty, he was there with his laptop. He pushed the screen around when he saw her.

Wil ignored it and went looking for her shoes.

'I found a death certificate,' he called out behind her.

She stopped, despite herself.

'I guess we missed it because Thomas died in London, not here, and no one thought to look for a death we didn't know had happened.'

Wil didn't say anything. She was bruised in her head and heart, and heavy with the secret she didn't know what to do with. That John was her father. That there was a letter under a flagstone, waiting for her. When she didn't have the first idea what to do with it. And in a church that David was wanting to show on national television. Oh, and that he'd betrayed her, too. Secretly copying her mother's letters. The ones leading to all the secrets.

She wasn't sure which gave her more palpitations—the idea that her real father was a baron with a bad attitude or that her mother's last love letter might end up shared around Twitter.

'Coffee?' David asked.

'No.'

'Can we talk about it? I feel awful.'

But Wil couldn't even look at him. She needed to leave. She just needed her thoughts in enough order to work out how to do that. She was dimly aware of David talking about having something else to show her and him heading upstairs, but she wasn't listening. She was caught in her churning thoughts, watching the steam rise from the coffee maker.

A knock came at the door.

Then another.

Probably Rose Maxwell again. Wil broke her loop enough to slowly go down the hall and pull the door open. But it wasn't Rose. It was a man she'd never seen before and, behind him, something large and black.

'Miss Mann, care to comment on your relationship with David Hunter? How does he feel about your past? Miss Mann? How do you feel dating an England soccer striker going through a personal crisis? Miss Mann?'

Wil shut the door, shaking, as they continued to ask questions through the letter slot. She backed away. That black thing had been a camera. Through the high window over the mud room, she could see a white van out in the lane.

At the end of the hall, she ran slap into David. 'Who was that?'

'They knew my name,' she said. 'How do they know who I am?'

David walked calmly to the mud room window. He took one look at the lane and pulled out his phone. Wil watched him scroll with his finger, his face setting hard. Then he dropped the phone on the bench and paced to his office desk. She heard him pick up the landline.

Wil crept towards his phone. The screen was still lit. He'd opened several browser windows, tabloid sites with big splashy photos. There was a photo of her, looking seedy with a cigarette in her hand, and a headline that read 'Former England great David Hunter's "crisis" dating latest bad girl with criminal past'. With a shaking finger, she swapped windows. 'Meet Wilhelmina Mann, twice arrested bricklayer from Oz now engaged to David Hunter'. Flick. 'David Hunter moves from Candyland to Jailbait. Is she pregnant with David Hunter's baby?' asked another, answering its headline with another photo of Wil on an unflattering angle, with her hand suggestively angled over her stomach. She scrolled down through the text in cold horror. Rob, named as an 'ex-flame from Australia', was quoted as saying she was 'a bit wild'. *Rob!*

Worse, there were links at the bottom to older articles. 'David Hunter: fallen star' had seedy photos of David in a baseball cap, the text detailing party drugs and rehab. 'Naughty DH!' declared another about a lurid sex tape doing the internet rounds.

David was now shouting into his desk phone. Wil braced her hands on the bench. She wanted to run more than ever. But that van was blocking the road. She'd was cornered, and it was ten times worse than the incident in London, because she hadn't understood what was happening then. Now, she saw new awful angles.

Oh god. Tabloid reporters, sniffing around the village where the lord was a fraud, and she was his illegitimate daughter.

Wil wanted to burrow into the ground, to burn her mother's letters so their secrets could never come out. She would never speak of them to anyone, but Lord Elston didn't know that. He would only know what she had said at the beck and that now there were reporters in the village. He would think she had told them. And what would David do?

Her phone started ringing. Wil's cheeks burned as she stared at the screen: private number. The usually cheery ring sounded menacing. She dropped the phone and rushed back upstairs, away from David.

By the time he came up, she was half-crazed, folding the copied letters and unfolding them, trying to make them small enough to force into her pocket. Her case was a mess of half-finished packing.

'Mina,' he said. '*Mina.*'

'What if they drag the fen for the pieces? What if they, I dunno, tape them together?' she yelled. Her phone rang again downstairs. 'How do they have my phone number?'

'They make half of their crap up,' David said. 'Please, stop. This is just how they operate.'

Wil did stop, staring at him in a moment of clarity. 'Wait a minute. All that stuff in London that I asked you about—what Graham said—this is what he meant? You being in rehab and dating hookers, or something?'

David looked abashed. 'Look, this is my fault. I wasn't careful enough. I should have realised this could happen. Are you telling me you really don't know?'

'Know what?' she said, exasperated. 'All I knew about you was what you told me. I thought you were just a footballer who was now on TV.'

'I am.'

'So none of that other stuff is true?'

He hesitated, just enough for her to know.

She turned her back, shaking with humourless laughter. This morning, she'd known who she was. Who he was. How the world was. Now, all that was collapsing. And there was a horde of cameras and microphones out in the street ready to expose her to everyone.

'You don't understand,' she said.

'I really do, Mina—'

'You *don't* understand! They know I was arrested. They have my ex-boyfriend giving them quotes,' she said, clutching at her chest. 'Nothing will be the same again. Don't you get that? *Nothing.*'

She gave up on her pocket and pressed the letters into the bottom of her bag, then began stuffing her clothes on top. The drama of packing was dented by the fact that half her clothes were down in David's room, but at least she had the chance to stomp down the hall. Saint Barbara eyed her as she snatched her toothbrush from the bathroom. Patron saint of those under threat of violent death. Well, anything she and David had was dying a violent death, right now.

'Please, don't leave like this,' he said. 'At least wait until the vans clear out.'

Wil's phone started ringing yet again. She couldn't stand it anymore and went downstairs after it. She was bloody well going to smash the thing. The only thing that stopped her was knowing how much she'd have to pay to replace it.

David had followed. 'Will you let me deal with them?'

When she didn't refuse, he picked up her phone and answered the call.

'Hello?' he said, then took an inhale of air, ready to give whoever was on the end a blasting. Only he didn't. A moment later, he let a relieved breath out. 'Oh, yes,' he said. 'Just a moment.'

He held the phone out. 'It's Bridget from the V&A,' he said.

Wil hesitated before taking the phone. And when she pressed it to her ear, her own 'Hello' sounded hollow and defensive.

'Wilhelmina Mann, is it really you? Ann Mann's daughter?' The voice on the line was warm and expectant.

'Yes,' she stammered, her voice still clogged with fear this was some kind of ruse.

'I could not believe my messages. Tell me you're still in London?'

Wil managed to say that she wasn't. After all, if this was a tabloid, her whereabouts were hardly a secret.

Bridget laughed heartily. 'But of course, you must be in the village? It's only a few hours on the train. Can you come back?'

'Well,' Wil said, feeling despair morph into black humour. 'See, there's this little problem of reporters camped outside my door. I don't know if you've seen, but they seem to have taken an interest in me. Something about a footballer.'

'What, tabloids?' Bridget said. 'There's only one way to treat them, and that's not to rise. They're just bullies with big cameras. Now, chin up. Dye your hair if you need to, put on a pair of dark shades, and come see me.'

Chapter 25

Bridget McClaren looked exactly like her picture in the article: she wore oversized glasses in a sunset shade of orange, long hair in a wild angle from her head and a woven striped scarf draped artfully about her shoulders. Her office was small, but in a treasure-cave kind of way, with one wall full of bookshelves, another with a vast window that lit up the curios and boxes stuffed into every shelf. The other walls were covered in posters from past exhibitions. It all smelled of paper and black coffee.

'Anyone give you any stick on the way down?' Bridget asked, after she'd ushered Wil in. She was brisk and energetic, taking Wil's bag and stowing it under her desk. Wil could hardly believe Bridget was fifty-seven. She had more energy than Wil felt on a good day.

Wil shook her head. 'I took a cab all the way from the station.'

'What about at the village end? I remember when the reporters camped out after Susie died. Had everyone in a flap.'

'Lord Elston drove a tractor down the lane at full speed, so they scattered for a while,' Wil said, but with little joy in the memory. She'd spend much of the journey in a muddle over how to think about Cameron, what to do about what she knew. It had left her with a kamikaze feeling, accepting the crash that was coming. 'I made a run for it.'

Bridget grinned. 'Well, he'd have fair practice at that, I suppose. Probably the best approach. I've seen the tabloid pieces. Beastly codswallop, all of it. But they probably think they're onto a good thing with David Hunter being there. He was a darling of theirs for a long time.'

Wil didn't want to talk about David, but she was fascinated with the way Bridget used her words with such authority. She seemed a woman utterly comfortable in her skin, in owner-ship of this office and everything else in her life. Wil was taken aback to realise that she was the same age her mother would have been now. Would her mother have been like this, with this certainty and energy, had she still been alive? Wil found the possibility a devastating loss, adding into all the others she was drowning in.

'You're very quiet,' Bridget said, removing her glasses and setting them on the desk. 'Are you thinking about her? Or about those tabloid sharks?'

'Her,' Wil said. What was there to lose now? 'I . . . was wondering if she would have been like you.'

Bridget didn't laugh or make light. She tipped her head a little to the side, as if seriously considering the question. 'I don't know how to answer that,' she said. 'I'm not really anything like

I was when Ann and I first lived in London. I was a flyaway spirit with a fashion addiction. I know Ann thought I was terribly worldly, having lived overseas because of my father's work, but I really didn't grow into myself until my late thirties. I think she would probably have been the same . . . if she'd had the chance. I mean, we both had no idea what we were doing back then, knocking around and thinking we were so grown-up. Not that I'd have changed any of it.

'She had a huge influence on me, but I doubt she understood that. She always thought she was this nobody from a nothing village. But she was a lot more ambitious than I was. Bolder, too. The only thing was, she didn't know what she wanted. Then again, neither did I. So I think she'd have found her place in things, too. Never imagined I'd end up at the V&A.'

Bridget raised her shoulders philosophically, acknowledging the happy accident of where she was. Then she brought her gaze back to Wil and sighed. 'You know you look so much like her,' she said. 'And I'm sorry to say that, because people must tell you that all the time.'

Wil felt her eyebrows rise, at the same time Bridget's words choked her with tears. She cleared her throat. 'Actually, no one tells me anything about her.'

'Really? Why on earth not?'

'I have no idea. My—' Wil caught herself about to say *father*, meaning Cameron, and stopped because there was a deep rip in that particular piece of herself now. She swallowed and began again. 'It's like everyone in the family wants to forget she existed. Even my sister. And our father.' The last part she managed to get out because sharing Cameron with Kate made it seem less of a lie.

Bridget tapped her blue-painted fingernail pensively on the desk. Finally she sighed again. 'You know what they say: people don't want to remember what hurt them. Ann wasn't the nobody she thought she was. She was extraordinary. Maybe not the kind of extraordinary that's hung in a gallery, but you didn't forget her. She had energy in her soul, an infectious want for living. She was my dear friend, and she made me better. I've never really got over her being gone. I know John never did, either, even though he married Susie. I suspect it was a source of some tension between them.'

Wil had to suppress a jerk on hearing John's name.

Bridget went on, 'Maybe your father just doesn't want to feel her loss all over again.' She smiled gently. 'Do you remember her?'

Wil shook her head.

'You were so young. It's so unfair.' Bridget gave her another kind smile. 'Is that why you went to the village? Looking for someone who knew her?'

'She wrote me letters,' Wil said, then paused. 'Did you know that?'

'No?'

So then Wil had to tell Bridget about the letters, from start to end, pouring out the story to her mother's oldest friend. Everything from the first one to coming to the village to find the others. Bridget wordlessly plucked a tissue from a box and handed it across. The only thing Wil left out were the parts she couldn't speak of: Lord Elston's secret, hers, and David's betrayal.

Bridget sat back in her chair. 'Oh my, how incredibly hard for you. Those letters must have brought up so many memories.

And forced you into a whole lot of recalibrating. And now, to boot, the tabloids got wind of you. You'll need a year to recover.'

'I don't know that there's much to recalibrate. I've been a disaster zone since I was a kid. This is just the latest thing I wish I could, you know . . .'

'Erase from your personal history?'

'Yeah.'

Bridget looked down at the desk briefly, then gave her a wry smile, as if she knew more about this than she'd admit. 'What's the worst you've really done?'

Wil laughed, bitterly at first. But as she told Bridget about the kitchen demo-gate, and her strained relationship with Kate, and bumming around the Gold Coast aimlessly for years, and all her other transgressions, she found herself beginning to laugh, as Bridget was, at the absurdity of it all. Somehow Bridget seemed a safe person to tell.

'I feel rather guilty about the fact I lost touch with you,' Bridget said finally. 'I always had this twinge, like I should have done something more.'

'What do you mean?'

'In those last years before she died, I had Ann's address in Australia, but I was going through an awful marriage break-down and then a divorce, and we weren't as in touch as I meant to be. But, then . . .'

Bridget sighed, and looked out the window, as if she might cry. 'I didn't know she'd written you letters, but she did send me a letter that she asked me to put at the church in the village. She didn't say what it was for. I don't know if you knew about that one?'

Wil gave a quick nod. 'Yeah. But it doesn't matter now.'

'Well, after she sent that, I felt awful I hadn't realised how sick she was. But by the time I knew, it was too late to come out. Her passing away washed into the awfulness of that year. But I've always regretted that I didn't see her, and you. I tried to call Cameron the year after she died to find out how you were all doing—I felt I needed to, because of what she meant to me. But the number had been disconnected. So I wrote, and eventually the letter was returned. I figured Cameron had moved. I didn't blame him—I should have realised he wouldn't have wanted to stay in the house that held memories of her.'

'He remarried the next year,' Wil said, feeling flat about the whole thing. This was why she couldn't remember the house with the blue door, because they hadn't stayed there long enough. It was why she'd never gone to the school her mother thought she'd go to. Maybe it was part of why she was as messed up as she was. 'I think his new wife had something to do with the move.'

Bridget looked surprised. 'Fast,' she said. She rubbed at her eyebrows with her thumb and finger. 'I feel just awful, Mina. What happened with the letters . . . Ann would be horrified. She would have wanted you to have them growing up, to be there as much as she could be through them. I guess it's good you finally got them, even if it was later than she intended.'

All Wil felt was resentment at the conspiracy of events that had kept all of these letters from her for so long, and that had now dumped such turmoil into her life.

'Having said that,' Bridget said, 'if it was me, I'd be raving mad about it.'

Wil glanced up. 'You would?'

'Sure. What an upheaval. I don't know what she wrote, but you've had a long while to make your way without having her in your life. I'm sure someone would try to tell you that maybe this happened for a reason, that now was the perfect time, or something like that to make themselves feel better. But it can't be anything other than a body blow.'

Wil snorted in agreement. To be perfectly honest, she didn't know if she would rather have never known about the letters. If she had continued on without ever receiving them, how bad could it have been? She could have kept thinking that Cameron was her father. She would never have gotten into a heartsore tangle with David Hunter.

Her stomach dived just thinking about the awful photos, the provocative headlines and all the people she knew in Australia seeing them. The humiliation was so heavy, she could hardly breathe.

'It does feel like that,' Wil admitted after a long pause. 'They were too late to do any good.'

'So why was it that you contacted me?' Bridget said. 'I got the impression there was something you needed.'

Wil quietly sighed. 'I was trying to find out what she wanted me to do for her. Before I had all the letters, that was.'

'So you know the answer now?'

Wil nodded. She just wasn't ever going to do it. Her mother had said she didn't have to. She would stay as far away from the secrets of those letters as she could. She wished that nothing of the last few weeks had ever happened. She couldn't stay in England, not with people sticking cameras in her face. But the prospect of going home was equally awful. In fact, she had the feeling Bridget's office was the last place she was going to feel safe.

'You know, not everything in those tabloid stories is codswallop,' she said to Bridget as she prepared to leave. 'I did get arrested twice.'

'Only twice, darling?'

Wil gave a short laugh.

Bridget grinned back. 'Oh, I have more than a few sordid moments in my past, too, don't you worry,' she said. 'I was quite the protestor in my time. My husband was always awfully embarrassed. Maybe one of the reasons we divorced.'

Wil grinned despite herself. 'Really?'

Bridget gave her a wink. 'How much longer are you staying? We could have lunch this week. I like you rather a lot.'

'Actually, I'm flying back tomorrow.'

'You are?' Bridget sounded disappointed. 'I was hoping to show you the exhibition.'

Wil forced a smile. 'Maybe another time.'

Bridget's hug as she left was warm, enough to make Wil cry.

Bridget patted her back. 'You know, sometimes all the stuff we wish we could rid ourselves of is what ends up teaching us the most,' Bridget said. 'But people who say things like that are incredibly annoying, don't you think?'

❧

On the platform at Waterloo early the next morning, Wil was still thinking about the things she'd like to rid herself of. Too many to count. But one kept rising to the surface: what her mother had wanted her to do. It was the reason she'd come. And despite all the turmoil, she loved the woman she'd come to know from the letters, whose laugh she sometimes heard at night. Meeting Bridget had only stoked that. And her mother had only asked for one thing.

Wil saw a postbox in the station. Carrying out that last wish was as simple as buying an envelope, writing the address for the manor house and shoving the last letter into the post. She couldn't bear to read it again anyway. Lord Elston would have his letter and know that she knew everything. What did she care anymore?

The only good thing about returning to Australia was burrowing into her seat for the long-haul. She hid behind her sunglasses the whole time—it really was tiresome how flights now had wi-fi and so anyone could be reading an article about her. Bridget had told her not to worry about the whole thing, like David had; that the tabloids would move on in a week. But that wasn't the point. Those things would be findable forever.

And, then . . . David.

Wil twisted in her seat, trying to find an angle where his name didn't make her chest ache so much. He'd lodged deep in her heart, and she'd had to rip him out. The wound refused to heal, and it wept with all the other hurts.

She'd been stupid to trust him. She'd known it all along, that's why she had all those doubtful feelings about his interest in her. But she'd fallen in love with him anyway. Stuffed it up like she always did.

She screwed her eyes shut, trying not to think about the slew of messages on her phone. From an irate Tony and probably Cameron, too. No doubt they'd been rung up for comment. She felt awful for them, and for Rose Maxwell and Bill, who must also have reporters on their doorsteps. And if she was honest, she might even feel a little bad for the lonely and fatally proud Baron Elston, should he become fodder for a Twitter-cycle about his illegitimate daughter and life of fraud.

Illegitimate.

Fraud.

Dear god, what a mess. She shouldn't have expected less.

⌒

The Gold Coast didn't feel like home. A cruel wind was blowing in off the ocean, making her shiver after the warmth of the English summer, and the sky was a smudge of dirty grey. She felt beneath rocky bottom when, jet-lagged to her toenails, she had to knock on Shonna's door.

'Wil!' Shonna said, opening the door. 'I had no idea you were back!'

Wil felt utterly unworthy of any welcome. 'I didn't want to bother you,' she stammered. 'Especially if you were getting calls from tabloids, too.'

'Oh, we told 'em to get stuffed,' Shonna said. 'Colin and I coordinated our message. Col said your dad got a new phone, but I don't know why. Cameron's usually very good at telling people to piss off. Come in, come in.'

Wil felt a tiny smile lift her lips as she stepped through the door. 'Yeah, he is. Just not when it's about me screwing up.'

'I think he was surprised more than anything,' Shonna said, with a confidence Wil didn't share. 'Besides, I have news for you. Colin and I had a success.'

'Did you find my dignity?' Wil asked, peering moodily at the heavy sky through the window. 'I think I left it here. Maybe it's down the back of the couch.'

Shonna laughed. 'Something better, I promise. I'm going to call Col. He'll want to be here.'

❀

'What do you mean, you don't want to?'

Colin gaped at her across the coffee table, and Wil had the agony of watching her brother's enthusiasm morph into hurt. He'd just spent ten minutes telling her how he and Shonna had sleuthed their way across the Gold Coast construction circles, from the demo crews to tradies and commercial builders, to find out which hospice Ann had lived in, and then started a social media campaign until they found Marionette. The whole time, all Wil could think was, *He really isn't my brother anymore. Not even my half-brother.* Her place as the outcast of the family was well and truly cemented. She didn't share blood with any of them, except Kate.

'But she remembers you,' Shonna pleaded. 'She remembers your mum. You'll be able to find out what your mum wanted to tell you.'

'I already know what she wanted to tell me,' Wil said.

Shonna and Col sat back in unison. 'You do?' They looked at each other. 'Well, what was it?'

Wil got up. She couldn't bear disappointing them again after all they'd done, but she couldn't explain to them that she now felt as though all her insides were on the outside. 'It's private,' she said.

'All right, well, can you tell us how you found out then?'

Wil shrugged. 'I found the letters. Eventually.'

'Details! How?'

Wil heard the hurt in their voices now that she was the one keeping secrets. But they didn't understand how big these secrets were. 'I really appreciate everything you did,' she said, hearing how flat she sounded. 'But I just don't know where to start.'

'This is because of those articles,' Shonna said, as if she'd just worked everything out. 'I can't believe anyone gave them quotes. Who the hell is Rob?'

'Her ex,' Colin said. 'A certifiable arsehole.'

He was searching Wil's face in a way that said he knew something was horribly wrong. After Shonna declared she was going out to fetch drinks for them all, Wil escaped to the bathroom. She was still sitting on the edge of the bathtub with her face in her hands when Colin knocked and pushed the door open.

'That stuff they said about you being with David Hunter— was any of that true?'

Wil flicked a look at him. 'Yes. Sadly.'

Colin put a hand over his grin. 'You're serious? *David Hunter*. You shacked up with David Hunter?'

'Don't say it like that.'

Colin gave a soft whoop.

'Don't.' Wil closed her eyes. 'Everyone must hate me.'

'You mean Dad,' Col said. 'I know that's what you mean. Come on, he could never hate you. Hey, you don't need to take all this so hard.'

Wil stood and gripped the edge of the sink, fixated on a drying blob of toothpaste on the porcelain. 'You don't know what I found out in the letters, Col,' she said. 'I don't know how to walk around with what I know and not be able to tell anyone.'

Colin crossed his arms and leaned against the jamb. 'You think I don't walk around with secrets I wish I could tell?'

Wil was about to chastise him for making fun of her, but something in his pause told her he wasn't joking. She glanced up. He looked as serious as Cameron did when he was watching Man United trailing by a goal. And sad, too, right at the corner of his eyes. 'What secrets?'

'Well, now, if I told you they wouldn't be secrets, would they?' he said.

Wil chucked a washcloth at him and covered her eyes again. 'Col, what am I going to do? I'm a screw-up, and looking for these letters has only made everything worse. Somehow I got splashed across the papers like I'm some law-breaking skank who's banging England's favourite retired footballer.'

'Well, aren't you?'

This time, Col was ready and ducked the soap bar Wil lobbed at him. They stood facing each other, Wil with her hands on her hips, Col laughing his arse off.

'Maybe,' she said. 'Just not the skank part, okay?'

Col reined in his amusement, his eyes becoming sombre. 'Look, Wils, I got another idea for you, but you're not going to like it.'

'What?'

'Talk to Mum about it.'

Wil screwed up her face. 'I'm not talking to Carol.'

'Why not? She might know something that could help.'

'I know everything. Mum wrote it down.'

He stared at her. 'Well, then, I guess you've got it all figured out.'

Wil immediately wanted to cry. She turned back to the sink, her head hanging between her shoulders.

Col's hand was on her back. 'It'll be okay,' he said.

'No, it won't.'

He laughed. 'You don't see yourself, do you? Whatever you found out, it doesn't change you. You're still my sister—'

Wil gave a great hiccup.

'—*and* the girl who got David Hunter in the sack.'

'You're awful,' she wailed.

'Yes. But you must be a class act. I've been watching that *Saving History* show since you left and he has some serious smarty chops. But he chose you. Somehow.'

'Oh, somehow!'

'You know what I mean.'

Wil shrugged, trying not to think about it. 'But I chose to leave,' she said. It was just one of the many things that could never go back to the way it had been.

Chapter 26

The grey skies hung around for the next week, with rain showers pelting into the surf and making holes in the soft sand up the beach. Wil spent many mornings huddled in a hoodie at the edge of the esplanade, moodily watching the waves, still not feeling she was home. She was exhausted from working late shifts at a bar where she knew the manager, something she'd done in years past when building work had been slow. Even so, she couldn't sleep in. She would wake early and stare at the ceiling, visited by all the disasters.

Colin came round to Shonna's and tried to convince her to ask about coming back to work, but Wil couldn't face Cameron, not after two of the tabloid stories had run photos of him, too. And especially when he'd been so silent. She'd expected annoyed texts or phone calls, asking what the hell she was doing, even if from a new number. But there'd been nothing, which was so much worse.

The halfway arrangement with Shonna couldn't go on forever. Wil would have to find somewhere to live, and another job to cover rent and bills and all those adult things that she'd avoided in Cameron's house and while gallivanting about the English countryside. During the days, she worked on those things. At night, she thought about the unfinished sketches of the manor house kitchen, which she'd left behind. She thought about the fields and the church, of the letter under that porch stone. The impact of having sent that last letter to Lord Elston weighed on her, as did the thought of David's crew revealing the secret she'd told him . . . and the one she hadn't.

The letters themselves—the ones she had—she left in the locked pocket of her travel bag. She couldn't bear to touch them.

She was early to work that night, dressed in the same black pants and shirt for the third night. She slipped in the back door and ducked under the hatch. There were always glasses to put away. Better to be busy than thinking.

'Wil? You're not on tonight.' The manager, Brett, stuck his head out of the office.

'Yeah, I am.'

'Nope. Check the roster.'

Wil muttered to herself as she pulled out the book on the back counter. Dammit, he was right. She'd misread and was on tomorrow. The evening loomed ahead, grey and empty of distraction. What could she do? Not another night of Netflix with Shonna. She needed something physical. She briefly entertained finding Rob to throw a drink in his face, but he wasn't worth it.

'What's up, kiddo? You need the cash?' Brett said, strolling over.

'Always need cash,' she said, because that was acceptable. And true.

He checked his watch. 'If Olivia doesn't show, shift's yours. I'll pay you until she turns up either way.'

Wil went to it, taking orders until the few people waiting at the bar had all been served. It was a nasty weeknight in winter, hardly time for a crowd. But she was unreasonably disappointed when Olivia arrived fifteen minutes later.

'Didn't think you were on,' Olivia said.

'I'm not, now,' Wil said, undoing her apron. She'd just slung it into the basket under the back counter when somebody walked up to the bar.

'Can I get a drink?'

Wil froze. David's voice. Unbelieving, she straightened and saw him, all six foot three of him. He looked rough, as if he'd just spent two days crammed in a small airline seat and had come straight from the airport, but somehow he managed to exude an undeniable glamour.

'What are you doing here?'

'You weren't returning my calls or messages,' he said.

She looked around, wondering if the paparazzi were about to spring out at them again. 'How did you even know I was here?'

'Well, I went to your father's house—'

Wil groaned and put her hands over her face. 'How did you even know where it was?'

'The address was on your luggage tags,' David said. 'I paid attention.'

'By looking at my *luggage* tags? What, some kind of research reflex?'

He raised his hands helplessly. 'More like making sure you know how to contact the woman you're into. When I knew I was going to want to see you again, and that you were only in the country for a short time, I made a note. I must say, your father's a real football fan, isn't he?'

She groaned again. 'Tell me he didn't—'

'Recognise me? He invited me in for a drink. And a tour of the house.'

Wil dropped her voice, aware of Olivia hovering. 'He must be so pissed at me. I never told him where I was, and then there were the tabloids.'

'Fairly sure he's caught up now.' David looked around the bar. 'Your brother Colin was the one who told me you were here. Seems he's a pretty big soccer fan, too.'

'Oh my god.'

David gave her a tentative smile. 'I may have even suggested I would be coming with you to some kind of barbecue on the weekend. Making up for one you apparently missed.'

Wil looked at him in horror. The idea of seeing Cameron was too much. He would be absolutely furious with her—for the tabloids, for leaving, for everything—and she didn't want to be anywhere near that anger, especially with what she knew now. How could she face him? She wanted to crawl away and die, and to have never known anything about David Hunter.

'You need to go now,' she said, despite the kick from her heart at the idea of never seeing him again. 'Before this gets any worse.'

'Any worse than what? You leaving the country was about the worst thing I could imagine.'

Wil didn't answer. She picked up a glass and pretended it was curiously difficult to buff.

'Look, if it makes any difference, I don't think your dad's that mad. He asked after you a few times.'

'Probably wants to send me a bill.'

'And I need to show you something, too.'

Wil put the glass down and took a long breath. She couldn't unpack everything that sentence required. 'The last time you said that it didn't turn out well,' she said, folding her arms over her chest. 'What is it?'

'What time do you finish? I was hoping to go somewhere nicer,' David said.

'Oh, she's done now,' Olivia chipped in, giving Wil a wink that said, *You go, girl.* 'Though, if you want to stay, *I'm* happy to get you that drink.'

Wil sent uncharitable thoughts to Olivia, but she ducked out under the bar hatch. If she stayed any longer, Brett might come asking if she thought she was still being paid.

'Where do you want to go?'

'I just spent a day on a plane. Isn't there a beach around here someplace?'

'You did notice it was winter and miserable out there?'

He shrugged. 'You've clearly never seen the English winter.'

⁓

Half an hour later, Wil and David were sitting on the edge of the Broadbeach esplanade, watching the last daylight fade into the grubby horizon.

'Bit cold to be out here,' Wil grumbled. She really didn't want this conversation. Didn't want him to have come all this way.

'That's the beauty of living in England. This is positively balmy.' David dug his toes into the sand. He stared out at the water for a good minute. Wil felt the joking fade, like the surf disappearing into the sand. 'Were you never going to talk to me again?'

Wil heard the hurt in his voice, but her despair was stronger. 'I couldn't think about anything except getting away. I'm angry with you.'

'Fair,' he said.

'You bet it is. My life was already bad. I'd lost my job and my house, and then there were all the letters to deal with. And then I learned all these things I didn't want to know, and now I have people writing lies about me across the internet. You were the one thing in all of that—'

She broke off, not wanting to cry again. 'Look, what was it you wanted to show me? Because I've got a hot date with Netflix later and I'd like to get to it.'

She hated how pathetic she sounded.

David offered her his phone. Wil took one look at the screen, saw more tabloids and pushed his hand away. 'I don't want to see any more of that stuff, okay?'

'It's not stuff about you,' he said. 'This is what they wrote about me.'

'I've already seen it.'

'Not the drugs and the reality star tape. This is before that, when my career ended.'

Wil caught his eye. He had such a sadness in him now, she took the phone. It showed a grid view of text and photos taken from old newspaper articles. She read through headline after cutting headline about his injury, the surgeries, the end of his contract. Photo after photo comparing him at full fitness with him on crutches. His face in every photo told Wil how much he was hurting. It was so much more raw than the sordid shots of him later.

'I'm not making excuses for what I did after this,' he said. 'When you asked me if any of it was true, almost everything was. I was a tabloid reporter's dream back then—they hardly had to make anything up. Addiction. Partying. Questionable friends and girlfriends.'

'That . . . doesn't seem like you,' she said. It was hard to reconcile the clean, confident man she'd known in the village, who conversed effortlessly in French about ancient stonework on TV, with a washed-up, self-destructing playboy.

'It wasn't me,' he said. 'My career ended very suddenly. One day I was successful, healthy, living the dream. Football was all I ever wanted to do. All my family dreamed about, too. Overnight, all that was gone. I went from the peak of my career, representing my country, playing in premier clubs, to surgery and painkillers and nothing to do but regret the moment I made that move. I think I was in shock for six whole months. It wasn't pretty.

'Even before that, I was interesting to the tabloids—playing for England, the rivalry with Becks. But they love it more when you're into something juicy, something that sells on the front page. And boy, did I give them juicy.'

He paused, as if waiting for permission.

'Go on,' she said.

'I came away from the injury with a raging pill addiction. And a raging need to keep filling the hole football had left in my life. Drinking was never a problem for me, but the narcotics were, and how I spent my time. There were lots of nightclubs that I didn't leave until dawn. Partying with high-flyers. Fights I don't remember. Then the rehab time. It was my dad who pulled me round into that. I don't know what I'd have done without my family. They never gave up on me, even in relapse, but I did give up on myself for a while.'

In the midst of her own family disconnection, Wil felt a twinge of jealousy. But she also knew what it felt like to screw things up. 'What else?' she said. 'What about the tape?'

David looked up at the sky. 'After rehab, I pulled back from public events for a long while. The press went away gradually. But then I dated a woman who won one of those celebrity shows. I met her at a charity event. I thought she was a nice girl, but she had a certain . . . image. Platinum hair, long nails, lots of make-up, very glamour model.'

Wil could almost see the type of woman he meant, buxom and curated. Nothing like she was. She felt a stab of irrational jealousy. 'So what happened?'

He shrugged. 'I'd been out of the public eye, studying, trying to stay away from all the memories of playing. Trying to pitch the show to networks and be taken seriously, not just as some washed-up footballer. But she was an up-and-comer, going to all the parties, all the red carpets. I went with her to a lot of them. Like I said, I thought she was a nice girl.'

'But?'

'But she was into some heavy stuff. Cocaine, and other things. I never touched it. I could see the road she was going down, because it had happened to a few of my teammates in the past. But the tabloids assumed I was into it, too, so they started printing stories about my second sad decline.'

'And that's why she wasn't so nice?'

'Not at all. Addiction's a beast. I knew all about that myself, and how hard it is to kick it, and how lonely a place fame is. I could sympathise with all that. I wanted her to get help. Only she didn't want help. By the time I pushed the idea, she thought I'd fulfilled my usefulness in her social climb. So we split, and she released the tape.'

He looked down at the ground, clearly embarrassed. 'I never even knew she'd recorded it. My guess is that she kept it as insurance against her star fading. Which is calculating. But the worst thing was the shade it threw on the show. It didn't do so well in the first season. I had to work double time to avoid being cancelled, and I started using pills again to cope with all that. I came very close to spectacular disaster. The consequences of the bad publicity still follow me around, but the pills the second time . . . that could have ended all the good things that were going on. My point in telling you this—as well as mortifying myself—is that I should have told you about it earlier. Especially when you asked what Graham was talking about. If I was going to offer an excuse, it would be that I didn't want to be that person anymore. I didn't want to have to tell you. You might have been the only person in the universe who didn't know, and I liked it that way.'

Wil grunted and handed the phone back. She hugged her knees. The temperature was dropping with the night, the dog walkers on the beach huddling in their puffer vests. Even the waves sounded cold.

'I suppose,' she said, 'I can understand that. But . . .'

'But, the letters,' he said. 'Yeah, I screwed up. I should have asked you. I know you'll think I was going to use them for the show, but I honestly wasn't. I don't know how to ask your forgiveness or how to convince you to trust me again, but that's why I'm here.'

Wil kicked at the sand, torn. He was right—he'd scrubbed her trust by copying the letters. But then, if he hadn't, she'd have lost them all. And then there was the fact she still loved him despite everything. It was the reason this all hurt so much.

'Do you really mean that?' she said. 'I thought you didn't care. That everything you did was about the show.'

'You didn't think waking up in my bed was evidence I cared?' Then he dropped his voice. 'Are you telling me there's no hope?'

Wil remembered the mornings with him, all too vividly. So different to Rob, who'd scuttle out before she was awake. She didn't want to never experience that closeness again. Slowly, she leaned her shoulder into David, testing the tiniest sliver of good feeling she had for him. They sat like that for a long time, the dusk gathering around them.

'What did you do after the tape?' she asked eventually. 'How did you get from there to here?'

'You mean, how did I go from Shitsville to television host, rivalling Kevin McCloud?'

She laughed but heard the hope in his voice. 'Yes!'

'Little by little. First I had to acknowledge I wasn't where I wanted to be. That took a while, because sometimes being high at ten in the morning felt really good. But I'd end up hurting people, and myself. Once I knew I had to change, then the only thing I could do was go towards the thing I loved. Which was history.'

Wil sucked a breath; his words were so close to her mother's about living a life that moved towards what you love. 'You told me you didn't read the letters.'

'I didn't. Swear to god. Only what you'd showed me. Why?'

Wil kept that to herself. 'I don't know how to think about you now. Or what to do, about you, or even myself. I've hurt a lot of people.'

He blew out a long breath. 'Well, I won't give you some crap about it being easy. It wasn't for me. Especially when I had to learn how to do things without being praised all the time. I was a real natural at football. Not so much at architecture or TV.'

'I don't think that's an issue I'm dealing with,' she said wryly.

He chuckled. 'I'm sorry about that, really. I'm not sure what's worse. I had to learn a whole new way of being me—reading, paying attention to details, convincing people I could do more than run down a field and kick a ball into a net. And the second time I got into my addiction, I also had to carry the worry I'd blow everything up, because I had before.'

'Okay, that one I get.'

'But I loved what I was doing. And I just kept heading towards it. Taking the next step.'

Wil stared out at the waves, mulling. Her mother may have given the same advice, but Wil had never felt able to land the basics of life, let alone know what she loved.

'You still make it sound easy,' she said.

'That's because I'm in television,' he said. 'You're not supposed to see how hard it is. Calm on the surface, mad paddling underneath.'

'And what if I don't know what to go towards?'

Five waves crashed into the sand through his silence. Then he said, 'You've had a lot to process. Give it time. Think about it. Just don't do Vicodin while you're thinking.'

'I shouldn't laugh.'

'Go ahead. The guy who made all those mistakes seems like a long-ago person who isn't really me. Another reason I didn't want to talk about it with you.'

'Will I ever feel like that?'

David drew her into him, warm and reassuring. He gently kissed her temple. 'I'm sure of it.'

A heavy set of waves rolled in, scattering walkers who wanted to keep their feet dry. But the sky seemed less bleak. Wil nursed a spark of hope. She had no idea what to do, but he was right—she wanted to change. She didn't want to be here, doing the same things, in another ten years. Her mother had told her about her past, but the future was open.

Finally, she took a breath. 'I don't know where I'm going,' she said. 'But maybe I can start with someone I used to love.'

'Sounds fine to me.'

'It would. You're not related to her.'

David laughed, but Wil didn't. Somehow, she'd always known she would have to do this difficult thing. That she'd been running away from it most of her life. Now as she looked David in the eye and saw whatever they had wasn't dead, she knew it was time: to be brave enough to circle back and face it.

Chapter 27

K ate's terrace house in western Sydney had a wilting geranium pot by the front door and smelled of pine disinfectant. A cloud of it hit Wil as soon as Kate opened the door, still in her nurse's scrubs, clutching a sponge in a rubber-gloved hand.

'I thought you were joking,' she said, her gaze darting to David. 'I texted Neil to say I bet him twenty bucks that Wil did *not* just call me to say she was dropping round.'

'Can we come in?' Wil asked, her heart rate refusing to settle. She hadn't been to Kate's house since the wedding, and all their past conflicts seemed as solid as the brick front wall.

Kate pointed a pink rubber finger at David. 'You're that footballer. The one I saw in *Hello!*'

'David Hunter,' David said, offering his hand, then holding it up in surrender when Kate offered him the rubber glove with a cocked eyebrow. 'I'm moral support only. I'm happy to stay out here.'

Kate looked from Wil to David, and then back again with an absolutely inscrutable expression. 'Don't be silly. Come on into the chaos.'

Wil remembered the house being minimally furnished, but neat and clean, with potted plants on shelves and benches; even in the bathroom. Now, as she looked around at the stacks of papers shoved to the end of the dining table, the Lego and building blocks strewn across the carpet and unfolded washing spilling out of two baskets at the end of the couch, she felt ashamed. She hadn't realised how much things had changed for Kate. She had never even wondered about it.

'Neil's taken Ashleigh out for a few hours, so I'm jumping on the chance to clean out the fridge,' Kate said, returning to her post in the kitchen. 'We must have three months of take-out and leftovers growing legs in there.'

'You have a lovely home,' David said, managing to sound sincere.

Kate narrowed her eyes at him. 'You're kidding, right?'

'Not at all.' David pointed up to the ceiling. 'Crown mouldings, original cornices. Those chair rails over there are a pure delight, don't you think?'

Wil glanced around. David must have some architect super-power, seeing hidden history and grace. As if all the chaos was just a passing fad within a beautiful shell. Amazingly, Kate thawed.

'I think that's what we must have thought when we bought it,' she said, ruefully. 'We wanted to do it up, but now it just takes both of us to keep the mortgage, and I can't even think about pulling up carpets or removing walls. The idea just makes me tired.'

'Do you know what you'd want to do?'

Kate shrugged. 'To be honest, no idea. You watch enough reno shows you think you know, but I don't.'

'So it's just not the right time,' he said. 'Sounds like you have enough on for now. Maybe in a few years it will all be different. How old is your daughter?'

They continued on like this, making easy conversation, Kate answering David's questions as she pulled containers from the fridge and dumped the contents into a thick black garbage bag. Occasionally, she brought one up to eye level and declared that there was *no way* she was opening that one, before dumping it whole. Wil watched, licking her lips, aware she would soon have to stop being a coward.

Then David glanced at her and said, 'Well, I've been going on. I'll let you ladies catch up, if you wouldn't mind me going out the back to make a few calls?'

Kate was only too happy, offering drinks and snacks to take along, which David refused. Once Wil and Kate were alone again, David's absence felt as though an oak had been felled in an open field, and now there was no shade from the sun. Kate began running a sink of hot water.

'You are going to have to explain to me how it is that you ended up with that man,' Kate began, squirting suds into the tub. 'Last I heard you were dating some dropkick who booty-called you at eleven every night, unless he was off stoning for weeks. And now it's deliciously attractive and sparkling conversation man?'

'Rob wasn't . . .' Wil began, and sighed. She didn't want to slip into old patterns. 'I mean, yes, he was a dropkick. But . . . it wasn't *every* night.'

'Ha, ha,' Kate said.

Wil stared at the bench and ploughed on. 'To be honest, I don't know how it happened. I didn't think he'd be interested, with my lack of charm.'

Kate gave her a raised eyebrow. 'I know there's more to it than that.'

'Well, I fell into his duck pond. And that was after I blundered into some nettles. Which was after being chased by a farmer on a tractor.'

Kate laughed. The only reason Wil didn't was because she remembered that the farmer on the tractor had been Lord Elston. Her father. She picked at her nails, conversation limping to a stop.

'So, did you just come here to show him off? I mean, I don't blame you. If I had a hot piece of stuff like that I'd take him everywhere,' Kate said, then she looked up from the sink with an oddly vulnerable expression. 'Oh, please don't repeat that to Neil, okay? You know I'm only joking, but he's had a tough year and I wouldn't want him to be hurt.'

Wil was able to meet Kate's eye. 'I won't say anything.' She was more startled by the declaration. She knew nothing about what manner of tough year Neil had had. And shouldn't she know?

'So, how are you, Kate?'

Kate paused in dunking plastic containers but didn't look up. 'Look around. I think you can see for yourself.'

'I knew you were busy, I just didn't know you were *this* busy.'

'I didn't know you cared.' No trace of the charming Kate now.

'Of course I do.'

But even as she said it, Wil knew that there was little evidence that she actually did. So she wasn't even shocked when Kate began her rant, still savagely scrubbing at a Tupperware lid.

'Could have fooled me, Wil. You've only visited twice since I moved down here. You froze me out, and then you acted like my wedding was the hardest thing in the world for you. I'm always the one having to make the effort. And now, I'm the one with a little kid, who's always working. Neil and I hardly see each other, did you know that? No, because you only call about Tony or Colin, or Dad's back. If I call you, because I'm desperate to hear a friendly voice, you always seem like you're angry with me. And then I become this horrible person somehow. You don't ever see how I am.

'Well, I'm exhausted. I go from work, to cooking, cleaning, to feeding Ashleigh, to bathtime and being up at night, and then to work again. And then I've got you suddenly calling and asking about old letters, and texting about kids' books, and other things I don't have a single second for. Or, to be honest, that I really don't want to think about, being a mother now myself and without mine. But I'm sure you haven't thought about that, have you? You're just here for something else you need from me.'

Kate's fury made her voice thick and her eyes brim. Guilt choked Wil like a tight scarf. She wanted to reach out to Kate, but she was convinced Kate would shrug her off.

'I'm not here for that,' Wil whispered.

Kate shot her a look, still angry, but with hope in her red eyes, too. 'You're not?'

Wil shook her head. 'If I take over washing this stuff, will you stop and sit down or something? I know I'm useless at this, at talking to you. But I'm trying. And I'm better when I'm doing something.'

'Have at it.'

Kate handed over the sponge like a university degree, and then grabbed a bottle of water from the gutted fridge. She flopped onto a stool at the end of the counter and dropped her head back on the wall. 'I'm still mad at you. I think I'm the one who's allowed to be.'

'I know.'

'You can't fix it by doing dishes.'

'I know.' Wil dropped a cleaned container into the drainer. She paused, swirling a teething ring through the bubbles in the water. 'I'm sorry I treated you like that, and that I've made things harder for you.'

Kate didn't respond.

Wil grabbed another container before she could be distracted by the bubbles. 'I didn't know you were unhappy.'

'I'm not.'

Wil lifted her head. 'Didn't you just—'

'I'm not unhappy. I love Sydney, I love Neil and Ashleigh. I love my job. Am I overworked? Sleep deprived? Questioning my choices? Hell, yes. But I'm not unhappy. I just wish my sister had a bit more . . .'

Wil waited with desperate hope for whatever answer Kate was about to say. 'A bit more what?'

'I dunno. Whatever it is that you don't have right now.'

Wil slumped as she went back to scrubbing. This was the cue to say the things she didn't want to. She closed her eyes.

'You remember when you left home?' she started. 'And moved down here?'

'Of course.'

'I don't know what it was like for you,' Wil said, carefully. 'But for me, it was like the world ended. I was so mad at you for going and at Carol for pushing you to leave. I think that's why I behaved like that, why I got in trouble back then. I didn't know how to be without you. And it's been like that ever since.'

'So it's my fault?'

Wil shook her head. 'No, it's not an excuse. But you always seemed so much better than me. I didn't know how I could ever be like you, and trying seemed to make it worse. I think I just gave up. Going to your wedding was awful. You and Neil were so together and beautiful, and I couldn't even hold a job down. That's why I didn't come to Ashleigh's christening. I just . . . didn't want to feel that again. It seemed better if I wasn't here. Even though it was selfish.'

Kate was silent for a long while. 'I didn't know you felt like that. That's not . . . that's not what I wanted for you at my wedding.'

Wil dunked another container. 'I couldn't have told you that, then. And I'm not saying I feel perfectly fine now, because I don't. It's still hard to look at you and what you've achieved, and still be me. I mean, come on. I've been arrested and in tabloid magazines, and the year's only half done.'

Wil set a container in the rack and watched soapy water run off its surfaces. She wished it could be so easy to clean up her own life.

'Those letters Mum wrote you,' Kate said suddenly. 'Did they mention the books she wrote? Is that why you were asking?'

Wil bit her lip, grateful that the new container in her hands had a stubborn stain. She was afraid of starting down the path of talking about the letters, that it might end up with her and Kate being only half-sisters at the end of it.

'I didn't come here because of the letters,' Wil said.

Kate rubbed at a mark on the bench with her finger. 'Do you remember that photo we used to have? The one of us with Mum, and the truck?'

'I have it,' Wil said, grabbing a tea towel to dry her hands. She dug in her pocket, fumbling where her damp hands caught the fabric. Her hand shook as she offered the photo to Kate. 'Here.'

Kate took the photo gently. 'Gosh, I remember this, a little bit. Stopping at roadsides. Having stories in the bunk.'

Wil paused. 'You never said.'

Kate turned the photo over. Wil watched her run her finger down the side of the little mouse drawing, as she'd done so many times herself. Kate sighed and looked up. 'Sometimes it's much easier not to remember those things.'

They caught each other's eye, a moment of shared speechless understanding where Wil felt as though Kate was still the same sister she'd grown up with.

'Did you know that Mum sent a baby photo of you to someone in her village?' Wil said. 'This lady called Rose Maxwell. Mum used to turn the pages of her organ music. Rose showed me the photo. She keeps it on her wall with her family pictures.'

'Really?'

Kate looked away, but Wil saw tears in her eyes. Her sister didn't say anything for a long while, cradling the polaroid in her hand and staring out the window while Wil washed up two more semi-rancid containers. Then Kate sighed and said, 'I'm sorry for what I said before. It's just all that stuff about Mum out of the blue . . . it made me think of that day when she died. And I find that awful now, after having Ashleigh. Carol says maybe I need to do some work on it, but I don't really want to think about it. At all.'

Wil gripped her hands on the sink, afraid to look at Kate, her stomach folding in knots. 'I don't really remember much about that,' she whispered. Only she did remember, in the way her heart trembled. In how she felt like running. And like a shock, she realised she *had* been angry, long before Kate had left home. She'd been angry all the way back to that day.

'Well, I remember being scared,' Kate said. 'Of everything. The equipment, the room, even her. Maybe that's why I ended up as a nurse. My way of mastering it, if you want to overanalyse. But still, I've learned not to think about it. That's probably why I never showed you my letter when we were kids. And I still find them really hard to read, the ones I have.'

Wil watched Kate pluck unseen fluff from her nurse's scrubs. Finally, she dropped her hand. 'Put that last container in the rack. I have something you might want to see.'

Kate led Wil down the hall to the tight cupboard under the stairs. She pulled open the door and slid out a dusty cardboard box from deep on a low shelf. It rattled as she plonked it on the floor.

'What's this?'

'Mum's tapes,' Kate said. 'There are a few photos in there, too, tucked between them. And some of her books, in the bottom. I should have mentioned it when you asked. I just . . . didn't.'

Wil reached a hand into the box and came out with a cassette tape, its handwritten label full of Beatles songs. The writing was faded, but so familiar.

'You're welcome to take them,' Kate said. 'If you'd like to go through them all. I mean, I have no idea if any of them would still play, but that's not really the point, is it? Actually, I'd prefer you took it all. If that's okay. I'll keep my letters.'

She and Kate looked at each other again, and something in that barrier of old conflicts had shifted: less fear, more hope. And from that place, Wil could see for the first time how much her own fear danced around her mother's death. The unanswered questions about what had happened that day. Why she had been taken away? Who had been there when her mother died? Had anyone been there? Kate might not want to discuss it, but Wil knew that night was a wound in her barely formed memory. One that she couldn't ignore anymore.

Wil sat back on her heels, facing Kate across the box of their mother's things, trying to see her sister again as a little girl, as she'd been in that photo, and not this woman that she'd had such trouble relating to.

'I'm really happy that you're happy,' Wil said. 'I'll try to be a better sister, okay?'

Kate smiled down at the floor. 'Okay.'

'And also, would you mind very much if I went by Mina now? I'm trying to shake the whole Willy thing.'

Kate gave a quick eyebrow that she dropped just as fast. 'Sure.' She paused. 'You know, that's what Mum used to call you.'

'I know,' Mina said.

'Oh, god, see what happens?' Kate sucked a breath, tipping back her head so the tears wouldn't run out of her eyes. In that one moment, Mina saw all the layers of emotion in her sister's own experience, all the years of healing and conversation that might still need to pass between the two of them because of what had happened. But she was prepared for that, if that's what it took. She'd started.

'I'm going to come down here more,' she said. 'Maybe I can take Ashleigh out sometimes, give you guys some time together?'

Kate laughed. 'Okay, steady on. You're going for a medal now.'

'Well, kids are easy, right? You just give them sugar and let them watch TV.'

Kate rolled her eyes. But she leaned over the box and wrapped Mina in a hug. 'Now, how about you get that gorgeous man back in here? I want to take a photo as evidence you brought him here.'

⌒

Much later, after David and Mina had stayed long enough for Neil and Ashleigh to come home, and Neil demanded Kate pay up on the bet, Mina closed the cab door and dropped her head back on the rest.

'That seemed to go well?' David asked.

'Kinda,' Mina said, deep in thought. 'I have a lot of fixing to do though.'

The cab pulled away, heading east towards the city. David's idea was that they play tourist on the shores of the harbour, stroll by the bridge and the Opera House, and find a nice wine bar for a late afternoon drink.

But as they approached Circular Quay, with the bridge towering over the water and the sails of the Opera House peeking through, all Mina could think about was her mother, in the middle of the New York winter, seeing that same sight on a television. About her mother and Cameron meeting on a beach, not so terribly far from here. Where that had all ended up.

She managed to step out of the taxi, but then she couldn't go any further. She needed to fill that place where Kate didn't want to go, to get answers while she had the courage to chase them. And she couldn't do that here. She leaned back into the cab and asked the driver to wait, the box of tapes clanking under her arm.

'Something wrong?' David asked.

'I need to do something first. And I'm sorry, but I need to go by myself.'

A small smile crept onto David's face. 'You're coming back, right?'

Mina nodded.

'Good. Because you see that pub over there? That's where Prince Frederik met Mary Donaldson. If you don't come back, I'm sure I could find another good sort around here.'

'Comparing yourself to royalty, now?' Mina said. 'Very humble.'

David laughed and put his arms around her, kissing her slowly. 'See, that's how you know everything is going to be all right . . . when you can laugh again,' he said.

Mina clung to him for a heartbeat, then pushed back before she lost her nerve. 'I'll text you.'

'Take care, Mina.' He kissed her once more then stepped away. 'Don't get yourself arrested.'

Mina threw up her hand. 'Why would you *say* that?'

'Too soon?' David laughed again and blew her a kiss. Mina watched him stroll away, shaking her head, but laughing too. Maybe it would be all right.

She slid back into the cab and pulled out her phone to text Colin.

'Can you head north, please?' she told the driver. 'I'm just getting the exact place.'

As the taxi pulled away, she messaged Colin. *Can you send me your mum's address?*

Immediately he typed back: *Jeebus. Did hell just freeze over?*

Chapter 28

Mina's stepmother Carol lived in a smart little cottage on the northern beaches, boasting a well-tended front garden behind a white picket fence and décor straight from the pages of a beach house mood board: pale wood, soft blue and crisp white, complete with seashells and macrame hanging baskets.

If Carol hadn't been home, Mina's courage would have failed her. But she found her stepmother in the front garden, wearing a sunhat and weeding an azalea bed. She gave a cheerful wave as the taxi pulled up. *Colin the rat*, thought Mina. But she got out of the cab.

'This is a *lovely* surprise,' Carol said, dusting off her hands as she opened the gate. 'Kate was just telling me you'd been visiting. How are you?'

All right, Kate the rat.

Mina awkwardly professed to be fine and let Carol lead the way inside, chatting the whole way about a new iced tea she was loving and biscuits fresh from the oven. Mina had always found her stepmother difficult to relate to. Something about Carol's openness and constant offering of food and drink, the way she never got angry and had all those inspirational Bible quotes on the wall around the house. It left Mina feeling unsettled.

But now, in her stepmother's perfectly tended living room, perched on the pale blue sofa with its bright yellow print cushions, Mina thought about how Carol had been the one who'd realised her mother wasn't well and had welcomed her into the house. Maybe that was just how Carol was.

'Are you feeling quite all right?'

Mina shook herself. 'Sorry. I was somewhere else.'

Carol gave her a tentative smile. Mina thought she saw nerves in that smile, as if Carol didn't know what she was doing either. Wait . . . was Carol uncomfortable? 'It's been a while since I saw you last. Do you still prefer Wil? Tony was trying to convince me to call you Willy, but I think he's stirring.'

Mina grimaced.

'Ah, I see I was right. He is a dreadful stirrer.'

'Actually, I prefer Mina now,' she said quickly.

Carol, whose iced tea had been halfway to her mouth, put the drink down. 'Oh, how lovely. That's what your mother always called you.' And without missing a beat, she looked Mina right in the eye and said, 'She'd have been so proud of you.'

Mina was caught by a sudden urge to cry. She pretended to chew a biscuit, inhaled and coughed on the crumbs.

'I'm sorry, I didn't mean to upset you,' Carol said, annoyingly perceptive, as Mina recovered. 'It's just I think of her a lot. Even after all this time.'

Mina swallowed in surprise. 'You do?'

'Yes. I think under different circumstances we might have been quite good friends. And she was utterly devoted to you girls. Every time I had a hard day with my boys, I would think of how she was with you and Kate. Endless energy.'

Mina took a big breath, feeling as though she were outside her own body. 'It's actually her I wanted to talk about.'

Carol gently raised her eyebrows, as if she'd been long expecting this. 'How can I help?'

'Well . . .' Mina began. 'This year I received some letters she wrote to me. I was supposed to get them a long time ago, for my birthdays.'

'Ah,' Carol said, leaning back. 'I thought she was writing something in those last weeks. She was very protective about it, though. I knew that you and Kate got a letter, but . . . sorry. Go on.'

'No, actually, that's what I'm interested in. The letters told me all about her life, things I never knew about, but they stop when she stopped writing. And I keep thinking about her last day. I don't remember much except . . . wanting to be with her so much. But Cameron . . .' Mina waved a hand, unable to put this into words, '. . . and then she died, and I never saw her again, and it's like this great black hole inside me. And then Kate—'

Mina exhaled a great breath, pinching her hands between her knees to keep herself anchored. She shook her head. She couldn't finish.

Carol put down her cup again and took her own breath. 'Have you been wondering about this a long time?'

Mina nodded, teeth crushing her lip, feeling the weight of this buried memory that shifted underneath everything else in her life. Terrified of what she might find out, and yet terrified to never know.

'I can tell you anything you want to know,' Carol said, very matter-of-fact. 'I was there that night.'

'You were?'

Carol nodded. 'You were so young, I wouldn't be surprised if your memories are all fragments. But you were with your mother almost constantly in those last few days. Snuggled up beside her on the bed. It was lovely, and heartbreaking. If I was a superstitious person, I'd say that she was waiting for something, and somehow you knew it, too, and wanted to help her until whatever it was came to pass. I think she held on for so long because you were there.'

Mina thought about what her mother had said in the letters, about having to be strong around her and Kate all the time, and how exhausting it was. 'Was that why I wasn't there when she died?'

Carol sighed. 'Not exactly. I felt awfully for both of you. See, you were never fazed by all the medical things. I think you looked at Ann and just saw your mother, so you wanted to stay. But Kate couldn't do that. Cameron ended up taking Kate out because we could see that it was distressing your mum to see her so upset, especially as Ann was needing to slip away. Then Cameron came to get you, too, because he thought that Kate needed you. And we both thought that your mum wouldn't be able to let go if you were there. I've seen that before in my career, many times. Sometimes people wait until they're able to leave on their own terms, whatever those are.'

'So . . . she was alone when she died?'

'Oh, no.' Carol took a hesitant breath. 'Did your mother ever mention a man called John Elston in her letters?'

Mina jerked in surprise. 'John?'

'He was someone she was close with once. I think perhaps he might have been her oldest friend. Perhaps more than that, once. I—'

'I know who he is,' Mina said, almost breathless.

Carol nodded. 'I think she was waiting for him to come, because it wasn't many hours after he arrived that she passed. I wasn't in the room, because it was obvious they needed some privacy, but I was there right at the end. She seemed to have lifted a huge weight from herself after she had spoken to him. A peace had come over her, and she was able to drift into sleep.

'I remember being so grateful to him at the time. Whatever they said to each other, or didn't say, it seemed it was what she needed to hear. Cameron, for all his good qualities, wasn't good with sickness. He doesn't know how to express those kinds of feelings. But John . . . look, I didn't know him from a bar of soap, but he didn't flinch. He took her how she was, as if she was exactly how he'd last seen her. I think that's what love does.

'So in the end, she passed very peacefully, Mina. I'm so sorry if you wanted to be there, and if that's been on your mind all these years. But I know Cameron was doing what he thought was best for you girls. When I went to find him, you and Kate were both asleep, with your arms so tight around each other. I know it doesn't change anything, but I believe you really helped her that night, Mina.'

Mina sat, stunned, her cup forgotten. John had been there. He had come after all, even when her mother had clearly thought she would never see him again. That night, which had been dark in her memory, was now a vivid picture, her own memories stitched together with Carol's and Kate's and her mother's peace. Mina felt an intense relief.

'What about John?' she croaked.

'By the time I came back to the room, he was gone. Your mum had a rose from one of the bouquets resting on her chest, which I think he must have put there. But I never saw him again and after that . . . well, life eventually went on.' Carol unexpectedly reached across to clasp Mina's hand. 'She wasn't alone, darling. And she wasn't distressed. We held her hands and she just slid away into whatever comes next.'

Mina took a great breath and bawled her eyes out. Carol squeezed her hand as she cried, but she didn't let go.

'There, now,' she said eventually. 'You obviously needed to hear that. And I'm sorry that it's taken this long for us to talk about it.'

'I'm sorry that I was always so difficult,' Mina said, still hiccupping.

Carol smiled. 'You were different,' she said firmly, as if this might have been something she'd told herself over and over until she believed it. 'Not difficult. You'd been through a harrowing experience at an age when you couldn't make sense of it. Of course it wasn't going to be easy. You and Kate held each other up for a long time.'

'I thought you made Kate go away when she moved to Sydney. I was so angry with you. But it wasn't your fault.'

Carol looked surprised, but then her expression shifted. 'Anyone could see how hard it was on you when she left.

I wouldn't blame you for that. It wasn't an easy decision for Kate, but I think it was a good one.'

'But Kate always got on so much better with you. She always held it together.'

'Everyone has their own problems, Mina, and Kate has her own burdens from what happened. She is naturally anxious and a perfectionist. She finds it difficult to ask for help. But she also wants to do the right thing, and she's easily moved. We all have those assets and challenges.'

'And what am I like?' Mina asked hopelessly, needing Carol to tell her.

Carol hardly paused. 'Your heart is difficult to touch, I think, and you're not easily impressed, speaking from experience. But you're incredibly loyal and hard-working when there's something that has caught your imagination.'

Mina laughed and narrowed her eyes. 'I don't remember my report cards ever saying anything like that.'

Carol gave a bird-like laugh. 'No, because school never much impressed you. But I remember you sitting up late at night, finishing those models you built. One was a Victorian mansion, made of paper. Do you remember what happened to it?'

Mina's mouth dropped open. She'd completely forgotten about that. 'Tony dropped it in the bath one night and ruined it,' she said. 'I was so angry with him.'

Lord, it seemed she'd been angry with everyone. A quiet, insidious anger, lurking like a pilot flame around the edge of her soul.

'I can only imagine. And then you went off to jobs with your father, as soon as he'd let you along. I don't think I've ever seen Cameron prouder. I know you working for him wasn't a success in the way he would have wanted, but Cameron's standards for his office are a bit extreme; that's part of the reason our marriage didn't work out. And I could never see you doing administration for a builder as your career.'

Carol smiled and sipped her tea.

Mina pushed her cup away and heaved a sigh. She might feel a new peace around her mother's death, but it didn't change all the secrets she was holding. Carol didn't seem to know there was more to the story. No one seemed to know except Mina herself . . .

. . . oh, and John, who she'd lobbed the secrets grenade at, courtesy of the Royal Mail. What consequence would that now have for Cameron?

Maybe it was better to come clean.

On the journey back to the Gold Coast, Mina endlessly rehearsed what she could say to her father. To Cameron. Argh, she still couldn't get used to thinking of him that way.

She felt very different approaching his house than when she'd been living there. She'd been oblivious to so much. And now she was about to have the hardest conversation she could ever imagine having.

She glanced back to the street, but David had gone. She'd told him to come back in an hour so she didn't chicken out. She knocked, and waited. When she heard steps come down the stairs, it felt like two fists were jammed in her stomach.

Cameron opened the door and paused when he saw her. He was still in a work shirt, and he looked tired.

'Hi,' she said, faltering, 'I'm sorry I haven't come earlier.'

'Okay,' he said.

'And I want to say I'm sorry. About . . . everything.'

That much, she'd rehearsed on the drive over and, now it was said, she hadn't a clue how to go on.

He considered her as the clock in the hall ticked through the seconds.

'What's everything?' he said finally.

'Well . . .' This wasn't what she wanted to bring up, but now she was groping for an answer. 'Demolishing that kitchen. And getting arrested. And the shoplifting. Oh, and that I didn't tell you I was going overseas.'

There, that was closer to the reason she'd come. But now he was frowning.

'You didn't have to tell me squat about where you were going,' he said, with a touch of exasperation in his voice. 'I kicked you out, remember? And you're thirty-one. You can go to the moon as long as I'm not paying for it.'

She laughed despite the nerves. 'Yeah, I guess so. But, still.'

'Are you coming in?' he said finally.

Mina followed him upstairs to the kitchen. He put a beer in front of her, which she took so she could hold something, and then she fretted over saying, *So, there's something I need to ask you.* 'Where are the boys?' she asked, completely failing.

'Tony took the truck to the wash. Not sure about Col. Maybe over at Shonna's. Seems to be hanging out there a bit.' He paused. 'Did you find what you were looking for?'

'Where?'

'In England. Figured you didn't come to discuss your sock drawer.'

Mina took a breath. This was it. This was her opening to say, yes, she'd found more than she'd been looking for, actually, and she had to tell him about it.

'Well . . . more than I expected.' She took a breath.

'You look different,' he said suddenly, then shook his head. 'You know, I didn't think those letters would lead to anything good.'

'They didn't really,' Mina said.

But Cameron was still shaking his head. 'I'll admit the whole tabloid thing was a shock and a bloody nuisance, but Kate said you'd been to visit her. Carol, too.'

Mina started in surprise. 'Carol called?'

'She does, sometimes,' Cameron said, then added with a wry smile, 'and not just for the boys. Still trying to reform me, probably.'

Mina returned the smile. 'Yeah, I did visit. I owed them both an apology.'

Cameron paused, considering her, and Mina couldn't help doing the same. He was leaning against the counter in the kitchen he had built himself. He had bleeding nicks on his fingers and forearms from work. Cameron didn't believe in Band-Aids. She smiled, sadly, thinking about how much she knew about him, as if laying down a last record of how they were before she told him he wasn't her father.

Then he said, 'I think I owe you one.'

'One what?'

'I didn't think anything good would come of those letters. I always believed that. But I didn't realise what having them might mean to you, when you couldn't really remember her. I'm sorry I kept them from you. I thought it was the right thing.'

Mina stared at him. He was still completely restrained, but it was more concession than she'd ever heard from him in her life. And she believed him.

'Hell,' he said, 'if I'd known they'd have you off overseas, finding jobs in stately houses and landing one of England's greatest footballers, I'd have given them to you years ago!'

Mina laughed, aware he was making a joke to cover the discomfort of admitting he'd been wrong. That was another thing she knew about him: how he prided his strength, and how strength to him was all about how much he could hold inside, and never concede any weakness.

She had a fleeting glimpse then of how much she *didn't* know about him. What things had gone on in his heart and soul. She wanted the chance to know him better and to make him proud—not because she was doing what he wanted, but because of the things she had learned from him. She didn't want to destroy that with her secret. What did it matter, now, to ask him if he'd known she wasn't his daughter? He had been her father, in all the ways that mattered.

'I'm still sorry,' she said quickly, her heart beating in fright for what she'd nearly done. 'Actually, I wondered if I could ask your advice.'

He raised his eyebrows.

'I want to start a business,' she said, and stopped because, for just a moment, she was sure his eyes had sparkled.

'What kind?' he said.

'Well ... designing and building, kitchens and bathrooms maybe. I like designing, and I don't want to just do the same things everyone is doing. So for people who want something different, you know?'

'Do you mean like that avant-garde architect stuff?'

She shook her head. 'No, more like restoration and recovered materials. Remaking from what was there before. Telling a story. What do you think?'

She held her breath, afraid he'd shoot her down.

He dug his fingers into his chin, rasping through the stubble as he thought. 'I know one or two contractors dealing in recycled materials on the coast, but not exclusively. And one of them's a right pack of wankers. I don't know how they keep clients.'

Her hopes leapt. 'So it's a good idea?'

'I didn't say that. It's half an idea at best. What about a business plan? Starting capital? Suppliers?'

'No idea. I was hoping you'd be able to fill me in.'

He chewed his lip, then grabbed a fresh beer from the fridge. 'Come and pull up a pew. I'll give you a rundown on how the other operators work. That can be a place to start. But you don't want to jump into these things unprepared. I spent a few years preparing to open my business.'

Mina watched him, taking a deep breath. 'Will you tell me about that, too? When you started your business?'

'I suppose so, but the market's completely different now.'

'Well, what about when you were a diver? And how you decided to change to building.'

He paused. 'That's going back a long way. But yeah, maybe. Later, after this stuff. Grab that pen there, Willy. I've got paper.'

Mina could hardly breathe as she followed him. For the first time in her life, she was sure this was going somewhere. That it wasn't just an empty promise, a desperate hope that she'd inevitably muck up tomorrow. This felt like cutting a road completely new.

He talked at her for half an hour, and she took the best notes she could, knowing she'd have to come back and ask him to go over most of it again. The scale of things he thought about—accounting, opportunities, maintaining contacts, tools and inventory, licences—scared her. But she thought, maybe, just maybe, she could learn it. Because she wanted to.

Into the second hour, when Mina hadn't touched her beer and Cameron was onto his third, she looked up from her notes to find him eyeing her.

'What?' she said.

He shrugged slightly. 'Just wondering what it was in the letters. What she said that changed you. I couldn't do it with anything I said.'

Mina tried to smile, happy and sad at once. 'I guess when I was done with the letters, I decided I didn't want to be where I was anymore, and someone told me I just had to take the first step to start doing something different.'

He grunted. 'Wasn't David Hunter, was it?'

'It was,' Mina said. She looked at the wall to avoid his eyes. 'I always wanted to be more like Kate, but I couldn't see how to make up the gap between me and her. But maybe I don't have to. I can just be a better me.'

He sighed heavily. 'Jeez, Willy, it's not like I meant to compare you. I just wanted you to stand on your own feet.'

'I know that.'

He paused, and Mina sensed that his thoughts were travelling way back, thinking of her and Kate when they'd been little, maybe even allowing himself to remember Ann. To feel all the weight of what had happened, and all that had changed since.

'I know I haven't been a good sister, either,' Mina said softly. 'But I'm not just trying anymore. I'm doing. I'm making it up to Kate.'

Cameron chuckled. 'You and David suit each other, you know that? He had his troubles when his playing career ended. Had to make up for a lot of things and the press didn't do him any favours. They make things up all the time. Look at Lady Di and what happened to her.'

Mina snorted. 'Oh yes, David Hunter and Lady Di and me. We have so much in common!'

Cameron thumped his fist to his chest. 'Any daughter of mine can stand shoulder to shoulder with royalty. I won't have it otherwise. Now, David, he was destined to be one of the best. That match from the Premier League back in '06? Magic.'

Mina smiled, another anxiety ebbing away as he spoke. She *was* his daughter, in all the ways that mattered. Maybe he did know the truth, or suspected, and chose to ignore it. Or maybe he never knew, and the whole idea of their family rested on it. Either way, he would always be home.

'Dad,' she said, when she could get a word in. *Thank you. For everything.* 'If you're intent on putting me next to royalty, I want to go by Mina from now on. I'm sick of being called Willy.'

⁓

When Tony came back from the car wash, there was a round of the usual jibes. But by then, Mina and Cameron had mapped out the start of her idea, and Cameron told Tony to pull his head in and they went back to their notes.

'Don't just leap into it,' Cameron said again, as they downed tools to organise dinner. 'Think about it. Work out what you need, how to afford it. Before I started, I saved a good while to make sure the business had a good backing.'

I know, Mina thought, *more than you know.*

'Why's David Hunter outside?' Tony asked, clearly annoyed to be silenced.

'Shit!' Mina said, leaping up. 'I completely forgot!' She spun on Tony. 'Why didn't you say that first?'

'I wanted a beer.'

Mina raced back down to the car to find David reclining on the bonnet, sunning himself as if it were January.

'I'm so sorry,' Mina said, out of breath. 'You should have come into the house. What on earth are you doing? It's not T-shirt weather.'

'It is back home,' David said.

'I'm sorry, we got distracted—'

'Don't worry about it. I think I'm quite entertaining for the neighbours.' He waved towards the second storey of a house across the street, where a curtain rapidly pulled closed. He laughed and jumped down.

The day seemed to set the tone for the week. Mina researched and planned, and the family came back together. But as David's departure date approached, Mina thought increasingly of the church in South Bandinby, and what had happened to the letter she'd sent to the manor.

'Surprisingly I think it helped,' David said when Mina asked one day about how the tabloids had affected his prospects in the village. 'It's almost an enemy-of-my-enemy-is-my-friend situation. Lord Elston's had two meetings with the producers last week. Or maybe it's because of the structural issues—he wouldn't want the place to fall down. Either way, it's looking like we'll have the chance to run a story there after all.'

This did nothing to reassure Mina. She tried and failed three times to call the manor house. The first time, she hung up while the phone was still ringing. The second, she heard Bill pick up, then hung up on him. The third time, she spoke to Bill for a minute, pretending to ask how he was and to thank him for his help. When he began to ask if there was any chance she was coming back to finish the kitchen, Mina muttered lame excuses about being back in Australia.

But the issue nagged at her, sucking energy from her attempts to find ways to kick her new venture into gear. She needed to talk to the demolition crews, to see if they would give her a heads-up on any useful materials before they put an excavator bucket through them. Her father had agreed to point any potential clients in her direction. Or Cameron had. Despite deciding not to tell him, she still wondered how to hold him in her thoughts. And how to ensure the niggling worry didn't stop her moving forward.

She was hunched over the coffee table at Shonna's, ringed in pages of notes and dreading David's departure in a few hours, when there was a knock at the front door. Mina stuck her pencil behind her ear and trotted across to answer it. She swung the door open and got the fright of her life.

'Oh my god, Lord Elston,' she said.

He was dressed for a gentlemanly day out on the water, in bone-coloured trousers, white shirt and a blue blazer. For once, the flat cap was absent.

'Baron Elston,' he said, dryly. 'God is still a few rungs above me.'

'Funny,' she said, her heart thumping. What on earth was he doing here? She was intensely afraid of what might happen and couldn't summon the anger she'd had when they'd last met. He seemed so much less grandiose without the backdrop of the manor, and she worried what his arrival might mean for Cameron.

'Would you invite me in?' he said.

Mina hesitated. 'What do you want?'

'Well, I was having my kitchen renovated, you see, and I seem to have lost my contractor. I wondered if she was here.'

Mina dropped her hand from the door. 'Maybe she didn't much like the working conditions. It's hardly a thing to fly around the world for. Most people call first.'

'Most people aren't the subject of interest for a nation mad for tabloid newspapers,' Lord Elston said. 'And where said newspapers are apt to get hold of phone calls. Much safer to say things in person. They also seem to lose interest the further from England one goes. And my father always told me that an apology was worth any journey.'

Slowly, Mina pushed the door open and allowed him in. He looked around before selecting the sagging armchair across from the couch and coffee table. She sat opposite.

'Your, um, apartment?' he said.

'A friend's. I'm crashing on her couch, saving some cash for a new place. I got kicked out of my old one a few weeks back because I demolished the wrong kitchen.' Mina shrugged. What did it matter now that she couldn't hold her tongue? 'And I also have to pay my brother back for the trip to England.'

'I see.' He allowed the silence time to settle before he drew an envelope out from the inside pocket of his blazer and slid it across the table. The paper was worn and yellowed on the edges. Chills ran over Mina's skin just looking at it. She'd seen envelopes like that before, many of them.

'What's this?' she said.

'I'll come to the point. That letter you sent was a shock.' He paused, obviously grasping for words. 'I last saw Ann twenty-six years ago, which was also the last time I was in this country. Even that long . . . wasn't long enough.'

Mina stared at the letter. 'Long enough for what?'

His eyes flicked to the letter, then he let his breath go, leaving the thought unsaid. 'You can read it, if you want to.'

'This is the letter from under the flagstone at the church, isn't it? Under the stone that says—'

'*Remember, man, as you pass by,*' he said. 'She used to joke about it, when we were young. Remember Mann as you pass by. She said it meant I'd never forget her. And I never have. Every time I walk over that stone, I think about her.'

'You called her a fantasist.'

'Yes.'

'But—'

'I'd have called her worse in that moment, if I thought it would sway you from your questions. She was a fantasist. She had more imagination than anyone I've ever known. But Ann was never a liar. Quite the opposite. Overly frank, like you, was how she was. In fact, holding my secrets must have been the hardest thing she ever did.'

Mina reached for the envelope and turned it over. 'It hasn't been opened.'

'No.'

She pushed it away again. 'This one wasn't for me. You were supposed to read it.'

He looked up at the ceiling, his jaw working, clearly distressed. 'Ann . . . she was fading that last day. Sometimes she made sense, but mostly not. The parts that made sense were all about when we were young. But there was one thing she said that I got rather wrong.'

His gaze flickered over her. 'She said that I had given her the greatest gift. I didn't think anything of it at the time. But now I realise she meant you.'

Mina shifted in her seat. 'I—'

John held up a hand. 'I'll admit that my behaviour towards you in the village was hot-headed and ill-considered. I didn't expect to react that way after all this time. But I knew you were her daughter, that first day I saw you in the field. I could see her in you. I felt as though the clocks had turned back, and I didn't want that.'

'So you wanted to run me over?'

'I don't know what I wanted,' he said, wryly. 'Except I think to forget. But I was curious about you, and you made me feel as though she was here again, at least in part. But when you came with those letters, asking about Thomas . . .'

'You thought it best to throw them in the river.'

'Yes,' he said, looking away. 'That was a terrible business, what happened to my brother. But the lie was not a choice I would have made. Our mother had very strong ideas about it, and I deferred to her, in the end. But I regret destroying Ann's words because of that. I had the river dragged afterwards. Bill said he tried all the spots that the current catches things coming down the flow, but he says he only found one piece, where a duck had dragged it up into a nest. The rest, I'm afraid, are lost.'

Mina half-smiled. 'There were copies.'

'Ah,' he said, seeming to relax. 'Bill finally admitted to me that he'd given you the letters. How Ann asked him to place them in the church, and how he'd taken them out for safe-keeping. He's been with me a long time and I thought we knew everything about each other, so it was surprising to find a secret after all. But having lived one so long myself, I know how they can become as binding as truth.'

Mina's eyes fell on the letter again. 'But you didn't read it. Why not?'

He paused a long time before he answered. 'She wrote that letter when she thought she wouldn't see me again. But I was there at the end of her life, though in quite a different way to what I'd once hoped. And as terrible as that was, it removed all the doubts I'd ever had about her. I don't need her words to know what she would have said, and I don't want that peace changed by what's in this.'

'That seems . . . terribly sad,' Mina said, her voice cracking, looking over the envelope again. 'What if you only think you know what someone's going to say and you're wrong?'

He caught her eye, and she glimpsed the fear in him.

'I think you're worried it won't say what you hoped,' she whispered. 'But if you don't read it, you'll wonder.'

He snorted, softly. 'You are so like her,' he said. 'All right. If you read it, I will, and then we'll agree to take it back to the church. It can stay there long after we are dust. I could never have my life with her, because of faults we both had. But the stones can witness the end of it. As you will, being ours. Maybe you're the only thing that truly is.'

Mina put her head into her hands, moved by the depth of feeling John obviously still had for her mother. She felt more than ever at a crossroads, with so much confusion on what to do now.

'I never expected you to say that,' she croaked.

'Nor I,' he said. 'But somehow, after all these decades of strife, you being my daughter seems the easiest thing to accept.'

Mina burst into noisy tears. 'But this is terrible!' she sobbed. 'What am I supposed to do now?'

'Well, for a start, I want to know if you would consider coming back.'

Mina stifled her sniffles. 'Why?'

'To finish the work you began, for a start. And maybe, if you choose, to learn something of the estate. It is your estate, too. You have a half-brother you have never known and land our family has presided over for generations. That is no small thing.'

'No one here knows anything about . . . us,' she said carefully. 'I don't think it's right that they do. It was hard enough for me. It's unfair to them.'

'And I have the same problem, being as I'm John and not Thomas,' he said. 'I'm well practised at living in secrets, Mina. Your family never need know there is anything other than a professional relationship, if you so choose. I had my secret thrust on me by my family, because they were too ashamed of Thomas to admit to the truth.'

'David knows,' Mina said, feeling bound to warn him. 'It was in the letters, and I told him about it.'

John grunted. 'That's the thing about secrets—someone always knows. Perhaps we'll have more tourists if it comes out. This one between us, though, is not my choice, and it doesn't change the truth. You *are* my daughter, regardless of what anyone knows. Just the same way Ann was the love of my life, regardless of what my actions suggest. I'm not proud of it, but marrying Susie came from wanting to be connected to Ann.'

Mina was attempting to digest this when she heard footsteps coming to the front door. She reached for the envelope and slid it quietly into the pocket of her cargos, just as David opened the door.

'I'm back—er, Lord Elston,' he said.

'David,' John said, rising to his feet and extending his hand. 'How are you?'

'At the end of the holidays,' David said. 'And you?'

'Quite the same.'

John turned to Mina. 'You'll consider what I asked?'

Mina could only nod as John Elston, a man everyone thought lived in Jamaica, and who everyone would think she had no connection to, walked out the door. But there was connection. There was the long history of family tying them together.

And so she knew that she would go back, not to aspire to be a lady of an old estate but because it would be part of making something entirely new.

Epilogue

Spring came late to England the next year, but even the frigid air and the skeleton trees didn't keep the crowds away as the film crew set up in the churchyard. From her perch on the manor wall, Mina watched David striding towards the camera, which was fixed on the grandest angle of the church. Out of shot, a crowd of villagers and visitors held court. Rose was moving among them, her antiques roadshow and bake sale raising funds between takes.

'You've probably never heard of this place,' David was saying. 'After all, it's just a tiny village in the fields of Lincolnshire, with no pub and no shops, no reason to stop in. But there are surprises here that make it worth the journey from London. This church, for example, just happens to be one of the oldest examples of Anglo-Saxon architecture in the country. And just out there in the fields are the remains of an entire village, lost to the plague but remembered in local stories. All that on the lands of a noble family with both a long, long history and a very modern controversy. Welcome to South Bandinby.'

He stared hard into the camera, and Mina stifled a giggle. 'It seems much more ludicrous in person than on TV,' she said.

John grunted beside her. 'Speak for yourself. All seems ludicrous to me.'

'But you still let them do it.'

'Yes,' he said, sounding doubtful as to his sanity.

The crew were recording all the introductory pieces today, before scaffolders arrived tomorrow and covered the church façade. David was in a huddle with the producer on whether they should go again.

'Are you having second thoughts?' Mina said to John.

His eyebrows twitched. 'I'm an Elston,' he said. 'I don't have second thoughts.'

Mina laughed at him. 'Sure you don't.'

He smiled, just a small one. The time Mina had known him could only be counted in months, but she had the feeling that smile had been in retirement for a long time. And she knew he'd been having second thoughts his whole life. Now, he was finally acting on some of them.

'The town meeting went well last night,' she said.

John grunted. 'Maybe I should have given you the microphone.'

'And have your secret daughter tell everyone that you've been pretending to be another man for thirty years?'

'Careful,' he said, dropping his voice to match hers. 'If you intend that secret to hold, you ought to know that Rose Maxwell keeps her hearing aid turned up. Bill warned me.'

'Speak of the devil,' Mina muttered. Rose had detached

herself from the crowd and was sneaking close behind David and his producer, on her way towards them. She waved.

'Good morning, Your Lordship,' she said. 'And Wilhelmina. This is rather a lot of visitors, isn't it? Not that I really approve of the quiet being so disturbed, but we have sold all the jam.'

'Excellent,' John said. 'What will you do with the proceeds, now that the production company is covering the roof?'

'I've an idea,' Rose began. 'What if—'

They broke off as the crew held up their *Quiet please* paddles and David began walking along the south wall of the church, trailed by a camera operator.

'The Elston family of South Bandinby have always been royalists,' David began, 'a steadfast loyalty that sometimes brought rich rewards—land, titles, positions of influence. But it also brought consequences in times of political turmoil, with the family mausoleum defaced during the Civil War.' David paused. 'Defaced or vandalised?'

'Defaced,' said the producer. 'And the angle's not right. We'll mark it. Let's go again.'

Rose swung back to John. 'Perhaps the funds could be used for the mausoleum, Lord Elston?'

'Kind of you, but the family should be responsible for that. Find something the whole village can take part in.'

'I expected there to be more reaction last night,' Mina said, when Rose had headed back to the bake stall. 'Especially Rose.'

John paused. 'Rose has been here longer than anyone else, and she's my grandmother-in-law. We've always had . . . tacit understanding. Though I imagine some burden is now released for her, too.'

Mina considered Rose, though on the scale of surprises of the past year, this barely moved the needle.

'As for the rest of them,' John said, 'I doubt they really care about what goes on behind these walls, when many of them live elsewhere most of the time. Or they're too polite, more likely. It's probably all they can talk about over there.'

'So they're all gossiping to each other, just not to your face?'

'As it should be.'

Mina laughed. The last months had been a steep learning experience on so many different fronts. She'd carried through the kitchen design alone, organising contractors and ensuring it was done exactly as John had approved. That had been intense, but nowhere near the scale of learning how to relate to John when they had little in common. The winter months had sometimes been bleak with how unalike they were. But she eventually worked out to keep things light and not to expect perfection.

Except perhaps in her work.

The kitchen had turned out better than she had imagined. It was eccentrically beautiful with its hand-coloured tiles and the painted mural stretching up to the wood-panelled ceiling. Distressed recovered pieces, like the oak bench and cabinets, framed the contemporary appliances. But Mina's favourite feature was her mother's hand-drawn fairy, now framed on the wall below the stairs.

She'd caught John, more than once, pausing by that picture. Mina saw it as a change in him, a willingness to let the past back in. Those signs of change were all around the estate—the stables and rose garden were being restored, and the land over Middle Bandinby barred from ploughing again. As if all the things John had done to forget Ann were being let go.

Twenty-Six Letters

'Lord Elston.'

Mina looked up and smiled at David, walking towards them in his dashing trademark long coat. He looked ready to vault onto his horse and go galloping off on a campaign. She still couldn't quite believe she went to sleep with him every night.

'We're hoping to move up to shoot the new manor kitchen,' he said. 'We have everything we need in the churchyard for now, and we're ahead of schedule. If we could do the kitchen, the crew can be out of your hair early.'

John flicked his eyebrows. 'Sounds reasonable. Bill will let you in the gate.'

'I'll do it,' Mina said, before John could yell out for Bill. She gave David a wink as she threw her legs around the wall and jumped down. 'Have to earn my keep somehow.'

As she strode across the gardens and past the gleaming red manor door, she knew that, to anyone else, it might seem that she was simply enthusiastic about her work being filmed for a national show. After all, what kind of budding designer *wouldn't* want such a chance?

But as she glanced up the front of the house, at the window where John had looked down on her mother so many years ago, she thought of the twenty-six letters. Her mother had been right—the stories had changed everything, but they hadn't defined what was next. The past was only as big as she wanted to make it. Some of her mother's past connections she'd sought out, like Marionette and a retired publisher who'd replied to her email. But without dwelling, so that she could do what her mother had really wanted: find where she fitted and have a life that meant something.

409

The final letter was always in her pocket these days, along with the pressed rose her mother had taken from the garden. When the TV crews were gone, she would return them both under the flagstone in the church porch. Her mother's words could then remain at the centre of the village where her story had begun. Mina would carry them only in her heart.

That heart was full, now, soaring as she passed under the trees that were bursting into spring and listened to the gurgle of the beck. Then she lifted the latch on the huge gates to let the new world in.

⌒

Dear John,

Is it the wrong time to make a joke about that opening to a letter? We made it so many times before, you and I, but somehow, because this is the last, I'm not sure whether to be as we always were or whether to let the moment have a gravity it probably deserves. You know I could go on about it for an hour. But I don't have that time, now. All the hours are winding down, where once I thought there would be so many.

You might think I blame you for the lives we had, and perhaps I did for the longest time. Because what we had felt so unique, and so powerful, I thought it was wrong for us to never have had more than just fleeting grazes of time together. I couldn't imagine why gods or universes, or whatever it was that drove our fates, would have done that to us.

Why we would have done that to us.

But, after everything, I have to believe there are so many stories like ours. Of hearts that found each other in times

that were wrong or impossible for more than just wanting.
Hearts that never managed to be what they could have been.
And now that I'm facing down that place where I'll never
know such sorrow or joy as you brought me again, I can only
be touched that I found you at all. That I had those grazes of
time with you. That, because I knew you, I moved inexorably
away from the life I was probably meant for and into the
one I actually had. That we made memories together, and a
beautiful daughter, that I will cherish forever.

So whatever is waiting for me now (I don't forget all our
arguments about life after life, I know we are still unresolved),
I'm prepared to go, and go alone. I trained well for that.

But I'll not go empty, for you have filled my heart since
the day we met. You have made me understand why wars
were fought for love, both grand and oh so private. And ours
was private. I used to think that was a failing, to not have
declared it to anyone. But now I think the declaration that
matters is the very kind we had—that we knew ourselves
how deeply we ran together. A well that will never be dry, no
matter how long we draw from it.

I was drawing from it every day of my life, and now I will
do the same beyond. Beyond when this church crumbles into
the dirt. And when its ruins are covered over. Beyond the next
fated pair who meet in the lumpy field, and however their
story ends. You were the start and end of mine. The rise and
fall of my time.

With all my love, unending.

Ann

Acknowledgements

*T*wenty-Six Letters was a twisting vine that grew out of stories my mother told and experiences of real places and people—even the anonymous confessions of internet redditors. My own father died young and, as I now approach the age he reached, I've thought a lot about what you might do with your remaining time if you knew it was limited (at least, much more limited than our already limited lives). What you might choose to say. In writing that kind of story, which is a mosaic of fiction and experiences, I acknowledge the story is owed to many people, even if the words are mine (and any mistakes).

I want to especially thank my mother Isabella and my step-father Vic, who have always told me stories and been wonderful supportive people. Also, my writing buddy Rebekah Turner, who is a constant friend and an amazingly strong person who often inspires me. I also thank my husband Kevin and my son Alec, who not only put up with me and my writing but encourage it. There are many others to thank, for all the large and small things you did or said that ended up in these pages (beware befriending the writer . . . or even having a conversation with one)—for me, these connections are most of the immeasurable joy of art.

I also want to express my immense gratitude to my agent Alex Adsett and my publisher Annette Barlow for giving this book a loving home at A&U. The editorial team including Courtney Lick has been wonderful. The project was also made possible by a grant from Arts Queensland, and even more so by the time that my workplace made for me to take up that grant (thanks, David Hartigan . . . not everyone would be cool with someone they really just hired disappearing for most of five months, but I'll be forever grateful you were).

These are really so few words in which to fold the years spent and the thanks owed, but, seeing as we know language can't express the deepest things in us (the irony of writing!), you'll just have to imagine the things I can't say and know I'll carry it all into the next thing.